Harry Bentley's

Second Sight

Harry Bentley's

Second Sight

A Yada Yada Brothers Novel

Book 2

Dave Jackson

CASTLE
ROCK
CREATIVE
Evanston, Illinois 60202

© 2010 by Dave Jackson

Published in Evanston, Illinois. Castle Rock Creative, Inc.

Scripture quotations are taken from the following: THE HOLY BIBLE, NEW INTERNATIONAL VERSION®. Copyright © 1973, 1978, 1984, by International Bible Society. Used by permission of Zondervan Bible Publishers.

Words attributed to the "radio broadcast" by Dr. Tony Evans, came from his book: Tony Evans, *No More Excuses* (Wheaton, Ill.: Crossway Books, 1996), pp. 12-13.

"Pass Me Not, O Gentle Savior," written by Fanny Crosby, 1868, first printed in *Songs of Devotion*, by Howard Doane (New York: 1870). Public domain.

"Anywhere with Jesus," words by Jessie B. Pounds, 1886, and music by Daniel B. Towner, 1887. Public domain.

Publisher's Note: This novel is a work of fiction. Names, characters, places, and incidents are either products of the author's imagination or used fictitiously. All characters are fictional, and any similarity to people living or dead is purely coincidental.

ISBN: 978-0-9820544-2-0

Printed in the United States of America

For a complete listing of
books by Dave and Neta Jackson
please visit www.daveneta.com

What Is a Parallel Novel?

Dave and Neta Jackson are doing something new in Christian fiction—"parallel novels," two stories taking place in the same time frame, the same neighborhood, involving some of the same characters living through their own dramas and crises but interacting with and affecting one another ... just the way it happens in real life.

Growing out of Neta Jackson's best-selling Yada Yada Prayer Group novels came two brand-new stories sprinkled with familiar faces and places from the Yada Yada world: Neta's *Where Do I Go?* which began her Yada Yada House of Hope series, and Dave's *Harry Bentley's Second Chance*, a Yada Yada Brothers novel.

Reader enthusiasm was so high, that we've done it again. This book, *Harry Bentley's Second Sight*, parallels the third book in Neta's House of Hope series, *Who Do I Lean On?* And it goes even further to give a glimpse into events in the fourth book of that series.

It's something a husband-and-wife writing team is uniquely equipped to pull off.

Each of these novels stands alone, and they can be read in any sequence. However, if you would like to read them in order, it would be:

- *Where Do I Go?* Book 1, House of Hope.
- *Harry Bentley's Second Chance*, Book 1, Yada Yada Brothers.
- *Who Do I Talk To?* Book 2, House of Hope.
- *Who Do I Lean On?* Book 3, House of Hope.
- *Harry Bentley's Second Sight*, Book 2, Yada Yada Brothers.
- *Who Is My Shelter?* Book 4, House of Hope.

Have fun reading in 3-D!

To Rachel, my
ever-encouraging
daughter.

Prologue

DaShawn Bentley was tall for a nine-year-old, but to rest his knees on the dash of his grandfather's SUV, he still had to slide way down in the front seat while he texted his friend, Robbie. "R—u—g-o-i-n-g—2—c-a-m-p—2-m-o-r-r-o-w-?" He hit Send. Except for that brief stay in a foster home in the suburbs, DaShawn had never been outside Chicago, especially not way out in the country, in the woods, by a lake with canoes and horses. So he was counting on some of the other guys from SouledOut Community Church going with him.

"You ever been to camp, Grandpa?"

When Harry Bentley didn't answer right away, DaShawn looked over to see his grandfather turning from side to side as if he were trying to read the address numbers on the passing storefronts. He kept closing one eye and then the other with exaggerated winks that contorted his face like a rubber mask.

"Grandpa?"

"Yeah, what?"

"I said, did you ever go to summer camp?"

"Uh ..." The searching and winking continued. "No. We only had day camps down on the Southside. But they were pretty good."

Realizing his grandfather wasn't watching where they were going very carefully, DaShawn sat up just in time to see them closing too fast on a stopped truck.

"Grandpa, LOOK OUT!"

Harry Bentley hit the brakes. Tires screeched, then *WHAM!* The little RAV4 slammed into the back of a huge red pickup.

There was a moment of silence, like dust settling, as DaShawn realized he'd just been in his first-ever car accident. He turned to look at the baldheaded black man next to him. "You okay, Grandpa?"

DaShawn's grandfather was staring straight ahead. "Yeah. You all right?"

"I think so. What happened?"

Grandpa shook his head. "I was just …"

His response was cut short by the cursing of two burly white men getting out of the pickup. They both wore sweat-stained T-shirts, yellow hardhats, and looked to DaShawn like twin construction workers.

"Uh-oh. You wait here!" Grandpa opened the door and went to meet the men inspecting the damage. But a few moments later, DaShawn was surprised to hear the construction workers' curses turn to laughter as they pointed to the back of their truck and then the front of the little SUV.

"So what happened?" one said, throwing up his hands. "Are you blind or something? Isn't this truck big enough for you to see it?"

"Yeah," said the other man. "We were stopped at a red light, for Pete's sake! What's the matter with you?"

DaShawn relaxed a little. At first the men had seemed really angry at his grandpa, but now it was more like they were making fun of him.

In a few moments, the loud voices quieted as the drivers got down to the business of exchanging licenses and insurance cards.

The other driver began shaking his head as if he didn't care about all that, and DaShawn heard him say, "We can report this if you want, but my truck ain't even scratched. That big hitch can take a hit and keep on truckin', know what I mean?" He pointed at the RAV4. "You're the one with the messed-up bumper, and it was your fault, so reportin' it'll only raise your insurance rates. Do what you want. But if it were me ..." He shrugged.

"You sure neither of you are hurt?" Grandpa asked.

The two men looked at one another. "Nah. We're good." Then with a smirk, the driver added, "But run into me again, and I'll claim whiplash and sue ya dry."

"Hey," Grandpa held up both hands in surrender. "I'm really sorry, guys. Thanks."

"No problem. Just watch where you're goin' next time."

The men returned to their truck and drove off as DaShawn's grandfather came back and got in his car. He sat there, pulling at his gray, horseshoe-shaped beard until the car behind beeped its horn.

"You okay, Grandpa?"

"Yeah, yeah." Harry blew out a lung full of air as he stepped gently on the gas to cross the intersection and pull to a stop behind some parked cars along the curb. He sat there staring out the front window, then glanced momentarily over at DaShawn. "Can you read that parking sign up ahead there?"

"Sure. Says, 'No parking when snow is over two inches deep. Tow zone.'"

"But ... none of the letters are smeared or anything?"

"Uh, no. But don't worry, Grandpa. It don't snow in July."

"Course not." Harry laughed as he continued "winking" at the sign, then began rubbing his eyes with the back of his hands. "Musta got somethin' in my eye. Left one's all blurry. But ... hey, it's probably nothin'."

"That why you didn't see that truck, Grandpa?"

"No ... well, maybe. I was distracted, I guess, tryin' to read signs."

DaShawn grinned. "I know. I know what you were doin'. You lookin' to find some nice restaurant to take Miss Estelle to for dinner tonight, huh?"

"Hey, that's none of your business." His grandfather grinned and put the car in Drive as he pulled away. Then he turned back to his grandson and arched his eyebrows while pursing his lips. "Actually, I already got plans for tonight." He bobbled his head from side to side. "Big plans."

"Oh yeah? What's up?"

"Promise you won't tell?"

"Promise."

"I'm gonna ask her to marry me." He slapped his breast. "Got a ring in a little box, right here in my pocket."

"Really?" DaShawn's eyes got huge.

"Yep. After dinner I'm gonna take her sailing on the Tall Ship *Windy*. And right during the Chicago fireworks, when they're lighting up the whole sky, I'm gonna pop the question. Whaddaya thinka that?"

"The Tall Ship *Windy*! Can I come?"

"Ha! Not likely! You're going over to your great-grandma's house."

"Aww, no fair!" But DaShawn grinned at his grandpa's secret. He couldn't wait 'til he could tell Robbie."

"HARRY, THIS PLACE IS TOO EXPENSIVE," Estelle Williams whispered as she scanned the menu for Riva's Restaurant on Chicago's Navy Pier. Their table looked out over the harbor as the sun's golden rays ricocheted off the glass and steel of the city's magnificent skyline.

"Don't worry 'bout it. Just order what you want."

Estelle shrugged and returned to the menu. But there'd been an edge in Harry's voice. In fact, ever since he'd picked her up this evening, he'd seemed uptight. She shot him a look. "Harry Bentley ... you tryin' to wink at me?" She closed her menu and lowered her head to position herself more in his line of sight.

"No, I'm not trying to wink at you. Why would I be doin' that? Haven't we been seein' enough of each other to be beyond flirting?"

"Well, I should hope so. Harry ..." She reached across the table and pushed his menu down, forcing him to look at her. "What's the matter with you?" The frown lines in his forehead were deeper than usual. "DaShawn told me you were in a car wreck this afternoon, but I didn't see any damage. You okay?"

Harry leaned back in his chair and stared out at the boats. Then he closed his eyes, and rubbed them with the knuckles of both hands. "Yeah, I'm okay. It was nothin', Estelle. No one was hurt. Just messed up my bumper a little."

"Hmm." She studied the man she'd come to love. Something wasn't right. "Harry, what's the problem? Come on. Somethin's troubling you. Is it Mother Bentley again?"

"No, she's doin' fine. You know that. You take care of my mom more than I do. It's just ..." He closed his eyes for a moment. "My eye has been bothering me a little. Think I'm getting allergies or something."

"Your eyes?" The implications clicked through her mind like a calculator. "Is that why you had a wreck? Maybe you shouldn't be driving, Harry."

"It wasn't a *wreck*. Just a little fender-bender. And I can see quite well enough to drive. Besides, it's just my left eye. Probably

5

got something in it." He flipped open his menu and squinted at it. "Now, come on. Let's put that behind us and have a nice dinner."

"Maybe you need glasses, Harry. Most people our age do need glasses, at least to read. I should get some myself."

"I already have a pair of reading glasses, Estelle."

"Then why don't you use them? I've never seen you wear them."

"Estelle … don't worry about it, okay? Just order."

She stifled her next comment and opened her menu again. The man was nothing if not stubborn. Well, if he insisted on paying for it, she'd enjoy her meal. "I think I'll start with some lobster bisque and one of these salads—baby greens with balsamic vinaigrette and sliced almonds."

When the sun had finally set and they'd finished their dinner, Estelle was so full of scallop fettuccine and asparagus Parmigiano—not to mention the bites she'd snitched of Harry's double-cut pork chop with black current sauce and his garlic mashed potatoes—that she passed on the dessert, and they just lingered over coffee. But their conversation mostly involved brief answers from Harry every time Estelle tried to introduce a new topic. She noticed he'd actually turned his chair slightly away from her and spent most of his time looking out at the boats as they came and went across the lights of the city shimmering off the water. Occasionally, he checked his watch as it approached nine o'clock and then, resting an elbow on the table, he held his head in his hand for a moment, shaking it back and forth slightly as though he were deciding the course of the universe.

She had to do something to pull him out of this funk.

"Harry … Harry, let's top off the evening with a ride on the Ferris wheel. I've always wanted to do that, and it's such a beautiful night. I bet we could see the whole city from up there."

He stared at her blankly for a moment, then nodded. "Yeah, yeah. Why not?" He sat up in his chair as though relieved. "Let's do it. I'll call for the check."

BY THE TIME HE GOT HOME, HARRY FELT BUMMED. His special evening with Estelle had crashed and burned … at least in terms of what he'd planned. Why hadn't he taken her for a sail on the *Windy*? Why hadn't he given her the ring?

It was that episode of *Grey's Anatomy*—the one where they discovered that a guy who was going blind in one eye had an inoperable brain tumor. Memory of it had popped into his mind just as he was turning into the Navy Pier parking garage with Estelle. He wished he'd never seen that show, but he had, and all evening he couldn't get it out of his mind.

What if that was happening to him?

It was nearly eleven after he'd taken Estelle home and picked up DaShawn from his mother's. He'd been tempted to let the boy spend the night at Great Grandma's, but tomorrow was Sunday, and Harry had to have him packed and over to SouledOut Community Church an hour early to catch a ride in the van with the other kids going to summer camp. If it was a church camp, why did it start on Sunday? It made no sense to Harry.

Harry dumped the boy onto the bed, pulled off his shoes, and let him fall back to sleep in his clothes. He could take a shower in the morning.

Harry knew he should go right to bed himself, but he couldn't … not yet. Not until he had a better understanding of what he might be facing. He couldn't ask Estelle to marry him if he was going blind! Or what if he died of a brain tumor? The ring in his pocket nearly burned a hole in his chest. Passing up his plans for a romantic proposal on that sailing ship tore him up. He wanted so badly to declare his love for her, but he couldn't go through with it, not until he knew.

He sat down at the table in the living room where he and DaShawn shared a computer and turned it on. When the browser came up, he typed "blind spot in eye" into the search engine and clicked the Return key.

One website said everyone has two blind spots, one in each eye, but they were over to the side and corresponded to where the optic nerve connects to the eye. There was even an on-screen demonstration: "Close one eye and position your face close to the screen while focusing on the large 'x.' Then move your head slowly back away from the screen." When Harry tried it, the three large letters a few inches to the side disappeared and reappeared, one after the other as his natural blind spot passed over them. *Why haven't I noticed that before?* he thought. "Because the other eye compensates and fills in the missing image," the web page explained.

Cool, an interesting distraction ... but it didn't account for the blind spot right in the center of his vision. He tried another website ... and another ... and another. Just as he feared, several mentioned the possibility of a brain tumor as the cause of a blind spot. And he couldn't find anything to rule it out in his case.

By the time he finally shut down the computer at one o'clock in the morning, his mind was spinning with other scary possibilities: a detached retina ... macular degeneration ... diabetes ... a stroke. On the other hand, he found a few less frightening causes of temporary visual problems ... stuff like migraine headaches or excessive fatigue and certain medications.

As he finally crawled between the sheets, he tried to relax. Maybe he was getting worked up over nothing. In fact, he'd probably feel better after a good night's sleep. Maybe something blew into his eye and scratched it without him noticing it. It had to be something like that ... didn't it?

But sleep wouldn't come. *Please, God. I don't want to lose my sight. How would I take care of DaShawn? Didn't you give him to me? And Estelle ... don't You know we've got a good thing going? I couldn't saddle her with me as an invalid. In fact, God, I don't think I could stand myself as an invalid. I'm too old to learn Braille. I couldn't adjust, not at this age.*

His heart pounded as he stared up into the gloom of his bedroom.

If it were a tumor, what other havoc would it wreck inside his skull before it killed him? How long would it take? Would he suffer? Would the doctors shoot him so full of morphine he'd be a zombie by the time he died? In his mind, he already had himself in the hospital, pincushioned with tubes and monitors. *Huh! At least they won't have to shave my head before operating!*

But who would care for his elderly mother? He couldn't leave that responsibility to Estelle. In fact, he probably ought to break off his relationship with her completely. He couldn't entangle her in something like this. She already had enough problems, like that schizophrenic son of hers. She deserved a life of her own, not the burden of looking after a blind man. He couldn't do that to her.

Harry turned over on his side and stared at the window, covered by Venetian blinds. Fine strips of light from the city glowed between each slat. He closed his right eye. At the point of focus for his left, the otherwise straight lines of light detoured around his blind spot like water flowing around a rock sticking out of a river. Yeah, now he was calling it *his* "blind spot," not just blurry vision. He squinted, trying to evaluate what he could see. Maybe it wasn't as bad as it had been earlier that day. He was tempted to sit up, turn on the light, and see what happened if he tried to read words from a book. Would the "missing" letters have returned? Maybe there'd be only a slight fuzziness. Maybe he was getting better.

But Harry resisted with all his will power.

Checking on it wouldn't change a thing. He needed sleep.

"O God," he groaned, "help me! Help me calm down and just go to sleep. Please!"

Chapter 1

THE ENGAGEMENT RING IN ITS LITTLE BOX ON HARRY'S DRESSER had teased him for nearly a month. Most days he left it there, thinking he should return it to the jeweler and get his money back. How long did he have … a month? Two months? But then there were days like today when it tempted him to put it in his pocket and take it with him. Maybe his eye would be better. Maybe he'd find some romantic opportunity to ask Estelle to marry him.

"Grandpa! Hurry up!" His grandson pounded on his bedroom door. "I'm gonna be late for basketball camp!"

Harry grabbed a pair of socks from the top drawer. "Finish your breakfast and leave me alone, DaShawn!" he yelled back. Harry was never late for anything. Twenty years on the police force had made sure of that. He sat down and put on his socks and shoes, then went through the little ritual he'd fallen into each morning: checking his vision by staring at the slats of the Venetian window shades, then picking up the *Readers Digest* to try and read something with his left eye. Nope. The blind spot was still there. Apparently, more rest wasn't the answer—what little he got of it, worrying through night after night—but the blind spot hadn't gotten worse either.

So, maybe he wasn't going blind. Maybe it was just something he'd have to learn to live with. He could do that. It wasn't all that bad, and his right eye compensated in most situations.

But it still worried him. He had to keep busy, get his mind off it. He'd quit his job as doorman at Richmond Towers at the end of July so he'd have more time to spend with DaShawn, now that the boy had come to live with him. He hadn't really needed the job for the money. He had his policeman's pension from when he'd been a Chicago cop. And while it wasn't that much, he knew how to manage his money ... at least he *had* known before taking on his grandson. How was he to know an Xbox 360 cost over three hundred dollars? And why did DaShawn *need* a $135 pair of Air Jordan XXIs, anyway? Wouldn't something cheaper work just as well?

But now that he had his new routine—taking DaShawn to basketball camp each day, grocery shopping for two, cleaning the apartment, and checking on his elderly mother, who had recently moved from Evanston down to Rogers Park—there still seemed to be too much dead time when he ended up fretting about his eye.

Which is why he drove over to the Manna House women's shelter that afternoon to see what needed doing. Volunteers ... the homeless shelter always needed more volunteers. Kept his mind occupied by helping out where he could—not to mention giving him an excuse to check in on Estelle Williams who worked at the shelter part time as lunch cook. It used to be a volunteer job for her, but now they'd hired her to teach some life skills classes as well—cooking, sewing, that kind of thing.

Lunch was over when Harry poked his head into the dining room on the lower level of the shelter, but Estelle was still busy in the kitchen with four of the residents. He caught her eye and waved her a greeting. She stopped mid-sentence and rolled her eyes at him. "Harry Bentley! You here again? Can't you see I'm teaching my class? Go find yourself somethin' to do!" Shaking her head, she turned back to her class. "Now where was I? ... Right. See here? It's marked on the wrapper of this stick of butter. There are eight tablespoons of butter in every quarter-pound stick."

Harry grinned to himself. What a woman! Instead of the ugly hairnet kitchen staff usually wore, she had piled her black-and-silver hair on top of her head and encased it in a green African-print wrap that set off her caramel-colored skin. Her large white apron had the words, "Kiss the cook," beside a pair of red lips across the front. For half a second, Harry wondered if he dared try ... then chuckled to himself as he climbed the stairs and headed for the closet off the large multipurpose room on first floor. Inside was a stack of old folding chairs that had been donated to the shelter. Most needed repair, and Harry spent the next couple hours sorting through them, fixing those he could salvage and carrying the hopeless ones out to the dumpster in the alley behind Manna House. But Estelle was still busy in the kitchen when he had to leave to pick up DaShawn from basketball camp.

HARRY DIDN'T SEE ESTELLE AGAIN UNTIL SATURDAY when he and DaShawn picked her up to go over to Gabby Fairbanks' apartment for her boys' welcome-home and belated birthday party. Harry had become friends with the "Firecracker," as he called the redhead who was always popping with wild ideas, when he still worked as the Richmond Towers doorman. But when her husband, Philip, kicked her out of the penthouse, Gabby went from a do-gooder who worked at Manna House as the shelter's program director to a homeless resident there herself. When Philip added insult to injury by sending their two sons back to Virginia to stay with his parents in a seeming demonstration of his power over her, Harry

13

was amazed how quickly the Firecracker rebounded to establish a home of her own so she could get her boys back.

After "losing them" for six weeks—during which time each boy had had a birthday—the Firecracker had finally worked out a deal with Philip that brought them back home to live under her own roof. It was time to celebrate!

"So you got the hot wings?" Estelle asked Harry as he held open the door of his SUV for her to climb in.

"Yep. Got two big pans in the back. They're on the floor right behind DaShawn."

Estelle pulled the folds of the loose yellow caftan around her and slid into the front seat, then glanced back over her shoulder. "Oh, hi, DaShawn. How you doin'?"

"I'm good, Miss Estelle. An' you?"

"I'll be fine soon as I get this seatbelt fastened." She clicked the snap. "Mm-mm. Those wings smellin' mighty good. Where'd you get 'em, Harry?"

"They're Hecky's, the jumbo wings." He closed the door and rested his arm on the open window, a twinkle in his eye as he leaned his head in closer. "Cost me as much as takin' you out for dinner, too."

"Ha!" She tipped her head up and closed her eyes. "I ain't even gonna dignify that comment with a response." She sat there with her eyes closed until Harry withdrew and went around and got into the driver's seat. Then she opened her eyes and turned to him. "Well, we goin' or what?"

As Harry started the car and pulled away from the curb, Estelle waved her hand in front of her face. "Can't we put up the windows and use the air, Harry? You know we can always put those wings in the oven when we get to Gabby's. We don't need to reheat 'em here in the car."

Harry grinned at her. "Be glad to put on the air." He pushed the buttons. "But it didn't seem all that warm to me this afternoon. You sure you ain't havin' one of your hot—"

"Harry Bentley!" She swatted his shoulder. "You watch your tongue, now."

Harry ducked. "Hee-hee. Okay. Okay, Babe. Whatever. If you say it's the weather, then it's just the weather. Hee-hee."

When they got to the six-flat, Harry and DaShawn each carried one of the large covered aluminum pans of hot wings and followed Estelle as she stomped across the street and up the steps. Harry wondered if he'd teased her too much. Her nose still seemed a little high as she pushed the doorbell.

Gabby Fairbanks was there in a moment. "Harry, Estelle, come on in." She opened her arms wide for Estelle. "And hi, DaShawn."

"Too hot for a hug, honey," said Estelle as she brushed past her. "I'll make it up to you this winter. C'mon, Harry. You too, DaShawn. Bring in those wings and stick 'em in the oven."

Harry gave the Firecracker a wink as he followed Estelle into the first-floor apartment. Behind him, DaShawn said, "Hi, Miz Fairbanks. Your kids here?"

"Not yet. We want all the guests to get here first."

It wasn't long before more guests began to arrive. Mable Turner, the director of Manna House, came with her teenage nephew, dressed in a skin-tight, collarless knit shirt with a long scarf wound around his neck. He looked just too "pretty" with his cornrow braids. Harry shook his head. Maybe things had changed these days, but Harry suspected the kid still got persecuted at school. Then came Denny and Jodi Baxter, a middle-aged white couple. Denny was a high school coach and Jodi taught school at Bethune Elementary, which reminded Harry that he needed to enroll DaShawn there in the next few days ... as a fifth grader. The last school his grandson had attended out in the suburbs had threatened to hold him back because he'd missed so many days of class even though he'd been able to do the work. But Harry had promised DaShawn he'd fight to be sure he'd be admitted as a fifth grader.

"Hey, Harry," Denny said as the two men greeted each other with a quick hug and a slap on the back. "Saw you at church the other day, but been missin' you at Bible study. Everything, okay?"

"Oh yeah. Just busy. You know how it is." Which wasn't exactly true. Everything wasn't "okay" with Harry. Prayer for his eye might be just what he needed. It was a cinch he wasn't getting very far praying by himself.

"You know the guys been missin' you," Denny continued. "Think you can make it next Tuesday?"

"Yeah. I'll do my best." He might need prayer, but could he really tell these men how he'd been feeling? After all, it wasn't that long ago he'd had to own up to his crime of breaking into the house across the alley from Denny Baxter to get back something that belonged to DaShawn. God had helped him get out of that mess, but it was rather embarrassing to admit he was in another one.

When the front door to the apartment opened across the room, Harry saw Denny's son and his African-Honduran wife come in. Glad for a chance to change the subject, he said, "Hey, Josh ..." That was his name, wasn't it? "How's that baby girl?"

Josh took a couple of strides across the room and thrust the baby into Grandpa Denny's arms. "I think she needs changin', Dad." He turned and smiled at Harry. "Gracie's fine. Here for her first big birthday."

Birthday? That was the first Harry had heard about someone else sharing this party. Estelle had only mentioned Gabby's boys.

"And how you doin', Mr. B?" the tall young white kid asked.

"Oh, I'm good. I'm good." Harry was about to ask how Josh and Edesa's adoption of little Gracie was proceeding when the Firecracker asked for everyone's attention.

Philip, her estranged husband, had just pulled up out front of the apartment building with the boys. "Everyone come away from the windows," Gabby said. "And Jodi, when they buzz the intercom, I'll go out and let them in from the foyer, but when the boys get to the apartment door, you pull it open and everybody yell 'Surprise!' Okay?"

Harry caught Denny's eye and made a grimace as he glanced at the baby Denny still held. Yep, Josh had been right. From three feet away, Harry could smell the little tyke. He imagined DaShawn as a baby.... He could live without any diaper changing memories, but he hadn't even known he *had* a grandson until a couple of months ago when the social worker from the Department of Children and Family Services had called and asked him to take nine-year-old DaShawn.

Everyone moved together into a group facing the apartment door as though they were a choir waiting to sing.

The door buzzer sounded. "Quiet! Quiet. I'm going out." Gabby slipped into the hall to let in her boys. Harry could hear the normal greetings, but there was an obvious tension in Gabby's voice as she spoke to the boys' father. Funny, ever since he'd begun worrying about his eyes, Harry had been paying more attention to his other senses—smell, hearing, touch. It was like entering a new world.

He held his breath and strained to listen. If Fairbanks messed up this party, Harry wasn't sure he'd be much of a gentleman about it. In fact, Harry was about to step out of the "choir" and go see what was happening, when the door swung open just as Fairbanks was saying, "The boys want me to see their 'new digs' anyway—"

"Surprise!" … "Happy birthday!" … "Welcome home!" everyone shouted.

Harry had to play catch-up to join the chorus as the two boys pushed past their father into the apartment where they were greeted with hugs and handshakes. He overheard Philip say to Gabby, "So … am I invited?"

Harry saw the enthusiasm melt from the Firecracker's face. Didn't blame her. This was supposed to be *her* party for the boys after her ex had sent them away for six weeks under the guise of visiting the grandparents. Oh, yeah, he wasn't technically her "*ex*." They were still married, but …

Just then Paul bounced between his mom and dad. "Oh, could Dad stay too? Please, Mom? That'd be great! Please?"

To her credit, the Firecracker quickly regained her composure and turned to her guests. "Uh, everyone, this is Philip, the boys' dad. Paul, uh, wanted him to stay for a few minutes." Others might not have noticed it, but Harry picked up the slight inflection that said she was only agreeing to "*a few*" minutes. Then she broke away from Fairbanks and began introducing her sons to some of the people they may not have met before.

"P.J. and Paul, you remember my boss, Ms. Turner, the director of Manna House. And this is her nephew, uh … Jermaine. He's starting ninth grade at Lane Tech, too, same as you, P.J. Thought you might like to meet a few kids before you start school."

The slender black boy gave a hopeful nod, but P.J. didn't react … at least not at first. Gabby ignored the awkwardness and turned to me. "And you boys remember Mr. Bentley, the doorman at Richmond Towers." While she was speaking, Harry watched over her shoulder as a sneer crossed P.J.'s face and he reached his hand out to Jermaine. The boy took it only to find his delicate fingers caught in a painful vice. Harry shook his head—like father, like son. When

P.J. released his grip and caught up with his mother's introductions, Harry only barely resisted the temptation to show the kid what a real crusher felt like.

"And this handsome young man is his grandson, DaShawn," continued the Firecracker.

Yeah, and you mess with my grandson, and you won't even have a hand, telegraphed Harry with a steely stare.

Thankfully, DaShawn was oblivious to the whole exchange. "You dudes got a cool crib here. Thanks for inviting us to your party!" Then he looked up at Harry and whispered loudly, "We gonna eat soon, Grandpa? I'm hungry!"

It wasn't long until Estelle came in from the kitchen and announced, "Food's ready! It's all laid out on the dining room table. Somebody want to say a blessing over the food and over our birthday boys?"

"It's Gracie's birthday, too, don't forget!" said a vivacious young black woman, her hair done in tight little twists. Harry had seen her at Manna House, but wasn't sure if she was a volunteer or a "guest."

"That's right," added Estelle. "And you just volunteered to say the blessing. C'mon now, everybody join hands."

Soon the guests had filled their plates and were standing around schmoozing. It was what Harry hated most about parties like this—trying to look casual while not spilling food off paper plates that were too flimsy even if you snuck two of them. And how were you supposed to hold a drink? Furthermore, Estelle was too busy to help him make small talk with people.

It was just plain awkward.

"So, Bentley," said Philip Fairbanks as he sidled up to Harry, "haven't seen you around the past couple of weeks. You working the night shift now?"

19

"No, *Fairbanks.*" Ha! He didn't have to call him *Mister* anymore. "I quit the job." Harry turned and looked out the window as though something outside was far more interesting than conversing with Fairbanks. "Now that I've got custody of my grandson, I wanted to spend more time with him before school starts."

The Firecracker overheard him. "Mr. Bentley! You quit your job? How—"

Harry shrugged. "It was just a job to supplement my retirement anyway."

A puzzled look crossed Gabby's face, but Harry changed the subject. "By the way, DaShawn and I are going to go to the zoo and some of the museums before school starts. Was going to ask if P.J. and Paul might want to come along too."

"Oh, Mr. B! That would be great! I'm only working half time at Manna House until school starts—maybe we could go together."

"Pick you up when you get off work then." When Gabby nodded, Harry tapped his shaved head a couple of times with his finger. "It's on my calendar."

Harry turned away from Philip's condescension and drifted toward the door. He'd had enough of this.

Outside on the porch steps, he breathed deeply of the afternoon's humid air, exhaling tension as he gazed at the door of the building across the street. He closed his right eye to measure how much was covered by his blind spot. About the same, he guessed. Then his hand absently found the little box in his pocket. He fingered it open and felt the smooth gold and sharp diamond of the ring he wanted to give Estelle when he asked her to share his love for the rest of their lives.

But he couldn't do that ... not until he knew for sure what that life might be.

Chapter 2

MONDAY MORNING, HARRY CRANKED UP HIS COURAGE to go over to the For Eyes store on Peterson. Maybe all he needed was a pair of glasses. He sat in the chair reading the eye chart causing the optometrist to "Hmm" when Harry was able to decipher the smaller type. As far as he could tell, his right eye did just fine.

But when she told him to hold the patch over his right eye and read the chart with his left eye, he quickly knew he was in trouble. As his eye scanned from letter to letter, the shapes distorted and then disappeared into the smudge that was his blind spot.

It was still there!

"Uh, 'A,' 'P,' 'X,' … uh, give me a second. Uh …" If he focused on the letter before or after his blind spot, he could make it out. But was that what the doctor wanted to measure? If not, whom was he trying to fool? "I think the next letter is a 'Q,' but I really can't read that line," Harry admitted.

"That's okay. Now if you'll just lean forward a little and put your chin in this cup, with your forehead against the rest, we'll take a look inside your eye with the slit-lamp."

Harry complied only to have the doctor shine a light so bright into his right eye that he could hardly keep it open. "Hmm, hmm."

She moved the light back and forth. It hurt most when she was looking straight into his eye.

"Okay. Now we'll take a look into your other eye. Just focus on my ear with your right eye while I check your left eye."

Focus on her ear? Harry couldn't see anything with his right eye, the light had been so bright, but he tried while she searched the innards of his left eye. She searched ... and searched ... until Harry couldn't help but close his eye for a moment of relief. "Sorry.... Okay, go ahead again."

"All right, Mr. Bentley. You can sit back now." The optometrist swung the apparatus away from him and began writing something on her clipboard. In contrast to the bright light she'd been shining in his eyes, the whole room looked black to Harry.

"So, Mr. Bentley, have you been having any problems with your left eye?"

"Well, yeah."

"Describe them for me."

Harry did, telling himself he shouldn't leave anything out. After all he wasn't trying to impress the doctor. He was here to find out what was wrong ... as much as he didn't want to hear it.

When she was finished her notes, she stood up. "I think that 'blind spot' you've been experiencing, Mr. Bentley, may be the result of a retinal problem. I want you to see an ophthalmologist who specializes in retinal issues." She was writing rapidly on her pad. "Here's the phone number of the clinic at the University of Illinois at Chicago. You can go elsewhere if you want, but they're one of the best. And I recommend you make an immediate appointment."

Harry stood up. "'Immediate' as in...?"

"Today, Mr. Bentley. Today, if at all possible! Give this referral to the doctor. It'll indicate why I've sent you."

Harry left the glasses store with his mind spinning. What was the rush? He'd been dealing with this blind spot for a month now. And he didn't have time to spend all day in doctors' offices. But, Harry told himself, he wasn't the kind of guy who ran from problems either, so when he got in his car, he took out his cell phone and made the call, not really expecting to get an immediate appointment, hoping, in fact, that he'd have a few days to think about all this. But the receptionist told him to come right in, and in a matter of minutes Harry was heading south on Western Avenue toward the University of Illinois' Chicago campus.

THE MAGAZINES IN THE WAITING ROOM were months old and held no interest for Harry. He looked around at the other patients, some bent over as though they were almost asleep, some with a patch on one of their eyes. Only one woman in the corner was reading, but she kept squinting at her book as though she couldn't see. Everyone seemed as much in shock as Harry felt. How could this be happening to him? He was healthy and not that old. He liked his silvery beard, and as for his bald head, he didn't have much hair, but it was smooth and shiny because he shaved it. It was the sexy way to go. Even guys with plenty of hair shaved their heads these days.

So God, why is my eyesight failing me?

"Mr. Bentley?"

It didn't sound like the voice of God, but Harry looked toward the door and held up his hand anyway.

"Follow me, please."

The technician ushered Harry into a dimly lit office and to a barber-type chair like the one he'd been in an hour before in the For Eyes store. Same routine with the eye chart, and then a bunch of questions about his general health, especially focusing on whether he had diabetes. Then the technician put some drops in his eyes and said the doctor would see him shortly.

"*Shortly*" took a half hour, just sitting in that dim room with nothing to do but rehearse all his worst fears—brain tumor, macular degeneration, stroke. He kept flipping through the horror stories like a deck of cards. Finally the doctor came in and introduced himself as Dr. Howard Racine. He repeated the slit-lamp exam, which was even more uncomfortable now that the drops had dilated Harry's eyes. Then the doctor performed a number of other exams, including testing the pressures in his eyes and looking into them in every way possible, some of which hurt as the doctor pressed on his eyeballs from the side to seemingly look into the very "corners."

Finally, he stood back and turned up the room lights slightly. "Well, Mr. Bentley, I think I can tell you why you have a blind spot in your left eye. You have what's known as a macular hole."

"A what? That's not macular degeneration, is it? I've read about that."

"No, not macular degeneration. I see no sign of that, fortunately. But the eye is a marvelous and complex organ. In the back of the eye there is a layer of cells known as the retina that is attached to the wall of the eye. These cells are sensitive to light and send messages that the brain can interpret as images. That's how we see. We call the very center of the retina, where our vision and focus is most acute, the macula.

"Now,"—he held up both hands, fingers splayed as though he were holding a basketball—"the whole eye is filled with is a clear jelly-like substance, known as the vitreous. When a person approaches the age of sixty, the vitreous begins to shrink. As it does so, parts of it can stick to the retina and begin to tug as the vitreous contracts. If it sticks too strongly, it can actually tear holes in the retina. When that happens right at the macula—the very center of our visual focus—we call it a macular hole. If it happens away from the focal point, we just call it a retinal tear. You following me so far?"

"I guess so. You sayin' that's what's happenin' to me?"

"We've got some more tests to run, but that's what I'm seeing." The doctor held his left hand out, palm down, and pinched the loose skin on the top of his hand, pulling it up like a tent. "Before the vitreous tears a complete hole, it tugs on the macula like this, raising the center until it is so out of focus you perceive it as a blind spot, while lines and images immediately around are distorted. Does that describe what you see?"

"Yeah. Yeah, that's pretty much it," Harry said, recalling how the lines from the window blinds appeared to curve around his blind spot. Somehow, understanding more about what was happening within his eye gave him a sense of hope. Surely, if the doctors knew so much, they would know enough to fix it. Right?

"So, what happens now?" he asked.

"Like I said, I want to run some more tests, but at this point you seem to be in Stage 1, and your vision is only down to about 20/80."

"You mean it could get worse?"

Dr. Racine smiled. "The good news is that about 50 percent of Stage 1 holes resolve spontaneously. That is, the vitreous pulls loose and the macula returns to a normal smooth surface before the cells in that spot die from having been pulled away from their point of nourishment. The bad news is, 50 percent go on to get worse. So, this is what I'm thinking: If it doesn't resolve in the next few weeks, we can do a vitrectomy—that means taking out some of that gel, especially where it's tugging on your macula."

"Will that fix it?"

"Can't say 'fix.' It will stop the traction that is causing this specific problem, but then we have to heal that little wound, flatten the tent, so to speak. We do that by injecting a gas bubble into your eye, and then having you remain face down. The bubble floats up—or when you're face down, to the back of your eye—and gently holds the macula in place while it reattaches to the wall of your eye."

The doctor stood there as though there was more to say while Harry imagined the gruesome prospect: poking holes in his eye, injecting gas, yuk! He'd heard people talk about eye surgery—Lasik surgery, cataract removal—like it was nothing, but he'd never imagined actually cutting into the eyeball, putting something inside it. He felt queasy, almost sick to his stomach. He held his breath for a moment and then swallowed. "So, what about my vision?" That, after all, was the real question. He could tolerate anything if it would restore his sight.

"That depends on how well the hole heals … and that has a lot to do with how disciplined you can be in maintaining a face-down position to let the gas bubble do it's work."

"Oh, I can be disciplined. I was in the Army, and I'm a retired Chicago Police Officer." But he'd also had a drinking problem, which for years hadn't yielded to mere will power even as he watched it destroy his marriage and cause him to lose his relationship with his son. But surely this was different. "So, how long's this face down business last? Will I have to stay overnight in the hospital to do it?"

The doctor started to chuckle then caught himself and sobered his face. "As long as there are no complications, the surgery can be outpatient. You can go home within a few hours. But the face down part …" His eyebrows went up and he took a deep breath like a swimmer preparing to dive in. "We're talking at least two weeks, but—"

Two weeks? Had he heard right? Harry's mind was swirling, causing him to feel so dizzy he was glad he wasn't standing up. How could he possibly remain in such a strange position for *two weeks*? He'd end up looking like a ninety-eight-year-old man all curled over into a hump with arthritis. He couldn't do that. There was just no way, blind or not.

"Mr. Bentley? … Mr. Bentley, there are devices to help you maintain face down. Have you ever gotten a backrub, perhaps in the mall or at a convention where you had to sit on one of those forward leaning chairs while you got the massage?"

The room slowed its swirling as Harry focused on the doctor's question. "No, but I've seen 'em."

"Well, you can rent one of those chairs. They include a face rest that enables you to stay in a face-down position quite comfortably. And at night, there are foam wedges and a foam donut pillow that lets you sleep comfortably on your stomach."

"Sleep on my stomach? You talkin' twenty-four/seven?"

"That's right … maintaining a face-down position is crucial for the best chances of recovering your sight."

"Wow. And for two weeks, you say?"

"At least two weeks."

"But how would I eat? What about walking to the bathroom? Do I have to sit in that chair all the time?"

"Oh, you can eat. You just have to keep your head bowed. You pray before you eat, Mr. Bentley? This would be …" he shrugged, "just praying through the meal."

Harry laughed nervously. "Well, Estelle's gonna love that."

"Who?"

"Never mind. It's just that I don't usually pray that long."

"Well, it's better than fasting. And as for walking around, it's best if you stay mostly in the house unless someone's with you."

He's already presuming I'm going to have the surgery, thought Harry.

"When you're standing up, just keep watching your toes and be careful not to run into anything. And when you're sitting in your massage chair, you might want to use mirrors so you can see other people in the room or watch TV. I had a patient who kept working on his laptop by putting it on a low table under him where he could look down on it all day. It's possible.... but we're not there yet. Let's give your eye a chance to resolve spontaneously. Okay? For now, I'm going to send you next door for some more tests, but then I want to see you again in a week. They'll schedule you out front."

The doctor closed the folder he was holding, shook Harry's hand and turned to leave. He was halfway out the door when he turned back. "Just one other thing, Mr. Bentley. If you should note any significant changes in your vision, give us a call. Especially if you experience bright flashes off to the periphery or a shower of floaters—you know what they are, don't you?" At the dull shake of Harry's head, he continued. "Sometimes they appear as little spider-web things or a black dot that seems to float in your vision. We're not worried about a small one or two, but if you begin seeing a lot of them, or—and this is really crucial—if anything like a gray curtain begins to close over your vision, you call us immediately and come right in. All right? Okay, you have a good day, now." And he left.

Good day? Yeah, right! The man had just announced Harry's personal apocalypse, and he was supposed to have a *good day?*

Chapter 3

HARRY DROVE OVER TO WESTERN AVENUE and turned north. The clouds from the morning were breaking up, and his still-dilated eyes couldn't take the brightness. Even his shades weren't enough to keep his eyes from involuntarily squinting and closing so tightly that he had to force them open again and again. He probably shouldn't even be driving like this, but he had to get home. In the back of his RAV4 somewhere was his White Sox cap. Maybe it would help. He pulled over to stop and went around to open the back. After shuffling around for a few moments, he found the old thing and pulled it low over his eyes. Ah ... slight relief. It was even better when he "saluted his nose" with one hand, creating nothing but a small slit between the edge of his hand and the brim of his cap. *Kind of like the snow goggles Eskimos wore*, he thought. But he couldn't drive like that.

Back in his SUV, Harry eased away from the curb. He knew he was driving like an old man in a huge 1960 Oldsmobile "boat," all hunched up over the wheel, squinting to see where he was going so he wouldn't hit anyone. Ha! If he so much as scratched another car again, Estelle would confiscate his keys. He loved that woman, but sometimes, sometimes ...

The driver behind honked long and loud and flipped Harry the bird as he roared past. This was terrible. Everything Harry did depended on being able to see clearly, and right now he felt like he was looking through the bottom of a milky glass—everything too bright and white, and nothing very distinct!

Hadn't Jesus healed a lot of blind people when He was on earth? He put mud on the eyes of one guy and told him to go wash it off, and he could see again. Someone else only got partially healed—he said men looked like trees walking—until he came back and Jesus finished the job. Harry had been reading his Bible. And he knew crowds of people—many of whom were blind—had followed Jesus all over the country to witness or receive healings.

"So, Jesus, how 'bout me?" Harry shouted at the roof of his SUV. "Hey! How 'bout *me*? … Oh man, I can't do this!"

For days, even weeks he'd been praying, but God hadn't even sent back a text message. Had God forgotten him totally, or—Harry didn't want to think about the possibility—perhaps there was no God after all.

He tried to think back to what had restored his faith after so many years. It had happened a couple of months before, when DaShawn had come to live with him. On his own, Harry had tried and failed at every attempt he'd made to get his grandson back. But when he prayed with the brothers in the men's Bible study, God had seemed to make a way. But was that God, or had he just been fooling himself? He'd been so sure it was God that he'd started going to church again—with Estelle's encouragement, of course—started praying again, started reading his Bible … couldn't really say "again" on that one 'cause he'd never been much of a Bible reader before. But now he was trying, keeping up with the men's Bible study, and even reading other passages on his own.

But what good had it done him? Now that he desperately needed God's help, where was He?

Harry blinked and looked around. While wondering where God was, he'd lost track of where *he* was. He knew these streets, nearly every one of them, but he couldn't place the businesses and buildings he was now passing. He'd intended to turn on Peterson, but … uh, he squinted at the next green street sign: "Greenleaf?" How had he gotten this far north? He didn't recall passing the cemetery or even Warren Park. To go to his apartment, he should have turned east before this. Well, he could turn on Estes, but it had stop signs every block. Might as well wait and take Touhy Avenue over toward the lake.

The Bakers Square restaurant on the corner of Western and Touhy was easier to see than the green street sign hanging from the signal. Harry turned right. At least now he knew where he was. Yeah, and up ahead on the left was "The Office," that friendly little bar he and his partner, Cindy Kaplan, used to stop at all the time when he was on the police force and they were working Special Ops. Harry remembered it being nice and dark inside, free from the glare that was still hurting his eyes. On impulse he pulled into the string of open parking spaces. Why not? He needed to unwind and let his eyes return to normal. After all, it wasn't safe driving like this.

Inside, the dim lighting soothed his tired eyes. He saw only two other customers in the bar—a couple huddled over their table in the back, twittering the nonsense of young love.

Harry slid up on a barstool.

He was going to say, "Just give me a Coke." But then he noticed the Sam Adams handle for the on-tap beers. A cool one would taste so good right now. Surely he deserved a break after what he'd just been through. It had been a year and a half since he'd had a drink. He'd broken the back of his drinking problem, no question. Besides, now he wasn't in that pressure-cooker of a job that had caused his drinking to get out of control. Every day, every day, wound tight as a bowstring. It was insane. And his wasn't the only family that had crumbled under the pressure. Nearly every cop he knew had issues at home because of the tension on the job.

But now he was free from it. He'd learned a lot about himself in AA, enough to handle just one glass of beer.

"How 'bout a Sam Adams?"

"Comin' right up."

Harry had never met this bartender, so he wouldn't remember the times Harry'd made a fool of himself at "The Office," requiring Cindy to throw his arm over her shoulder as she helped him out the door. For years he'd kept his drinking to after hours, but when it had finally started interfering with his work, he'd been lucky to have a partner like Cindy to cover for him when necessary and to urge him to seek help. And AA had worked.

But now, things were different, and the cold Sam Adams tasted so good.

Harry stared at the White Sox game on the TV for a while as he sipped his beer. "What's that score? Just been to the eye doctor, and can't see too well."

The bartender checked the screen. "Top of the eighth. White Sox eleven to one over the Kansas City Royals."

"*Eleven to one*! All right! Go White Sox!" He pushed his cap up a little.

"That why you still wearin' your shades?"

"What?" Harry pulled off the sunglasses. "Oh, yeah." He grimaced and put them back on. "Still too bright. My eyes are as dilated as a crackhead's, but it's just those drops the eye doctor put in 'em. I got tested real good this afternoon."

" 'Nother beer?"

"Oh, yeah. Thanks."

Harry sat through a couple more beers until the White Sox wrapped it up, twelve to two. Harry removed his shades. He hadn't thought about his eyes even once during those last two innings. But it was time to get home. DaShawn would already be there. He settled his tab and slid off his stool, holding onto the bar as he started toward the door.

"You okay, buddy? Want me to call you a cab?"

Harry looked at him and frowned. "Ah, no. I'm good. Must be those eye drops. Kind of make my eyes go ..." He held up his hand, fingers splayed, and waved it back and forth. "You understand?"

"Oh yeah, I understand. What I understand is, you need a ride. Look, this is just a quiet neighborhood bar, and I can't risk my license. I probably should've cut you off, but you didn't really have that many. I didn't realize ..." He picked up his phone and dialed while Harry stood there staring at him, feeling his world waver.

If he took a cab home now, how was he going to retrieve his car? He'd have to walk all the way up here later tonight or tomorrow morning.

It was when he was climbing the stairs to his apartment twenty minutes later that it struck Harry how much like "the bad ol' days" this was—holding on to the banister to keep his balance, wondering what excuse he'd give his wife and son. He'd lost them because of the drinking. Now he had DaShawn. Would the boy notice? *"Oh, I've been to the eye doctor, and he put drops in my eyes"* ... yeah, right!

He was at his door, ready to put his key in the lock when he heard Estelle's voice from within, laughing and talking with DaShawn. Oh no! What was she doing here? She'd certainly understand the implications of his condition, and there'd be no excuses for her! He'd started drinking again! Drinking again? But he'd only had three or four beers, half of what he used to chug down in an evening, and no hard liquor. Harry was a cop. He knew the alcohol consumption chart. He should still be sober enough to drive. Maybe it was true what they said in AA: If an alcoholic returns to the bottle after an extended abstinence, he'll have no tolerance.

Oh, the heck with it! Why not just go in there and tell them: "Whatcha see is whatcha get: I'm drunk!" But he wasn't quite that far gone. He still cared what Estelle would think. He turned from the door and crept quietly down the stairs, willing the cobwebs out of his mind.

Estelle was caring for DaShawn. Harry needed to think. He started walking around the block. The sun would be setting in another half hour or so, but he could tell his eyes were returning to normal … all except for the blind spot. That was definitely still there. But without realizing it, the way he'd chosen to escape worrying about his eyes had only created more problems. Why hadn't he stopped with just one beer? Obviously, he'd welcomed the warm buzz that dulled the horror of his day, all the gruesome talk about cutting into his eyeball. He turned the corner and kept walking. Unfortunately, reaching for the liquid escape had been what he'd always done when the pressure got too great.

He had to face it: He'd fallen down but … but he wasn't "back on the bottle." He wouldn't accept *that* characterization of himself. One mistake was enough. He'd learned his lesson: He was still an alcoholic and couldn't have "just one beer." That might be fine for other people, but not for him. It wasn't the way for him to cope with his pressures!

But how could he be sure he wasn't back on the bottle? What would keep him from getting hammered tomorrow night? Wait a minute … tomorrow was Tuesday, men's Bible study night. That's it. He'd go hang out with the guys. He hadn't been to an AA meeting in a long time, but perhaps they could be his support group. Of course, he'd have to confess what had happened, but maybe they'd have some ideas about how to handle Estelle.

He'd gone around the block. The walking—and the time—had definitely sobered him up. He'd go get his car. It was only a couple of miles away. He picked up his pace as he passed his apartment building and headed for Touhy Avenue.

As for Estelle, he'd better call her at least. As it was, he knew she'd be fit to be tied. He dialed his cell …

"Oh, hi Estelle. It's me."

"I know it's you. Where you been? DaShawn came home, and no one was here, so he called me. Where you at, Harry Bentley? You shoulda been—"

"Estelle, Estelle, just listen to me a minute. I went to the eye doctor today, like you wanted me to. But they saw some problems and sent me down to the eye clinic at the University of Illinois at Chicago—"

"See, I knew it, Harry. I knew you needed to see a doctor. It's—"

"Estelle, please. Let me explain." Harry took a deep breath and turned a corner, walking a little faster. What was he going to explain? What *could* he explain? What did he even know? That was the scary part. But he had to try. "It turns out I have what they call a 'macular hole' in my left eye—"

"A hole in your eye? How could there be a hole in your eye? I've never seen a—"

"Estelle, it's not a hole like that. I'll explain later. But it's … well, it might get better on it's own, and it might not. And … and to be honest, it's all kind of scary. I … I haven't been handling it too well. I need a little more time to think about what the doctor said. You follow me?"

"I guess so, but Harry—"

"Look, I'm on my way to get my car right now, and then I need to stop and get something to eat. Could you hang in there with DaShawn? I'll be glad to give you a ride to your place when I get back."

"Why don't you just come straight home, Harry? I'll fix you something to eat here, and we can talk about it then. You just come home, okay?"

"Not yet, Estelle. Can you just give me this? I'll be there in an hour or so."

Except for a TV laugh-track Harry could hear in the background, there was a long silence on the phone. Finally, Estelle said, "Okay, Harry, but you shouldn't keep this all inside yourself. I'm here for you, Harry. You know that, don't you?"

"I know it, Estelle. I'll see you in a few."

He knew he'd have to tell her soon. Neither of them wanted a relationship with secrets, and his "fall" this afternoon couldn't be the first one.

Chapter 4

ONCE HE'D PICKED UP HIS RAV4, HARRY SWUNG BY the McDonalds on the corner of Clark and Pratt—one of DaShawn's favorite feeding troughs—and ingested enough calories and salt for a week, but it gave him time to sit and think. Estelle would want to know what the doctor had said as soon as he got home. And he could tell her about that. He could even tell her how scared it made him. She'd understand ... once she'd lectured him two or three times about how she'd told him so, about going to an eye doctor. But he could see that one coming, and he knew how to handle it: Don't argue and don't get defensive. Just thank her for caring enough to get him to go.

And that was the truth. Her concern had been part of convincing him he needed to check out his eyes. Whether it ended up doing him any good—anything other than scaring the wiggle out of him—was yet to be seen.

He'd also go to Bible study tomorrow night and tell the guys. Ask them to pray for him. Pray that God would do another miracle for him, like He had when He arranged DaShawn's return, and this time heal his eye. But maybe he didn't need to say more to the guys ... at least for now. They were a cool group of men, a lot more spiritual than he was. What would they think of him if he told them he fell off the wagon? After all, they weren't an AA group. He shouldn't put that on them. Besides, he was sober now, and he wouldn't make such a stupid mistake again. Why embarrass himself by airing his dirty laundry? Just being with the guys would be enough. And it would ensure he didn't drop by "The Office" again, at least not tomorrow night.

But he shouldn't fool himself. His problem wasn't "The Office." The last time he'd been in that bar his former boss, Lieutenant Matty Fagan, had threatened him for blowing the whistle on Fagan's corrupt use of Chicago's elite anti-gang unit, but Harry had held his ground. "Ha, ha!" Harry chuckled to himself. He'd more than held his ground. Too often he'd witnessed Fagan confiscate drugs, money, and weapons and beat up kids … without arresting them. It was his little scheme: Keep the money and sell the drugs and guns while the criminals went free to gather more. But Harry had actually tricked Fagan into providing him with concrete evidence of his corruption, and soon Fagan would be indicted. It had been a stressful evening, and Fagan was a dangerous enemy, but Harry hadn't even felt tempted to drink.

So why had he buckled today? And what about next time? What if his eye didn't recover spontaneously? What if God didn't do a miracle? Well, he'd cross that bridge when he came to it. He threw his trash in the McDonald's bin and stacked his tray on top. He'd go face Estelle, then tomorrow night he'd go to Bible study.

ESTELLE WASN'T NEARLY AS HARD ON HARRY as he'd expected. If he still smelled like stale beer, she didn't mention it, and there were no I-told-you-so's when he reported the eye problem the doctors found. In fact, once he'd reported what Dr. Racine had said and answered what questions he could, she gave him a hug. "Well, I think we need to pray. Mind if I pray for you right now?"

"No, not at all. That'd be good."

They were sitting side-by-side on Harry's old couch, and she put her hand on his knee. "Father, You know all about our eyes. You made us, Father. You are *Elohim*, our All-Powerful Creator, so You know what's going wrong with Harry's eye. And You are *Jehovah-Rapha*, our Healer. So in our time of need, we are turning to You for healing, Father. And this problem frightens us, too. But You are greater than any of our fears. You are *Jehovah-Shalom*, our Peace, so right now we ask for your peace. And please give us both a good night's sleep tonight. In Jesus name, Amen."

Harry sat there for a moment with Estelle's hand still on his knee. The whole time she'd spoken of *we* and *our* and *us both*. Something he didn't quite understand had just happened, and he had to wipe tears from the corners of his eyes.

"Well," said Estelle as she stood up, "Gotta get home. You did say you'd give me a lift, right?"

"Oh yeah! Of course."

Harry checked on DaShawn—who was still reading in his bed—and told him he'd be out a few minutes. "I'm glad to see you reading, but it's time to turn out the light. Okay, buddy?"

THE NEXT MORNING, HARRY WAS ON HIS WAY BACK from delivering DaShawn to basketball camp when his cell rang, and the caller ID showed it was Estelle. He glanced around—no cops—so he pressed Talk.

"Yeah?"

"Harry, it's Estelle. I just tried to call Leroy, but some stranger answered and wouldn't tell me a thing. I'm worried, Harry. But I can't do nothin' 'bout it 'cause I don't have a car, and I have to cook lunch at the shelter and—"

"Hold on, slow down a minute, Estelle. Who you talkin' 'bout?"

"Leroy, my son, Leroy. He lives in my house on the Southside. You remember, I told you about him."

"I thought you said his name was Michael."

"Well, it's actually, Michael Leroy Williams. I don't know, maybe it's his illness, but he up and decided he doesn't like the name Michael anymore, so I'm trying to honor his request and call him Leroy—"

"You call him back? Maybe you dialed the wrong number."

"I didn't get the wrong number, Harry." Her voice got level, explainy. "The guy *knew* Leroy, he just wouldn't let me talk to him … or tell me anything about him. And, yes I did call back, but no answer. That's what worries me. Anyway, there's no time to get down there and back by public transportation …."

"So … you want me to go check on him. That it?"

"If you got time, Harry. If you got the time. I know this is awful last minute."

"Don't worry, Estelle. I can do it." There was something about the way she'd prayed for him the night before that made Harry ready to do anything for this lady, even if he couldn't marry her. "But you gotta tell me again where he lives. Do you have a key or something in case he's not there?"

"I got a key. Can you drop by Manna House? It's in my purse."

"See you in a few."

Harry glanced at his watch. If it didn't take Estelle too long to find the key in that big bag of a purse she carried, he ought to have plenty of time to get down to the Southside and back before DaShawn got out of basketball camp. But if he had to, he'd call DaShawn and tell him to go over to his great-grandma's house. He hoped he wasn't imposing on her too often, but she seemed to like having DaShawn visit, and DaShawn usually had a good attitude about helping out his great-grandma. But he didn't want to push it too far. After all, when he was that age, he wanted to play with his friends, not hang out with old people whose idea of fun was watching soaps and napping in front of the TV.

THOUGH IN OBVIOUS NEED OF MAINTENANCE—cardboard in a broken front window, unmowed patches of grass instead of lawn, trash everywhere, no flowers or shrubs—Estelle's brownstone was classic Chicago and worth enough to have kept her out of the shelter if she hadn't left it to her abusive son.

As Harry recalled the story, Michael—or rather Leroy—was probably schizophrenic and had begun pushing Estelle around one day, causing her to fall and hit her head hard enough that she had to go to the emergency room. Though she didn't think he'd ever get violent with anyone else, she didn't want Leroy to get institutionalized, so when a friend told her about Manna House, she left her home to her son and fled north to the shelter where she checked in as a victim of domestic violence. But she quickly got back on her feet as the paid lunch cook, teaching various classes at Manna House, and doing in-home elder care part time. That gave her the resources to move out of the shelter and share an apartment with Leslie Stuart, the social worker who had helped Harry get DaShawn back.

Estelle was doing well enough on her own, even continuing to pay the taxes on her place. But it made Harry grit his teeth as he climbed the steps—to think, a fine woman like her with a house like this, but she couldn't even live in her own home. He shook his head and punched the doorbell.

41

No sound from inside. Maybe the bell was too quiet, but more likely it didn't work. He didn't bother pushing the button a second time. Just knocked on the door.

He waited … still no response. This time he banged with his fist, loud enough for the neighbors to hear. Finally, he heard movement, something was being slid to the side, and then the door opened two inches.

"Yeah."

All Harry could see was some unkempt, nappy hair, one eye, and a slice of face with a week's growth of beard. "You Leroy Williams?"

"Who's askin'?"

"Harry Bentley, a friend of your mom."

"I ain't Leroy."

Harry smiled. "Ha! You gotta be kiddin'. You Michael today?"

"Don't know no Michael."

Oka-a-a-y, this wasn't getting very far. "So, can I come in?"

"Have to ask Leroy." And the door closed.

Harry raised his hands in helplessness and spun around to face the street. So what was that about? Had Estelle's son split into three personalities now? A couple of minutes passed as Harry stood there closing one eye and then the other. Checking his blind spot had become a habit. Should he try the door again or just leave and tell Estelle he'd seen her son, but he didn't want to talk?

The door creaked again, and Harry turned back as it opened a crack.

"He say he don't know you."

But Harry hadn't been a Chicago cop for twenty years for nothing. He jammed the toe of his shoe into the opening and smiled as warmly as possible. "That's because we never met, so step back.

I'm comin' in to get acquainted." And with one mighty lunge, Harry pushed his way through the door.

Whether the guy fell back on his own or from Harry's shove, he was no longer in the small entryway but standing in the darkened room just beyond, hands before his face as though he feared being hit. Harry caught the sweet scent of burned Styrofoam: crack cocaine. If Leroy was on the pipe, who knew what his mental state might be?

Harry shrugged, palms up. "Hey man, everything's cool. I ain't gonna hurt you. Just wanna talk." The guy lowered his hands a few inches and stared at Harry, eyes wide. Then tentatively he dropped his hands to his sides as Harry stepped into the room.

They weren't alone. Half a dozen people were scattered around the room—blacks, whites, Latinos. Drugs integrate anyone. Some were stoned. Some asleep. The underwear-clad body of a very pregnant young white woman shook with sobs as she lay on her side, hair hiding her face.

"Oh no, Leroy. Whadda you doin' here? How could you do this to your mama? I know she raised you better'n this!"

"I ain't Leroy!" the guy who'd opened the door said. "He's upstairs."

"You what?"

"I said, I ain't Leroy. He's upstairs."

Harry looked around at the other bodies in the room as if they could confirm or deny this bit of information. But no one moved. "All right." He looked back at his ... *host*. "Lead the way."

Harry followed the man into a dark hall. "How 'bout some lights?" he said.

"No electricity."

"Figures."

At the top of the stairs the man took a key from a hook on the wall and unlocked a large padlock on the first door. Harry put his hand on the guy's shoulder. "Whadda you doin'?"

"You said you wanted to see Leroy."

"You got him locked up in there?"

"Yeah. Whadda you expect? He's crazy. The Mick said we gotta keep him locked up."

"Oh, yeah? Who's the Mick?" Harry stepped into the room as the door swung open but as quickly reached back, grabbed his guide by the collar, and dragged him in too. "No, no, no! You're not gonna trap me in here, too. Give me that padlock."

He took one whiff of the stale air heavy with smell of urine and sweat. "Get over there and open a window." He gave the guy a shove.

"He's liable to jump out."

Harry studied the frail shell of a man on the bed. "You Leroy Williams? Estelle's boy?"

The man nodded.

Harry stepped forward and extended his hand. "I'm Harry Bentley, friend of your mama's. This is terrible." He surveyed the room again. "Can you stand up?"

Leroy swung his feet off the bed and stood up, only slightly relying on assistance from Harry's firm grip.

"You been smokin' dope with these people?"

"No sir."

"Hmm." Harry studied Leroy's eyes, and after a moment nodded his head. He grabbed his arms to check for tracks. "Okay. How long you been locked up in here?"

Leroy shrugged.

"They feed you? Want somethin' to eat?"

He nodded.

"You like Mexican? Saw a Mexican place back down the street." When Leroy nodded again, Harry said, "Get your shoes and wash your face. I'm gettin' you outta here."

Once Leroy had cleaned up a little and put on some sneakers, Harry ushered him out the door. "You get that hasp off the door," he said to the punk who had let him in. "And you get everybody outta here before we get back, or I'm gonna have the cops up in here to clean you out so fast you'll think they came on a bolt of lightning. Understand?"

The guy nodded, but as they went downstairs, Harry realized he had no idea where he would take Leroy on such short notice to get him "outta there." Navigating the Department of Human Services and the Division of Mental Health to get the boy the help he needed could require a lot of red tape and more time than Harry had right now, given his own problems, especially with his eye.

Chapter 5

Leroy didn't want to talk much while they ate lunch, and Harry hesitated to push it. The guy was obviously hungry and confused—and embarrassed about both. But something had to change.

Harry spooned some of the *salsa picante* onto his rice and beans and reached for a tortilla. "So whadda we gonna do here, Leroy? Even if we kick 'em out, those guys'll be back. Shuttin' down a crack house takes more than me yellin' at 'em."

Leroy shrugged and kept shoveling in bites of his *chile relleno* without looking Harry in the eye.

Harry studied him a few moments, estimating that Leroy was close to thirty. "You know you could be charged under the federal crack house statute for what's going on up in there. You live there. That makes you responsible. Now, you might beat the rap given you didn't have much choice about them lockin' you up and all, but it could get ugly, especially if some of those guys fingered you in a deal with the DA. You understand what I'm tellin' you?"

Leroy nodded, but kept his head down.

"I think you oughta get out. Whaddaya say?"

"Can't do that."

"Why not?"

"Ain't got no place to go. Besides, I'm lookin' after my mom's house."

Harry laughed. "You what? You think you're lookin' after it? Son, I got news for you: You're puttin' her at risk, too. If the cops come in to shut that place down, it could get condemned. Then she'd lose everything."

Leroy finished the last couple of bites without responding.

Harry wiped the corners of his mouth with a napkin. "You need to find a safe place to live and let your mom bring in a rehab crew so she can sell that brownstone and get something out of it." Harry watched Leroy for a few moments without much hope that he was getting through to the kid. "Well, you think about it. I gotta go to the restroom. Be back in a minute."

But when Harry returned to his table, Leroy was gone, and the busboy was clearing away the dishes.

"Where'd that other guy go?"

"*No lo entiendo.*" He shrugged. "*No Inglés.*"

"Yeah, yeah. The other guy ... how do you say? *El otro hombre? Dónde?*"

"*Ah, sí—*" He rattled off a string of Spanish too fast for Harry to catch even a word, but he was pointing toward the front door and Harry got the message.

He tossed a twenty and a ten on the table to cover their lunches and ran outside, but Leroy was nowhere to be seen. Ten minutes later, Harry was back at the brownstone. This time he didn't bother to knock, just shoved open the door and stormed in. "Leroy! You in here? Don't play with me, son."

The only answer was the continued sobbing of the pregnant woman, who finally had some clothes on, probably as much as she ever wore this time of year. To Harry's surprise, everyone else had cleared out.

"Leroy here?"

The woman shook her head, stringy blond hair looking like it hadn't been washed for weeks.

"You need some help?"

She shook her head again and gulped to curtail her sobbing.

"Well then, got a place to stay?"

"Yeah, my mama's."

"Well, you better get on home then, and lay off that pipe! It'll destroy you and the baby." He nodded toward her stomach but didn't have much hope she'd take his advice. "Now get outta here!"

The young woman stuffed a few more things in a plastic shopping bag and grabbed up her whimpering baby as Harry started toward the stairs. "'Scuse me, mister," she called after him. "Any chance you could help me out a bit? I ain't got no fare money to get home. I'll be glad to mail it back, first thing. Mama's good for it."

Harry turned back to her and snorted. "Bet she is, but you ain't." He ran his hand over his bald head. What to do? "Look, I got some more stuff I gotta take care of here. You wait out there on the stoop. When I'm done, I'll put you on the bus, but I ain't givin' you no cash money. Where's your mom live, anyway?"

"Wheaton."

"Wheaton? Lord have mercy, girl! Whadda you doin' up in here anyway?"

She shrugged.

Harry sighed deeply. "All right then. I can go through the Loop, put you on the Metra, and send you straight home. You wait out there. I'll be along shortly."

Harry went upstairs shaking his head. That crack was a demon, no respecter of persons. It'd take anyone down!

The hasp was not off the door of Leroy's room, but neither was he locked inside. In fact, no one was upstairs. There had to be a screwdriver somewhere in the house to remove the lock. If not, Harry had one out of the car. He grabbed an old pillowcase while making a sweep through the house looking for a screwdriver and filled it with drug-related trash—burned scraps of aluminum foil, old candles, small mirrors, razor blades, scorched spoons, a couple of old needles, empty packets of blunt wraps, a roach clip, empty weed bags, and a broken glass pipe. Someone needed to clean out all the empty beer cans and booze bottles, too, but they weren't evidence of illegal activity, and he didn't have time now. As he carried the pillowcase out the backdoor and down the alley to a dumpster, Harry knew his search hadn't found everything that could be used against Leroy, but at least it wouldn't be so obvious. A screwdriver finally turned up in one of the kitchen drawers, and Harry went back upstairs to remove the hasp.

It was half past two when Harry finally came out of the house. He looked around. The woman and her baby were not waiting on the stoop or anywhere else. Figured … sadly. At least he wouldn't get caught in Loop traffic and should make it to the Northside in time to pick up DaShawn from basketball camp. Leroy wasn't back yet either … though Harry was sure he would return sooner or later. Where else could he go? He hung around for ten more minutes, then left. Leroy would have to fend for himself. At the moment, Harry didn't have anything better to offer him anyway. He started to lock the door, and then thought better of it. If Leroy didn't have a key, it would just be a hassle for him to get in. If the crackheads came back first, they'd just break in.

As he drove north, Harry decided he'd have to return later when he had enough time to try and get Leroy some help—maybe Thursday. No, he'd promised to take DaShawn and Gabby and her boys to the zoo on Thursday. He'd have to wait until Friday. Maybe in the meantime he could do a little research and have something concrete to suggest. But he couldn't do that this evening. He still wanted to go to the men's Bible study and get some prayer for his eyes.

His cell phone rang. He glanced at the caller ID. "Hi Estelle. I'm on my way home. See you in a few."

"But did you see Leroy?"

"Yeah, I saw him, and I took him out to lunch. There are some things we gotta work on, but right now I'm driving, Estelle. Can't be talkin' on the phone. Also, this evening I'm going to Bible study, but I'll get with you tomorrow. Okay?" He closed the cell. How would he tell Estelle? It was not a pretty picture, and it wasn't going to get any brighter either.

PETER DOUGLASS BUZZED HARRY INTO HIS APARTMENT building on Pratt Boulevard that evening and was waiting with the door open once Harry had climbed to the third floor.

"Am I the first one?"

"Looks like it. Come on in. The other guys should be here soon."

Harry had first met Peter Douglass last May when Harry dropped by Manna House for a "fun night" ... where he'd also met the enchanting Estelle Williams for the first time. Peter Douglass owned Software Symphony, served as one of the board members for the shelter, and his wife, Avis, was the principal of the school DaShawn would attend in the fall. She also led worship at SouledOut Community Church. Peter and Avis were one of those classy African American couples one might see at some gala fundraising ball.

It looked to be a *very* small Bible study that evening: just Peter, Denny Baxter—the white high school coach who had nudged Harry to return to the group—and Harry. Then Carl Hickman and young Josh Baxter showed up … better late than never. If Peter and Avis looked like Chicago society, Carl and his wife, Florida, were veterans of the streets. In fact, if Peter hadn't offered Carl a job as shipping manager at Software Symphony and urged him to get some more training at DeVry University, Carl might still be unemployed and defeated.

Harry had actually met Carl at that same Manna House fun night. It was Carl who had cut through the smokescreen Harry had put up to keep his distance from these men. But Carl knew what he was doing, and Harry needed a new circle of friends to replace the old companions he'd hung with when he was on the police force.

A *small* small group was fine with Harry. He'd just as soon not spread his stuff too wide. Instead of sitting in the living room, which could accommodate a larger number, the five of them gathered around the dining room table and opened their Bibles.

They were studying First Peter, chapter four, and Carl Hickman read the first few verses.

> Therefore, since Christ suffered in his body, arm yourselves also with the same attitude, because he who has suffered in his body is done with sin. As a result, he does not live the rest of his earthly life for evil human desires, but rather for the will of God. For you have spent enough time in the past doing what pagans choose to do—living in debauchery, lust, drunkenness, orgies, carousing, and detestable idolatry….

Carl read on, but Harry's mind focused on the first verses. When Carl finally stopped, Harry asked, "Does this mean if you suffer, you won't sin anymore, that you're supposed to be 'done with sin'?"

Everyone was quiet for a few moments, as though Harry had asked an awkward question. Finally, Peter Douglass said, "You're right, but I think the operative words are we're *'supposed to be.'* We're supposed to be done with sin. Check out what comes just before it. The apostle tells us to arm ourselves with Christ's attitude. He wouldn't have to say that if we didn't need an attitude adjustment."

"Yeah but, what does suffering have to do with it?"

"I don't know 'bout you," said Carl as he scanned the group, "but suffering had a way of forcing me to face what's really important in life. I really had to *go through it*, brother. Know what I'm sayin'? I had to go through it before I saw how stupid I was livin.' I had to decide I didn't want to live that way the rest of my life. Only then did I really turn to God for help. Every day I gotta *arm myself*—as the Word says—with the attitude of Christ who knew what suffering was, or I can't make it. Doin' it on my own never worked for me."

Harry looked back at the passage and all he saw was, "For you have spent enough time in the past … living in … drunkenness." Yeah, well, Harry knew about that. He'd lost his marriage to Willa May and his relationship with his son, Rodney—who now sat in Cook County Jail—and the whole mess was pretty directly connected to his drinking. But had he really learned his lesson? He thought he had … until yesterday.

The guys continued talking about the passage while Harry thought about Carl's claim that he needed to arm himself with the attitude of Christ in order to change. Was that what AA meant by appealing to a "God as we understand Him"? Perhaps, but Harry knew that when he was working the Twelve Steps, he didn't understand God very much at all. To him God was way off, up there somewhere. He'd never understood Him as Jesus Christ who'd lived on this earth and had experienced his kind of suffering.

Could that have made a difference yesterday when he felt so overwhelmed about his eye? He *was* suffering, no question about it. Not physical pain but in the sense that his whole future felt threatened. But any day now, it could end up being *both* eyes. He needed to talk about this.

"Excuse me, brothers, but I got a real-life issue here."

The conversation stopped as the others looked back and forth to one another. "That's okay. That's what we're supposed to be about," said Josh Baxter. "Lay it on us."

Oh yes, the boldness of youth. If he only knew! Well …

Harry took a deep breath and dove in. He hadn't intended to get so frank, but the more he talked, the more his fears about his vision came tumbling out until they lay there on the table like his whole hand of cards.

But there was still a card up his sleeve. He wiped his eyes with the back of his hand and studied the guys around the circle. Some were nodding their heads with a sober look on their faces, getting ready—Harry knew—to pray for him, which he needed and wanted. But … "There's one more thing. I don't know whether you guys know, but in the past I've had a problem with drinking." All right, be bold enough to say it like you did in AA. "Fact is, I'm an alcoholic … and yesterday after the doctor told me all this stuff, I kinda … well, I actually *did* fall off the wagon." Harry pulled at the horseshoe-shaped beard that outlined his jaw. "I walked out of that office feeling like I deserved a break. I stopped in a bar and ordered just one beer, feeling certain I could handle 'just one,' don'cha know? But before I was done, the bartender had to call a cab to take me home."

"After only one beer?" Denny frowned and sat back in his chair.

"No, no. I had a few more, but only about four. Used to drink more 'n twice that much all the time, but guess I'm more sensitive now, after being dry for a while."

"Wow!" Denny's eyebrows went up. "Hope we didn't cause you to stumble or anything."

"You? How could you have had anything to do with it?"

"Well …" Denny looked back and forth to the other guys. "I occasionally have a beer, and—"

"What's that got to do with me?"

Denny held out his hands. "Maybe … maybe we tempted you."

Harry shook his head. "Nah! That wasn't it. You weren't there pushin' more beers on me when you knew I had a problem. This was my issue. I appreciate your concern, but nobody was tempting me." Harry sat there a moment, then tapped the place where they were reading in the Bible with his finger. "This, this says something to me. Somethin' 'bout how Christ used suffering to defeat sin rather than letting it be an excuse to go back to the old ways of coping."

"Now you're talkin'," said Carl, "'cause that's what used to happen to me. I'd have a rough day—or maybe I'd even have a good day, didn't matter—and I'd think, ah, I deserve a break. 'Cept in my case it was a break from what was good for me."

Peter nodded his head. "Yeah, and it doesn't matter who you are either. I've seen businessmen, politicians, even pastors do it. Somehow we men think if we work real hard—whether it's doing something good or suffering something really hard—then we deserve a break from doing what's right. Well, we might need a rest, a chance to kick back and put our feet up, or a steak dinner or some other *good* reward. But where'd we get off thinking we 'deserve a break' from doing's what's right?"

Carl snorted. "Yeah! And taking a break from doing what's right don't give you no rest from whatever you're goin' through either. Just adds on to your problems."

Harry's head was swirling. It kind of made sense. "But, but what if you're really tired of doing what's right?"

Denny Baxter rested his elbows on the table. "Is that what you were facing? Were you tired of bein' sober?"

"No, no!" Harry shook his head. "That wasn't it at all. When I sat down at the bar, I was planning on having a Coke, but … but that draft beer just looked *so* good. That's when I said to myself, I need a brea—"

"Yeah," Denny jumped in, "that's it! It always looks good. It's like sex. There're plenty of women out there who 'look good,' right? And we've all heard about preachers fallin'."

Everyone nodded. "Oh yeah, way too many of 'em," added Peter.

"Sometimes we think they're total hypocrites—preachin' what they don't really believe—but I'm not so sure that's always the case—"

"But ain't that what a hypocrite is?" put in Josh. "Sayin' one thing and doin' another?"

"Yeah, but a lot of times I think these guys *do* believe what they're preaching. And a lot of times they claim that they never wanted to lose their marriage."

"Oh yeah," Carl sneered. "Afterwards, when they get caught and it's not just their marriage but their whole career goin' up in smoke, *then* they're sorry!"

Denny raised his hand. "Hold on, now. I'm sure that's true in some cases, but I've seen other preachers lose their pulpits and their reputation and they still are willing to go through whatever it takes to save their marriages. That tells me they weren't tired of being married or tired of their wife. I think Peter's onto something. If, when we're going through it, we think we deserve a break from the hard work of doing what's right, we're likely to fall."

Peter nodded. "And it doesn't matter whether you just ran ninety yards for the winning touchdown or closed a million-dollar deal or preached your heart out or were told by your doctor that he may have to cut your eyeball"—he looked at Harry—"it's all the same. If you think you deserve a break *because* of what you're goin' through, then it better be a break *from* what you're going through and not a break from doing right."

"Wait a minute," said Josh. "Run that one by me again."

"I said, if you think you deserve a break *because* of what you're goin' through, then it better be a break *from* what you're going through and not a break from doing right."

"Amen, amen. Right on!" declared Carl. "That's it!" He paused. " 'Course, can't always get a break *from* what you are going through, but that's just life. Ain't no excuse for doin' wrong."

Peter Douglass took a deep breath and turned back to Harry. "Hey, sorry, man. Didn't mean to preach at you, it's just that I've been trying to figure this out, too. And what you asked earlier about what suffering had to do with sin, that was the key for me. Suddenly, the whole thing began to fall into place."

The men around the table sat there in silence for a few moments. Then Harry shook his head. "Hey, I know you weren't tryin' to preach at me, but I can tell you I was more than a little shocked that I fell off the wagon. I thought I was over that stuff, but I tell ya …" He wiped his smooth head with his hand.

Carl Hickman began flipping through his Bible. "Got a verse for you, man. I have to go back to this one more often than I'd like to admit." He flipped a couple of more pages. "Here it is: Proverbs twenty-four and sixteen. 'Though a righteous man falls seven times, he rises again.' That's for you, Bro. Get back up again and again and again, however often it takes. That's what makes you a righteous man, not whether you never fall."

"Yeah, like what's that song we sometimes sing at SouledOut?" said Denny. " 'We Fall Down.' How's it go? *'Get back up again, Get back up again, Get back up again.'* I think that's our song, guys."

Chapter 6

To Harry's surprise, Estelle didn't bug him about his visit with Leroy. In fact, when he dropped by Manna House the next morning to talk to her, she waved him off. "Wait 'til we get these potatoes peeled and in the pot." Maybe she just didn't want to talk about a sensitive subject in front of the two shelter residents helping her in the kitchen. "In fact, if you want to help us, Harry, there's another peeler over there in that top drawer."

Harry rummaged around in the drawer until he found it. But still, how'd she do that? He knew she was probably itching to know every detail of his visit with her son, but she held off. Perhaps it was her way of coping with the sorrow and the struggle of not knowing how to care for an adult son with mental problems.

"There, Harry. That ought to be enough. Tawny, turn these potatoes down once they begin boilin'. I don't want a mess all over the top of my stove. And while I'm gone, the two of you can wash up those pots and pans and clean up this kitchen."

She took off her apron and turned to Harry. "Okay. Let's go for a walk."

Harry was tempted to give Estelle the "lite" version of his visit, but if he didn't mention Leroy's "guests" and how they'd locked him in his room, then it would look as though Leroy had condoned all the drugs and the mess. So he dove in.

"WHAT?" she yelled loudly enough for the people back at Manna House to hear. "You tellin' me my boy's locked in a room by a bunch of drug addicts? I thought you said he was okay. Whadda you mean, 'okay'?"

Harry put his hand on her shoulder. "Estelle, Estelle—"

"Don't be *Estellin'* me, Harry Bentley! Bein' locked up in your own house ain't okay! It just ain't okay, no way!"

"Estelle, listen to me. I chased out all those junkies. I took him out to lunch. But … like I tried to tell you on the phone yesterday, there's some things we gotta work on. Mostly, we need to get him out of that building and into a more supportive living situation."

She quieted herself after that, Harry presumed because she was still ambivalent about forcing Leroy to move. They walked on until she finally turned to him. "You don't think Leroy invited all those people into the house, do you?"

"I don't think so, Estelle. I think he just didn't know how to say no when the creeps started leaning on him. Know what I mean? He probably met one of 'em somewhere. Maybe the guy befriended him, then asked if he could crash for a night. One night turned into permanent. One guy turned into a dozen. He was probably locked up in that room precisely because he tried to get rid of 'em at some point. Anyway, he's really too vulnerable to live on his own, Estelle. We've got to find an alternative."

"But what, Harry? Every time I suggest something to him, he gets upset. And I don't want to commit him. I mean, I've got to think about his future. A record of mental problems could make it hard for him to get a job. Maybe I should move back home and take care of him … or bring him up here."

"And then what? That apartment you share with Ms. Stuart isn't big enough for him, too."

"Well, maybe I need to get a place of my own then."

"Maybe …" Harry couldn't help thinking how Leroy's inclusion in Estelle's life could seriously cramp his dreams of marrying her. But that was a selfish concern. Besides, with his one bad eye and the other in such an unpredictable state, the whole marriage thing was on hold … maybe even out of the question. "Still, Estelle, your son does need professional help wherever he lives. I mean, they've got a lot of new medications out there these days. Maybe all he needs is the right prescription, and then he could function normally."

"You mean, a pill for everything? That's what our society has come to these days, hasn't it?"

Harry shrugged. What could he say?

"I guess you're right," Estelle finally mumbled. "He does need help. And I've been too proud … or afraid to insist he get it. So what should I do, Harry?"

"I'm not sure. But I'll make some inquiries. I was planning on going back down on Friday to check on him. We can see where we go after that."

"You're really goin' down there again? I really appreciate that, Harry."

They walked on in silence for half a block before Estelle changed the subject. "So how's your eye doin'? You haven't mentioned it lately."

Harry shrugged and then did his wink-wink at a parking sign up ahead. "Guess they're 'bout the same."

"When did you say you're gonna see the doctor again?"

"S'pose to see him on Monday afternoon, but what's the point if nothin's changed?"

"Harry Bentley, I'm tellin' you! I listened to you about Leroy. Now you need to listen to me. You keep that appointment! You hear?"

Harry grinned at Estelle as they climbed the steps of Manna House. "Yes ma'am. I hear you."

Thursday afternoon, Harry followed through on his invitation to take Gabby Fairbanks and her boys to Chicago's Lincoln Park Zoo. Basketball camp wasn't over yet, but Harry figured it wouldn't hurt DaShawn to miss one afternoon. They arrived at the Firecracker's apartment at 2:30 to find—as Harry expected—the older Fairbanks boy in his usual sullen mood, the younger one upbeat and open, and Gabby downright eager to climb into the front seat of his RAV4. They roared off for Lake Shore Drive.

It was at the zoo while they were trying to decide which exhibits to visit first that Gabby caught Harry squinting and winking at his hand-held map. "You having trouble with your eyes, Mr. B?"

"Nah. It's nothing." He had to stop doing that. Checking his eyes all the time was becoming a habit. "Just get this weird blind spot now and then." Of course, it was certainly more than *now and then*, but why worry her?

"A blind spot! You should get it checked out. An ophthalmologist or somebody might be able to do something before it gets worse."

He shrugged. He had gone to an optometrist who had sent him to an ophthalmologist where he had learned the frightening prognosis. But what good had that done other than give him more to worry about? He didn't want to have to tell the Firecracker the whole story. "I dunno. Don't really have time now that I got DaShawn—"

61

"Grandpa! Grandpa!" Ah, saved by DaShawn. The boy was hopping up and down at the top of a ramp that led to an underwater window in the polar bear exhibit. "Come see!"

DaShawn's announcement brought more than Harry and Gabby to stare into the great bear's tank. Soon a small crowd gathered to watch the massive body slide like a white ghost past the underwater window again and again, turning and thrusting with so little effort he seemed to mock the gaping landlubbers. *If only it was as easy for us to slip through life,* thought Harry. On the other hand, that bear was confined in an environment smaller than a pixel of its natural twenty-thousand-square-mile range. Perhaps freedom was worth the price of its hardships.

Harry followed Gabby and the boys around for the next couple hours as they examined the giraffes and elephants, the big cats, the reptiles, and the apes. Finally, to relieve his aching back, he sent the boys off on a paddleboat to explore the lagoon while he sat down on a bench. "Whoo-ee!" he patted the bench beside him to invite Gabby to join him. "I must be crazy thinkin' I can raise a nine-year-old." He watched the paddleboat, hoping the boys didn't get so rowdy they'd tip it over. "How you doin' with the single parent thing, Firecracker?"

Gabby sighed. "I don't know. I'm afraid I let Philip take care of a lot of things, never thought I'd have to know stuff—like how to buy a car. And I need one, like, yesterday! But a savvy car salesman could sniff out in two seconds that I'm a sucker." She turned toward Harry. "You got any advice?"

"You really askin'?" Harry grinned. "Buy used. Just a year or two old can save you some big bucks, and it'll still have a lot of miles left on it. Less of an invitation to car thieves, too. But you gotta know what to check out so you don't get a lemon."

She rolled her eyes, then cleared her throat. "You know what I'm going to ask you, right?"

He brushed his hand over his head, feeling the beginning of stubble in the few places where baldness wasn't natural. He'd sure walked into that one! "All right, but I can't do it tomorrow. Tomorrow I promised Estelle I'd check on—"

"Oh, neither can I. Work, you know! Saturday would be as close to 'yesterday' as I can come. But would you? I'd be forever grateful."

"Saturday it is, then."

As he drove to check on Leroy the next day, Harry's expectations were low. He'd be lucky if Leroy was still there. He'd be even luckier if all the druggies hadn't moved back in. Estelle was going to have to make some hard decisions. There was no way they could monitor the situation from all the way across town.

The door of the brownstone was locked, but Leroy himself opened it after Harry had been banging on it for only a minute or two.

"Oh, hey," Leroy said as he melted back into the darkened interior, leaving the door open for Harry to come in on his own.

Harry surveyed the living/dining room. It looked pretty much as it had when he left. "So how you doin'?"

Leroy shrugged, avoiding eye contact with Harry as he rocked from side to side. Darker than Estelle, the dull skin over Leroy's gaunt face reminded Harry of the Lost Boys of Sudan.

"Any of your … 'friends' try to move back in?"

"No. But I thought you was …" His voice trailed off.

"Was who? Who'd you think I was?"

"The Mick. Said he was comin' by to pay the rent."

"The what? … Wait! Did you say 'The Mick'? Isn't that the guy who had you locked up in your room the other day?"

"Yeah, but …"

"But what?"

"He … he … he's The Mick. Gotta do what he say, ya know."

"We'll see 'bout that! Ain't nobody gonna be locking you back up in that room if I can help it." Harry went from room to room, then headed upstairs to search, just like he had done so many times as a cop. Satisfied that no one else was in the house, he stood in the doorway to Leroy's room. Amazingly, the boy had actually cleaned it up.

When he heard the front door open, he turned back to the stairs.

"What's going on here?" A gruff voice came from below. "How come you put my people out?"

Harry hesitated at the top of the stairs. Harry knew that voice!

"I didn't put 'em out," answered Leroy. "That was Mama's new friend."

"Mama's what? Who do you think you are, boy?"

"Fagan!" It was Matty Fagan, his corrupt old boss on the police force. "Is this another of your shakedowns?" he roared, charging down the stairs and around the corner into the living room … to face Fagan's 9mm SIG. Harry stopped and raised both hands to shoulder level. "Put away your new toy, Fagan. You already showed it to me … remember? The evening you made yourself at home in my apartment … without my invitation."

"Oh, I remember," said the bull-necked Irish cop, his flat-topped red hair appearing grayer than the last time Harry had seen him. "But I never got the chance to demonstrate how well it shoots." Fagan kept his pistol pointed steadily at Harry while he looked back and forth between Leroy and Harry. "Let me guess. This boy's mama is your new friend. Do I got that right?"

"Ain't none of your business, Fagan. Now get outta here!"

"Don't get bossy, Harry. The way I see this, I'm holding the heat, and you're holdin' nothin'." He looked around, breathing hard, until he found a straight-backed wooden chair, which he pulled in front of him, turned it backwards, and swung his leg over it as though he were mounting a horse. Then he used the back of the chair to steady his aim on Harry.

His extra weight is taking a toll on him, thought Harry. *I might get lucky. He could collapse right here in front of us.*

Fagan licked his lips, lips that didn't look like lips at all, just the rim of a black slit in his flushed, chapped face. "You know, I'm glad we hooked up here, Harry. I think we still got some serious business to deal with. You promised me you were going to retract those nasty lies you told the Review Board about me." He arched his eyebrows, which were nothing but hairless folds of flesh in his forehead.

"You heard me call Captain Gilson, Fagan. You dialed the number yourself, and then you sat right there and heard me withdraw my complaint."

"Ah yes, but there are different ways to file a complaint. You think you're some kind of hero, Harry, but nobody likes a whistleblower. I'm discoverin' you went behind my back and turned in a video that puts me in a bad light. Why'd you do that, Harry?"

Harry pursed his lips and said nothing.

"I don't think you understand the seriousness of your situation, Harry. You double-crossed me. And now we're sitting in a crack house way down here on the Southside where no one even flinches when they hear a gunshot." Fagan flicked his hand to the side and fired a shot through the front window, the blast so loud in the confined room that Harry's ears rang. Leroy tumbled to the floor, whimpering as though he'd been hit, and slithered into a corner.

Fagan slowly brought his aim back to line up on Harry's chest. "You see, I could shoot the both of you and walk out of here, and *if* anyone found you before winter, they'd attribute it to some drug deal gone bad. Whether they thought you were involved or trying to intervene wouldn't make any difference. My name would never come up, 'cause today I'm in Philadelphia at an anti-gang initiative seminar—signed the attendance roster, paid my hotel bill. You think you're somethin', but I'm one up on you. No one would ever guess that I can be in two places at the same time. I got it figured, Harry."

"So what's your point, Fagan? How would shooting me benefit you?"

"Oh, it wouldn't … not directly. I'll beat my charges on that dumb video. It'll never be admitted. If you remember, the chain of custody is rather sloppy. But I can't let people double-cross me and get away with it. Not good for the reputation, you know."

Fagan turned to Leroy and barked a command. "Hey boy, what's your Mama have to do with this place? She own it?"

Leroy nodded without looking up.

"And this guy's her 'new boyfriend,' huh?" He glared back at Harry, a grin spreading across his face. "Aint' that sweet? You love her, Harry? And you'd do anything for her, right?"

Harry didn't respond, but Fagan started nodding his head. "Gotcha!"

Suddenly, he stood up, holstered his gun and pulled his wallet from his pocket. He took out a couple of twenties, wadded them up, and flipped them toward Leroy. "Here's the rent we agreed on. And I *always* get what I pay for. You let those people back in here. You hear?"

He started toward the door and then turned back to Harry. "And you, Mr. Whistleblower. We had an agreement! Either you make it right, or I will. You got … let's say, two days."

"Or what?"

But Fagan was already out the door.

Chapter 7

Harry walked over and extended his hand to help Leroy to his feet. "Don't worry, son. That man's a rogue cop. He's gone bad, but he won't bother you no more. We'll get you outta here."

Leroy stood, arms to his side, head slightly down as he studied the floor. "I don't wanna leave, Mr. Bentley. This my home, know what I'm sayin'?"

"That's the point, Leroy. It's not really your house. It belongs to your mother, and she don't want you stayin' here alone anymore, especially not under these circumstances. You don't have electricity. People come in and take advantage of you. And I already told you, if this place gets raided, you're likely to go down just like the rest of 'em."

What Harry didn't say was that if it was an actual drug raid, Fagan would likely be involved, and what might come of that was anybody's guess. He'd seen Fagan beat people up—claiming they were resisting arrest—even though he never arrested them. It was his way of exerting power. Fagan was not someone to mess with. But if the neighbors called the cops over other complaints, regular uniformed police might show up without Fagan. They'd arrest people on whatever charges were obvious. Either way, it wouldn't be good for Leroy.

"Now get upstairs and pack your stuff. I'm takin' you ..." Where would he take Leroy? Harry touched his shoulder. "I'm taking you to see your mom. Okay?"

Like a five-year-old, Leroy pulled his arm away from Harry's touch and stood there pouting.

"Come on, Leroy. Hey, I bet you miss your mama's cooking. I know she's just waitin' to fix you your favorite ... whadda you like best?"

"Catfish. I like deep fried catfish, but I can cook my own. I'm a good cook. I'm gonna be a chef someday."

"Well, that's good. It's good to have ambition, but you can't cook no catfish with the gas turned off, now can you?"

"My gas ain't off. And ... and the only reason the lights is off is 'cause ComEd made a mistake. I done paid my bill, and they're s'pose to turn 'em back on any day now. But I ain't leavin', Mr. Bentley. No way!"

Harry was getting the picture. Short of physically manhandling this thirty-year-old "child," there didn't seem any way to convince him to move out. He'd have to bring Estelle with him next time. Perhaps together they could talk some sense into the kid.

He made a couple more attempts, and then left. There wasn't much one could do without involving the law.

As he drove home, he thought about Fagan. It wasn't unusual that he was involved in maintaining a drug house. That fit his method of operation: steal drugs from the dealers—without arresting them—then sell it back to junkies. Harry knew that was what had been happening. That's why he'd reported his boss to Internal Affairs ... and why the Review Board had suggested he take early retirement while they assembled the case against Fagan. But Harry had never known how Fagan managed to sell the drugs he collected. Now he knew. The elite anti-gang/anti-drug unit Fagan led worked the whole city, wherever the action was. A drug house—perhaps several of them—made it easy to dump the product without funneling it back through the gang networks he'd stolen it from.

Pretty smooth. But Fagan was going down. Captain Gilson of Internal Affairs had informed Harry the indictment was likely to come through in the next couple weeks. What a relief it would be when that guy was actually put away.

He called Estelle that evening to give her a report on Leroy … without mentioning Fagan. "I don't know how we're gonna get him out of there, Estelle. I see why you chose to just walk away from the situation. He's a very determined young man."

"Stubborn, Harry. You know that's the word. Don't be afraid to use it."

"Okay. He's stubborn, so stubborn you might have to get a court order to evict him. I'm not sure—"

"Harry, I'm not gonna evict my own boy from my own house. That's just not gonna happen. You hear me?"

Harry let the silence hang for a few moments. Stubborn is as stubborn does. "Well, I hear you. But the situation is serious. Perhaps we could go together and try one more time to talk some sense into him."

"Just tell me when."

"All right. I'll let you know, Estelle. See you soon."

SATURDAY, HARRY LET DaSHAWN SLEEP IN—kids ought to be allowed to sleep in at least one day a week, shouldn't they? Cindy Kaplan, Harry's old partner on the police force, had promised to take

DaShawn to the Cubs game, which started at 12:20, so he couldn't let DaShawn sleep too long. Cindy had invited Harry to go, too, but he'd promised to take the Firecracker car shopping. *Agh!* He'd sure rather spend the afternoon in the friendly confines of Wrigley Field, but he'd promised.

After fixing coffee, Harry relaxed into his recliner by the window to read his Bible. Too often his good intentions were thwarted by the hectic demands of the day, but today he had a little time for "the Word," as his Bible study brothers called it.

He turned to John 14 where he'd last read.

Wink, wink—eyes the same. God hadn't done a miracle overnight ... or maybe He had. At least his eyes weren't worse. Hmm, how could you tell when God miraculously protected you from something worse—the truck that barreled through a red light seconds after you cleared the intersection, the virus from someone's sneeze that settled out of the air before you breathed it, the macular hole that did *not* develop overnight in your right eye? He knew he ought to be more grateful ... every day.

In John 14, Jesus was explaining that He would soon be returning to His Father to prepare a place for his disciples. Harry read, "I am the way and the truth and the life. No one comes to the Father except through me." Yeah, he understood that part. The guys in the Bible study had helped him put his faith in Jesus as his only access to God. And it had made a world of difference in his life.

But as he read on, Jesus reminded His listeners of all the miracles He'd done and then said, "I tell you the truth, anyone who has faith in me will do what I have been doing. He will do even greater things than these, because I am going to the Father. And I will do whatever you ask in my name, so that the Son may bring glory to the Father. You may ask me for anything in my name, and I will do it."

Wow! What a promise! *Greater works ... whatever you ask in my name ... ask me for anything in my name, and I will do it?* Could he believe it?

Harry recalled the "Have Faith in God" message Pastor Cobbs had preached last Sunday at SouledOut Community Church. It, too, proclaimed a similarly mind-boggling promise. Harry flipped to where he'd left the Sunday bulletin as a bookmark in Mark 11 and found the pastor's text: "Therefore I tell you, whatever you ask for in prayer, believe that you have received it, and it will be yours."

Could he pray like that? Did he believe like that?

Harry knew there were people who didn't believe major portions of the Bible. Some didn't think Noah's flood covered the earth, or they explained away Jesus' miracles as merely symbolic or slight-of-hand tricks. Some liked Jesus' "warm-fuzzy" teachings but considered His harder words "impractical." According to Pastor Cobbs, Thomas Jefferson had literally used a razorblade to cut up the New Testament, pasting together the verses he liked and discarding sections he found too incredible—specifically all references to angels, prophecy, miracles, the Trinity, the divinity of Christ, and the Resurrection.

The only point of faith, as Harry saw it, was to connect beyond human experience, so why dumb down the Bible, reducing it by mere human opinion and humanly explainable interactions?

Harry knew there were challenging passages that could benefit by scholarly interpretation, but these straightforward verses weren't parables and didn't seem culturally vague. Jesus was offering plain instruction: "No one comes to the Father except through me," a succinct summary of the Christian faith. A minute later, in the same teaching and without changing tone, Jesus said, "Ask me for anything in my name, and I will do it." Both promises required

71

faith, which by definition surpasses human comprehension, no doubt about that. But neither was confusing.

Had Jesus said what He meant and meant what He said? There were probably skeptics out there who explained away one or both statements, but—Harry scratched his beard—he didn't want to live in the world of the skeptics. And what was the point of affirming Jesus' statement about approaching God (which we can't prove) while dismissing His other promise simply because it was more measurable in the here and now?

Of course, the obvious test for Harry—and he was not a man to ignore the obvious—involved his eye? Would Jesus grant his request for healing?

The verse Pastor Cobbs used had emphasized that our faith plays a part in God answering our prayers: "Therefore I tell you, whatever you ask for in prayer, *believe* that you have received it, and it will be yours." And even this passage in John 14 said much the same thing: "Anyone who *has faith* in me ..." Did he have that kind of faith? Could he believe? The doctor's explanation of his macular hole clearly described its physical characteristics—it was definitely not a psychosomatic problem. For God to heal him, God would actually have to reverse the damage that had already occurred. Could he believe it?

Of course, he *had* been praying God would heal his eye. But he knew his kind of prayer didn't require much faith. It was more like: "You probably could fix my eye if You wanted to, God. So I'm just askin', but I have no expectation that You will." That seemed a far cry from the kind of positive confidence Jesus seemed to encourage.

Maybe he should practice with a more modest faith request. God had helped him get DaShawn back. He was sure it had been God. He would look for similar ways God might build his faith and pray for those. Today! He would look for things he had faith to pray for right now.

HARRY PULLED UP IN FRONT OF GABBY FAIRBANKS' apartment and muttered a quick, "Lord, help us find a good car for the Firecracker today." He'd done some checking online, and most dealers had several "Don't-Miss Bargains!" But he still wasn't sure where to start.

He flung open the door of his RAV4 and was about to jump out when he recalled his earlier commitment to look for more *modest* faith requests he could ask God for. Not that finding a good car would be any harder for God than healing his eye, but if he could "pray believing"—he'd heard that phrase somewhere—it might build *his* faith.

"Okay, God. If you're trying to teach me something, this is as good a time to learn it as any. So seriously, Father ..." Harry took off his tweed slouch hat and closed his eyes to shut out distractions. "Help me find a good car for Gabby Fairbanks today. She needs transportation, and she's got too much on her plate to fuss with breakdowns all the time. So, help me see the right one." He put his hat back on and sighed as he stepped out of his RAV4 and headed across the street with a spring in his step. He *did* have faith that God would show him the right car.

As he went up the steps to the apartment building, he thought about the wording of his prayer: "Help me *see* the right one." And he believed God would *show* him. He shook his head. *Even our language presumes "sight,"* he thought.

"Oh Lord, my eyes. Please—"

Before he said more, the Firecracker came bouncing out the door, ready to go car shopping. As effervescent as usual, she began telling Harry about her idea to buy the six-flat apartment she lived in with the inheritance money from her recently deceased mother's estate and turning it into transition housing for families who came through the women's shelter.

Harry shot her a sideways look. "Young lady, do you have any idea what you're doing?"

The Firecracker snorted. "No. Not really."

"Good!" Harry laughed. "In that case, you might just have a chance with this crazy scheme ... if you realize that."

She shrugged as though she didn't understand his drift. "So, where are we going?"

"Uh ..." Harry hadn't made a decision about where to start, but he was heading west. "Guess we could start at the Toyota place out on Touhy." It wasn't the closest dealership, but he could still visualize the used car lot there where he'd found his own RAV4. And even though he couldn't recall much about any of the other cars he'd seen online that morning, one came to mind—a metallic burgundy Subaru Forester—and he was pretty sure it'd been at this dealer's lot.

Once they arrived, he herded the Firecracker quickly through the maze of cars toward the back corner ... ahead of the salesman, who was quickly gaining on them. And there it was: the burgundy Subaru. "I was looking online at this little wagon earlier today. It might be worth considering." He shielded his mouth from view with his hand. "But let me do the talking."

"How ya doin' today? It's a mighty nice vehicle. Only twenty-seven thousand *eeeasy* miles on it."

For $16,999, it ought to be "mighty nice," but Harry was not going to let the Firecracker pay that much for a three-year-old Forrester. "Can we take it for a drive?"

By the time they got back, Harry was certain God had shown him the right car for Gabby, but he wanted to make sure. "It's a steal, Gabby. Good, solid car. I know a mechanic who can check it out for you, to be sure. But as far as I can tell, somebody probably just wanted to upgrade. A lot of people do that, even though the car they got is still perfectly good."

"But shouldn't we look at some of the new Toyotas?" she said. "You drive a RAV4 and like it. Wouldn't a new car be smart in the long run?"

Wait a minute. Had God shown him the right car or not? Why wasn't she delighted? He scratched his beard and squinted his eyes at her. Something else was going on here. He took a deep breath. "Well, sure, if that's really what you want to do. But a new car in the Wrigleyville neighborhood … well, just more of a temptation for car thieves. You'll spend a whole lot less on a pre-owned and still get a good car for you and your boys. No shame in that. All my cars are at least a year old when I buy—even the RAV4. And pardon me saying so, but you're on your own now, Gabby girl. Doesn't hurt to cut your expenses where you can."

Her face flushed, and Harry wondered if he'd said too much. Then she sighed. "You're right. Guess I got a little greedy. Should I—?" She dug her checkbook out of her purse.

"Put that away! No way are you going to pay that sticker price. C'mon, let's go talk to that baby-faced salesman, who's probably only been on the job a month." He chuckled. "He ain't had to deal with Harry Bentley before!"

Once they'd finished haggling, Harry was able to get a thousand knocked off the price, and the Firecracker drove home happy as a puppy.

As Harry followed, he thought back over what had just happened that afternoon. True, he'd been familiar with that particular dealership, but he'd also been completely open to going elsewhere. He'd even looked online at other dealers. It was just that

... the vision of that car lot had come so strongly to mind, as had that particular vehicle, even before they got there. And he hadn't known where it was parked, but he somehow felt compelled to head toward the back corner where, in fact, he found it. Not a big coincidence, but could he believe God had led him? Is that what faith was, believing God was active even though some skeptics might explain the same events by other means? He could see that if he honestly attributed all good things to God—even though other people explained them as chance—his faith might grow to where he could believe God would do other good things when he prayed for them. Was thanksgiving the key to faith?

"Thank you, God, for showing me that car. And I do believe You led me right to it and that it will provide reliable transportation for that young woman. Bless her and her boys, Father. And ... and keep building my faith, too, please. 'I believe, but help my unbelief!' In Jesus' name. Amen."

"*I believe, but help my unbelief!*" Now where had he heard that line before? He couldn't recall, but somehow it described him perfectly.

He flipped on the radio, and ten minutes later pulled in behind the Firecracker as she parked in front of her apartment. When she got out and came back to his RAV4, he rolled down his window. "So whaddaya think?"

"It's great. Drives like a dream, really!"

"Take it in next week, have my guy recharge the air conditioning, see what happens. He'll do right by you."

"Thanks, Mr. B. Don't know what I'd do without you." She paused a moment. "The boys will be home soon. You want to stay for supper or something?"

"Can't. Gotta pick up DaShawn. My former partner—a great gal named Cindy—took him to a Cubs game today." Harry reached to start his engine and arched his eyebrows in a smug grin. "Radio just said they beat the Cardinals, 5 to 4. Go Cubbies!"

"Wait! Your former partner? What do you mean, partner?"

Oh, yeah. He turned away for a moment with a little laugh. All Gabby Fairbanks knew about him was his recent job as the doorman in her former high-rise apartment. Probably presumed he'd been nothing more than a friendly "helper" his whole life.

"You know … partner." He gave her a tolerant smile. "Two to a car, got my back, all that stuff. She was the best on the force. Still is. I'm a retired Chicago cop, Firecracker. Didn't you know that?"

He left her standing on the curb with her mouth open, eyes wide, as he drove off. White people! He liked that girl. Would do anything to help her, but O, Lord …

Chapter 8

A T FIRST, HARRY THOUGHT IT WAS THE ALARM on his cell phone waking him in time to go to SouledOut Community Church. And this morning he was eager for church, an occasion to praise God for guiding him in his little faith-growing venture of finding a good car for Gabby Fairbanks. But it was an incoming call from Estelle and not his wake-up alarm.

"Morning, Estelle," he yawned as he sat up and swung his feet to the floor. "What time is it, anyway?"

"Time don't matter, Harry. Leroy just called. Had some kind of a fire in his kitchen. Said he wasn't hurt but it made a mess. Lotta soot and burned one of the cupboards. Can you take me down there? He sounds real shook up, and I'm worried, Harry."

Harry pulled the phone away from his ear and checked the time—8:02. "Sure, Estelle. Be right over." He started to close his phone. "Oh, Estelle. You still there? Look, if it's okay, I'll bring DaShawn with me. Could you check downstairs and see if the Baxters can take him to church and look out for him 'til we get back?"

"Sure, either them or Stu, one of the two. Just hurry, Harry. Okay?" And she hung up.

78

Harry hoped it would be the Baxters rather than Estelle's housemate, Leslie Stuart. "Stu," as everyone called her, was certainly nice enough, but she was the caseworker with the Department of Children and Family Services who'd actually arranged for DaShawn to live with Harry when his father—Harry's estranged son—had gone to jail. She'd been in Harry's corner all the way, but she was still part of "the system," and Harry didn't want DCFS to think he wasn't caring for DaShawn himself, no matter how legitimate the occasion.

Ah well, this *was* a legitimate request. "Lord, I'm gonna keep practicing my faith and believe that You're in control."

"DaShawn!" he yelled. "Get up. Gotta hurry. Gotta get over to Miss Estelle's right away. There's been a fire."

"What?" Came the groggy voice from DaShawn's room.

"I said we gotta hurry. Get your clothes on."

"What about a fire? She okay?"

"Not her, DaShawn. Her son, down on the Southside. Now get dressed. We gotta go."

LEROY WAS SITTING ON THE PORCH OF ESTELLE'S BROWNSTONE on 35th Street. According to Estelle, he'd called 911 as soon as the fire broke out, but by the time she and Harry arrived, the fire trucks and police cars had come and gone. So the fire couldn't have been very bad.

Estelle hopped out of Harry's SUV and half-ran to Leroy with her arms wide. Harry followed, his head shaking slightly. He loved that woman—including her protective concern for her son—but the situation was getting out of control. The boy was obviously not able to manage on his own. He needed a supportive environment. A solution needed to be found.

Estelle was all over her son, holding his face between both of her hands, and planting kisses on his forehead. "You sure you're okay, Baby. No burns? No smoke inhalation? You know that smoke can mess with your lungs later on. You sure, now?"

"Come on, you all," Harry said. "Let's get inside. I'm sure the neighbors have had enough drama out here for a week." Though no one seemed to be paying any attention. Across the street a new condo building had recently gone up, probably filled with yuppie-types minding their own business and taking no responsibility for anyone round them.

Inside the brownstone, the place stank of smoke. The floor was filthy with muddy trails where the firemen had dragged in a hose. Harry went immediately to the kitchen and was grateful to see that they'd knocked down the fire with an axe and a fire extinguisher rather than using the hose. The cabinet above the stove had been torn off the wall, and a few pots and pans and broken dishes were scattered around the floor. The kitchen was a mess and would need a thorough cleaning, replacement of the cabinet, and paint. But Leroy—and Estelle—had been fortunate.

"You got insurance, don't you Estelle?"

"Oh yeah. Had to keep that up."

Harry scanned the ceiling, soiled with soot. "Insurance should cover most of this, and it might be a blessing. Redecorating the kitchen could be the first step in getting the place ready to put on the market."

"What?" Leroy gaped back and forth between Harry and Estelle. "Oh, Mama, you can't sell my house. This is where I live. Where would I go?"

"Don't worry, Baby, don't worry." She gave him another hug. "I ain't gonna put you out on the street."

Come on, Estelle, thought Harry. *This is no time to go soft. We gotta settle this situation—completely!* Of course, they wouldn't put him out on the street, but they needed to focus on Leroy's inability to take care of himself. "How'd the fire start, anyway, Leroy?"

He shrugged. "I dunno." And scanned away.

"No, no, no. That's not good enough. Fires don't just start by themselves. What were you doin' in here?"

"Nothin'."

"Were you trying to cook somethin'?" Estelle prompted.

"Yeah. I was gonna fix a special breakfast. Had some bacon in the pan, but I couldn't find the eggs." He stopped, as though that was the end of the story.

"So," said Harry, "whaddya do then?"

"Went to see if Johnny O's was open."

Estelle drew back her head and frowned. "Johnny O's? That's just a bar and a hotdog stand."

"Yeah, but they sometimes give me stuff. You know, if it's gettin' past the sell date."

"And then what?" asked Harry.

"Well, they weren't open, so I came home, and … and smoke was all pourin' out of the house."

There didn't seem to be much use continuing to grill the boy. He'd obviously forgotten the bacon on the stove with the flame on under it, and it had finally ignited.

They went out and bought cleaning supplies and trash bags and spent most of the day cleaning up the kitchen, carrying the burnt cabinet and broken dishes out to the trash, and scrubbing down the walls and ceiling. When they were done, it looked ready to paint. To Harry's amazement, Leroy worked right along with them, without slacking off at all. Perhaps there was more hope for the young man than Harry had given him. Still, it seemed only wise to get him into some kind of a supportive program where he could build a stable and productive life. Harry wished he'd had the time to look for a program before today.

As they were finishing up, Harry noticed that if Leroy wasn't doing something specific, he soon ended up standing in one place, rocking from side to side, wringing his hands and looking around with a frightened look on his face.

Harry had just tied up the final trash bag when Leroy grabbed it. "Uh-uh. Lemme take that out to the garbage."

"Well, okay then!" Harry shook his head as Leroy ran out the back door. "That boy's wound as tight as a guitar string. But …" He looked around "… guess that does it for now." He turned to Estelle, who was wringing out the last few rags. "What you gotta do, Estelle, is get one of those companies that do major cleanup after a fire or flood. Have them come up in here and clear everything out. Then you can get the place painted and put it on the market."

"Harry, I have no idea what the value of this place is. I wouldn't know what to ask for it."

"That's what real estate agents are for. They know the market, and they can help you select a price that moves the property while getting' you the best return."

"But what if it doesn't sell?"

"Oh, it'll sell. This is Bridgeport, after all, less than a mile from the White Sox stadium. What do they call it now? Cellular Field. I liked it better when they called it Comiskey Park. But anyway, it'll sell, and Leroy'll be a whole lot better off some place else."

He followed Estelle as she walked through the cluttered living room and stood looking out the widow at the condo building across the street. "I don't know, Harry. I hate to let it go. It's all I really got, you know." She threw up both hands. "The neighborhood has changed. Nothin' like it was years ago. You said there were crackheads all up in here, right here in my own house, but how could that be? Look at that nice new building over there. This isn't a depressed neighborhood."

"No, it's not. But like you said, it's changed! The old relationships have broken down. I bet people don't even know one another any more—don't look out for one another."

She was quiet a moment. "Mmm. Guess you're right. It had already gotten that way long before I left a couple years ago. A shame, though. I love this old house."

Harry stepped closer and slipped his arms around her from behind, sensing her sorrow over fading memories and dying dreams. "But ... I believe God's got good things to come in the future." It was part of the lesson he was trying to learn for himself, but the moment he'd said it, the dread of his eye problems rushed in. Did he really believe God had good things for him in the future? Would Estelle be a part of *his* future?

"You're right, Harry." She untangled herself from his arms and turned around to face him. "Still an' all, I really don't know what I'm going to do with Leroy."

"Well, first thing's to get him outta here." He peered back toward the kitchen. "Where is that boy, anyway? It don't take that long to carry out a bag of trash." He walked through the house and out on the back porch. "Leroy! Where you at, anyway? We gotta go! Leroy!" Harry went out to the alley and checked both ways. Not a sign of Leroy. "Did it again," he mumbled to himself. "Just like before."

HARRY SPENT AN HOUR CRUISING THE STREETS AND ALLEYS while Estelle stayed at the house in case Leroy came back. Harry stopped in various sports bars and convenience stores along 35th Street, but there was no trace of Leroy. Finally he called Estelle on his cell. "I can't find him anywhere. Has he shown up there?"

"No. He's not here. I think he must have his cell, though. I've tried calling it but can't hear it ringing anywhere in the house. I left a message, but I haven't heard a word from him."

"Do you know of any friends in the area? He might have gone to someone else's place."

"Like we said earlier. The neighborhood's so changed, Harry, I don't even know anybody 'round here anymore."

"Well, I'm headin' there now. See you in a few."

When he got back to the house, he could tell Estelle was struggling with leaving without Leroy. The fire had convinced her he shouldn't be left alone, but what could they do?

"It's the same thing he did to me the other day, you know."

"What do you mean?"

"Like I told you. I took him out to eat at that Mexican place down the street, but he split while I was in the restroom. Guess he was afraid I was goin' to make him leave."

Estelle rolled her eyes. "I'm about at the point of *makin' him* myself. Invitin', even beggin' him hasn't worked. I don't know, Harry, what kind of steps would one have to go through to force him to come with us."

"Hard to say. As long as he hasn't done anything illegal, it's not easy to get the law involved. I know social workers have a list of criteria they gotta apply before committing anyone against their will ... stuff like posing a danger to himself or others, unable to adequately care for oneself, expressing acute symptoms of mental illness—guess some of those might fit Leroy. But ..."

Estelle shook her head. "Lord have mercy! I can hardly imagine forcing those kinds of things on him. Lord have mercy!"

"Yeah, I understand. Not easy! Not easy! But we probably better go now. He's made his statement. He might even be watching the place to see when we've gone. Whatever, he deliberately split to avoid us tryin' to take him with us. We gotta face it, Estelle. Before we can do anything more, we need professional help."

Chapter 9

B<small>Y THE TIME</small> H<small>ARRY HAD PICKED UP</small> D<small>A</small>S<small>HAWN</small> from the Baxters's and got home that evening, he felt a little foolish. So where was God today? Or maybe the question was, what made him think God had led him to help Gabby find a car yesterday? Who did he think he was? Was he so important God bothered to guide him at all?

He flopped into a chair and thought about it. Every step of the car search *could* be explained by coincidence: He'd searched online, obviously looking at the dealer where he'd found his own car, a car he liked. He'd noticed the Subaru, which appeared as though it might suit the Firecracker's needs. He'd checked out other dealers too, but it made sense that the Subaru stuck in his mind. He drove to that dealer first because … well, his car was pointing west and he knew the route without thinking about it. When he got to the lot and noticed the salesman approaching, it was natural to walk away, gain a little distance so he could look around without the man hovering. And the Subaru sat in the corner of the very direction he was headed: coincidence.

"Hey Grandpa?" DaShawn was standing in the hall. "We gonna have something to eat?"

"Eat? Didn't the Baxters feed you this evening?"

"Yeah, but I was wantin' a snack."

"How 'bout microwavin' some popcorn?"

"Want me to do two?"

"Two? What for?"

"Thought you might want some."

"Of course, but ..." The kid must be having a growth spurt. "No, you can have the whole bag yourself. I don't need any."

DaShawn punched the air with his fist as he went into the kitchen.

Harry shook his head. Now what was he thinking? Oh yeah. Was finding that car for the Firecracker just a coincidence? It was a good car, but then he was a fairly mechanically-minded guy, had bought several cars in his lifetime, knew what to look for. No rocket science in choosing a good car ... perhaps no miracle in finding one either.

So, if God had been leading him on Saturday, why hadn't he and Estelle received more help today?

Did you ask? Did you even pray?

What? Pray? Well ... come to think of it, he guessed he hadn't prayed! *They* hadn't prayed, at least not together! In all their frantic running down there, with something as scary as a kitchen fire, with Estelle's troubled son running off so they couldn't take him to a safe place ... no, they hadn't stopped to pray. Maybe Estelle had prayed—she was a praying mother, after all—but he hadn't prayed. And he hadn't taken the lead for them to pray together.

On the other hand, if he intended to take this faith thing seriously, he'd at least have to practice it by turning to God rather than trying to handle everything on his own. He took a few deep breaths to calm himself down. Now what was the first step? Oh yeah, *thankfulness*! He needed to thank God for every good thing so that he could become more and more aware of how much God *was* at work in his life. That would build his faith in what God was like, and build his confidence that God would *continue* working all things together for good.

But the second step was prayer. If he really believed God was the source of everything good, then he needed to turn to God for that good. He needed to pray for it.

"Yeah, well. Sorry, God. Guess it's kind of easy to slip back into my old ways of thinkin' and actin', tryin' to do everything on my own. *I do believe, but help my unbelief.*"

There it was again. Where had he heard that phrase before? Must've been one of those TV preachers his elderly mother always listened to. He'd ask some of the brothers at Bible study if they knew where it came from.

"Hey, Grandpa." DaShawn came bouncing up to him with a small bowl. "Here's some popcorn for you, anyway."

"Ha! Thanks, DaShawn." Now there was a boy to thank God for. "If you want some more, do a second bag."

MONDAY AFTERNOON WHILE DASHAWN was playing at his friend Robbie's house, Harry sat at his kitchen table opening envelopes from a pile of bills. He frowned at his ComEd bill. Why did it seem higher every month?

"Seven twenty-four," came the metallic female voice from the police scanner on the bookshelf, "you're looking for a twenty-year-old white male. He's in the ER, room G-39."

"Do you have any photos of him?"

"No, but he has a tattoo of a dragon on the right side of his neck ..."

Harry glanced over at the scanner. Maybe all the electronics in the house were causing his higher bills. But even though it was little more than background noise, it was hard not to listen to his scanner after twenty years on the force. It squawked and squealed as the dispatcher fielded another call, this one about which routes fire trucks and other vehicles should take to a fire on 35th Street.

Did she say 35th Street? Harry jumped up and increased the volume.

The dispatcher repeated it, adding the address ... the *exact* address of Estelle's brownstone. "Yeah, it's a two-alarm blaze," the dispatcher explained in a disinterested voice, "but the street's so blocked with gawkers, emergency vehicles can't get in there. Is there someone in the area who can assist with traffic control?"

A car volunteered, and the dispatcher thanked him, but Harry was already dialing Estelle's phone number.

Not Leroy again! But had he heard correctly? Was it really Estelle's house? He didn't dare call with a false alarm about something this traumatic. He stopped before he punched in the last number, listening closely for another mention of the address. But the dispatcher had moved on, managing calls about someone who'd pulled a gun on a repo man for trying to tow away his new luxury SUV. "Yeah, black 2006 Escalade with dark-tinted windows. License: BOOGY DO, that's Boy—Ocean—Ocean—George—Young—David—Ocean. Can you give me an assist?"

"Come on! Come on!" Harry stood there, shaking his fists in the air, trying to will the dispatcher to get back to the fire on 35th Street, but she said nothing more about it.

He couldn't call Estelle without being sure it was true. And he couldn't find out if it was true if he left his scanner. Oh, man! He needed a portable one, one he could plug into his car. But if it was Estelle's house, if it was Leroy, he needed to get down there ASAP.

He waited five more minutes and then zipped out of his apartment, thundering down the stairs to his car. He had to get down there. As he punched his RAV4 up to speed on the Lake Shore Drive, an idea came to him, and in spite of Chicago's law against using a cell phone while driving, Harry called his old police partner, Cindy Kaplan.

"Hey, Cindy? Harry. Hey, I need some help. You in your car?"

"Yeah. What's up, Harry?" She sounded skeptical. "Ya know, now that you're retired, you're all the time wanting me to do something for you that's on the edge. So what's up this time?"

"No, no. Nothin' like that." Harry knew she was referring to the time he'd asked her to search her boss's cruiser for a missing and incriminating cell phone. "All I want you to do is to tune in to the dispatcher for District 9. There's a fire goin' on down there on 35th Street, and I need to know the exact address."

"I don't trust you, Harry. What's this about?" But Harry could hear her switching channels.

"Come on, Cindy. This time it's all legit. It's a friend of mine. She owns a house down there, and I think it's on fire. I'm headin' that way myself right now, but I had to leave home before I could confirm the address." Harry gave Cindy the address. "If they mention it again, call me right back. My friend's son may be inside or hurt. I should be there in less than thirty minutes, but I haven't told her yet … and I don't want to if I got the address wrong."

"Okay, I'll monitor it, Harry. Don't drive too fast. We're out there everywhere, you know."

"You just get the bad guys, Cindy, and let me sail on through. Thanks."

Harry was driving too fast and watching his mirror and every side street to avoid the blue and white. But if Leroy was in that house, he wanted to get there and be sure the kid got out. The dispatcher had said something about emergency vehicles having trouble getting through the traffic, but they always sent an ambulance to a serious fire. And if this was a two-alarm fire, that meant the first responders hadn't been able to put it down or it was threatening other buildings.

The *Law and Order* theme chimed from Harry's cell phone, and he grabbed it up. "Yeah."

"That's your address, Harry. Dispatcher just gave it again. Sounds like they've got the fire under control and are releasing one of the stations."

"They say anything about injuries?"

"Didn't hear anything. Hope that's good news."

"Thanks, Cindy. I owe you one."

"Harry, you owe me so many I'm gonna need a bank pretty soon. Take it easy. And get off that phone while you're drivin'!"

He hit "End," then pressed his speed-dial key for Estelle. Now he *had* to tell her. He waited and waited while he weaved through traffic until her phone went to voice mail. "Estelle, Estelle, this is Harry. Phone me back right away. This is an emergency."

Should he have said it that way? She'd be in a frantic panic! But it *was* an emergency. How much more of an emergency could it be than your house burning down and your son possibly trapped inside?

Monday ... Monday. What would Estelle be doing this time of day on a Monday? Probably teaching her sewing class down in the basement of Manna House. He knew she often left her phone in her big purse because the reception down there wasn't very good. But he had to get through to her! At the next stoplight, he called the Manna House main number: Busy!

He kept redialing as he drove west on 31st Street, thinking it would be easier to get to the brownstone from the north if 35th was congested with fire trucks and other vehicles. But he was still two blocks away when he could see he could get no closer and pulled his car to the curb to walk the rest of the way.

Finally, his call was answered at Manna House. "This is Harry Bentley. I need to speak to Estelle Williams immediately. Could you get her for me?"

"Uh ... I'm not supposed to leave the desk, but I'll be glad to take a message if—"

"NOW, girl! Get up outta that desk and run downstairs to get her 'fore I reach through this line and whap you upside the head. This is an emergency!"

Harry could hear things crashing around and knew his warning had worked, but it still seemed to take forever before he heard a breathless voice say, "Yes, this is Estelle Williams."

"Estelle. This is Harry. I'm almost at your place, and there's been a fire, a big one—"

"My apartment?"

"No, your house on the Southside—"

"Oh no! Is Leroy okay?"

"I don't know yet. I'm just comin' up to it now, but I don't see no ambulances, so maybe they've already taken him. I'll call you back soon as I know."

"No, Harry! Don't hang up. What happened?"

"I don't know, but this was no little kitchen fire. There's still lots of smoke boiling out of the roof, and it looks like they've punched out most of the windows. They've even got a water cannon pourin' down from one of those snorkel trucks." He ducked under the police tape, held up his wallet as though it were his badge case and mumbled, "CPD," to the cop who was supposed to be on duty. Harry didn't see a fire chief right off, so he stepped up to the nearest red helmet. "Hold on, Estelle. I'm asking about Leroy ... Sir! Sir! You get everybody out?"

The fireman was cleaning soot from his face with a Handi Wipe. "Yeah, made a full search before it started cavin' in on us."

"Anyone hurt?"

"Just one guy, a civilian. Took him to the County already."

"How bad?"

"Hard to say, but he was a little toasty."

Harry slammed his cell phone to his stomach, hoping Estelle didn't hear that crude description.

"How long ago?"

"Maybe five minutes. Took 'em a while to get him stabilized. Why, someone you know?"

"Yeah. You could say that. Know how it started?"

"Hard to say. But fire was pretty much everywhere by the time we got here, and we're only a few blocks away."

Harry noticed the big 29 on the side of the engine. He nodded at the fireman. "Thanks." And he left, heading back to his car.

"Hello, Estelle? You still there?"

"Of course, I'm still here! Wha'd he say? Is Leroy okay?"

"Don't know. They took him to the hospital. I don't know any more 'n that, but I'm headin' over there right now."

"But Harry, Harry. What about me? I gotta get down there."

"Yeah. Look, if you can't find anyone to give you a ride, take the El. Transfer to the Blue Line—"

"No, no. I'll take a cab, Harry."

"Whatever you want. Just call me when you get close, and I'll meet you. But right now, I'm goin' on to the hospital to see how he is."

"Harry …" Her voice broke. "Call me soon as you find out anything."

"I will, and … and I'm gonna pray, too, Estelle. I'm gonna pray for him."

"Yes … please." The phone went dead.

Harry was halfway to the hospital when his phone rang again. Without looking at the caller ID, he opened it. "Yeah."

"Hey, Harry, my man! What's happenin'?"

Harry pulled the phone away and checked the name on his screen. "Fagan? That you? Where you at?"

"Ah, Harry, I'm glad to see you care so much. Actually, I'm pretty close to your place. Sittin' right here in the 24th District Police Station, talkin' with some of the old gang."

Harry exhaled the breath he was holding. Somehow, Fagan's call at a time like this felt too much like a bad dream, but if his old boss was way up on the Northside in Rogers Park, then he couldn't have had anything to do with—

"Harry, you still there? I'm not interruptin' anything am I? You sound preoccupied or something. But it's a little early for a *tête-à-tête* with your lady friend, isn't it?"

"Whaddaya want, Fagan?"

"I think you know what I want, and today was your deadline, Harry. Haven't you figured that out yet?"

"I don't have time for this, Fagan." He slammed his cell phone closed and pulled into the parking lot for Stroger Hospital of Cook County.

Chapter 10

NOTHING HARRY DID AT THE EMERGENCY ROOM DESK seemed to gain him entrance to the ER until he saw Joe Garcia, a fellow police officer back in the day when they were both beat cops.

"Hey, Joe. How you doin'? You on duty here?"

Joe checked his watch. "For the next hour and forty-eight minutes. What's up, Bentley? Haven't seen you around for the longest."

"Yeah, well, I retired. Tell ya 'bout it some time. Right now, can you get me through those doors? Paramedics just brought in a burn victim. You see him?"

"Yeah, 'bout ten minutes ago. You know the guy?"

"Son of my ... of a lady friend of mine. Can you get me in?"

"No problem. Here ..." He pushed the doors open, and held up his hand to the frowning woman at the side window. "It's okay. Off-duty cop."

Harry found Leroy alone in the fourth curtained booth, lying on the gurney with his clothes removed and a towel draped over his middle, an oxygen tube in his nose, and an IV already in his right arm. The burn was obvious, all up and down his left side—singed hair on the side of his head, angry blackish-red patches on his arm, torso, and leg, some blisters, and a few places where the skin had actually peeled off. *Too much third-degree,* thought Harry.

"You awake, Leroy?"

Leroy's eyes opened slightly, and he searched through puffy slits until he focused on Harry. "Mama here?"

"Not yet, but she will be soon." Harry shook his head. "You in a lot of pain?"

Leroy closed his eyes again. "Not so much, now. They give me somethin' in the ambulance."

"You know how this happened?"

"No sir. I was jus' watchin' TV when the whole place exploded. Didn't do nothin', I swear, Mr. B."

A nurse, followed by a tech, pushed past Harry. "Excuse me, sir. Could you step out for a few moments. We're gonna have to intubate him."

"Intubate? How come? He seems to be breathing okay, especially with the oxygen."

"Just precautionary. He had smoke inhalation, so there'll be some edema. We wouldn't want to take a chance on his airway closing down. So … could you please …" She jerked her head to the side like she was rooting Harry out of the way. "I need to draw the curtain."

He stood on the other side of the thin barrier listening while Leroy sounded like he was choking. The nurse said, "Okay, let's try it one more time."

Harry wasn't usually the queasy sort, but he was grateful for the distraction when his phone rang … until he saw it was DaShawn.

"Grandpa, where are you? Basketball camp's been over for twenty minutes. Weren't you gonna pick me up?"

Oh, no! The thing about crises was that they create more crises! He'd totally forgotten about the boy. "Sorry, DaShawn," he said as

96

he went out through the swinging doors into the ER waiting room. "There's been a fire at Miss Estelle's, and—"

"Another one?"

"Yes, another one. And this time her son got injured … burned pretty badly. I'm at the hospital with him right now. So listen … hold on a minute. I got to find a phone number, and you get something to write it down with." He fumbled with his phone until he found the number for Josh Baxter. As a student, Josh was the most likely person Harry could think of who might be free at this time in the afternoon, that is if he wasn't on duty with his little daughter. He gave DaShawn the number, then said, "See if he can give you a ride over to Great Grandma's, then phone me back."

As he finished the call, Estelle came rushing into the waiting room like an avalanche. "Thank God you're here!" She fell into Harry's arms as he slipped the phone back into his pocket. "Have you seen him? How … how is he?"

"He's awake, and they've given him something for the pain. We spoke briefly, but then they had to put one of those tubes down his throat to be sure he can breath freely if anything starts to swell. He was askin' for you, though."

"Well then, I'm goin' in there!" And she marched around Harry.

"Wait a minute," said the woman at the window.

Estelle paused long enough to confirm her relationship to Leroy and answer some meaningless questions before the woman waved her on.

"And you already know who I am," Harry said, herding Estelle through the doors without giving the "gatekeeper" a chance to stop him, even though she was pointing to the "No Admittance Beyond This Point" sign as the doors swung closed.

Twenty minutes later, DaShawn texted Harry: "At GGs. All OK. See you."

Kids! Now why didn't the boy just call? Harry fumbled with the keys on his phone, trying to figure out how to send a return text saying that he had received the message. Finally, he gave up. All that mattered was that DaShawn was safe.

IT WAS TEN THAT EVENING BEFORE THEY MOVED LEROY from the ER up to the Intensive Care Unit in the Burn Center. They'd given Leroy enough painkillers that, through the window of his room, they could see he was resting quietly.

The doctor, who appeared and sounded like he might be from Pakistan, came out and removed his mask and gloves. "The next twenty-four hours will be the most critical in terms of how his body manages the buildup of fluids. Once we are through that phase, we'll be—how do you say it?—out of the woods. After that comes the long process of fighting infection and helping him heal. But," and his eyebrows went up as he nervously transferred his stethoscope from one pocket to the other, "he's a very lucky young man. I don't think his lungs were damaged."

"Not luck! That was God," Estelle insisted.

"Perhaps," the doctor admitted with a shrug. "But there's nothing more you can do here tonight, so why don't you be taking yourself to your house for getting some rest?"

Estelle shook her head. "Nope, I'll be stayin' in the waiting room 'til I can go in and see him." The doctor shrugged and left as Estelle turned to Harry. "I'll call Stu and have her pack me a little bag of necessities."

She didn't say it, but Harry nodded, knowing what she needed. "Have her leave it downstairs with Jodi Baxter, and I'll drop by and pick it up tomorrow before I come down." He looked at her a moment. "I do have to go home tonight, though. DaShawn's at my mom's, and I've got to put together a plan for him for tomorrow. Then I'll come back. You got money? You need to get yourself something to eat. No good you gettin' sick. They won't let you in there to see Leroy if you do."

"I'm good, Harry."

He walked her to the small waiting room—which was empty at that time of the night—gave her a hug, and was halfway down the hall to the elevator before he realized he'd forgotten something and turned back. When he reentered the waiting room, she was sitting in a chair, bowed over, her head in her hands.

"Estelle." He smiled when she looked up, surprised to see him standing there. "Wanna pray together?"

IT MIGHT HAVE BEEN A LITTLE SHORTER to go up Western Avenue, but Harry chose to take Lake Shore Drive. He put down the windows and let the cool evening's air purge the tension from his body as he glanced out over the water. It was only then that he remembered the eye appointment he'd missed that afternoon. He had questioned the need for a doctor's visit if nothing had changed— he winked his left and then his right eye, still the same—but he'd promised Estelle he'd go anyway. The fire had changed all that, of course. Oh well, he'd reschedule for some other day. Estelle would understand.

She was an incredibly understanding woman, and he was glad that he'd gone back to pray with her. He'd been a little embarrassed that he'd gone through such a traumatic day and only thought about talking to God after everything calmed down. He snorted a laugh. Seemed like he was still managing big hunks of his life without even thinking about God, but at least he'd finally remembered this evening and had the courage to act. Maybe he was changing a little. Maybe his faith was growing. Now what was that spiritual lesson he'd learned the other day? Oh yeah: By thanking God for all good things, he could become more and more aware of God's presence, and that would build his confidence in God's providence. And that was the essence of faith, wasn't it ... the belief that God cared and was involved in our lives?

As he passed Montrose Harbor, he spoke out loud. "Okay, God, what can I thank You for today?" It'd been a rough day. Well ... at least Leroy hadn't died ... Estelle had gotten down to the hospital safely ... and there *was* a hospital, even if it was only the County ... DaShawn was safe, at least as far as he knew. "You know what, God? I'm sorry, but I'm gonna get real honest here. It's actually been a beast of a day." He thought about it a moment, pressing his lips into a hard line. "And you know what? The good stuff's only 'good' in contrast to how much worse it might have been. So ... so thanks for nothin'."

His heart was pounding as he took the Foster exit from Lake Shore Drive. He felt guilty for his sour attitude and briefly wondered if God would strike him with a bolt of lightning. But once he got home, he managed to get to bed and fall asleep without thinking about God anymore.

THE REST OF THE WEEK WAS TAKEN UP with all the logistics of supporting Estelle—calling Mabel, the director of Manna House to explain why Estelle wouldn't be coming in for a couple of days; arranging care for DaShawn while he went down to be with Estelle; and trying to encourage Estelle that she needed to get back into the routine of her life. "You can't sleep down there every night Estelle. It's wearing you out, and Leroy is getting good care. You don't need to be there every minute."

"Yeah, but he doesn't have anybody else, Harry, and I don't want him to feel like I forgot him. That's what I worry about most."

"I know what you're sayin', but behind your concern I think there's more … like maybe you're feeling some guilt?"

"Guilt … what's with you, Harry Bentley? You gone from cop to doorman to what? You a shrink now? You have no idea what it's like to realize your son—your own flesh and blood—is suffering because you weren't there for him."

Harry dropped his head to resist responding defensively. She wasn't really attacking him. When he looked up again, his heart filled with the compassion of someone who'd been there, done that. "Actually, Estelle, I might know more about guilt than you're remembering. I've got a son, too. And right now, he's sittin' in jail, and I gotta live with the fact that I was the poor father who didn't spend enough time with him to start him on the right path. But that's not the only consideration here. Both of our sons are adults. We're foolin' ourselves if we think we can keep them from all the consequences of their bad decisions."

"But Harry, Leroy may be thirty years old, but he's just a child in his mind."

"Well …" Harry shook his head and scanned away, "that's why we gotta get him into a supportive living situation." He locked eyes with Estelle again. "But you can't blame yourself for that fire. It wasn't your fault, and blaming yourself won't do Leroy any good. The only way outta this is to go forward."

She heaved a big sigh. "Yeah, I know."

Finally—realizing Leroy was going to be in the Burn Center for weeks, not just days—Estelle agreed to go home Wednesday evening … provided Harry would bring her back for a visit Thursday afternoon as soon as she prepared lunch at Manna House.

On Saturday morning they took DaShawn with them when they went to the hospital for another visit, and then they stopped by the house to try and salvage anything they could from the fire. The windows were boarded up with plywood and there was a crime scene seal on the door warning, "No Trespassing," but it had already been broken, and the door stood ajar, so they went in. Within a few minutes, Harry was sorry they had. The place was a discouraging mess. They filled a couple of black plastic garbage bags with the few things that hadn't been damaged or stolen, but every room brought grief to Estelle. "Oh, no. This was my favorite end table, and now it's completely charred." … "That was my mother's flower vase, but it's broken now." … "I think we can save the silverware, don't you?"

"I'll put it in the bag if you want, Estelle. But it's only old stainless, and most of it looks pretty bent up to me."

It was that way in every room, and with each damaged item, Estelle grew more and more depressed. "I think we've been through every room, now, Estelle. Got about everything worth … DaShawn, put down that old basketball. It's gettin' soot all over your shirt."

"Yeah, but Grandpa, couldn't we just blow it up again?"

"You've got a nearly new basketball. What do you need that for?"

Estelle smiled wanly. "I think that was Leroy's, but DaShawn can have it if he wants it. Leroy never played much."

"Okay, but put it in a garbage bag. Come on, you two. Let's get otta here."

As they went out the door, Harry noticed the crime scene seal again. Why would they consider this a crime scene? Arson, maybe? Did they think Leroy lit the fire on purpose? He'd never have done that. What had he said? He was just watching TV *"when the whole place exploded.*" And Harry had believed him when he said he hadn't done anything that could've started a fire.

Maybe he just didn't remember doing it. After all, the day before he'd gone off—left the house, even—with a pan of bacon unattended on the stove. Yeah, Leroy could have done something like that again, but would another mistake like that have caused the whole place to burst into flames?

BY THE TIME THEY GOT BACK TO ROGERS PARK, Harry knew he had to do something to get Estelle's mind off the horrors of her destroyed house and her son's injuries. "Hey, I know what let's do this evening. Cindy, my old partner from the CPD, gave me some tickets for a nighttime cruise on Lake Michigan. The department's always getting tickets to one thing or another. So, how 'bout us takin' a cruise this evening? This is a fireworks night!"

Harry never would've gotten Estelle to go if it hadn't been for DaShawn. He was ecstatic. "Yeah, and can we take Paul, too?"

"Paul? Paul who?"

"You know, Paul Fairbanks, and maybe P.J., too? That way there'd be someone my age along."

"P.J.'s hardly your age, but … I guess, if we have enough tickets."

"Oh, that's okay," said Estelle. "I'm bushed. You just take the boys."

"No, no, no! Look in that glove box there. I think I threw the tickets in there. See how many there are."

Estelle found five tickets.

"Great!" said DaShawn. "That means we can all go."

Estelle protested some more, but DaShawn begged, "Please, Miss Estelle? I want you to come, too!"

Chapter 11

HARRY SMILED TO HIMSELF WHEN HE PICKED UP ESTELLE after they'd all showered and changed clothes. She was dressed in a bright yellow-and-black caftan, looking more like an African queen than a sailor decked out for a yacht cruise. No problem. The lakefront sightseeing boats catered to passengers in any attire, and Estelle's bright outfit suggested his plan of getting her mind off the fire for an evening might be working.

"I sure hope it's cooler out on the lake." She slid into the front seat of Harry's car, waving her hand at her face. "You got the air on?"

"It's on, but it's not really that hot, is it? Maybe you're just having one of those—"

"Harry Bentley, I done told you 'bout that, so don't you say it again!" She glanced back to see if DaShawn was paying attention.

Harry checked his mirror. DaShawn was texting, so who knew how much he'd overheard?

When they got to the Firecracker's apartment, she seemed surprised to see them, but invited them in. The boys weren't home yet—it was their regular weekly visit with their dad—so Estelle propelled Gabby into the kitchen to quiz her about how she was going to respond to her husband's request for a short-term personal loan—twenty-five grand, it turned out—to cover his gambling debt.

What? A loan? Harry couldn't believe it. The nerve of the man! While working as a doorman at Richmond Towers, he'd developed a simmering dislike for Fairbanks. The man was a racist stuffed suit—though he usually dressed GQ-casual. And when he'd kicked his wife and her mother out of their penthouse apartment, causing them to seek shelter at Manna House, that was too much. Harry had lost all respect for the man.

But this! He shook his head at the news of the loan request. So now Fairbanks had come to Gabby, all contrite, hinting at a possible reconciliation. As far as Harry could see, Fairbanks was just leveraging her for the loan. He gritted his teeth, forcing his face to remain stoic. It wasn't any of his business. When his cell phone rang and the caller ID showed it was his old police partner, he gratefully excused himself. "Sorry. Gotta take this. Be back in a minute," and he escaped down the hallway toward the dining room.

"Hey, Cindy. What's up?"

"Just thought you'd want to know. They arrested Fagan today. Indictment came through this morning."

"That mean he's locked up for awhile?"

"You kidding? He'll be out before breakfast. But at least he's suspended—with pay, of course—pending ..."

"Yeah. Figures. How you doin'? Any repercussions in the unit?"

"Oh, you know, everyone's speculating on how they got the indictment, who blew the whistle and all. But ... haven't heard your name come up, so just hang loose. Everything's gonna be okay."

"Yeah. Maybe. But Fagan knows. He tried to lean on me again the other day, made some kind of threats about me havin' only two days to clear his name."

"How'd he know?"

"Gotta be a leak in Internal Affairs. I mentioned the possibility weeks ago to Captain Gilson, but …"

"Well, at least now it's official, so maybe that'll cool Fagan's jets for awhile."

"We can hope. We can always hope. Thanks for callin', Cindy."

Harry closed his phone and sauntered back to the kitchen, hoping the conversation about Fairbanks was over.

Estelle looked up. "Oh, Harry's back. Everything okay?"

He sat down. "Yep. That was Cindy. They've picked up our man. Indictment came out this morning."

"Oh, praise Jesus!" Estelle said. "I'm glad that dirty cop is off the streets."

Harry grunted. "For 'bout one hot minute. He'll pay his bond and be out by tomorrow. But at least he'll be on leave from the force until the trial."

The Firecracker leaned forward and waved her hand like a flag between Harry and Estelle. "Hello-o. What are you guys talking about?"

"Sorry. Just some old police business. This guy Fagan used to be my boss, but—"

Estelle touched Harry's arm. "You can tell her 'bout Fagan some other time, Harry. Gabby says everybody's tellin' her don't go givin' Philip a loan. But she wants to know what *you're* thinkin'."

Nothin' like being put on the spot. He stared dead-eyed at Estelle. Should've stayed down the hall. Oh well, he took a deep breath. "Sounds to me like Fairbanks is a classic 'problem gambler.' I've seen it take down guys on the force again and again. He's addicted, just like a drug addict." *And just like me and alcohol.* The accusation interrupted his train of thought for a moment. "Uh … He doesn't know when to stop. Even if you did loan him money out of the kindness of your heart, you wouldn't be doing him a favor. He'd just gamble it away. And you'd just be enabling a bad habit."

"But he promised to pay it back. I think he honestly realizes—"

Harry shook his head. She didn't understand. "Maybe your husband *thinks* he sees the light, even promises himself he won't do it anymore. I don't much care for the man, but I'd be the first one to cheer if he actually got some help, turned things around, decided to treat you right. But throwing money at a gambling problem is the worst thing you can do. If you care for your husband at all, don't loan him that money. Any money."

Estelle leaned forward and put her hand on Gabby's arm. "Mm-mm-mm. Outta the mouth o' babes ... an' old men." She gave Harry an exaggerated wink. "Now *that* sounds like a God-reason to say no. Now that we got our petty little selves outta the way, maybe we're ready to pray 'bout this? What do ya say, honey?"

As they prayed, Harry realized that in spite of Estelle's occasional feistiness, the two of them were usually on the same page. If only he didn't have that problem with his vision, they could make a good team together.

THE THOUGHT PLAGUED HIM ALL EVENING: *If only he didn't have that eye problem ...* he would've taken Estelle on this cruise the last time they were down here, and he'd have asked her to marry him then. He would've given her the ring that now sat on his dresser at home while he hoped with the thinnest thread of faith that God would somehow heal his bad eye and save his good one so he could get on with his life.

He laughed under his breath when he closed his right eye during the fireworks display and watched the rockets explode in blurry distortion. With all the technology the manufactures used to obtain unique displays, he could create them just by using his left eye.

He gripped the rail of the Mystic Blue cruise boat as it rocked gently in the swells of Lake Michigan.

"Oooo! Now there's a pretty one, Harry!"

"Look! Look! A happy face!" yelled DaShawn, standing on the other side of Estelle with the Fairbanks boys. "How do they do that, anyway?"

"Ha!" said a manly voice from down the line, causing Harry to lean forward to see whether it really came from P.J. Fairbanks or not. The boy's voice flipped back into his pubescent higher tone. "Don't you know? The guy in the helicopter paints 'em like that."

"Rea— Ah, there ain't no helicopter up there!"

"Ha, ha! Had ya goin'!" This time his new deep voice held until the word, *goin'*. Harry smiled. Did the Firecracker know what phase of parenthood she was entering?

It was a great evening, and when the crisp material of Estelle's yellow dress brushed his side, Harry involuntarily slipped his arm around her and drew her close.

Later, as they rode home, the boys were quiet, and Harry figured they'd fallen asleep. He didn't want to wake them, so he didn't talk. And he also didn't want to break the spell of the hollow feeling that had settled in the middle of his chest ... like the melancholy of a sad movie. If he could just ride it out, maybe he could see a deeper meaning for why things weren't working out for him and Estelle the way he wanted. He stole a peek at her. She'd turned toward the side window, watching the boats bob in Belmont Harbor and the nighttime fitness addicts jogging along the bike path. Was she also wondering about their relationship, longing, perhaps, for something more? His eyes got a bit misty ...

ah, come on Harry, enough of that! He took a deep breath and pushed himself back from the steering wheel, his arms locked straight.

When they arrived at the Fairbanks apartment shortly before midnight, both boys jumped out with the bounce of a couple puppies, no evidence of sleep. "Thanks, Mr. B," Paul said as Harry walked them to the door.

"Yeah, that was pretty cool," added P.J. in a gravelly baritone.

When he got back into his SUV, Harry turned to Estelle and shrugged. "They might turn out all right after all."

WHEN HE GOT TO BIBLE STUDY at Peter Douglass's apartment Tuesday evening—even before the guys had finished greeting one another and exchanging small talk about their week—Harry blurted, "Have any of you heard the phrase, 'I believe, but help my unbelief'? Where'd that come from? I'm sure I've heard it before."

"Ha," said Ben Garfield, the older Jewish guy Harry suspected came to Bible study mostly to get a break from caring for his baby twins. "I've heard that one, too—every time I promise Ruth I'll clean out the den. But if I clean it and make it all nice, she'd be in there bugging me. As it is, it's my mess, and she stays out. So, what's *alter kocker* like me to do, eh?"

Denny Baxter chuckled. "Don't think that's the source, Ben. He opened his Bible and started flipping through the pages. "It's from the Bible."

But Carl Hickman beat him to the reference. "Here it is, in Mark nine and twenty-four. 'And straightway the father of the child cried out, and said with tears, "Lord, I believe; help thou mine unbelief." ' "

"You still using that old King James Version?" asked young Josh Baxter.

"Of course. It sounds more ... more holy to me. Know what I'm sayin'?"

"You mean, you think all the *thees* and *thous* make it more holy? Whatever ... long as you can understand it."

"And what was so hard about understanding that verse?"

Harry held up both hands like a cop trying to stop traffic. "Hey guys! I got the words, but what's the point? What's the saying mean?"

After a moment of silence, Peter Douglass spoke up. "Well, the context was a father of a boy who was tormented by an evil spirit. The disciples had already tried to cast out the spirit and failed, so he brought the boy to Jesus. Start at verse twenty-one:

> Jesus asked the boy's father, "How long has he been like this?"
>
> "From childhood," he answered. "It has often thrown him into fire or water to kill him. But if you can do anything, take pity on us and help us."
>
> "'*If you can*'?" said Jesus. "Everything is possible for him who believes."
>
> Immediately the boy's father exclaimed, "I do believe; help me overcome my unbelief!"

Harry scanned the following verses. "Wow! Jesus still healed the boy, even after the father said that? That's amazing, man. That's amazing." The healing was great, but Jesus didn't even seem angry over the father's shaky faith. "Thanks," he muttered to the guys as he leaned back in his chair. "I was just wantin' to know where it came from."

"All right, brothers. We ready to get into the Word? Denny, would you open us in prayer?"

110

Denny Baxter asked the Lord's blessing on their evening and prayed that the Holy Spirit would open their hearts and change them. But after his "Amen," he said, "Peter, I just wanted to ask Harry if there was some reason that verse was on his mind tonight. What about it, Harry?"

Harry shrugged and his breath came a little shallower. "Guess I been thinkin' 'bout it for several days now, but … Well, you guys remember about my eye and all? I've been tryin' to pray, you know, thankin' God so my faith will grow stronger, but things keep happenin'." He stopped and looked down.

"What kind of things?" prodded Carl.

"I suppose you heard about Estelle's son and her house gettin' burned—that's one. That's why I wasn't here last week, and, well, nothing's changed with my eye. Ha! I kind of let God have it the other day 'cause it seemed like everything was goin' wrong. You know, I *want* to believe … but somehow it's hard, don'cha know? That's when that phrase—I mean, that verse—came to mind. That's all."

The guys were quiet for a few minutes. Then Denny said, "You know, it's okay to tell God what you're feeling. He knows it already, anyway. A lot of the psalms in the Bible are like that. David often complained because it didn't seem like God was answering his prayers."

"Really?"

"Yeah. I'm sure you've heard 'em before. For instance …" He flipped some pages. "Here, in Psalm 22 …

My God, my God, why have you forsaken me?
    Why are you so far from saving me,
      so far from the words of my groaning?
O my God, I cry out by day, but you do not answer.

"He says much the same thing in Psalm 10, too: 'Why, O Lord, do you stand far off? Why do you hide yourself in times of trouble?' And there're others. But the writer also remembered to thank the Lord for all the times and ways he does see God's answers and His care."

"Yeah, that's what I was tryin' to do. I was tryin' to thank God for all the good things, but one time when I was comin' back from the fire, it seemed like nothin' was really good. At least, it was only good in relation to how much worse it could've been—like Leroy could've *died* in the fire. Instead, he just got third-degree burns. Guess that's better, but … it's hard."

"That's okay! That's okay," said Peter. "The point is to keep talkin' to Him."

"And keep listenin' for Him to speak to you," added Carl, "in every circumstance of your life, in every word from the Word"—he held up his Bible—"that He burns into your heart."

"*Oy vey.*" Ben Garfield threw up both hands and rolled his eyes up toward the ceiling. "I have no idea what you guys are talkin' about. You sound like you think God's gonna talk to you like you were a prophet or something. Hey, I'm just a retired Buick salesman, after all. How's He gonna speak to me? I'd like to know."

Josh Baxter began laughing, not just a little chuckle, but a side-grabber that rolled him back in the overstuffed chair where he sat. "I bet I know one way He speaks to you, Mr. Garfield. And you listen, too … though you may not know who's speakin'."

"What are you talkin' about?"

"Your kids, Ben! Your kids! What else gets through to your heart faster? I know, I know, because that's how God gets my attention sometimes, through Gracie. Now you can't deny that."

Ben sat there blinking with a blank look on his face. "How can that be God?"

112

"Well, I'll admit it's probably not 'the still small voice' God used to speak to Elijah, but I bet they get your attention."

"Well, yeah. But who's to say that's God? Sometimes I think they're little devils. Uh … don't tell Ruth I said that."

Peter cleared his throat. "God works through—and can speak through—any circumstance in our life, but you're right. That doesn't mean we get the message. When we think God is speaking, the first test is whether the message lines up with the Bible and whether it's consistent with God's character. Because God never contradicts Himself. That's why we need to get to know the Word, so … let's move on. How far'd we get last week?"

Chapter 12

WHILE IT WAS STILL DARK THE NEXT MORNING, Harry saw flashes of light. Another big storm must be coming. He waited, counting the seconds to divide by five and calculate how many miles away it was ... but the thunder never came. He flopped over in his bed, and there was another flash, but other than the normal hum of traffic on the street below, the city was silent. Strange. No cloud-ripping cracks. No boomers. No teeth rattling explosions so typical of Chicago's summer storms.

Harry opened his eyes in his still dim room and glanced toward his digital clock. A flash off to the side startled him, as bright as if the lightning had struck the building next door. It should have shaken the windows and doors and punched him in the chest with the concussion. It was that bright and close, but ... no sound.

The clock read 6:05. He got up and walked stiffly to the window where he turned the Venetian blinds open. The bottoms of the clouds were ribbed with pink announcing the sunrise, but it was a high, thin overcast, no thunderheads, no storm. Harry frowned and sat down on the edge of his bed. He blinked, and checked his blind spot. Still there ... but wait, there was some dark fuzzy lint over to the side, like a ragged spider web. He rubbed his eye to dislodge it, and the lightning flashed again.

He held his breath … but still the thunder didn't come. And then he remembered Dr. Racine's warning: "*Give us a call. Especially if you experience bright flashes off to the periphery.*" He'd also mentioned "*little spider-web things or black dots that seems to float in your vision.*" Harry flipped on his room light and stared at a blank wall. Yes, the ragged spider web in his left eye was drifting slowly down. "Floaters," that's what the eye doctor had called them. He shifted his point of focus on the wall, and the floater followed his gaze and then drifted down again.

The unusual quiet of the morning was replaced by the pounding of his heart, blood throbbing in his ears. Something was happening in his eye, and he knew it wasn't good. He squeezed his eyes shut. What had the doctor said about such warnings? How severe were they?

He checked the clock again: 6:15. Too early to call the doctor. But he knew he had to go to the clinic! No way to make an appointment ahead of time, he'd just have to be there as soon as the doors opened at eight.

"DaShawn!" Harry started pulling on his clothes. "DaShawn! Time to get up. We gotta go." He grabbed his shoes and noticed another flash off to the side of his left eye. "DaShawn! You hear me?"

"But Grandpa!" DaShawn's moan was mumbled from the next room. "How come I gotta get up so early? Basketball camp doesn't start 'til ten."

"I know, but I need to go to the eye doctor, first thing. So … so you need to get over to Great Grandma's."

The moan turned into a whine. "But I don't *wanna* go over there today. I hafta to go to her place almost every day. It's boring. Why can't I just sleep in and go to camp on my own?"

"Just 'cause, that's why! Now get up."

After a long silence, Harry still couldn't hear any sound of movement from the next bedroom. "DaShawn! I ain't messin' with you, boy. You hear what I said?"

"Yes sir. But …" There was a long silence, and Harry was ready to pounce on whatever came after that *but*. But when DaShawn continued, his tone was humble. "Uh, you think I could go over to Robbie's today? All Great Grandma does is watch those TV preachers. There's nothin' to do."

Harry sighed and walked down the hallway to lean in the doorway of DaShawn's room. "Look, you get up, get dressed, and get somethin' to eat. Then call Robbie. If he's up, and his mom agrees, I'll drop you by. But hurry up. I wanna to be leavin' out of here by seven."

Surprisingly, they drove out of the parking lot in the RAV4 at five minutes to seven to take DaShawn over to his friend's place.

By the light of day, the flashes weren't as noticeable, but if he closed his eyes while he waited at a stop light and scanned back and forth quickly, a flash would occur. And the little fuzzy floater still played around the edges of his vision. Something had definitely changed. By the light of day, he was also thinking more clearly. What would the doctor do? Would he schedule surgery? What if he wanted to do it today? What would Harry do with his car? He needed a change of plans. As soon as he dropped DaShawn at Robbie's, he raced back to his apartment building, parked his car, and headed to the El stop. It would take longer to go down by El, but he needed the flexibility. Should he tell Estelle? Not yet. She had too much to worry about with Leroy, and besides, he didn't have anything conclusive to tell her, anyway. He'd call after the doctor told him what was happening. He might need her to arrange for someone to pick up DaShawn.

DR. RACINE STOOD UP AND STRETCHED after examining Harry's eye through his grueling slit lamp. "Well, floaters and flashes are usually benign. But with your macular hole, we do have to watch more carefully. And I think you do have a small retinal tear in there. That floater you're seeing looks like a little blood that's leaked in. It's not bad, but I'd like to pin down the tear to make sure it doesn't get worse. We wouldn't want any vitreous to seep through the tear and get in behind the retina." He held his hands up and moved them like a mime artist. "Think of your retina as if it were new wallpaper on the wall. If fluid gets behind it, it could loosen and start peeling off, and we don't want that."

Harry nodded, trying to be positive and upbeat but understanding only about half of what the doctor was explaining. "Okay, so how do we—as you say—pin it down?"

"With laser." He shrugged as though it was just an option. "To be safe, I think a laser treatment would be wise."

"Woo, laser! I mean, I thought shining a laser into a person's eye could make 'em go blind."

"Depends. Of course, we control it carefully, focusing it on a tiny spot on the retina where it burns a little dot. That burn quickly begins to heal, and as it does, the scar tissue acts like a tiny rivet to pin the retina to the back of the eyeball. We'll actually do several shots all around the tear. It should keep it in place. But I also think we should schedule you for the vitrectomy to take care of your macular hole. It doesn't seem to be getting any better by waiting."

"Oh … oh, yeah." Harry sat there dumbfounded. All this was happening so fast. What could he say? "Uh, would you be doing both of those procedures at the same time?"

"Well, no. We can't do the vitrectomy today. I usually schedule surgeries for Fridays, and I'm full-up this next Friday, so maybe Friday a week. But I'd like to do the laser treatment today. I don't want to leave it any longer than necessary."

Harry wiped his hand over his shaved head, noticing it was a little prickly around the edges. "Today. Uh ... how long will I be in the hospital?"

"Not the hospital. We can do that right here in the clinic as an outpatient procedure. Won't take long, and other than some immediate discomfort, you'll be able to go home in an hour or so. But you won't be up to driving today. Do you have someone with you who could take you home?"

Harry shook his head. "Came by El."

The doctor frowned. "I suppose that'd be okay. We'll give you a patch to wear over your eye. Bright light might be uncomfortable."

Yeah, thought Harry, *like that slit lamp! Has anybody told him how uncomfortable it is?*

He agreed to the procedure. What else could he do? The doctor left, and an assistant came to collect his signature on several papers. Within thirty minutes, he was taken to another room where he was again seated in a barber-like-chair where he was told to lean forward, place his chin on one rest and his forehead against a strap, stabilizing any head movements. After some numbing drops were put into his eye, Dr. Racine showed him a lens that looked like it belonged to a camera. "This is actually a contact lens that I'll put on the surface of your eye to stabilize it and to help me focus the laser. You won't feel anything other than a little pressure."

Harry didn't feel it touching the surface of his eye, but it was so large that the doctor had to pull his eyelids open wider to position it. In only a few moments he said, "Okay, this shouldn't hurt too much. Here we go!" Followed by a loud *click, click, click,* each accompanied by a flash of green light in Harry's eye. And the doctor was right ... at least concerning the first few times the laser fired. But by the time it had fired five or six times in each spot before moving, the pain—more like an intensifying ache—became nearly unbearable.

Harry had imagined he'd need only six or eight laser shots, but the doctor kept encouraging him. "Okay, we're doing good. Just a few more, now." Harry hung in there, griping the arms of the chair tighter, hoping it would soon be over. It seemed to go on and on until Dr. Racine flipped the switch that turned off the aiming light and said, "Okay, that's 53 shots. I think that'll do it."

"Oh-h-h." Weak-kneed and shaky, Harry stood up, not caring very much that the only thing he could see through his left eye was a bright glare that made him want to close his eye.

"You okay? We'll get you an eye patch and some Tylenol 3."

The patch was not the cool black patch pirates sometimes wore. It was just a thick wad of gauze taped in place. Harry caught a glimpse of himself reflected in the glass door as he walked out of the clinic. He resembled one of the walking wounded coming back from the battlefront in a great war. He felt like that, too. But all he wanted was to get out of there before he lost it. He found a bench outside the entrance to one of the other UIC medical buildings and sat down—elbows on knees, head in hands—waiting for the Tylenol to kick in.

"Oh, God. This is too much," he muttered over and over under his breath. "Help me here, God. Help me."

He had no idea how long he sat there, but at some point, he realized that the pain had subsided to a dull ache—more like an average headache—and his pleas to God had shifted to wondering what was to become of him. Was he losing his sight? What if it started happening in his right eye? He'd been over those questions so many times, but there'd been no answer. Where was God, anyway?

Finally, he took a deep breath and pulled out his cell phone. Two-twenty. He ought to call Estelle. As it was, he knew she'd be furious that he hadn't told her earlier.

After five rings, Harry was about to give up, and then she answered. "I'm tryin' to teach this knitting class here, Harry. Can this wait?"

"I'll only take a moment. I need to tell you I came down to the eye clinic today because I was having some problems. The doctor gave me a laser treatment, but I'm okay, and am heading home now."

"You what?"

"I said, I came in to the eye clinic because I was having some more trouble with my eyes—flashes and floaters."

"Both eyes now?"

"No, just the one, but … the doctor gave me a laser treatment."

"What's that mean?"

"I'll tell you when I get home. I need to go now, catch the El. Talk to you later."

"What? Wait … Harry? You still there? How come you're taking the El?"

"I figured before I came down here that I might not be able to drive home, so—"

"Oh, Harry, why didn't you tell me?"

Harry sighed deeply. His eye still ached. "I'll explain when I get home, Estelle." He closed his phone before she could answer.

It was only about a four-block walk to the El stop, but by the time he got there, Harry felt as if he'd walked miles. Maybe this wasn't such a good idea. Maybe he should've taken a cab. Sometimes it didn't pay to be so cheap. There were only a few riders waiting, and he found a vacant bench to sit on while he waited. His eye throbbed with every beat of his heart. And when the El finally came and he got aboard, the train's vibration as it jostled along the steel tracks into the Loop hurt his eye with every jolt.

Chapter 13

ARRY HAD INTENDED TO TELL ESTELLE about his doctor's visit as soon as he got home, but he was so exhausted after picking up DaShawn that he kept putting it off. She was the one who finally called him that evening. Even then, he ended up giving her an abbreviated version. After all, she'd just been through the trauma of losing her house and having her son severely burned. She didn't need to cope with anything more.

"I'm okay, Estelle. It really doesn't hurt anymore—"

"How would you know? You're on those painkillers. They work, Harry, and that's good, but when you're on them, you can't say you don't hurt anymore."

"Estelle, I'm tryin' to tell you …" He rocked back in his recliner and glanced at DaShawn who was watching TV. "I'm tryin' to tell you I'm okay."

"Well, I'm comin' over to check on you." The phone went dead.

Now how was she going to do that? She didn't have a car. But if he knew Estelle Williams, she'd find a way. He went into the bathroom and gazed at himself in the mirror. He looked a wreck— big gauze patch held in place by long strips of what resembled transparent office tape, face haggard from pain, right eye a little bloodshot. The doctor had said the purpose of the patch was to protect him from bright light. But this was evening, no sun. He could turn down the lights in the house if need be. He pulled the tape off and gingerly removed the patch. Oh, man! If he thought the patch appeared bad, the sight of his left eye was right out of a horror movie, as though someone had tagged him with a right hook. He couldn't let Estelle see him like that.

"Hey, DaShawn," he said, hurrying through the living room, "I'm headin' over to the Walgreens. Be back in a few. Okay?"

DaShawn nodded without looking up from his TV show, and Harry headed out the door.

At Walgreens—just two blocks away—he found what he was looking for: a small black eye patch with an elastic band attached. He had it out of the package and on his head by the time he left the store. And it did the intended job, keeping the glare of car head-lights from punching right through to the back of his head.

He got back to his apartment building just as a taxi pulled up and Estelle got out. Oh no! She's gonna grill me about why I'm out walking around when she probably thinks I ought to be in the hospital. "Hey, Estelle, you made it. I was about ready to come get you since I figured there was no way I could talk you out of comin' over here tonight."

"What you doin' out here, Harry Bentley?"

He laughed. "Sayin' hi to you. Come on up."

"Oh, Harry." She reached out and touched his cheek. "Your poor eye."

"So, whaddaya think? Do I make a good pirate?"

"Pirates aren't funny, Harry. They rape and pillage. Let's get upstairs."

Harry balked and stared after her. He didn't like it when she spoke to him as if he were a kid … and yet … he loved that she cared about him. So what was the difference? He shook his head and followed, stepping around her to open the door. She marched through, and they climbed the steps to his third-floor apartment.

Funny how the stairwells of apartment buildings blended the smells of the residents and their lifestyles—a hint of curry from the Indian family on first floor, stale cigar smoke from the three students trying to be cool on the second floor, dust and paint fumes from the empty second floor apartment that was being redecorated. He noticed these things more now that he knew his sight was threatened.

Once inside his apartment—it smelled … neutral, or was he just used to it?—Estelle dropped her large purse on the couch while Harry stepped into the bathroom to inspect the black patch over his eye. Dr. Racine hadn't seemed concerned about him wearing it any longer than he needed for relief from bright lights. But as Harry turned this way and that, he thought the patch looked pretty cool. All right, all right. This wasn't Halloween, but it'd be better than having people fawn all over how ugly his eye looked underneath. He'd wear it until it appeared normal again.

"Harry, get back in here and sit down in that chair. Give yourself some rest. You've had a rough day."

He took his seat while she puttered in the kitchen, putting on coffee as though this were her own apartment. He'd be glad to make it so … if it weren't for his eye. And in practical terms, if they got married, they'd have to get a bigger place, anyway.

"So when do you get that patch off?" Estelle asked from the kitchen as she got out a couple of cups.

"Don't know. I'm supposed to go back on Friday for a check-up. And …" He'd better tell her. "And the following Friday, I have to go in for real surgery. "

"What? What are they gonna do?"

Harry didn't want to go through all the gory details. "They're gonna fix that little blind spot. Not a big deal. Just outpatient, so I'll come home the same day. But afterwards, I have to keep my head down for two weeks."

She came in and stood over him. "Harry, this is getting' outta hand—"

"Yeah, and I don't want to talk about it. Suffice it to say, I gotta go in this Friday, okay?"

She stood there as if she were deciding whether or not to push it. "Well, okay for now." She stretched and ran her fingers through her hair. "So, you gonna take the El down there again *this* Friday? You can't drive with that patch on your eye."

"Why not? Lots of people manage to drive just fine with only one eye. And some who think they have two eyes, can't see that well out of either of 'em."

"Humph!" Estelle shook her head. "Well, what time?"

"First thing in the morning. Friday's Dr. Racine's surgery day, but he wants to check me first. I'm supposed to be there by seven-thirty, even though the clinic doesn't open until eight. Someone's supposed to let me in early and dilate my eyes."

"I guess if it's just a checkup, and it's that early, you should have time to get back to Manna House by noon. I'm planning a back-to-school lunch for everybody—staff kids, too. So you and DaShawn better be there."

"Estelle!" He gritted his teeth. "You askin' me or tellin' me? I ain't staff, you know."

"Might as well be. We need you around there mor'n you know. Besides, Mabel needs someone to bring her nephew, Jermaine, over. So pick him up on your way. Okay?"

His shoulders sagged. If she wasn't fussin' over him, she was bossin' him. But what could he say?

FRIDAY CAME, AND HARRY MADE IT TO THE EYE CLINIC EARLY as instructed. He had to knock on the door several times before attracting the attention of a technician who let him in and put the drops in his eyes—the doctor always wanted to check both of them. There was still that risk.

Afterwards, as he sat alone in the waiting room waiting until his eyes had dilated, he thought about Estelle. He was always thinking about Estelle. Perhaps he ought to break off their relationship completely, explain to her it couldn't go anywhere as long as the future of his eyesight was so tentative. He knew she wouldn't accept that explanation, but he was clear about it: He couldn't marry her if he was about to become an invalid! And he wasn't being able to keep their relationship "on ice," either. He thought about her all the time, and she was treating him like family—for better or worse. He laughed to himself. Yeah, maybe it was best to break it off. But how could he do it without hurting her?

"Mr. Bentley," Dr. Racine leaned in through the door of the waiting room, "Why don't you come on back so we can take a look at that eye. Ah, I see you've got a more, uh … stylish patch. Does the light still hurt your eye?"

"Not necessarily. It was just more …" What could he say? That he didn't want to look like a train wreck victim with that taped-on piece of gauze? But the doctor didn't seem to expect an answer, ushering him instead into the seat and adjusting the headrest so he could look into Harry's eyes.

"Any more flashes?"

"No, not since the other morning."

"Good. Now just look straight ahead toward my ear."

The slit lamp came on, and Harry had to force himself not to close his left eye. Then he endured the exam of his right eye.

A few minutes later, after the "searchlight" had scoured the insides of his eyes, Dr. Racine turned it off and stood up. Harry leaned back, blinking. In reaction to the brilliance of the slit lamp, his eye returned only a black-purple "glow."

"So, what'd you see?"

"Things look pretty good. But I want to do an ultrasound to make sure there's no detachment, no fluid behind the retina."

Harry tipped his head down, covering both eyes with the palms of his hands. Not something else. He'd had an echocardiogram once where they did an ultrasound to observe the function of his heart. It wasn't so bad, but ... oh, God, would this ever end?

"Just relax for a minute," said the doctor. "I'll wheel the ultrasound machine in here and take a look."

After putting in the numbing drops, the doctor touched the surface of Harry's eye with an instrument, moving it round and adjusting the angle to provide an image of the wall of his eyeball on the nearby screen. The pressure wasn't actually painful, but Harry's every natural instinct revolted against allowing someone to poke something into his eye and move it around and around and around. When would it all stop?

Finally, the doctor leaned back and handed Harry a tissue to wipe the tears from his eye and cheek. "Okay. Well, it looks like there's a slight detachment. Here, I'll play it back on the screen so you can see."

Harry wasn't sure he wanted to see it, and when he studied it, the image was about as meaningless as the ultrasound he'd seen of his son thirty years before when his wife came home from the doctor announcing she was eight-weeks pregnant. But Dr. Racine pointed out the arc that represented his retina and the corresponding arc for the wall of the eyeball. "Now right here, you can see this little black line between the other two. That's a slight separation. Not much. Probably some fluid leaked in there before we did the laser the other day. I don't think we have to worry, but just to be safe, I'd like to add a few more shots of laser this morning. Won't take long."

Harry closed his eyes and exhaled. "How many?" He hoped he didn't sound too dramatic.

"Oh, no more than a dozen."

The pain from just two days before was still fresh in Harry's mind, but he had no choice. What wouldn't a person do to save their vision? He couldn't give up.

The procedure was the same, though not nearly so long, and consequently it didn't generate as much pain. In fact, when Harry left the clinic at about nine-thirty, his eye didn't feel much worse than a nasty headache. He popped a couple of Tylenols and sat quietly in his RAV4 for forty minutes with both eyes closed, just listening to music.

HE GOT HOME IN TIME TO PICK UP DASHAWN early from basketball camp and get Jermaine and take them both over to Manna House before noon. Estelle was as busy as a choir conductor directing the last minute details for the luncheon from the kitchen. When Harry waved at her from across the dining room, she just nodded, and that was good enough for him. He still wasn't ready for conversation, but he had to get beyond all this preoccupation with his vision.

After most people had eaten, Mabel Turner, the director of Manna House asked for everyone's attention and then named Paul Fairbanks, the Firecracker's youngest, Volunteer of the Month for helping out by entertaining the younger kids until school started. She also gave out backpacks filled with school supplies to all the kids, and then the Firecracker announced a Labor Day picnic— "On Sunday, not Monday!"—and invited everyone to sign up. She handed the sign-up clipboard to Harry and said, "You and DaShawn are invited too, Mr. B." Then she lowered her voice and said, "You used to be a cop, right? We could use some security."

Harry glanced at the clipboard for a moment. Yeah, if he wanted to get beyond thinking about his eyes all the time, he needed to fill his life with other activities. "Might just do that," he said to the Firecracker and signed his name.

SUNDAY MORNING, ESTELLE ASKED IF HE'D DRIVE HER to visit Leroy. It surprised Harry that she would miss church, but with the picnic in the afternoon, morning was the only option.

Three things struck Harry when they entered the burn unit at the county hospital: It was hot—perhaps high 90s—humid, and it smelled. The heat and humidity were intentional, to keep the patients warm until their bodily thermostats recovered and to keep their skin from drying out. But underlying the acrid scent of antiseptics and disinfectants was the unmistakable smell of burned flesh, more insidious than oven-charred meat or singed hair. It smelled like death.

Harry coughed and took Estelle's elbow as she fanned her face. "Good heavens, why don't they turn on the air in here?"

A man in a bed near them, shielded only by curtains, screamed in pain, and a male nurse walking toward them apparently noticed the horror that came over their faces. "It's okay," said the nurse. "They're just changing his dressing. Can't be helped. You looking for someone?"

"Uh ..." Estelle drilled Harry with a look, telegraphing her fear that the crying man might be her son. "We're looking for Michael Leroy Williams."

"Oh sure, Leroy. He's been moved from the intensive care unit to a convalescent bed. It's still part of the burn unit, but you gotta go through that door. Second bed on the right."

"Thank you, Jesus." Estelle stepped off like she was in a marching parade headed for that door, and Harry had to hustle to keep up.

The TV was going when Estelle parted the curtains and said, "Leroy, you okay?"

"Oh hi, Mama. Yeah, doin' better." The thin man lay on top of the sheets dressed in a pair of loose shorts to expose the burns along his left side to the air, all except for two places still covered by large bandages.

Estelle stared at the burns. "How come they look so black?"

"I dunno. It's the medicine they put on so it won't get infected." He searched Estelle's face like a child looking for release. "Mama. I'm ... I'm really sorry." He started to cry.

"There, there now." She stroked the good side of his head.

"They gonna fix it, Mama?"

"Not likely. The insurance is handling all that stuff. But how you doin'? You still in a lot of pain?"

"Not so much." He sniffed in a big sob. "'Cept when they change the dressings or make me stretch the skin."

Harry cringed, recalling the cries of the man they'd just passed.

Estelle sat on the edge of Leroy's bed, stroking his head for the next thirty minutes without saying much as the TV droned on and captured more and more of their attention. Finally, Estelle said, "We probably better be goin'. But Harry, would you pray for Leroy?"

Harry's jaw dropped. What would he say? He wasn't sure God heard him when he prayed for himself. So how was he supposed to pray for Leroy? That he would be instantly healed like Jesus had healed the ten lepers in the New Testament? Who did Estelle think he was? He recovered his jaw, and muttered, "Uh … me?"

"You're the only Harry in the room!"

"All right, all right. Let's bow our heads, uh …" He glanced at Leroy. How could he bow his head? "I mean, let's pray." He started to fold his hands, but Estelle grabbed one of his hands while leaving her other hand on the good side of Leroy's head. "Okay. That's good. We got a little 'touch and agree' goin' on here"—he'd heard that phrase in church but had no idea what it meant. Still …

"Uh, dear Jesus, Leroy's in a lot of pain, and he's sorry for what happened to their house, even though he didn't start the fire. So, we're askin' You to come and be with him right here in this hospital room." Suddenly, what Harry was praying seemed to get easier, just talking to Jesus about what was. "And I'm sure it's pretty boring for Leroy here in this hospital and scary not knowing what's in the future. So reassure him, Jesus. Reassure him that You won't leave him. And Jesus, protect him from any complications. And give him patience. Please bless the nurses and doctors for everything they do, and thank You for this hospital with such an advanced burn unit. And … and thank You that he has a mother like Estelle. Amen."

Estelle gripped his hand hard as she bent down and kissed Leroy once more before they left.

Chapter 14

I DON'T LIKE MISSING CHURCH." ESTELLE FROWNED as they got back in the car after visiting Leroy. She punched on the radio. Dr. Tony Evans was on Moody, and she sat back, crossed her arms, and closed her eyes in satisfaction as he preached. Harry listened too—for a few minutes—but then his mind drifted back to Leroy.

He knew Leroy hadn't started the fire, but there was something funny about how fast it had spread, overwhelming Leroy before he could escape. The raging inferno grew so quickly, it seemed more sinister than an accidental source like bad wiring.

When they'd first returned to the house a few days after the fire, it was sealed as a crime scene—even though the seal had been broken and the door stood ajar. Harry had wondered at the time whether the police suspected arson, but as far as he knew, nothing had come of any investigation. Had there even been one?

The thing that nagged at the back of Harry's mind was Fagan. He'd been at the house. He'd threatened Harry, said he had two days to neutralize the charges against Fagan as a dirty cop. That had been exactly two days before the big fire. And less than an hour after the fire started—while Harry was still at the hospital with Leroy—Fagan had phoned to remind Harry that Monday had been his deadline. And then he said, *"Haven't you figured that out yet?"*

Cold sweat broke out on Harry's forehead. Why hadn't he seen it before? He'd been so concerned about Leroy and so irritated with Fagan bugging him at the hospital that he hadn't paid any attention to what the man had said. But in retrospect, it seemed so obvious: *Fagan* had set the fire to punish Harry for not neutralizing the complaint against him!

Harry's foot slipped off the gas, slowing the RAV4. His insides were churning. If Fagan had retaliated with fire, it meant Harry bore some responsible for the harm that had come to Leroy and Estelle. His beef with Fagan had left them vulnerable. *He'd* been the connection. He glanced over at Estelle, his mind racing to find some release from the guilt of having put her in harm's way.

But maybe … maybe he was jumping to conclusions. After all, how could Fagan have set the fire if he was way up on the Northside calling Harry from the 24th District Police Station so soon after it happened? He might've had one of his goons set the fire, but that wasn't Fagan's style. Too risky. And any sort of a timing device would've left too much evidence.

"Harry, why are you slowin' down? Huh?"

"Oh, sorry." He stepped on the gas, bringing the vehicle up to speed again. But he had to find out where Fagan had been. He unclipped his cell phone from his belt. "Estelle, here … take this and go to my contacts. Punch in two, four."

"What? You know you're not supposed to use the cell while you're driving. And you, with only one good eye, Harry Bentley! What's got into you?"

"No, no. It's okay. I, uh …" He hesitated, not wanting to blurt out his fears in front of Estelle. If they were true, this was no way for her to find out! He'd have to be careful what he said. He reached forward and turned down the radio. "Go ahead and dial. Then put it on speakerphone." When, out of the corner of his eye, he saw Estelle was frowning, he added, "It's okay. It's legal if I keep both hands on the wheel."

Estelle shrugged and went ahead with the dialing. In a few moments, the tinny speaker announced, "Twenty-fourth District, Guzman here."

"Guzman? Jerry Guzman? When did you start driving a desk? This is Harry Bentley. How you doin'?"

"I'm okay, 'cept for my ankle. Broke it chasing some kid down an alley in the dark. Stepped in a hole." He swore a cascade of profanities to emphasize how bad it had been, then sighed loudly. "So how's yourself, Harry?"

"Oh, I'm good. I'm good. But tell me, when was the last time you saw Matty Fagan? Has he been around lately?"

"Haven't seen him all summer. I hear he got indicted, though. Why?"

"Can you remember whether you were on the desk Monday before last?"

"Can I remember? That was my first day as a desk jockey. And I'm gonna be stuck here for another four weeks, too." More swearing.

"So you're sure you were on duty that Monday, what was it—?"

"The twenty-first. No doubt about that! Got my calendar right here in front of me."

"Yeah. And you say Fagan didn't drop by in the middle of the afternoon? How 'bout later?"

"Like I said, I was here noon 'til after eight, and I haven't seen him all summer."

"Okay. Thanks a lot, Jerry. See you around."

Harry waved his hand for Estelle to close his phone.

"What was that about?" she asked. "Wasn't that the day of the fire?"

"Yeah. Just doin' a little police work. You know what they say, 'You can take the man off the job, but can't take the cop out of the man.' I guess that's me."

"Whatever. Can we turn the radio back up now?"

"Oh, sure." Harry turned up the volume, grateful she wasn't insisting on an explanation of his call to Guzman.

"… It's true," Tony Evans was saying in his characteristic bellow, "that circumstances beyond our control can sometimes make it difficult for us to be all God wants us to be."

No kidding, thought Harry, pulling to a stop in front of Estelle's building. *I certainly never imagined my actions could boomerang and hurt Estelle.*

She held up her hand to stop him as he reached to turn off the ignition, wanting to hear the rest of what Tony Evans was saying.

… It's high time that we stop blaming past circumstances or present pressures and start living as real men. Being real men means we don't allow our past to control our present by coming up with a "limp" to hide our mistakes…. Instead, we accept responsibility for our actions, identify what needs to be corrected, and set about being the men God wants us to be.

But *Harry* didn't hear the rest of Evans' message, which concluded a few short minutes later. He was thinking about what it meant for him to take responsibility for his actions, even if he hadn't intended any harm.

Once the radio was silenced, he put the window down and took a deep breath. "Estelle, there's something I've got to tell you, something I feel terrible about."

"Harry ..." She shook her head vigorously. "I'm not sure I want to hear this—"

"You probably don't, but I need to tell you, just the same." He raised one eyebrow at her. "It's about the fire." Her head wagging stopped and she visibly relaxed.

Oh, how he didn't want to do this! "I'm not sure, but I think Lieutenant Fagan may have set the fire in your house."

"What? What are you talkin' about, Harry?"

"Matty Fagan, that rogue cop I've been tryin' to help put away. He's one dangerous dude, believe me! And he won't go away!"

"But I ..." There was panic in her voice. "I don't understand. Why would he set fire to my house and nearly kill my baby?"

"To get back at me, Estelle."

"What?" She threw up her hands. "That doesn't make any sense. Why would he do that?"

"No, it does make sense. I just didn't see it before. When he found out who you were—that is, who you are to me—he figured he had some leverage. He hadn't been able to crack me by threatening me directly, but what if he threatened you? Don't you see? You owned the house, you are someone special to me, so he knew I'd care more about protecting you than myself. Except, at the time, I didn't get it." Harry smacked his forehead with the heel of his hand. "Too dense, I guess."

"Sweet Jesus." Estelle shook herself as though a chill had grabbed her. "Some people make it hard to keep hold of your religion. I'm just sayin'!" She paused and frowned. "Are you telling me he actually warned you, but you didn't take it seriously?"

"Yeah. That's what I'm tryin' to tell you, Estelle. The second time I went down there to check on Leroy, Fagan showed up. He was usin' your place to house a bunch of druggies, makin' money off them any way he could. That's how he learned my connection to you and Leroy and the house. But by then he'd also discovered that even though I'd withdrawn my formal complaint against him, I'd turned in DaShawn's cell phone—guess it technically belonged to his mother—and it showed him beating her up and shakin' her down for drugs. More powerful evidence than my earlier complaint."

"So what did he say?"

"He was mad as … Well, he pulled his gun on me again, and this time he fired it, shot a hole right through your front window, all to convince me to renounce the video."

"Humph!" Estelle crossed her arms and leaned back in her seat, as resolute as a statue. "I know you're not the kind of guy to let his threats faze you."

"You're right—but that's the problem. I was so intent on standin' up to him that his real threat didn't register with me."

"Bein' what?"

"That if I didn't do what he wanted, he was gonna hurt you."

Her eyes widened. "He actually said that?"

"No. But he might as well have. When he figured out who you were, he said, 'And you'd do anything for her, right?' And then he said, 'We had an agreement! Either you make it right or I will,' or something to that effect. Then he said, 'You got two days.'

Estelle was no longer a statue. She leaned toward Harry, her eyes flaming with rage. "And two days later, my boy almost died in his fire! Harry, how could you let that happen?"

"I know." He felt like a whipped pup … no, a whipped pup is just pitiful. But he deserved this. He'd hurt the woman he loved and her son. He'd let them down, failed to protect them when they needed it most. "I'm sorry, Estelle. I truly am. If I'd only …"

She sat back and gazed out the side window. After a moment, she said in a small distant voice, "Maybe it wasn't him. Maybe it was just an accident after all."

"No, Estelle. He did it! I see it all now. Hindsight's always better, don'cha know?" Harry adjusted the patch over his eye. "When I was at the hospital after they took Leroy in, but before you got there, Fagan called me on the phone. That's what I was asking Guzman about. He claimed to be calling from the 24th District Police Station, way up here on the Northside. And he was rubbin' it in. He even mentioned you—called you my *lady friend*—then said today was my deadline and asked me, 'Haven't you figured that out yet?' No, it was him. I briefly wondered at the time whether he had something to do with the fire, but I was just too preoccupied to think it through."

They sat there without speaking and without looking at one another while the cicadas droned at them in waves from the trees outside the car. Harry had to do something, say something. He cleared the lump from his throat. "Estelle, I know that was a terrible oversight, and I'm sorry. Can you forgive me?"

She took a long, deep breath and opened the car door. "Just give me a little time here, Harry. A little time, okay?"

"Yeah. Sure," he said as she closed the door—without slamming it—and, with her head bowed, headed slowly up the walk to her apartment above the Baxters. Harry watched her go, wishing she'd yelled or hit him or done something other than absorb all the pain into herself.

What a fool he'd been.

Just before she disappeared inside, he remembered. "Hey, Estelle! What about the picnic this afternoon?"

She gave him a dismissive wave. "If I go at all, I'll catch a ride with someone else." And she was gone.

Chapter 15

"WELL, THAT SURE WAS A BUST!" HARRY SNARLED to himself as he drove toward SouledOut Community Church to pick up DaShawn as soon as the morning service was over. The radio preacher's advice had sounded good at the time: "Man up! Take responsibility when you've made a mess of things, even if the circumstances were beyond your control" … or something like that.

And it *hadn't* been his fault. He hadn't started that fire, and there was no way he could've known what Fagan planned to do. No, no, he felt bad, but it wasn't his fault. Even taking responsibility for not anticipating it, for not reading Fagan's mind, hadn't worked with Estelle, not even when he said he was sorry. He was genuinely sorry about what had happened, but …

Maybe he ought to take a little detour by The Office and sip a cool one to calm down. He checked his watch. There was still twenty minutes before SouledOut would be over. Echoes from his former marriage reverberated through his head. He deserved a break. Back then he'd felt trapped, just like now! He'd been trying to do his police job but kept being blamed because it took so much time from home and family. But what could he do? He'd been in a bind. The circumstances and pressures of his life were incompatible. They were impossible! And he'd taken a … a break, a daily break, a long one … so long that he'd lost his wife and son.

Yeah. He had to admit that much.

He turned toward the church rather than Touhy Avenue and The Office. He'd been given a second chance, and he couldn't throw it away. What was it that Peter Douglass had said? *"If you think you deserve a break because of what you're goin' through, then it better be a break from what you're going through and not a break from doing right."* Well, what was "doing right" in this situation?

For him, he knew doing right meant not drinking just because he felt pressure. But was there a way to get some relief *from* that pressure?

Where did the pressure come from? It felt like it came from Estelle, like she didn't understand, wanted something more out of him before she'd forgive him. But is that how it was? He thought about it. Not really. She'd just said she needed a little time. Was she blaming him for the fire? She hadn't said so. She just wanted some time.

He pulled into the Gateway Center mall where SouledOut church was and parked where he could watch the front door.

Maybe it wasn't so hard to understand why Estelle wanted some time. She'd experienced a tremendous and frightening loss. And she'd been blaming herself a lot for that, too, saying she never should have left Leroy alone in that house. Now Harry had thrown her a curve: It wasn't an accident. Maybe Leroy had exercised poor judgment by letting all those people stay in the house, but he wasn't so far gone that he'd burned the place down, nearly killing himself in the process. Estelle knew Harry had done everything he could—as much as she had—to get Leroy to move out. So she wasn't blaming him for that.

In fact, when it came down to it, Harry was the only person who was blaming himself for not foreseeing the danger Fagan represented. Maybe he could lighten up on himself a little bit … and give Estelle that space she wanted, a little time to adjust to the new circumstances surrounding the fire. It didn't mean she was withholding her forgiveness, or even that she agreed he needed it from her.

He lifted his eye patch and gently messaged his left eye. He'd found a way to reduce the pressure on himself, a little at least, if he could manage not to blame himself. And he guessed he hadn't needed a break from doing what was right after all. A moment later when the kids started coming out of church, and DaShawn spotted his car and came running toward him with a wide grin on his face, Harry was glad he hadn't stopped by The Office.

"So, big man, what are you so excited about?"

"The Manna House picnic. We're goin' aren't we?"

"Yeah." Though there was a little grab in his chest as he remembered Estelle wouldn't be riding with him. "But first we gotta go by the house." He glanced over at DaShawn as they pulled out of the parking lot. "You need to change clothes, and I gotta do a little police work before we head out there."

"Police work? Whaddaya mean? How you gonna do that at home?"

"Ah ha! Have you never heard of Google?"

" 'Course I've heard of Google. Everybody has. But what's that got to do with police work?"

"Cops investigate things, and Google's a search engine. I gotta check somethin' out."

When they got home, Harry turned on the computer and called up the Internet. There was one more detail about Fagan he needed to check out.

The day Fagan had threatened him at the house, the day he'd fired a bullet through the window, Fagan had said he could pretty much do anything because he had an alibi about being in Philadelphia at some anti-gang seminar. Of course he wasn't, but maybe that was just another of his attempts to intimidate Harry into fearing and cooperating with him.

He checked the date on his calendar and typed in the relevant words, "Philadelphia, anti-gang, August, 2006" … nothing! He gave it several more tries, using different combinations. Still nothing.

It was a minor detail, but ten minutes later, he was satisfied there had been no anti-gang seminar in Philadelphia at that time. Now he was even more sure of Fagan's guilt.

"COP WORK" FOR HARRY CONTINUED THAT AFTERNOON at the Manna House Labor Day picnic. The Firecracker had asked him to provide a little "security" for the group of women in this isolated picnic area. And he and DaShawn were the first from Manna House to arrive at Sunset Bridge Meadow along the Des Plaines River, just west of the city.

But when they turned into the forest preserve, the parking area was cluttered with at least fifteen Harleys. Standing around the motorcycles and under the pavilion were a crew of men all decked out in their colors—sleeveless leathers, red kerchief skullcaps, scraggly beards, and wind-burned faces.

"Oh no," moaned DaShawn. "What are all these rednecks doing here?"

"Don't use that word, DaShawn. They're just bikers. Now you stay in the car while I see what's goin' on."

"But Grandpa, you can't go out there. What if they lynch you?"

"Where'd you ever get an idea like that?"

"Well, it's happened, hasn't it? And we're way out in the woods where no one would see us."

"DaShawn, you sure are a city boy, 'cause this ain't the woods. It's just a forest preserve, and besides no one's gonna lynch anybody. You been watchin' too much TV. Now just stay in the car. Hear?"

Harry slammed the door and sauntered toward the men, thinking that for the first time the black patch over his eye—along with his bald head and horseshoe beard—might be an asset. "Yo. How you doin'? Kinda warm, huh?"

"Yeah, kinda warm," one said, looking Harry up and down. "You from around here?"

"Not too far. What's happenin'?"

"We're just out cruisin' and stopped for lunch."

Harry looked back toward his RAV4, wondering if he ought to call the Firecracker on his cell and suggest they find a different picnic area, but just then a parade of vans pulled into the parking lot—the Manna House van, SouledOut's van, and the Baxters' minivan. Oh boy, too late! Harry turned back to the bikers, their attention captured by the little caravan.

He gestured toward the caravan. "Yeah. We're bringing a bunch of folks from a homeless shelter in the city out here for a Labor Day picnic. Uh …" he survyed the parking area as if searching for a sign, "this is the Sunset Bridge Meadow, isn't it? At least that's the spot we have a permit for."

"A permit?" said the biggest biker, who'd been acting as a spokesman. "You need a permit just to have a picnic here?"

By then, Gabby Fairbanks was approaching, followed by a herd of Manna House picnickers. "I told these fellows you have a permit for this picnic grove, Gabby." Harry leaned toward her and muttered under his breath, *"I sure hope you have one!"*

To Harry's relief, she pulled a folded paper out of her pocket. "Sure, right here." She offered it to the biker who probably weighed two-eighty.

The man frowned at it for a few moments, holding it at arm's length. "Manna House, huh? ... Is that like 'manna from heaven' from the Bible?"

The Firecracker's eyes got big and she shrugged. "Uh, I think so. It's a Christian shelter for homeless women."

"A *Christian* shelter," injected Precious, one of the Manna House residents—dark skin, hair in kinky twists as defiant as her pouty lip. Harry sucked in his breath. *Come on, sister, there ain't gonna be no lynching, but this is no time for an attitude. It could still turn into a racial incident if we're not careful.*

"Hey, wait a minnit!" Lucy, the old bag lady the Firecracker had first rescued from the park, elbowed her way to the front of the Manna House crowd and looked the biker up and down. "Ain't you the guy gave me a ride on that big bike t'other day in Michigan?"

What? Harry wasn't the only one who was startled. What did Lucy know about bikers? And when had she been in *Michigan*?

With a squint in his eye, the biker poked his finger at her like he was pinning something to a bulletin board. "Lucy Tucker, right? Yeah! You was hoofin' it along that two-lane road, tryin' ta find the bus station. I see ya made it back to Chi-Town okay."

Lucy grinned at Harry, proud as a Bingo champ. "Heh, heh, heh. You guys don't hafta worry. These dudes are all right. They just a bunch of Jesus freaks on wheels."

The big biker smiled broadly. "Show 'em fellas!" He turned around, along with the rest of his gang—and there, emblazoned in big red stitching on the back of their black leather vests, were the words GOD SQUAD and beneath them, CHRISTIAN MOTORCYCLE CLUB.

Harry sighed. Was this for real? He'd never heard of such a thing.

"Hey! That's fantastic!" Josh Baxter stepped forward, extending his hand toward the bikers. Within moments, Lucy was playing the host, introducing the bikers to each of the women from Manna House, some of whom still appeared as frightened as third-graders in a new school.

"Ma'am?" the big biker said to the Firecracker. "Sorry me an' the boys took your spot. We're travelin' from Michigan to a Christian Biker Rally and needed a place to eat our lunch. We'll be movin' on since you got a permit an' all that."

"Well, now, what's the big problem?" Precious butted in … *again.* "Lookit this shelter. 'Nuff picnic tables for a hunnerd folks or more, an' what we got? Forty … maybe fifty all together? We all God's children, ain't we? Well …" She reviewed the Manna House residents with a quick look. "Well, maybe not all of us, but enough to count. Jesus said if two or three folks get together in His name, He shows up, too. So to my way of figurin', we all just one big family. I'm gettin' hungry, so I say let's eat!"

The big biker shrugged and turned to the Firecracker for her decision. To Harry's surprise, she nodded.

"Well, now, isn't this a pretty how-d'ya-do." Harry hadn't seen Estelle sneak up to join the crowd. Their eyes met and she smiled briefly at him.

"Yeah, how 'bout that," Harry said tentatively. "Guess God showed up after all." But he was thinking of more than the picnic.

"Harry Bentley, if it hadn't been for God, none of us would be here right now. But God is good, all the time."

The Firecracker seemed as surprised to see Estelle as he was. "Thought you said you didn't cook on Sunday …"

Harry used the diversion to step off by himself, out of the throng that was laughing and getting to know one another. "Yeah, and all the time, God is good," Harry muttered the response under his breath. Estelle was right, and he knew it. The good outcome of this "confrontation" had nothing to do with him being a good cop.

And whatever relief he was experiencing from the guilt over the fire and Leroy's injuries was also from God. It was all God's doing, start to finish.

But why couldn't he remember that when his thoughts and speculations about his eyes sent him into a panic? Sometimes faith was obvious, but sometimes it was still, "Oh, God, I believe, but help my unbelief!"

"Harry." Estelle had come up on his left side—his blind side, as he now called it—without him noticing and touched his elbow.

"Oh, hi."

"I was just wantin' to follow up on … you know, earlier. I'm sorry I couldn't respond then, but I really do forgive you, Harry, though there's nothin' to forgive. I know you couldn't have known what Fagan planned. It's just that it … it was such a shock that someone might have started that fire on purpose. I still can't get my mind around it. In fact, Jodi was just askin' how Leroy was, and I still said something about him burning down the house."

"Did you tell her what we figured out?"

"Nah. Didn't seem the time."

Harry nodded. "Well, he still needs some kind of supervised living, but maybe it's a relief to know he didn't set the fire."

"Yeah. Yeah, it really is." She gave him a quick hug and headed back to the pavilion.

Chapter 16

HARRY HAD COMPLETED THE REGISTRATION DETAILS to enroll DaShawn in Mary McLeod Bethune Elementary School, the school where Peter Douglass's wife, Avis, was the principal and where Jodi Baxter taught third grade. But one issue remained: Would they admit him as a fifth grader, or would he have to repeat fourth grade?

Because of being bounced around between his parents and by the Department of Children and Family Services the previous year, before Harry gained custody of him, DaShawn had missed so many days of school that the Schaumburg School District—where he'd been at the end of the year—didn't want to pass him out of fourth grade. Harry had promised he'd do everything he could so DaShawn wouldn't have to repeat the grade. The kid was smart, and Harry was sure he could do fifth-grade work. Holding him back at this age might be the discouragement that caused him to give up on school as so many black boys about his age seemed to do. The experts floated all kinds of explanations, but all Harry cared about was that DaShawn not lose hope in school.

"You realize, Mr. Bentley"—Avis Douglass always spoke formally in the school setting, though she warmly called him Harry or Mr. B at church—"if we put him in a class where he can't do the work, that could be even more discouraging than repeating the fourth grade?"

"But I'll help him," Harry said. "He's my top priority now, you know. God's given me a second chance at being the parent I should have been with my own son, and I'm not about to blow it this time."

"That's good, Mr. Bentley. There's nothing like support from home to help a child succeed. I'll tell you what; we'll take another look at his test scores and see what we can do. I'd like nothing better than to see him advance, but I'm even more concerned that it be on a firm foundation academically."

That had been the middle of summer, but now it was Monday, September 4, the day before school started, and Harry *still* didn't know the answer. So today was the day. He'd call the school and get this thing settled, then he'd take DaShawn shopping for clothes and school supplies. Then they'd be all squared away.

After breakfast, Harry sent DaShawn to take a shower and get dressed. It was past nine o'clock, and the school office should be open. He dialed the number and waited while it rang … and rang … and rang. They were undoubtedly busy. He'd try back in a few minutes. But when he called again, the phone rang and rang until finally someone answered with a tentative, "Hello?"

"Is this the school office?"

"Yes … but I don't work here. I mean I'm a teacher's aid. I was just in the office here photocopying some papers, and the phone kept ringing so long I answered it, but …"

"Well, could I speak to the secretary or some one who's in charge?"

"There's no one else here today, sir, this being Labor Day, and all."

"Uh … Labor Day? Oh, yeah! Of course. Sorry to have bothered you."

Harry hung up and cradled his forehead in his hand, elbow on the table. It had been too long since he'd been a parent. No, that wasn't the excuse. This could've happened as easily with Rodney, he'd been so minimally involved in the raising of his own son. Now Rodney was in Cook County Jail, awaiting the conclusion of his "case." Harry shook his head. He ought to go visit Rodney. It'd been weeks. But he couldn't do it today. He had to take DaShawn shopping.

"DaShawn, hurry up in there. Come on, we gotta go!"

Harry circled the school twice the next morning before he found a parking spot three blocks away and walked with DaShawn to the school. Even though they were early, the office was a madhouse of activity—teachers coming in to pick up last-minute notices and forms, one asking if anyone had seen the janitor because all the windows in her room seemed to be stuck closed, parents of new kids wanting to register them, a girl about twelve with two younger brothers and no parents present who had no idea where the three of them were supposed to go.

Harry and DaShawn waited patiently until Harry realized there was no order to how the stressed secretaries served people—it was just the "squeaky wheel" routine. Okay, so he'd squeak. "Excuse me. Excuse me, please. I was wondering if I could see Ms. Douglass." He pointed at the office door with her nameplate on it.

One of the secretaries turned and looked, as if she'd forgotten there was an office behind her. "Uh, I'm sorry. Ms. Douglass is pretty busy today. Did you have an appointment?"

"She was working on something for me—something that should be finished by this morning." That was as close to an appointment as Harry could truthfully come. "Name's Harry Bentley. It's about DaShawn Bentley, a new student." He pointed toward the door as if he were asking her to deliver his message.

The secretary was a heavy woman but struggled more than seemed necessary getting out of her chair, making it clear how much trouble she was going to. *So what's that about?* thought Harry. *Does she expect me to tip her or something?* But as soon as the woman mentioned Harry's name, he heard Avis Douglass say, "Oh yes. Have him come right in."

When Harry and DaShawn entered her functional office, Ms. Douglass stood and reached across her desk to shake Harry's hand and then DaShawn's. "Well, DaShawn, we're delighted to have you at Bethune Elementary." Without inviting them to take a seat and without sitting back down herself, she turned to Harry. "Sorry I didn't get back to you on this sooner. It was my oversight, but we're putting DaShawn in Ms. Wagner's room. That's 219, second floor at the end of the hall." She pointed the directions. "It's a mixed classroom, both fourth and fifth graders." She looked back at DaShawn. "But we'll be starting you with fifth-grade work, DaShawn. And if you do well, that's where you will remain. Sound good?"

DaShawn nodded, and Harry had to nudge him before he said, "Yes, Ms. Douglass."

She again addressed Harry. "Even if he needs to go back and brush up on a few skills, it won't be as obvious as if he had to change classrooms, and by the end of the year, I'm sure he'll be performing up to grade level." She smiled and reached out to shake Harry's hand again, signaling that the meeting was over.

Harry felt good as they walked out of her office and headed for DaShawn's new classroom. As much as he didn't want his grandson to have to repeat the fourth grade, he recognized the wisdom of not overwhelming him with work he couldn't manage. Funny how God came through with a "better idea." "Thank You, Jesus, for this compromise," he breathed.

HARRY LOOKED FORWARD TO GOING TO THE MEN'S BIBLE STUDY that evening. He was getting more familiar with where to find stuff in the Bible and quickly found Philippians chapter 4, verses 4 through 7 as Denny read.

> Rejoice in the Lord always. I will say it again: Rejoice! Let your gentleness be evident to all. The Lord is near. Do not be anxious about anything, but in everything, by prayer and petition, with thanksgiving, present your requests to God. And the peace of God, which transcends all understanding, will guard your hearts and your minds in Christ Jesus.

"Twice we're told to rejoice," noted Denny Baxter. "And then we're told that even when we pray for things, we should do it with thanksgiving. Seems to me like rejoicing and giving thanks is pretty much the same thing. Whadda you guys think?"

Finally, Harry felt like he had something to contribute. "A few weeks ago, I helped Gabby—I mean, Ms. Fairbanks—find a new car, that little red Subaru she's driving around these days. I felt God really guided me to that specific car. So I thanked Him for helping me. And then it struck me: Thanking God about every good thing that happens is a way to acknowledge His involvement in my life. I can't prove it. In fact, the skeptic in me is tempted to explain away almost everything as a coincidence or the function of my subconscious or whatever. But when I do thank God, my faith kinda grows. I mean, it's easier to believe that He'll continue to be involved in my life, and that helps me 'pray believing.' You follow me? Maybe that's why these verses tell us to rejoice and include thanksgiving when we pray."

No one spoke, as though Harry had dropped some kind of heretical bombshell. He scanned the circle. "So, what? What's the problem? Haven't you ever heard 'pray believing' before? Pastor Cobbs says it all the time. Doesn't he?"

"Well, yeah," said Peter Douglass. "That's pretty much what he was talking about a couple of Sundays ago when he preached on Mark 11: 'Whatever you ask for in prayer, believe that you have received it, and it will be yours.'" Peter had a memory for detail like a computer and could quote verses just as easily. "That's 'prayer believing,' but I was just reflecting on that other piece you said, the way thanksgiving helps build our faith. I think you're onto something there."

Harry sighed audibly, slumping in relief. He knew he had a lot to learn about the Christian faith, but he didn't enjoy putting his ignorance on display. Could God have actually taught him something that his far more experienced brothers hadn't noticed before? It made him feel like a valuable member of the group.

Josh Baxter was flipping through his Bible. "Yeah, like it says here in James 1:17, 'Every good and perfect gift is from above, coming down from the Father of the heavenly lights, who does not change like shifting shadows.' Just like Harry was sayin', since we know where every good thing ultimately comes from, we really oughta thank Him all the time. But do we? Even at meals?"

"A good Jew always says a *berakhah* before eating," put in Ben Garfield, "and we recite the *Birkat Hamazon* afterwards. But hey," he turned up both palms, "who thinks about it?"

"That's what I'm sayin'. If we're not really thinkin' about it, how can it be a sincere thanksgiving?"

"At least we do it. That's something, isn't it?"

"I don't know. You tell me."

Ben shrugged and made one of his signature rubber faces.

The discussion continued with the guys finding verses in their Bibles that reminded believers to give thinks: Give thanks because God is good, give thanks in song, give thanks for his unfailing love, give thanks in all things … It went on and on and wouldn't have stopped if they hadn't run out of time.

"Sorry, guys," said Josh, "I gotta go home and relieve Edesa so she can get some studying done. I thank God for Baby Gracie, but she doesn't seem to understand she's not the center of the universe."

As the group disbanded, Harry headed over to Estelle's where he'd left DaShawn for the evening, thinking as he drove of all the things he was thankful for and saying them out loud to God.

He didn't plan to stay at Estelle's for long, but when he got there she insisted on talking to him about the Firecracker's husband.

"Harry, you gotta do something. Gabby told me her husband is involved with someone named Fagan, and I'm worried. Wasn't that your old boss's name?"

"Well, yeah. But what makes you think it's the Fagan I know? Certainly there's plenty of Irish guys with that name in Chicago."

"But this guy is some kind of loan shark or something. Philip's way over his head in gambling debt—he even tried to borrow money from Gabby, you know—and now he's gone to this Fagan guy for a loan."

Harry thought a moment. Since being indicted and suspended, Fagan wouldn't be able to continue running his street racket of taking guns and money and dope from drug dealers, so he might have changed his MO. Loan sharking would be a way to launder some of the dirty cash he picked up, and he probably still had plenty.

"Guess it could be Matty. I'll ask around. As much as I dislike that Philip Fairbanks for how he treated the Firecracker and her mom, I wouldn't wish Matty Fagan even on him. That guy's dangerous!"

"That's what I tried to tell Gabby, but I didn't have time to explain."

"Hmm. I'll give Cindy a call. See if she knows anything."

Chapter 17

THE ALARM JARRED HARRY AWAKE WEDNESDAY MORNING. *Uhh … Why in blazes had he set the alarm so early? Oh yeah, second day of school for DaShawn.*

He sat up on the side of his bed trying to wake up. A minute passed before he realized something was different about his vision. He blinked several times. Maybe it was some nighttime scum and would soon wash away. But after a few moments he realized it was just his left eye … and it did not blink away. Instead, a shadow had descended, darkening the upper-left part of his peripheral vision as if the lights in that part of the "stage" had gone out leaving the area so dark it faded to black.

He shut his left eye and looked around with his right. No shadow. The right eye was fine. But the left eye …

Was this what Dr. Racine had warned him about, his retina detaching and rolling down like wet wallpaper? *Déjà vu!* He stared at the picture of a Jamaican beach that hung on the wall of his bedroom and tried to calculate whether the dark area was "descending like a curtain," as Dr. Racine had described, or not. He couldn't detect any movement. The dark area was not notably advancing. Hopefully, that was good.

Except … there was no denying that something had dramatically changed in that eye. Before there had been the distorted, grayed-out blind spot in the very center of his vision. Now a curtain of darkness had reduced his field of vision. Not good! And why couldn't it have waited until Friday when he was already scheduled for that vitrectomy surgery?

"DaShawn, you awake?"

"Yeah, kinda," came the sleepy moan from the next room.

"You need to get up and get goin'. We've gotta leave a little early this morning."

"How come?"

"'Cause I said— Uh, I've got some more problems with my eye. Don't know why they keep hitting me in the morning, but …" He tried to sound matter-of-fact and keep the panic out of his voice. He didn't want to frighten the boy. How could he provide a secure family environment for his grandson if he were freaking out? "DaShawn, you hear me?" Oops, still too much snap in his voice. "I mean, come on, now. Time to get goin'."

"All right, grandpa. I'm getting' up. What's wrong with your eye now?"

Harry headed for the bathroom and peeked in on DaShawn. He *was* getting up. Good kid. "Uh, I'm not sure what's going on, but somethin's changed…. Gotta go down to the clinic and check it out, so I'll need to drop you off at Great Grandma's, and you can walk to school from there."

"Why not at Ms. Estelle's, Grandpa? It's closer to school."

"Yeah, but … well okay, I'll give her a call and see if she's good with that. But I don't want to presume on her too much."

DaShawn looked up at him with a neutral expression frozen on his face. "Yeah, I know, Grandpa. You want to keep things real cool with her."

Harry went on into the bathroom. Did DaShawn mean "cool," as in copacetic? Or had he detected that Harry was dialing down his relationship with Estelle? He felt so conflicted. He wanted to marry that woman with his whole being. His heart, mind, and spirit said they were meant for each other ... except, except for this eye business. He couldn't saddle her with that, especially not if he was going blind.

The thought gripped him like the hawk of winter blowing off Lake Michigan, its talons refusing to let go, making his heart beat so hard in his chest that his whole body throbbed.

But a short while later, when Harry phoned and asked Estelle if he could drop DaShawn off at her place, her first response was, "So, what do you have to do so early in the morning, Mr. Bentley? I thought you were retired."

He hemmed and hawed but finally told her about the shadow in his eye.

"Hmm, and you were gonna go off down there by yourself again? I don't think so. You wait right there. I'm comin' over. Hey, Stu—" And the phone went dead.

Harry slammed his fist down on the table. He had a mind to take DaShawn over to his mother's and head straight down to the clinic before Estelle could come. For one thing, if she got Leslie Stuart to drive her back over here to his apartment, then Stu would hear all about his eye problems. As the social worker who oversaw his care of DaShawn, her knowing too much brought up Harry's same old anxiety. He appreciated her keeping DaShawn "in the family." She was in his corner. But she still had to fill out reports, and if the Department of Children and Family Services decided he was too incapacitated to adequately care for DaShawn, they might take him away, and Leslie Stuart wouldn't be able to help.

But Estelle was coming, and right now he didn't need the hassle of working out how she'd feel if he ran off and left her, so he and DaShawn waited downstairs in the parking lot by his car until Leslie Stuart's candy-apple red Hyundai Accent pulled in and Estelle got out.

"Estelle, this really isn't necessary," he said as she came striding toward them. "I can take myself to the doctor just fine. You don't need to come along."

"Yes, yes. I know you think you can handle everything yourself, but I bet you have no idea what the doctor's gonna do about it. Do ya?"

"No, but—"

"Then I'm going down there with you. We're dealing with this thing together, Harry Bentley. You understand? And besides, it's late enough now that we can drop DaShawn off at school. I know because Jodi Baxter left the house before we did."

Harry nodded, dumbfounded, and the three of them got into his RAV4 as Leslie Stuart waved and sped out of the parking lot. Harry sat there behind the wheel for a moment. What had Estelle meant by, *dealing with this thing together*? He glanced over at her and saw her eyebrows go up as if to say, "Whatchu waitin' for? Let's go!"

DR. RACINE CAME OUT TO THE WAITING ROOM to directly ask what was the emergency that had brought Harry in without an appointment. The doctor nodded as Harry reviewed the details.

Then he touched Harry's shoulder. "You were right to come in. Look, I'll have an assistant take you back to one of the examining rooms and put drops in your eyes to dilate them. Then I'll squeeze you in as soon as possible."

When the assistant came to the waiting room door and called, "Mr. Bentley?" Estelle got up and followed Harry before he realized what was happening. He turned and frowned at her, but she looked away as though she hadn't seen it.

"If you'll take the examining chair, Mr. Bentley, and remove your eye patch, we'll get some drops in those eyes right away. In the meantime, Mrs. Bentley, you can be seated in that chair by the desk. Dr. Racine's pretty busy this morning, but it will take twenty minutes or so before your eyes are dilated anyway."

The drops in his eyes felt like tears and made everything swim in the semi-darkened examining room. Harry tried to focus on Estelle, who was reading an *Ebony* magazine by the dim light on Dr. Racine's desk. *Mrs. Bentley*, huh? Had she heard that? She hadn't even flinched. It had the right ring to Harry. Had it sounded the same to her? If only … He closed his right eye and scrutinized the room, trying to focus on various points to see if the descending darkness was still there.

It was!

The exam with the slit lamp and the ultrasound was as long and uncomfortable as ever, and Harry was about at the point of wishing he hadn't come in when the doctor swung the examining instruments out of the way and stood up.

He took his glasses off and rubbed the bridge of his nose and forehead as though this situation was giving him a headache. Harry's eyes were tired from the exam, as well, and he closed them until he heard Dr. Racine clear his throat, and he knew the doctor was about to speak.

"You do have a serious detachment in that left eye, Mr. Bentley, and normally I'd perform surgery right now, but the advance of the detachment seems to have stopped at the edge of the laser treatment we did peviously. I think we bought ourselves some time with it. So this is what I want you to do. I'm going to put patches on both of your eyes, and then I want you to go home and remain as completely still as you possibly can. Just sit in a chair or lie down—whatever's most comfortable. But I don't want you moving around or moving your head back and forth anymore than absolutely necessary. And no sudden movements. Then we'll proceed with the surgery as scheduled, early Friday morning."

"So ..." Harry didn't know what to say. "So, why patches on both eyes?" It was a way he had of coping when things got too intense: Shift to the practical, the mechanical, something comprehendible ... anything to escape the terror. He'd learned that as a kid in scary situations, like when the power got cut off in their apartment. And it sometimes worked: You could light a bunch of candles and drive away the darkness even if you couldn't understand why your daddy couldn't get hired just because he was black.

Perhaps Dr. Racine understood, because he quickly launched into an explanation. "Remember I told you your eye was filled with vitreous? Well, think of it like water in a jar. You shake the jar, and the water sloshes around, washing loose anything stuck to the inside of the jar. But we don't want that. We want your retina to stay attached to the wall of your eye. Make sense?"

"Yeah ... it makes sense. Okay, let's do it. Hey, Estelle, 'Here's looking at *you*, kid' ... maybe for the last time!" He said it, trying to sound like Humphrey Bogart, trying again to deflect the fear.

She waved her hand dismissively at him. "Get serious, Harry."

But to him, his situation was already far too serious.

ESTELLE DROVE THE RAV4 HOME WHILE HARRY SAT in the seat beside her, his head slightly bowed, trying to keep as still as possible.

160

So this was what it was like to be totally blind, unable to see anything. He'd played that game when he was a kid, tying a blindfold over his eyes and trying to walk around the house until his mama said, "Harry, you're gonna break your neck, and you're gonna break somethin' in my house. Now get that bandanna off an' do the dishes like I told you."

Back then he could always take the blindfold off. He tried to think about that now: He *could* take off the patches, and he *would* be able to see something. So it was just like the game when he was a kid, right? Except it wasn't! It wouldn't end in ten minutes or by supper or … But he was supposed to have his surgery on Friday. Then he'd get the patches off, or at least one of them. His right eye was still good, and maybe the surgery would fix things in his left eye. So, one day at a time, one day at a time. He could do that.

But this was no game, and he couldn't shake the horror of not being able to see. He'd always thought of himself as a brave guy— he was a cop, after all—who willingly put himself in harm's way, knowing he might get hurt or killed. But if he'd died on the job, it would've been all over—they always counted a fallen officer as a hero. But if he went blind, he'd have to sit around for … how long? Twenty years or more? He'd just be a burden on … no, not on Estelle. He'd already made his decision about that.

And what would he do? He was too old to learn Braille or a trade. He loved stories, but listening to the radio or audio story CDs all day … a guy can only take so much of that. What *would* he do?

Harry felt as if his whole world was closing in on him, like he was imploding into some kind of a cocoon while everyone else went on in life without him.

From somewhere in that other world, someone was calling his name again and again. He sat up a little straighter as he felt movement. He was riding in a car, his own car, and Estelle was driving ... and saying, "Harry, Harry. You asleep?"

"Uh, no. Just thinkin'. Why?"

"Sometimes thinkin's not such a good idea, Harry. And that's the truth of it! Now, I'm taking you to my place—"

"But—"

"No arguments, Harry Bentley. Just listen to me. You're gonna need someone with you most of the time, and I'm the one. It'll be a little tight, but if you don't mind sleeping on the sofa, we can work it out."

"But what about Stu? Doesn't she have anything to say about this?"

"Not a thing. And if she had the same need, I wouldn't have anything to say about her decision either. She'll understand."

"Estelle ..." Harry turned his head toward her, then caught himself, remembering he wasn't supposed to move any more than necessary. "Stu might not have anything to say about where I stay, but I do." His voice was calm and stern. "Take me home. It only makes sense. All my stuff's there. I know my way around my own apartment where I'd just be stumblin' over stuff in yours. After all, I will have to go to the bathroom and move around some, don't you know."

Harry felt the RAV4 stop and heard hip-hop music coming from a car beside them. They were at a stoplight. Which one? Hmm, didn't matter. "Estelle, you hear me? I wanna go home."

"Oh, Baby, I don't want you to be alone." He heard something different in her voice. His self-assured Queen was crying, crying over him. He knew if he checked, he might not see the tears, but her voice told him different. She cared that much?

"Okay. I appreciate it. What if you take me home, get me settled, get me somethin' to eat, then I'll be okay until DaShawn gets home from school. After that, he can help me with whatever I need."

Estelle drove away from the intersection. "I got a better idea. I'll drop you off, get you settled and feed you. Then I'll go home and pack up a few things for myself. While I'm there, I'll arrange with Jodi Baxter to bring DaShawn home and stay with them a couple of nights. Then I'll come back and sleep in DaShawn's bed so I can be there when you need me. There, now that's settled!"

Chapter 18

THE NEXT MORNING, ESTELLE HUSTLED AROUND getting breakfast for Harry and setting him up for the day in his recliner. "Here's your CD player on the table right beside you. I've put in a new disc of Fernando Ortega that I really love. Give it a try. And here's some other praise and worship CDs sittin' beside it—Bebo Norman, Jim Croegaert …" Harry heard her shuffling through the albums. "… and some gospel: Ron Kenoly, Donnie McClurkin, and, oh, here some oldies from the Blind Boys of Alabama."

Harry winced, *Blind Boys*, huh? Maybe he should audition.

"That should hold you. Now, you do what that doctor said and don't be peekin'. I've tried to clear everything out of the way, but here's a yardstick. Found it in your closet. It's leaning right here against your side table. If you gotta get up and go to the bathroom or somethin', use it to feel your way. Hear?"

"Yeah, like a *real* blind man. 'Cept they get to use a nice long white stick with a red tip so everyone knows they're commin' and makes way for 'em. But I gotta use this old yardstick?" He had intended it to be a joke.

"We're not goin' there. That's like speakin' death over someone. You're not blind yet, and we're trustin' God for a full recovery."

164

The faint waft of her perfume graced him as she moved toward the door and picked up her purse—he'd recognized the slight thump and a muted rattle of her keys. It *was* her purse.

"You got your cell phone now—right there on the table beside you." Harry reached out and touched it. "You be sure and call if you need anything. Okay?"

"Yeah."

"You want me to leave on this light?" The switch clicked. "Ooo!" Then clicked back. "*You* might not need it, but to me it looks too dingy in here without it." The car keys to his RAV4 rattled in her hand. "Be back as soon as I can, Harry."

She opened the door, and he envisioned her stepping out into the stairwell. "Bye, Estelle."

He leaned forward slightly as the door clicked shut and she descended the stairs. He listened to her every footfall, visualizing her turning at the landings as though he were at her elbow making sure she didn't trip—not that Estelle was clumsy, but it could happen, and he cared. There … both doors of the vestibule opened and closed, and in a minute he heard the thud of his car door and the sound of the engine starting. *Amazing!* He'd never imagined he could hear all that from behind the closed door of his apartment. A feather of air brushed his bald head, and he realized the windows looking out over the parking lot were open, but still …

Harry leaned back in his recliner, raising the footrest. She was gone. He deliberately nudged the flow of his thoughts away from the trouble with his eye or whether his retina was peeling loose or if tomorrow's surgery would be successful or whether his right eye would develop a problem, too. There were no answers to those questions right now, and he knew they would only stir up anxiety. But what was it Estelle had said before she left when he'd made that joke about being blind? *"We're not goin' there Harry. That's like speakin' death over someone."* Speaking death? What had she meant? Was she just trying to cheer him up with "the power of positive thinking"? Well, why not? He was doing that himself by trying not to think about his eye problems. Hmm, if you could speak death, could you speak life? Was Estelle talking about some kind of superstitious incantations—curses and charms? That wasn't like her! It had to be something deeper, some kind of a faith thing.

Faith, believe ... *"I believe, but help my unbelief!"* There it was again. He shook his head before he remembered he wasn't supposed to move. Still, it was getting harder and harder to believe when things kept going from bad to worse. And now he really was blind in both eyes. The temptation to lift the bandage—at least on his right eye, to make sure nothing had happened to it—was almost more than he could resist. And as he thought about it, he rationalized that the doctor's purpose in bandaging his eyes was to prevent him from swinging his eyes around or doing anything to shake them up. So what if he kept looking straight ahead and just lifted the corner of the bandage a little bit ... just enough to peek out? Wouldn't that be okay?

No, no! He'd do what he'd been told. He could follow directions. But ... maybe he could call the doctor and ask about a careful exception, just for a moment. He reached out and got his phone and flipped it open. Could he remember the number? Let's see, 312-555-1217. But ... did the numbers on the keypad go across, or did they go down? No, it was definitely across: 1-2-3; 4-5-6; 7-8-9; pound sign-0-star. Or was it star-0-pound sign. Yeah, star-0-pound sign. The star was on the left.

Boy, he'd never thought of those little details before. He closed the phone and put it back on the table. The urgency to call the doctor passed. Such an insignificant question seemed silly. If he wanted to peek, he'd peek. If he was careful, it couldn't hurt. Could it? He laughed at himself, realizing such vacillation betrayed his anxiety.

Uh … how long had he been sitting there? It seemed like hours, but maybe it'd only been minutes. Oops, there was another issue: He couldn't see a clock to tell time. He fumbled around until he found the TV controller and switched on his TV, cycling through the channels, hardly recognizing any of them since he didn't watch daytime TV. Finally, he stopped at what he thought was CNN, hoping they would mention the time. He knew it was on the screen—bottom right-hand corner—so why would a reporter mention it? And then one did, sort of: President Bush was going to have a news conference "at the top of the hour, twelve o'clock noon, Eastern Time." That meant that right now, it was probably somewhere between ten-thirty and eleven, Chicago time. He smiled at himself for figuring that out and switched off the TV.

What would Estelle be doing right now?

She'd be in her kitchen at Manna House, perhaps frying hamburger and opening cans of tomatoes and tomato paste to make spaghetti sauce. He'd seen her do that before, and now in his mind's eye, it was almost as if he were there watching her. The more he let his mind roam, the more he saw—some of the residents coming in for coffee, one of them, yeah, it was Precious, staying to help her. Estelle was telling her to put on a hair net and to fill a huge pot with water for the pasta. It was almost as though he were standing right in the dining room, off to the side in the shadows where no one would notice him. But Harry could see everything that was going on in the kitchen. Was this some kind of a psychic, out-of-body experience? Some second sight? Was he *really* seeing what was happening a mile away in Manna House?

What nonsense! And yet …

167

His cell phone rang, yanking him back to the reality of sitting in his recliner with his eyes bandaged. He fumbled around until his hand picked up and opened his phone.

"Yeah, Harry here."

"Hey, Harry, Denny Baxter. Heard you were laid up in your house. Want some company for an hour or so this evening? I could drop by."

"Ah man, that's good of you, but you don't need to do that. You guys are already doing enough by taking care of DaShawn for a couple of days."

"No, no. I don't mind. We could watch a game together or something .... Uh, uh-oh, sorry. Wasn't thinkin'. Anyway, I'd still be glad to come over. I could pick up some clean clothes for DaShawn while I'm at it."

Harry thought for a moment. "Sure, why not? That'd be great. I'd be glad for the company, though Estelle might be around."

"Well, we'll have a party, then. See you this evening. Oops, there I go again. Uh ... I'll be *over* this evening."

Harry closed his phone. He couldn't blame Denny for using the word *see*. That was just how central sight was to everyone. *I see*—when I actually view something. *I'll see you*—when we plan to meet somewhere. *Oh, I see*—when I finally comprehend something. *I'll see about it*—when I agree to consider something. *I'll see you to the door*—when I offer to accompany you. *Light, darkness, vision*, the metaphors of sight—at least for the sighted—permeated everything. It's the way we *see* the world!

But Harry knew he might be losing his!

HARRY SHUFFLED THROUGH THE CDs Estelle had left for him. *Ha!* Forest Gump was right: "Life is like a box of chocolates. You never know what you're gonna get." Wait, Estelle had already put one in the player she wanted him to hear. He fumbled with the machine until he found and pressed the Play button. Slow and plaintive, Fernando Ortega sang …

> *Pass me not, O gentle Savior,*
> *Hear my humble cry;*
> *While on others Thou art calling,*
> *Do not pass me by.*

Harry gulped and leaned forward in his chair. He knew this song. They used to sing it in his mother's storefront church when he was a kid. Strange how the mind can recall a song … while forgetting the three things you went to the store for.

> *Let me at a throne of mercy*
> *Find a sweet relief:*
> *Kneeling there in deep contrition*
> *Help my unbelief.*

There it was again: *"Help my unbelief."* Harry sat up a little straighter. Whoever had written this song understood the struggle to have the faith—not just to believe in Jesus, but to believe Him, that He would do just what he said He'd do. *"Help my unbelief."*

> *Savior, Savior,*
> *Hear my humble cry,*
> *While on others Thou art calling,*
> *Do not pass me by.*

It hit Harry with a thud. "Jesus, Jesus!" His head swirled. "Please, Jesus! You called on so many others when You walked this earth, and You healed them, blind people like me. *Do not pass me by.* I need You. I need You now! Please, please, please ..." He slipped into uncontrollable sobs that went on and on.

> *Thou the spring of all my comfort,*
> *More than life to me,*
> *Whom have I on earth beside Thee,*
> *Whom in Heav'n but Thee.*

What if ... what if *that* was the whole point of this ordeal? Did Jesus mean more to him than life itself? Could he say, "*Whom have I on earth beside Thee, Whom in Heav'n but Thee*"? Of course, he had Estelle and the guys in the Bible study and a church with a couple of good pastors and a skilled doctor with all the resources of modern medicine, but ... but really, as much as they all cared, what could any of them do for him for sure? In spite of all they might offer, he was alone. It was like ... like he was in a little room with all the world outside, and the door between the two was slowly closing.

On the last refrain Harry began to sing along in a thin, wavering voice.

> *Savior, Savior,*
> *Hear my humble cry,*
> *While on others Thou are calling,*
> *Do not pass me by.*

And this time he was not pleading for Jesus to heal his blindness, but that Jesus would make his presence known to him in his world of darkness, so he would no longer feel so alone: *"Savior, Savior ... Do not pass me by."*

"HARRY, HARRY, WAKE UP. HOW LONG YOU BEEN SLEEPIN'? You're gonna get a crook in your neck, you sittin' there like that. Here, I brought you some lunch. I made some great turkey rollups today and snuck a couple home for you." He heard Estelle walk into the kitchen. "You want me to pop a Pepsi for you?"

Harry pushed down the footrest of his recliner and sat up straighter. "You say you brought home turkey rollups? I thought you were made spaghetti today."

"Spaghetti? Why would I make somethin' as hot as spaghetti on a warm day like this? Who knows how much longer summer'll last? Cool foods for hot days. Hot foods for cold days. And those cold days'll be here all too soon."

"But I *saw* you makin' spaghetti—"

"Honey, I'm tellin' you, I ain't made any spaghetti since last spring. When the weather's like this, I don't like to cook any more hot stuff in that kitchen than I have to. They need better ventilation up in there, I'll tell you! ... Hey, wait a minute! What do you mean, you *saw* me makin' spaghetti? How could you—?"

"Forget it! Forget it, Estelle. It was nothin'. Guess I was just dreamin'."

"Well, you want those rollups or not?"

"Sure. And that Pepsi, too, if you would. That'd be great."

Chapter 19

Estelle went through Harry's mail, telling him about a couple of bills and asking if he wanted to keep any of the junk mail.

They sat in silence for a few minutes, and Harry wondered what Estelle was thinking. Then she spoke. "You know, I haven't seen Leroy since Sunday. Feel like I oughta check in on him, but …" He heard her get up and pace around the room. "Here, what if I read the paper to you." She snapped it open and rustled pages. "Uh, let's see, sports! 'Tigers' Free Fall Is Playing Right into the Hands of White Sox. When the White Sox visited Detroit in early August, there was—'"

"Estelle, Estelle! That's really okay. I don't need that now."

"Well, what do you want me to do? I can't just sit around here."

"I know. But you don't have to. You don't have to *be* here. I appreciate all you're doing, but it ain't right for me to tie you down like this. Why don't you just go on down to see Leroy. I'll be fine."

"You're not tying me down, Harry. It's my choice to be here. Besides, we gotta get you ready for your surgery tomorrow. So what can I do?"

172

"What's to do? I just go in. They do their thing, and I come home." Harry thought for a moment. "Uh-oh." He leaned his head back on the pillow of his chair and put a hand on his head.

"What?"

"Nothin'. It's nothin'. Forget about it."

"No, you remembered something. What still needs doin'? Tell me, Harry."

He sighed. "Can't do anything about it now, but I forgot to pick up that chair I was supposed to rent from that massage equipment store down on Ashland Avenue. What's the name of that place? Just north of Foster Avenue. I can visualize it, but ..."

"What are you talkin' about, Harry?"

"My surgery. After my surgery, I'm gonna have to remain face down for ... for a couple of weeks, and this chair is supposed to help with that. You know, you've seen 'em in malls and stuff. You sit down like you're sitting backwards on a kitchen chair, but they're slanted so you can lean forward with your face supported in this donut thing. Then they give you a back rub."

"How's that supposed to help your eye?"

"I dunno ... well, actually Dr. Racine did explain it. Remember? I told you. I'm gonna have this bubble put in my eye, but then I have to keep my head bowed so it rises to the back of my eye and pushes my retina back in place. The chair is supposed to help me stay in that face-down position."

"A *bubble in your eye*? Harry, you didn't tell me about any bubble in your eye."

"Yes, I did. At least, I told you I had to remain face down for two weeks."

"Well, yeah. I remember that, but then you said you didn't want to talk about it anymore! You didn't tell me about no bubble."

"Hmm. Maybe not. Well, I'm tellin' you now. I was planning on pickin' up that chair yesterday or today. Then I had that crazy detachment issue and ... forgot all about it."

He heard her slide out a table chair and sit down with a *whomph.* "Guess I better go down there and pick it up for you today."

Harry sat there feeling like nothing but a Big Problem. He didn't want to burden Estelle with all his stuff. That's why he'd decided not to marry her. But here she was getting tangled up in it anyway. He rubbed his head and realized he needed a shave—*ha*, another thing he couldn't do without his sight. But there had to be some way to get that chair without expecting her to run his errands.

He snapped his fingers. "Look, Estelle, got an idea. Denny Baxter called me earlier. He's comin' over this evening just to hang for a while. He works down that way. Well, not that far, but maybe I could get him to stop by and pick up the chair on his way home. How 'bout that?"

"Better call and ask if he can do it. What's the name and address of that place?"

"Just Google it."

"What?"

"Turn on my computer over there on the desk and look it up."

He talked her through the process, amazed that he was able to imagine what she was doing at each step and tell her how to do the next one. Huh. Maybe he ought to move to India and become a tech-support person. Yeah, a *blind* tech support person. How many times had he felt like he was talking to one of those on the phone? But he knew they *did* need to see their computer screens, whether they sounded like it or not. Everything seemed to require vision.

"Is this it?" Estelle asked. "BodyKneaders Rental and Supply, on Ashland?"

"Yep, that's it. Take down the address and phone number, and call Denny."

It took a while to reach Denny at the school where he was athletic director, but finally it was arranged. Harry leaned back in his chair and raised the footrest, finally able to relax.

"Hey, Estelle?"

"I haven't gone anywhere."

"Why don't you take my car and go on down to the hospital to see Leroy right now. Denny'll be along later. He can help with anything I need."

"Harry—" The tone of her voice was full of protest.

"I did just fine this morning. Go!"

She fussed and argued, but he could hear her voice start to change and knew she really did want to go. He kept insisting until she agreed.

"Okay, but first I gotta put together somethin' for you to eat. You need a decent meal. And while I'm at it, I'll fix something for Denny, too. How about that spaghetti you were dreamin' of? And I'll fix a salad to go with it."

"I thought you said it was too hot to cook. Besides, all I been doing is sittin' in this chair all day. I don't need much."

"It was just too hot to be cookin' up in that Manna House kitchen. But tomorrow's your surgery, and you need your strength."

BY THE TIME HARRY HEARD DENNY STRUGGLING and puffing up the stairs he actually was hungry and glad Estelle had fixed something for them to eat. The spaghetti had smelled so good while she was cooking, with all the garlic and basil and oregano wafting round the apartment. She had left everything on the stove or in the refrigerator so Denny could serve it up. And for the last twenty minutes, Harry's stomach had growled like a junkyard dog.

"That you Denny? Come on in. You got that chair?"

"Yeah. Where you want it?"

"Uh … I don't know. Is it big?"

"Not so big. Just awkward."

"Hmm." Harry was glad he hadn't sent Estelle to pick it up. "You think it would fit alongside my recliner here? I'm supposed to be able to watch TV from it if I use a mirror."

"A mirror? Wouldn't everything be backwards?"

"Hmm. Hadn't thought of that. Guess I'll just watch movies backwards, get the ending first."

They both laughed.

"You want to try it out? Here, let me unfold it." Harry heard a series of thumps and squeaks as Denny set it up. "All right. Get on and see whether we need to adjust it."

"Sure, why not?"

Denny guided him as he cautiously swung his leg over the seat as though he were mounting a motorcycle. Then he leaned forward until his chest was supported by the inclined, padded board and he could lay his head down on the headrest, all without any quick moves that might jostle the inside of his eyes.

"Here, put your elbows down here on the arm rests. Now, how's that?"

"Not bad. It's actually pretty comfortable."

"Looks like it, but I suppose anything gets tiresome after a time. Say, Estelle called me, said something about spaghetti … you hungry?"

"Yeah, it's all in the kitchen there." Harry heard him walk in there and lift the lid of a pan and open the fridge. "Hey, Denny, how's DaShawn doin'? I was worried about jerking him around without talkin' to him or anything, especially with him just start-ing school."

"Oh, I think he's okay. He's a bright kid. He understands. He's probably watching too much TV, but I hope you don't mind for a day or two."

"No. I just appreciate you guys takin' him in."

Denny helped Harry move over to the table and served up the food. But eating created more challenges for Harry: seeing where the food was, getting it onto his fork, and keeping it there while he lifted it to his mouth. He ended up with more than one strand of spaghetti in his lap.

"I was wondering …" Harry wiped his mouth and pushed himself slowly back from the table. "… earlier today I made this joke about being a blind man. Tryin' to keep things on the lighter side 'round here, ya follow me? Anyway, Estelle got all up in my face about it. Said it was like I was 'speakin' death over someone.' Then she said, 'We're not goin' there,' but I have no idea what she meant."

Harry waited for Denny's response, but for nearly a minute it didn't come. Finally, he asked again. "Well, do you know? What was she gettin' at, anyway?"

"Not sure, Harry. One possibility, though, might be a verse from Proverbs that says 'The tongue has the power of life and death.' That could just mean that what we say can have a lot of influence on people and events. Like a false accusation could destroy somebody's reputation or even condemn 'em in court. The Apostle James had quite a bit to say about taming the tongue, because when it's out of control, it can do so much damage. But Estelle may have been refer-ring to a deeper interpretation of that proverb. She may have been talking about being careful not to tear down faith. The other side of that would be 'speaking life' by building faith up."

177

"You talkin' about what we were sayin' in Bible study the other night, how thankin' God for every good thing helps us see His goodness and helps our faith to grow, expecting He'll continue to do good for us?"

"Yeah, kinda like that. But if you're all the time rehearsing the bad things by what you say, you could end up expecting more bad things and have a hard time exercising a strong faith that God will do you good."

"Sounds kinda like the power of positive thinking."

"No, no, no! That's just a psychological gimmick. It might work on the human level sometimes by boosting our confidence in our abilities so we perform at our best rather than being terrified that we'll make a mistake and fail, but—"

"Yeah. Any athlete knows that."

"Sure. I tell my coaches all the time to keep it positive with the players. But faith … faith is based, not on what we can do, but on what we believe God *will* do. Much different. Much different."

"What's 'speakin' death' over someone, then?"

Denny laughed. "Gee, Bentley! You ask more questions than a ten year old! I'm no theologian, you know."

"So? Just wanna know what you think."

"All right. I know it's not like a curse—whatever that might be. But I think … well, if you verbalize negative expectations, you might cause the other person to lose faith, just like you might lose faith yourself if you're not regularly thanking God for His goodness. And in the Bible, our faith *does* play a part in how God chooses to act. It's not like we can manipulate God and make Him do what we want if we have enough faith. But it might be connected with what He wants *us* to learn about Him through any situation."

"Yeah, well, I've been thinkin' about what He might want me to learn through this situation." Harry snorted. "Figured, the sooner I learned it, the sooner this might be over."

"And ...?"

"And what?"

"What'd you come up with?"

"Oh, well, not sure exactly. But earlier today I was thinkin'—actually it was a song I was listening to—that maybe ... I don't know, but the thing that seemed most important right now is that I need to be sure Jesus is with me. It was that song, 'Pass me not, O gentle Savior.' You know that one?"

Perhaps Denny nodded. Harry couldn't tell, but he went on. "I realized that song was ..." Harry stopped and swallowed the lump in his throat. "Anyway the 'Do not pass me by' part was about me and Jesus, don'cha know?"

"Hmmm." Denny said nothing for several moments.

Finally, Harry stood slowly to his feet and shuffled back toward his recliner.

"Need any help there?"

"No, I got it."

"So, you're goin' in for surgery tomorrow, right?"

"Yep."

"You wanna pray?"

Harry felt the recliner and sank into it. "Sure. Not much else I can do right now. Seems like everything has been going from bad to worse. To tell you the truth, Denny, I'm at that point where if God doesn't come through, I don't have much hope in anything else."

Harry felt Denny's touch on his shoulder. His friend spoke softly. "Yeah, and the strange thing is, most of us don't realize that we're at that point *all the time* in this life."

Chapter 20

THE *LAW AND ORDER* RINGTONE OF HIS CELL PHONE woke Harry Friday morning. Why wasn't it his alarm clock? But with the patches on his eyes, he had no idea what time it was.

"Yeah ... hello."

A voice so hushed, Harry could hardly hear said, "Hi, Grandpa."

"DaShawn? That you? You okay?"

"Yeah. I wanted to call you before you had to go to the doctor."

"Oh yeah? Well, thanks ... but why're you whispering?"

"So I don't wake up anybody."

"What do you mean?" Harry sat up, swinging his feet onto the floor. "What time is it?"

"Five o'clock. Mr. Baxter said you had to go in real early, so I set my alarm and called you to see if you're okay."

That lump caught in Harry's throat again.

"Grandpa, you still there?"

"Yeah, yeah. I'm here."

"And you're gonna be okay, aren't you?"

"Oh, sure. In fact, I'm supposed to come back home later this afternoon, so maybe you can come over after school. Whaddaya think about that?"

"That'd be cool." DaShawn was quiet for a moment. "Is it gonna hurt, Grandpa?"

"Hmm. Don't think so, but if it does hurt a little bit, they'll give me somethin' for it. Nothin' to worry about." But the memory of the laser shots was still fresh in his mind.

"Will you get those bandages off your eyes so you can see again?"

"I should. I should. That's what I'm hopin' for, anyway. But you know I'm gonna have to sit in a funny chair with my head down for a few days, don't you?"

"Yeah." DaShawn laughed. "Mr. Baxter told me all about it. Said you were all humped over like you were riding a crotch rocket motorcycle. But he said you had to use a mirror to see. How can you do that?"

"I don't know. You'll probably have to help me."

"I will, Grandpa." The boy was quiet. "Guess I better go."

"Okay. You get some more sleep, and you be good, DaShawn."

Harry ended the call and just sat on the side of his bed. What a kid! He must really love his old Grandpa to wake up that early. Harry needed to get through this ordeal so he could focus more on DaShawn's needs rather than his own struggles.

He got up and shuffled to the bathroom, feeling his way along the hall. When he came out, he heard Estelle in the kitchen and smelled coffee. Oh man, this is how it would be if they were married—to wake up and have her be there. He wanted to grab her and kiss her right then! But he just cleared his throat and said, "So, what's for breakfast?"

"Hmm. Glad to see you're up. Didn't know whether you'd set your alarm or not."

"Coffee smells good. And I smell banana. What're you fixin'?"

"I'm just havin' banana on my cereal. But you're not havin' anything, remember?"

"Whaddaya mean? I'm hungry."

"And you're goin' into surgery, Harry Bentley." He heard her coming toward him.

"But yesterday you said I need my strength."

"That was yesterday. Didn't you read that prep paper? 'Nothing to eat or drink before your surgery.'"

"I never read anything like that! What's the deal?"

"When you're under, they don't want you coughin' up something, you could choke on it and die. It's standard procedure for any surgery."

"But they're not supposed to put me all the way under. Dr. Racine said I'm supposed to be awake through the whole thing."

"I don't know what he said, but that's what the paper says. Right here ..." He heard her rattling some pages. "Surgicenter Instructions, number four: 'Do not eat or drink anything after 12 midnight the night before you are scheduled to be in Surgicenter.' I think that includes you, Harry, since that's where we're supposed to report. Now you better get dressed so we can go."

"Can't I even have some coffee?"

"I can't believe you! What don't you understand about, *Do not eat or drink anything*?"

He returned to his room, feeling his way to the edge of his bed where he plopped down. The day was not getting off to a very good start! His fingertips touched his cell phone that he'd left on the bed.... No, wait. He was wrong. What could've been better than the love expressed by that boy waking up early enough to call him and see how he was doing?

"Oh, Lord, forgive me ... and I thank You. Thank You for DaShawn. He is truly your gift to me."

Ten minutes later, Harry came out of his bedroom dressed and made his way to the end of the hallway. "Estelle, do I look okay?"

He heard her feet shuffle.

"Turn around."

Like a shaky model on a runway, he complied, though he had to touch the wall to maintain his balance. But it was how shaky he felt inside about the day ahead that troubled him more. *"Pass me not, O gentle Savior."* Would Jesus really be with him?

He heard Estelle sip her coffee. "You look fine, Harry."

"How much time we got?"

"About ten minutes before we need to leave."

"You all ready?"

"Yep. I got everything. How 'bout you?"

"I'm good to go, but I was just wonderin' if you could read to me from the Word before we leave?"

"You want me to …" Her voice trailed off in an amazed wisp.

"Why not? Been trying to keep it up regular like, but with these bandages …" He shrugged.

"Of course! Of course, Harry. Come on in here and sit in your recliner." Her hand touched his elbow as she guided him across the room. "You want any particular passage?"

"You choose."

He heard her get her small Bible out of her purse and flip through its pages.

"Here, how 'bout this? It's from First Samuel, chapter 17, where David was facing Goliath. Hmm, let's see …"

"Facin' Goliath, that's pretty much how I feel."

"Okay, here we go, verse 45.

David said to the Philistine, "You come against me with sword and spear and javelin, but I come against you in the name of the Lord Almighty, the God of the armies of Israel, whom you have defied. This day the Lord will hand you over to me, and

I'll strike you down and cut off your head. Today I will give the carcasses of the Philistine army to the birds of the air and the beasts of the earth, and the whole world will know that there is a God in Israel. All those gathered here will know that it is not by sword or spear that the Lord saves; for the battle is the Lord's, and he will give all of you into our hands."

"So that's the Word for you for today, Harry Bentley. The battle is not yours. It's the Lord's!"

THEY ARRIVED AT THE SURGICENTER for the University of Illinois at 6:30 to find a dozen other patients already waiting for various procedures, though, according to Estelle, no one else looked like they were there for eye surgery.

Once they took Harry into the ward and helped him onto a gurney in a curtained preparation stall, a nurse removed his eye bandages and washed his face.

Ahh, that felt good.

Harry checked his eyes. The right one was still good. Left one … same old mess. But that's why he was in here, right? He tried to remember what he'd been learning about faith and silently thanked God that his right eye was still good, that he lived in a time when there was something that could be done about the problems in his left eye, and that he was in a modern hospital, in the care of some of the best eye doctors in the world.

There were more forms to sign, questions to answer, and his IV to be hooked up. But when an African American introduced herself as Dr. Harding, his anesthesiologist, Harry let his head fall back softly on the pillow. He hadn't thought it mattered. But then he'd been a grown man before the Government stopped secretly experimenting on African-Americans in the Tuskegee Syphilis Study, and that forty-year atrocity had left a scar of uneasiness in the back of his mind. Would his doctors—if they were all white—take some subtle shortcuts, perhaps even unintentionally, because he was *just* a black man?

No, no, this was 2006, and we were past that in this country ... weren't we? And yet the smiling ebony face of his anesthesiologist provided a touch of reassurance. She would be there in the operating room, aware of everything, and holding his very life in her hands. He smiled at her and then glanced at Estelle.

Estelle frowned and shook her head. What was that about? Did she think he was flirting? Then, as though she'd read his every thought, she waggled her finger and mouthed, "It's the Lord's!"

"It's the Lord's"? What's the Lord's? Oh yeah, *the battle* was the Lord's!

Harry gapped at Dr. Harding. She was holding a small syringe upright, checking the level of clear liquid in its thin column. "So, I'll be giving you this little cocktail that'll leave you very, very mellow and relaxed. Sound good?" Without waiting for his answer, she injected it into his IV line.

Estelle, who was standing by Harry's bed, gripped his hand. "So, we have a little longer before you actually put him to sleep and take him in, is that right?"

"I think we're about ready to go in now. I just saw Dr. Racine. He'll be over to talk to you in a minute, and then I think we can wheel you in." She turned to Harry. "We weren't planning to put you all the way out unless you particularly want that. Sometimes the doctors like to communicate with patients during eye surgery, to ask a question or have you move if they need you in a different position. Is that okay?"

Harry shrugged. What did he know? He gazed up at Estelle. She was more beautiful than he'd ever seen her. And everything had become totally copacetic.

"How you doin'?" Dr. Racine seemed to appear out of nowhere, standing at the foot of Harry's bed. "How was your vision when they took the bandages off?"

"About the same."

"Good." He gestured toward a green-clothed man next to him. "This is Dr. Metzger. He'll be assisting me today."

"How you doin'?" Harry mumbled.

Dr. Racine clapped both hands together. "Okay. Ready to go? Got any questions?"

Harry moved his head from side to side, remembering only at the last moment to do it slowly and not shake his head.

"Well, I have one," Estelle said. "Could we pray with you doctors, before you take him in?"

"Of course." Dr. Racine's voice sounded as eager as it did surprised.

Harry felt Estelle's voice bathing him in the comfort of the Lord as she led out in a confident prayer, asking God's blessing and healing for him and wisdom and skill for the doctors and staff. When she finished, she squeezed Harry's hand one more time and leaned down. "Remember," she whispered, "'The battle is not yours. It's the Lord's.' And I'll be waiting for you."

HARRY NEARLY DRIFTED OFF TO SLEEP as they wheeled him down the hall to the glaring surgical theater. He'd expected to smell disinfectant and ether and other hospital odors, but the only thing that assaulted his nose was the cold—a clear, Chicago-winter-cold—to freeze all the microbes, Harry guessed.

He woke up enough to help the transporters and nurses move him onto the operating table. As he tried to get comfortable, he remembered one question that had been in the back of his mind. "Uh, Dr. Racine? Are you here yet?"

"Just over here, getting some things ready."

"Well, uh, I was wondering, if you're gonna poke three holes in my eye like you said, how you gonna keep my eye from moving around and messing up what you're trying to do?"

"Ha, ha. No problem. First we'll use some numbing drops and then some paralyzing drops that work on the nerves controlling the eye muscles. They won't move at all."

"Oh, guess that's good." Harry was fading again and had the vague sense that he would have said *good* to anything the doctor answered at that moment. Around him nurses were covering his body and head with drapes and positioning his head so it *couldn't* move. No drops for that, he guessed. Then they wrapped him in a preheated, comforting blanket. He was safe in his cocoon.

"Okay, I think we're ready to go in." The announcement came from very far away.

At first, all Harry noticed was that they were doing something to his eye—uh, no, it was *in* his eye. In his eye! But in spite of the doctor's earlier reassurances, Harry cringed from the memory of pain associated with the laser shots he'd had. But surprisingly, what the doctors were doing now really *didn't* hurt. Little tugs were all he felt.

Somewhere in the room, classical music played softly. And over the lilting notes, the doctors and nurses spoke to one another in calm, professional voices—everything under control, everything going as planned.

And although his right eye—his good eye—was grayed-out by the drape that covered his head and the rest of his body, Harry could see things happening in his left eye.

A warm light—not painfully bright like the slit lamp—entered the interior "room" of his eyeball on the end of a fiber optic probe. The doctors moved it around to illumine whatever they wanted. He felt another tug on his eye as the distant voice of Dr. Racine explained that a second instrument had been placed into his eye that would regulate the internal pressures and inject more fluid as needed.

"And now we are inserting the cutter."

Harry dozed for a moment until he realized he could see the cutter moving back and forth in his eye with the faint sound of a miniature Weed Wacker. A hollow needle, thinner than a toothpick, "ate" the offending vitreous membrane, chewed it up, and sucked it out of his eye. But he lay there watching, permitting it, without jumping up to try and fight off his "attackers."

"The battle's not yours. It's the Lord's!"

Okay. He relaxed and dozed again as the procedure continued.

He didn't know how long things had been quiet when he heard Dr. Racine's voice again. "Mr. Bentley, can you hear me?"

"Yes."

"Okay, Mr. Bentley, we have a problem here."

Chapter 21

"WE HAVE A PROBLEM HERE"? WHAT DID THAT MEAN? "*We have a problem here*"? It sounded like Apollo 13 announcing their potential doom. These were his eyes, after all! And he couldn't see a thing out of either one at the moment. Just a gray blur. He was blind! Totally blind in both eyes!

"*Pass me not, O gentle Savior,*" he mumbled, trying to stem his rising panic.

"Sorry. I didn't catch what you said, Mr. Bentley."

"Nothin', nothin'. What ... kind of problem?"

"It seems that the lens in your eye has developed ... well, in layman's terms, an instant cataract. This sometimes happens for reasons that are not entirely clear. It's the same thing that occurs to many older people in a much more gradual process. But when the eye is sufficiently traumatized, the lens sometimes clouds over in a matter of moments. As a result, you can't see out of it, and we cannot see in to finish our surgery." The surgeon stopped.

Just as he feared, he *was* completely blind in that eye. Defeat sat heavy on his chest, but ... "*The battle's not yours. It's the Lord's!*" Estelle's words echoed in his mind.

"And my right eye?"

"Oh, I'm sure it's okay."

He said my right eye's okay. Harry took a couple of deep breaths, trying to process the doctor's words.

"So ... what's this mean?"

"Ultimately, we'll need to take out the lens. Later, when your eye has healed from surgery, we can fit you with a contact lens on the outside like anybody who wears contacts. Or, if everything is sufficiently stable, we can implant a lens in your eye, replacing your natural one, just like they do for regular cataract surgery. You probably know people who've had cataract surgery, don't you?"

"Well, yes, but..." He could think of a couple, and they seemed to function all right.

"You don't have to make a decision right now if you don't want to. We can come back to this some other day if you'd rather."

"But you said that sooner or later, my lens has to come out, didn't you? There're no options here, right?"

"Right. If you want to see, there's no way around removing it."

Ha, if I wanna see? thought Harry. "Could you give me a minute to think about this?"

"No problem. Call us when you're ready."

Cocooned under zero visibility while breathing the frigid, surgical air, Harry tried to decide. Over and over, his eye had gone from bad to worse. What did that mean? Why was God allowing this? Hadn't Jesus heard his cry? Had He passed him by? Perhaps ... perhaps God didn't answer because He didn't even exist! How "unbelieving" was that! But if it was the truth, he had to face it!

But as he lay there, helpless, Harry realized a universe without God—a life without Jesus—was completely void, amounted to nothing, meaningless, drifting. It was worse than death, worse even than blindness.

He needed Jesus like he'd never before imagined! And not just a Jesus back there in history. He needed to know Jesus was with him now, that He hadn't passed him by. If he could be sure of that, nothing else mattered—not life, not death, not even sight. It was truth so deep it changed every game.

But how could he know Jesus was with him?

"Surely, I am with you always, even to the end of the age." Jesus' powerful promise, recorded at the end of Matthew's Gospel, trumpeted in Harry's mind from a sermon Pastor Cobbs had preached at SouledOut: *"I am WITH you always! I am with YOU always! I am with you ALWAYS!"*

Harry had heard those words—who could ignore Pastor Cobbs' powerful preaching?—but had he learned their powerful lesson in a personal way? Had he ever really understood how important Jesus' promise was? Well, he was learning it now!

Wait a minute. Could his need to *personally* learn the reality of God's presence be part of why God had allowed his suffering? If it was, then ... this whole crisis wasn't a meaningless random accident. If there was a lesson he needed to learn, it was because there was a Teacher trying to teach him. That meant God *did* exist! God knew, God cared, God *was* in control.

"The battle's not yours. It's the Lord's!"

The battle ... what battle? He'd assumed it was the battle to restore his vision. But, what if the battle being fought within him was a battle that would profoundly change Harry's relationship with the Lord? If so, maybe he was learning his lesson, and the Lord was indeed winning the battle.

He sighed as though he'd been holding his breath.

"Okay! Take it out! ... Hello?" Harry raised his voice. "Anyone around? I made my decision. Go ahead and take out that lens." He would surrender the *whole* battle to the Lord. Let God teach him.

DAVE JACKSON

Let God reveal His plans … or not. His little insight might be only a small portion of God's overall plan, but it was enough. The battle was the Lord's, whether he received his sight or not.

In a matter of minutes, the doctors were back around him, continuing their work. Their calm voices hovered over him as they probed inside his eye with their little tools. And when his lens came free and he could see it floating in the vitreous like a frosted Frisbee, he even got into the act himself. "No, no, a little more to my right. There you go! Now you're gettin' it."

The cutter nibbled at the edge of the lens, devouring it like Cookie Monster.

"Oops! You missed a piece. It's back the other way. Ah-ha! I think you got it all now."

Harry's surgery lasted only ninety minutes, even with the lens problem and his "time-out" to decide whether to proceed. When they were finished, Dr. Racine said, "I've bandaged both eyes again because I want you to keep them as still as possible for the next twenty-four hours. No reason to tempt fate here."

Fate? No, Harry knew fate had nothing to do with what had been happening to his eye for the last couple of months, and it certainly had nothing to do with what had happened today.

Dr. Racine touched Harry's arm. "They're going to roll you out to recovery now. I'll stop by and see you in a little while when you're more awake. Okay?"

"Okay. See ya later." Huh, he probably wouldn't *see* him until much later, but … there was that word.

When the transporter began to push his gurney, Harry had no idea where he was going, but when they arrived at recovery, the activity around him sounded similar to the stall where he'd been prepped for surgery. The transporter kicked the brakes on, and a young, street-wise voice said, "Everything cool, bro?"

192

"Um-hm."

"All right, then. You need anything, you just call. One of them nurses'll be right wi'ch you. Okay, my man?"

"Hmm." Harry let him go and fell asleep, interrupted only by the nurses who stopped now and then to check his vitals.

"MR. BENTLEY?" IT WAS DR. RACINE'S VOICE. "You awake enough to sit up?"

"Oh, yeah. I think so." Arms on both sides helped Harry sit up and then swing his legs over the edge.

"Like I said this morning. We put bandages on both eyes to reduce eye movement as much as possible, at least until tomorrow. There's also a small aluminum shield over your left eye. You can touch it." Harry reached up to check as Dr. Racine continued. "It's just to make sure you don't bump your eye while you're asleep. You won't need it after a couple of nights. And, like we discussed before, you're to remain face down for two weeks."

Harry tipped forward from the waist as though he were bowing before a king.

"No. Ha, ha. Just your head's all that needs to be face down. By the way, did you rent one of those massage chairs?"

"Sure did. Tried it out last night. Pretty comfortable. Me needin' to stay face down must mean you put in that bubble, but I don't remember you doin' it."

"That's understandable. You were kind of in the twilight. But yes, we put it in. Should last two or three weeks and help flatten that macular hole. Hopefully it will also hold your retina sufficiently in place so it will reattach. Right now, that is our greatest concern. If it continues to peel away, we may have to put on a Scleral Buckle."

"A what?"

"A Scleral Buckle. It's a thin silicone band that we put around the eyeball to constrain it and reduce the chance of further detachment. But I'm hoping we won't have to do that."

"You mean you'd actually put something around my eye?"

"Yes. It's like a little belt." The doctor touched Harry's shoulder. "But don't worry, Mr. Bentley. I'm not saying we need to do it now. It's just one further procedure if we can't arrest this deterioration you're experiencing."

All the calming influence of Harry's "cocktail" had worn off. "How long would you have to leave it on? Would it hurt?"

"Well, if we had to do it, it would be permanent. And no, it doesn't usually hurt. You'll get used to it and won't even feel it. And you can't see it either. It would be behind where your eye muscles attach to the sides and top and bottom of your eye, and you can't usually see those muscles on people. Actually, we would thread the band under those muscles like the belt loops on your pants."

Harry shuddered. "Okay. Like Estelle says, let's not go there."

"Estelle? Oh, yes, your wife. Well … we should call her in now that you're awake. But let's hope we don't have to use a Scleral Buckle."

To Harry, Dr. Racine didn't sound very confident, and he wondered if the doctor was just trying to prepare him for what was down the road. He took a deep breath. "So tomorrow, if everything looks okay, I get these bandages off?"

"If everything's good. And then you won't need to wear anything except an eye shield at night for a few nights while your eye is still vulnerable. After that, if you want to wear a patch during the day like I saw you had, you can, but you don't have to. The main thing is, keep your head down 24/7 for two weeks."

Harry again bowed his head, having inadvertently allowed it to come up.

"Yes, you keep it down. I want you to remember that. It'll take a little getting used to. I want to see you weekly for checkups. When all the swelling has gone and the bubble has been absorbed by your body, we'll talk about getting you a lens, either an implant or a contact."

HARRY WAS GRATEFUL FOR ESTELLE'S steady hand as she helped him up the stairs to his apartment. But he was getting more sure-footed even without his sight.

"Estelle. Think you could find something for me to eat?"

"Sure, Baby. I'll get you a little something now." She guided him into the apartment and helped him onto his massage chair. "There. How's that?"

He leaned forward, resting his face in the "donut" while flexing his shoulders to find the most comfortable position. "Not bad. I think I can do this. But what's this about a *little something now*? I haven't had anything to eat since last night, and I'm starvin'."

"I know, I know. But I gotta go out and get some clothes from my place. And while I'm out, I'll pick up something that won't disappoint you either. You can be sure."

Harry grinned into his donut. "All right. You do that." If Estelle was picking something up—rather than cooking herself—it had to be special.

To tide him over, she made him a turkey sandwich and set a can of Pepsi on the table beside him. "I put a straw in this can, Harry, because the little brochure they gave me said that was the way to avoid raising your head when you needed to drink something. They have lots of little suggestions in there, and tomorrow

I'm gonna get you one of those double mirrors. You need one of your pain meds?"

"No, I'm good."

"Okay, then." She grabbed his hand and guided it to the table. "Here, Baby, here's your food and the phone. And here's the CD player. Want me to put something in?"

"Sure, but how long you gonna be gone? Feels like you're settin' me up for the long term."

"Don't worry. I'll be back in a couple of hours with your dinner." She flipped through the CDs. "Hmm. I'm puttin' in Bebo Norman, and the others are sittin' here beside it. Okay? You need anything else?"

"No." But in a voice as morose as he could make it, Harry said, "Just send someone back who won't go off and leave me all the time."

"Harry Bentley! If it weren't for your eyes, I'd whap you upside your head …"

They both laughed and she pressed Play on his CD player as she left.

Harry leaned upright in his chair while keeping his head bowed and devoured his turkey sandwich, sipping occasionally on the Pepsi. The straw worked pretty good.

The second song on the CD caught Harry's attention: "I have nothing without You." Wasn't that the truth! Not an easy one to admit, but it sure was true. The song continued, identifying various ways we depend on the Lord for strength and time and even the ability to praise Him. But Harry was shocked by the last refrain: "I am nothing without You!"

Harry punched the Stop on the CD player and backed it up. He listened to the refrain again. Yes, the singer said, "I *am* nothing."

"Wow!" Harry muttered. "It's one thing to realize I *have* nothing except what God has given me, but to confess that I *am* nothing without Him…. Ooo, that's deep!" But as he thought about it, that's exactly where he'd been today. He'd gone all the way down to the bottom of himself and found nothing, nothing at all without the Lord. How had he lived so long without realizing that? How did most people go through life avoiding it? Thinking they really were something on their own. No wonder there was so little desperate hunger for God.

As a blind man, Harry was seeing things he'd never seen before.

He finished his sandwich as the other songs played and was surprised to find that "Nothing without You" was repeated at the end of the CD as a reprise.

When it ended, Harry slowly stood up from his chair and—while keeping his head bowed—stepped around the small side table where he could more easily feel the buttons on his CD player. He pressed the Back button to the beginning of that final song and hit Play again. It was a simple song—easy words, easy melody—and Harry sang along. When the line asked for strength to lift his hands, Harry raised both arms straight out from his sides, knowing he had no strength, nothing with which to serve God or even praise the Lord, at least not within himself.

Head bowed and arms stretched out to his sides, he sang the last line as though it were his last: "I am nothing. I am nothing without You."

Tears soaked his eye bandages as the CD ended, but Harry stood there, still as a crucifix, not wanting to lose the moment … until a clear voice broke the silence.

"The nightmare is over!"

Chapter 22

HARRY STOOD PERFECTLY STILL. Who'd said that?

"Hello? … Someone here?" Harry hadn't heard anyone come up the stairs or enter his apartment. But then he was so "into" the song, he might have missed them. "Hello?"

Perhaps it was the beginning of another song on the CD? But it hadn't sounded like Bebo Norman's voice. And nothing else followed. Just, *"The nightmare is over!"*

The more carefully Harry thought about it, the more he realized even though the words were as clear as if someone had spoken them in his apartment, he hadn't heard them through his ears. They'd been spoken inside his head: *"The nightmare is over!"*

"Hello?" He let his arms drop slowly to his side. "God? God? Is that You?"

Nothing.

"Come on, now. If that was You, don't be playin' with me … please." He knew he shouldn't be bossing God around, but … "You know I been through enough."

But maybe that was the point. God *did* know he'd been through enough and was reassuring him. *"The nightmare is over!"*

Harry re-bowed his head, which had slowly come up without him noticing. Yeah, not only for the sake of his eye, but if it was God, he *ought* to bow his head. Perhaps he should kneel down or fall prostrate on the floor. Instead, he felt his way carefully around the side table to sit on his massage chair. But before he settled in, he reached down and slipped off his shoes, thinking he might be on holy ground. Isn't that what Moses did when God spoke to him?

"Was that You, God? Did You actually speak to me? Is it really over?"

How could he be sure? And did he need to be absolutely certain before he believed? What was the role of faith even in something like this? *"I believe, but help my unbelief."* No, those words had been too clear. He believed! That was God. God had actually spoken to him! He had no unbelief about that.

The only thing that could possibly dissuade him would be if the words didn't prove true. And it would be a stiff test, too. Lots of things had gone wrong, and according to Dr. Racine, more could still go wrong—an infection, hemorrhage, or an ongoing detachment. He might need that buckle thing. He could remain blind in that eye. He might develop similar problems in his right eye. Any of those would continue the nightmare.

Only God knew if the nightmare was over.

"But I believe! I believe! Thank You, God. Thank You for being with me. Thank You for speaking to me. Thank You for ending my nightmare. 'Cause I know, I'm nothing without You! But with You … well, whatever You want."

THE DOORS BELOW OPENED AND CLOSED, one after the other, and someone began climbing the stairs. Harry heard only a few steps before he was certain it was Estelle—her pace, her rhythm, the weight of her tread—oops, he better not mention that to her. He smiled. He was sure it was she.

He made his way over to the door and unlocked it, and then shuffled back to his massage chair, being good to keep his head down. God may have told him the nightmare was over, but he wasn't going to test the Lord by falling down on his part of the job.

"Door's open, Babe," he called before she put the key in the lock.

"What?" The door swung open. "Why wasn't the door locked? It could've been anybody walkin' up in here on you."

"Nah, it couldn't, Babe. I knew it was you, moment you started climbing those stairs."

"Get real! How could you know it was me?"

"Mm-mm. Same way I know you brought me some Hecky's Ribs. Oh, Babe, am I ready for some of them right now!"

"What you talkin' 'bout? You done lost your mind up in here? And why would I go all the way up to Evanston to get some Hecky's?"

"'Cause ya love me, Babe."

"Hmm. Dream on, old man."

Harry heard the slight rustle of a plastic bag as she set something on the table. "You want to know how I know? It's like this: When you lose your sight, you begin payin' a lot more attention to your other senses, and no ribs smell as good as Hecky's. I knew the minute you walked in the door."

"Oh, you did, did ya? Well, I s'pose I can't get away with eatin' them all by myself, then, can I? But that don't explain how you knew it was me comin' up the stairs."

"You got your own way of walkin', Estelle. And it's the finest I've ever seen."

"Harry Bentley, you watch your mouth, now."

He chuckled. "I'm just sayin'... After all, I wasn't lookin' at nothin'... leastwise, not today."

"Good heavens, what's got into you? I leave outta here, and you're 'bout as sorry as a stray puppy, whinin' about when I'm comin' back. And when I do, it's like you been to the mountain top, or somethin'."

Harry couldn't help grinning. "Hmm. Just get me some of those ribs, okay?"

"Think you better come on over here to the table. But keep your head down."

Once Harry was settled with a dishtowel bib and plenty of napkins at hand, Estelle joined him and the only sound for the next several minutes were those of appreciative diners.

Finally, Harry wiped his mouth. "The Lord ever talk to you personally, Estelle?"

"Mmm. Of course. All the time."

"Really? How do you know it's Him?"

"God's Word is God's word. Who else would it be?"

"Yeah. Sure. *God's Word is God's word*, but ..." He didn't know whether he wanted to tell Estelle about the words he'd heard that afternoon. What if she thought he had just imagined them? And what if he had? No, as Estelle would say, he wasn't goin' there. He believed God had spoken to him, and the test would begin soon enough, tomorrow afternoon, as a matter of fact, when he saw Dr. Racine for his first checkup after the surgery.

They lost themselves again in the ribs.

THE NEXT MORNING, ONCE THEY'D HAD a leisurely Saturday breakfast and Harry was settled on his massage chair, he heard several people coming up the stairs. "DaShawn's here," he announced to Estelle. "Now you just see if I ain't right."

"How would he get over here by himself?"

"Oh, he's not by himself, but I can't tell who's with him."

Sure enough, when Estelle opened the door DaShawn came bouncing in. "Hey, Grandpa, how you doin'?"

"I'm kickin', I'm kickin'. Just not quite so high. And who you got with you?" He'd heard voices greeting Estelle. "Ah, that you Denny and Jodi?"

"Yeah," said Denny. "And we got Gracie with us, too."

DaShawn tapped Harry on his shoulder impatiently. "And I brought a game for you to play, Grandpa."

"A game? I don't know that I'm well suited for playin' games right now."

"Oh, this one you can play without lookin'. It's a smelling game."

"Harry," Estelle said, "why don't you move over there on the couch where the kids can get closer to you. You might like this."

Once Harry was situated, still keeping his head down and taking care not to shake it too much, DaShawn said, "Okay, Grandpa, I'm gonna hold something right up under your nose, and you guess what it is. Okay? ... Now what's this?"

"Whew! That's garlic!"

"Right. And this?"

"Mmm. Coffee! Smells good. How 'bout makin' up a pot, Estelle?"

"Sure. Anyone want coffee?"

"What's this one, Grandpa?"

"Bacon."

"No, bacon grease. But I'll give you a pass. And this one?"

Harry heard someone else coming up the stairs, but he concentrated on what was before him. "Hmm. That one's not so easy. Some kind of perfume, I'd guess."

"Harry Bentley, you *better* recognize that!"

"Why? What is it, Estelle?"

"You don't know? What's a woman to do? That's my lilac perfume."

"Oh, I knew it smelled good! Real good!"

"Yeah, but you didn't recognize it was mine. What other woman you been hangin' with? Oops, someone else is at the door."

Harry already knew someone was there to save him from his *faux pas*. As soon as he heard the new voice, he said, "Is that you, Firecracker?"

"Sure is, Mr. B. How you doin'?"

"Well, a lot better, now that we got a real party goin' on up in here. How's that coffee comin', Estelle?"

"Grandpa, come on. Guess what this next one is, Grandpa!"

"Uhh … cinnamon?"

"Aw, that was too easy. You'll never guess this one!"

Harry heard Jodi say, "Isn't that cute? DaShawn invented this smelling game since his grandpa can't see. Spent all morning at our house putting it together."

"What all does he have in those lids?" the Firecracker whispered.

In a few minutes, Estelle offered coffee all around and then said, "Okay, kids, that's all. Mr. Harry's got another visitor. So why don't you come into the kitchen and get a snack."

Yes, Gabby Fairbanks was here, and Harry needed to talk to her about her husband. "Come on over here, Firecracker." He reached out his hand and heard her slide the hassock closer and sit down as voices faded to the other room. Then he felt her hand on his.

"I'm really sorry about all this eye stuff you're going through. What did they—"

"Never mind that. I gotta ask what you know about your man Philip's association with Matty Fagan." He knew he was jumping in rather abruptly, but he'd been out of commission since Estelle had told him Gabby's husband was somehow involved with Fagan …

"I—I don't really know, Mr. B. Just that one time when he was on the phone, I heard him talking in the background to some guy named Fagan. That's it."

"Humph," Harry muttered. "It's never just 'one time' with Fagan." He swore under his breath and almost got up, then sagged back down on the couch, keeping his head bowed. "Sorry, Gabby. I'm just so *frustrated* to be laid up with these stupid eye patches right now. If this Fagan is who I think he is, whatever's going down with Philip can't be good—and could be downright dangerous. The man's always got some racket going on."

"But who is he, Mr. B?"

"He used to be my boss when I was on the force, but he's gone rogue, shaking down drug dealers and gangbangers, then reselling the confiscated drugs and weapons back on the street. I've been working with Internal Affairs to put him away for good, but the wheels of justice turn slowly. He's under indictment now, but it didn't take him long to get out on bail. Knowing Fagan, that hasn't stopped him from finding some other marks to go after. You think your husband is using?"

"Using? You mean, drugs? No!" She paused for a moment. "Only vice I know about is his gambling, which I told you about, and now he's in debt up to his eyeballs. That's why he came to me, trying to borrow money to pay it off …"

Harry groped for her wrist. "That's it!"

"Oh, Mr. Bentley, you don't think—!"

"That's exactly what I think. Fagan's got himself a new racket, loaning easy money to people like your husband—upstanding business types who've got themselves in trouble at the gaming tables."

"But where would this Matty Fagan get that kind of money?"

"Ha." Harry leaned back a little. "You'd be surprised how easy it is for someone like Fagan to get his hands on fifty grand, even a hundred or two hundred—mostly payoffs from the big drug dealers in exchange for his cops looking the other way. And you can be sure the 'interest' he's charging will set your man back even more."

"So why would Philip do that?"

"Quick money, no questions asked, no check into assets, all the stuff that banks do. But it's risky, because Fagan doesn't take kindly to people who cross him."

They were silent for a few moments as Harry imagined the shock and fear that must be going through the Firecracker.

Finally, she said, "But if Philip pays it back ..."

"I hope he does, Firecracker, I truly hope he does. Because Fagan isn't a patient man."

Chapter 23

THE VISITS FROM DaSHAWN, THE BAXTERS, and Gabby Fairbanks almost made Harry forget he had to go back to the eye clinic that afternoon, until Estelle jingled the car keys and said they needed to go.

Harry didn't know which was worse—trying to keep his head down while moving around or having both eyes bandaged as Estelle helped him navigate stairs, sidewalks, and getting in and out of the car. He felt so helpless!

But they made it to the clinic without any mishaps, and he finally relaxed in the padded exam chair as Dr. Racine removed the bandages. Harry blinked and took a deep breath as he gazed around the dimly lit room.

"Hold this little shield over your good eye, and tell me what you see."

The doctor retreated a few steps as Harry put the shield over his eye. "Uh, all I see is vague, blurry patches of light and dark."

"Can you tell me how many fingers I'm holding up?"

"I can't even see you, unless you're that whitish shape over there, movin' like some kind of a ghost." He pointed toward where the doctor had gone. But this was bad! Real bad! If this was all the sight he was going to get, what use was it? He was still blind in that eye.

"That's okay. That's okay. Without a lens, there's not much more you could see."

Harry watched the whitish blob come toward him. Discouraged, he lowered the shield. "Does that mean I'm legally blind?"

"In that eye?" The doctor shrugged. "Without correction, that eye is worse than 20/200. But to be considered legally blind it must be 20/200 or more *with* correction. So let's try this." He handed Harry another shield that resembled a little mask with a handle, the kind high-society people sometimes wore to masquerade balls. "Place the solid side over your right eye, and try to look through the pinholes on the left side."

Harry held it up to his face as the doctor instructed, bringing the pattern of a dozen, closely-spaced pinholes up to his bad eye.

At first the light shining through flashed like so many headlights on a nighttime freeway, but then he caught his breath. He was seeing images.

"I ... I can see some with it ... not very distinct, and it's hard to keep anything in focus. Most things are dark, but ... there you are ... and there's Estelle, over there by the door."

"Very good. Now how many fingers am I holding up?"

"Looks like three ... or maybe it's four. Can't be sure. But at least I can see that you raised your hand." He lowered the shield. "I don't get it. How can I see through those little holes, when I couldn't make out anything before?"

"You ever make a pinhole camera when you were a kid? The pinholes take the place of a lens, focusing the light so it creates an image on your retina. Right now, the image has to go through the bubble and the vitreous that's still in your eye. It's still cloudy. But at least you could see something. That's good. That's very good."

The doctor continued his exam—with the slit-lamp again, as well as other instruments—while Harry reveled in the words *"very good."* Perhaps this was the first confirmation that Harry had indeed heard the Lord and the nightmare truly was over! *Thank You, Jesus. Thank You, Jesus! Thank You, Jesus!* Harry repeated his gratitude silently as the doctor probed and examined and shined his lights in Harry's eye and then checked by ultrasound for any further detachment.

"I think it's holding," he pronounced. "But I'd like you to keep both eyes covered a little longer, just to reduce the motion. Come in early Monday morning, and if everything still looks good, we'll take the bandages off."

Uh, what was that? The doctor had said he'd only need weekly visits after the vitrectomy, and now he wanted him back in two days. Was that a setback? No, he told himself, just a precaution. But how much longer could he take not being able to see *anything*? Harry took a deep breath. He could endure it as long as it wasn't permanent!

"Here are some drops and salve and fresh bandages." The doctor put them in a Ziploc bag and handed them to Harry. "If necessary, your wife can help you put them in. Do it four times a day. One helps prevent infection. One keeps the pressure down, and the other moistens your eye. Any questions?"

"How about showers?" Estelle said.

What? Did she think he needed a shower? And he probably needed to shave his head, too. But how was he going to do that?

"Just keep his eye covered. Don't get any water in there. It wouldn't be sterile."

THEY'D RIDDEN SEVERAL BLOCKS TOWARD HOME in silence when he felt Estelle touch his arm. Her contact was electric, grounding him in the here and now—in his RAV4, riding home from the eye clinic, head down, while Estelle drove.

"You feelin' discouraged, Baby?"

He shrugged. "Kinda. But the doc did say everything was going okay, didn't he?"

"Oh yeah. But I know you were hoping to get those bandages off today. It's one thing to keep your head down, but it must be pretty hard not seein' anything either."

Harry thought for a moment. "You know what it's like? It's like I'm in a room by myself and all the rest of you—the whole world—are out there, and slowly, very slowly the door between us is closing, closin' me off. Did I tell you that before?"

"Don't think so, or I'd remember it."

"Well, I was thinkin' about it the other day, and that's what it's like."

"So, what can I do so you don't feel so ... so confined in that 'other' room?"

Harry thought for a moment. "You can touch me ... like you just did." He felt a little silly saying it like that and wondered how she'd respond. "I mean, any time you're nearby or walkin' past, just reach out and touch my arm or something. Somehow that makes more of a connection even than talkin' ... not that I don't want you to talk. Talkin' is good, too."

"Touch, huh?" The RAV4 came to a stop at an intersection. "I think you're just lookin' for some sugar, Harry Bentley."

"Ha, ha. Well, that wouldn't be so bad either. Anytime you wanna—" Wait! What was he saying? Hadn't he made up his mind to dial down the romantic stuff? Here Estelle was nursing him like family, the eye doctor was calling her his wife, and they were joking about smooching. He'd better get his head on straight, or he'd be delivering this woman into a world of hurt. He didn't want to do that!

THAT EVENING, HARRY PICKED UP THE ZIPLOC BAG of drops and salve and felt his way into the bathroom. He needed to take more care of himself and not rely so much on Estelle. He stood in front of the mirror and carefully removed his bandages.

"Oh ..." He was speechless. The only words that even came close to expressing what he saw in the mirror were words he'd flushed from his vocabulary in the last few months. His left eye literally resembled hamburger, as though a meatball had been crammed into his face. How could any organ so battered and bloodied do anything, see anything, or ever return to normal?

His shoulders sank. *The nightmare is over?* Not hardly. He stared at himself. He could never let Estelle see this. And yet ... there was the iris and pupil of his left eye right in the middle of the mess. And—he closed his right eye—he could still see vague blurs with that eye. It was working to some degree. He held up his left hand, making a loose fist with nothing but a tiny pinhole to look through like a miniature spyglass.

Ah-ha! There it was again, an image ... of the bathroom light reflected in the mirror and of his bald head, and his fist before his face. Everything was blurry, just like earlier at the clinic, but he *was* seeing ... at least a little.

He dropped his fist and grabbed the sink with both hands as he leaned forward for a closer examination using his good eye.

Three knocks rapped on the door. "Harry? You okay in there? What's takin' you so long? You keepin' your head down?"

"I'm puttin' in those drops like the doctor said."

"You need help?"

"No! No help! I'm handling it myself. Be out in a moment."

He hurried up with the drops, the salve, and the bandages, then bowed his head, opened the door and shuffled back to his massage chair.

TRYING TO SLEEP THE SECOND NIGHT AFTER HIS SURGERY became miserable. The pain pills he'd taken the first day and perhaps his exhaustion from the surgery had eased his first night, but sleeping on his stomach wasn't something he'd done since he was a kid, and even a pile of pillows didn't help much. Again and again he woke up to find himself partially on his side and not really face down. But how could he remain face down without smothering himself? Finally, he got up, grabbed a few pillows, and went out to the living room where he sat on one end of the couch. He turned sideways to lean over the large overstuffed arm. At least this way he could remain face down and still breathe.

He switched ends a couple of times, but morning took forever.

When he woke up—for what, the tenth time?—he heard Estelle puttering around in the kitchen, but he felt nearly as tired as he'd been when he went to bed. He got up and staggered around with his head bowed.

"What are you doin', Harry? You don't have to get up yet."

"What time is it?"

"A little after six."

"Well, I can't sleep no more. Tryin' to sleep face down just isn't workin'."

"But you gotta do it!"

"Yeah, I know, and for two weeks! Hey, you think there's some way to take that donut thing off my chair? Maybe I can use it tonight. I gotta do somethin' different."

211

She came over and fiddled with the chair for a few minutes. "Did Denny bring any papers when he brought that chair up here, maybe an instruction book or something?"

"How would I know, Estelle? I had my eyes patched."

"Oh, yeah."

Harry listened as she rummaged around in the living room.

"Here it is, BodyKneaders Rental and Supply. They sent a little instruction pamphlet for the chair, and … wait a minute, Harry. Their brochure says they've got something for sleeping. It's a sleeping wedge for your legs and chest and a special face pillow that lets you breathe. And they've also got double mirrors you can use in your chair so you can watch TV and see people. I'm goin' down there and get those things for you right now."

"Better call first. They might not be open on Sunday."

They weren't open. "But you know what, Estelle, you still got time. You could go take DaShawn to church. There's no reason for you to hang around here all day. We can stop by that rental place on our way home from the clinic tomorrow morning."

"I don't need to do that. Denny and Jodi are gonna take him to church. They'll be fine."

"Well, then, why don't you take the car and go visit Leroy?"

"No. I saw Leroy on Thursday. He'll be okay. I think I'll stay right here with you."

Harry wanted to protest, insist that she needed to get out. He didn't want her tied down because of him. And yet, he appreciated her being with him more than he could ever put into words. After struggling with himself for a few minutes, he just kept silent.

The rest of the day passed as slowly as when Harry was a cop and on stake out. They listened to a couple of church programs on TV—*I'm getting just like my mama*, thought Harry—and then they played all the music CDs. Harry considered telling Estelle what he'd heard after the Bebo Norman CD, but he wasn't so sure the words were as true as they had first seemed.

A call from DaShawn that evening was as good as Harry's day got.

THE NEXT MORNING, HE FELT MORE HOPEFUL. "I'm takin' my black eye patch with me, 'cause I'm getting' these bandages off, and I'm gonna drive you home."

"Well, take your eye patch if you want, but you won't be driving. You gotta keep your head down. Remember?"

"Oh, yeah. Forgot. But I'm going in this morning, 'faith believing' that I won't have to wear these bandages anymore."

They were both sitting at the table, eating bowls of cereal and toast.

"I believe, too, Harry." She grasped his hand. "Let's pray."

"Pray? Oh, yeah. That'd be good, real good!"

"Our Father, we come again, thankin' You for being so good to us. And we're thankin' You because we believe You are bringing Harry out of this dark wilderness of blindness he's been goin' through. Give us faith to believe Your promises, O Lord. And help us not doubt. For without You, we wouldn't be able to trust, we wouldn't have no faith at all, because faith is a gift from You, O Lord, and we thank You for it. You've been so good to us. So we thank You. You've been a light in our darkness, our only hope in this time of trouble. So on today, we are bold to ask that this nightmare be over. This we ask in the precious name of Jesus. Amen."

Harry couldn't believe what he'd just heard. She'd prayed almost the same words he'd heard God say. He sat there, not moving a muscle until Estelle gave his hand a little squeeze.

"I think we better get goin', Harry, if we want to be seen first in that clinic. I sure know I don't want to be waitin' around." She let go of his hand.

"Wait, Estelle." He reached out and caught her before she could rise from the table. "There's something I need to tell you."

"Well, maybe you can tell me in the car, Harry. We gotta get goin'."

But when they got in the car, she switched on the radio. As they headed down Western Avenue, with people honking horns and a lot of stopping and starting, Estelle seemed too busy with the traffic for a serious talk. Harry decided to let the test go a little longer before telling anyone what he'd heard.

Chapter 24

HARRY AND ESTELLE WERE THE FIRST PATIENTS in the door of the retinal clinic, and in a matter of minutes, Harry was sitting in a dimly-lit examining room waiting for his eyes to dilate from the drops an assistant had put in.

Estelle put down the magazine she'd brought in with her. "It's too dark in here to read." She stood up. "I'm going across the street to the cafeteria in the hospital and get some coffee. You want a cup?"

"No, I'm good." Harry didn't shake his bowed head. Even though both bandages were off, and it was very tempting to look around, he was trying to be good. Besides, he knew there wasn't much to see except an eye chart, some furniture, and various pieces of equipment. Except there was one large poster on the wall that diagrammed the interior of the eye. Dr. Racine had referred to it in explaining Harry's problem. He would have liked to study that more closely. But no, he kept his head down and studied the fascinating Berber carpet as Estelle left for coffee.

Several minutes later, the *Law and Order* ring tone of his cell phone *ta-dummed* him out of his doldrums.

"Yeah, Harry here."

"Harrrrry, my man!"

"Fagan, you know I ain't your man, and I never will be."

"Ah, Harry, lighten up. Listen, I got a deal you can't refuse."

"Wanna bet?"

He was in the process of taking the phone away from his ear and closing it, when he heard Fagan's faint words: "It's about Rodney …"

"What'd you say?"

"I got some good news for you about your son, Rodney."

"Fagan, you're never good news. I know you set that fire in Estelle's brownstone and nearly killed her son! And I'm gonna see you're prosecuted for arson and second-degree murder." Harry hadn't yet made a decision to formally accuse Fagan because he didn't have the proof to make the charge stick, but if he did … hmm, maybe he ought to dedicate himself to finding it. Someone needed to bust this Whac-A-Mole, and if Internal Affairs couldn't get the job done, maybe it was up to him! "If you're trying to use my son to leverage me—"

"Now Harry, calm down. I know you don't like me, but that's okay. We can still do business together, can't we? … especially when it's in the best interest of your own son."

The exam room door opened, and Dr. Racine walked in.

"Fagan, this isn't the time or the place. Look, I'm at the doctor's office … can't talk now." He slammed his phone closed and slid it into his pocket. He closed his eyes, his whole body shuddering with each beat of his enraged heart.

He took a slow, deep breath and opened his eyes. "Morning, doctor."

"Good morning, Mr. Bentley. How's it going?"

How was what going? His eyes or the homicidal pyromaniac extortionist he'd just hung up on? But Harry knew what the doctor wanted.

"Well, the pain's pretty much gone, but beyond that, I guess you'll have to tell me how it's goin'." He chuckled, glad to leave the chaotic streets of Chicago and enter the clinical world of eyecare where he prayed that *"The nightmare was over."* At least, that's what he was here to find out.

The exam was much the same as on Saturday—how many fingers do you see? glaring slit lamp, probing, ultrasound—the whole exhausting and sometimes uncomfortable battery of tests. Estelle slipped in at some point and sat down unobtrusively in the chair on the other side of the room.

Finally, Dr. Racine stepped back and crossed his arms while Harry watched him with his good eye.

"I think we're doing pretty good, Mr. Bentley."

"Thank You, Jesus!" Estelle burst forth as she threw up both arms toward the ceiling. "Thank You, Jesus. You been so good, so good!"

Dr. Racine turned to look at her over his shoulder. "Well, yes. I guess that's right, especially given what we were up against."

He went over to his desk and began writing on Harry's chart. "I don't think there's a need to keep both eyes bandaged any longer, but do keep your head down. That's going to be the key. Use the drops and the salve regularly, and come back in ... let's see ... how about Friday afternoon?"

"Fine with me."

The doctor stood up and put his pen back into the pocket of his white lab coat. "Once your body has absorbed most of the bubble, we'll probably want to do a little more laser work, just over there on the side where the detachment occurred."

Harry's horror must have shown on his face, because the doctor raised a reassuring hand. "It's just a precaution, just to strengthen it."

"But you're sure it's not coming loose again?"

"I don't see any evidence of that. I think we're good."

Harry stood up and pulled out the black eye patch he'd brought with him *in faith*, he'd told himself. He put it on and obediently bowed his head as he reached out to shake the doctor's hand. "Oh, got one more question. Even though my head is down, can I move my eyes around to look side to side, front to back, like I just did when I reached out to shake your hand? Is that okay?"

"Not really. The point is to look down so the bubble rises to the back of your eye to keep that macula in place so it can heal. So when you're looking at the floor, imagine standing inside a hula-hoop, and don't look at anything outside it. Even less is better. There are mirrors you can get that'll let you look all around the room—"

"Yeah, we're gonna pick one up on our way home."

"That'll be good."

"And, can I read?"

"As long as it feels comfortable and you aren't scanning over a wide page. Okay?"

They shook hands, and Harry and Estelle were out of there like kids fleeing school for summer vacation.

Estelle had gone to Manna House to cook lunch for the residents while Harry sat at home in his massage chair trying out the double mirror they'd picked up to see how it worked for watching TV. Pretty good! Words weren't backwards and images weren't upside down. At first, that last part had him stumped. He knew images were reversed when viewing them in a mirror—like the company name on a truck that was following you in your car's rearview mirror. But the upside-down part stumped him until he realized that *he* was the one who was "upside-down." In any case, two mirrors, mounted on an angle to one another solved both problems.

He got up from his chair, and used the mirrors to walk into the kitchen, take a Pepsi out of the refrigerator, and get a straw—all while keeping his head down. Pretty good! He might have been able to do it just by feeling around, but the mirrors gave him new freedom. "Amazing what I take for granted," Harry muttered.

Sitting on his chair again with a straw in the soda can, he aimed his mirrors at the TV and was channel surfing when his cell phone rang. This time he checked the caller ID and realized it was Fagan *before* he answered it. Should he ignore the guy? He wanted to, but … the scumbag had mentioned Rodney!

"Yeah?"

"You out of the hospital yet?"

"Just get on with it, Fagan."

"Okay, okay. Well, here's the thing: Being on leave has given me time to do a lot of stuff I've been puttin' off, you know, like painting the bathroom and fixin' that second floor window at the end of the hall. Someone burgled my place a while back and broke the frame. But you wouldn't know anything 'bout that, would you Harry?"

Harry squirmed.

"I don't know what this city's comin' to." Fagan sounded like he was playing a saw, his voice whining with melodrama. "Criminals just ain't as careful as they used to be. Know what I mean?"

Did Fagan suspect Harry had creeped his house—the night he'd gone there looking for DaShawn's pink cell phone—or was Fagan just running off at the mouth like he usually did?

"Harry, you still there?"

"What's this rehearsal of how you're spending your 'vacation' have to do with my son?"

"Oh, yeah. Sorry. Back on point, I've had a little time to do some research, and that's how I discovered that a Rodney Bentley is locked up in the County. I seem to remember you had a boy about that age. And sure enough, guess what—"

"So, Rodney caught a case. What's that to you?"

"Nothin', really. But I've got a little juice with the prosecutor who's handling his case and one of the cops who accused him of resisting arrest. Know what I mean? They owe me. So I'm thinkin' your son's probably been in there long enough to learn his lesson, and with the right leverage, everybody might agree to drop his case. You know how it works in Cook County Jail. They hold a guy a year or two while his case inches its way through the courts, then they drop it, figuring the guy's served enough time."

"Yeah, they get their pound of flesh without proving guilt."

"There you go. Now, Cook County may not be the worst slammer in the country, but some people swear it beats anything in second place."

"And that's why you want to stay out, right?"

"Hey, one way or another, I'll never spend a day in the County. You can be sure of that."

Harry stood up and began to pace around his living room. "You're sure, huh? That must be why you're always after me to pull the plug on any evidence against you, right?"

"Well, that's one way of dealing with the problem. But like I said, *one way or another, one way or another*. I'm just givin' you an opportunity to help out your son here, that's all."

Harry peered out the window as though Fagan might be out in the parking lot, staring up at him, and then he realized he hadn't been keeping his head down. With his head down, he walked back and swung his leg over his massage chair and sat.

"Harry ... you thinkin' about it? Don't take too long now."

Yeah, Rodney had messed up by missing his court date, and Harry wasn't the kind of guy to abort true justice. But the actual charges he'd been jailed on had been trumped up and should have been dismissed if he'd had an even halfway competent Public Defender. Harry knew his way around the system, but Rodney hadn't asked for help, and Harry hadn't offered. Was this just one more instance of not being the father to Rodney he should've been all along?

"Harry, I'm waiting!" Fagan's sing-song voice trailed off.

Without a word, Harry removed his phone from his ear and slowly folded it closed. He needed time, but he wasn't willing to ask for it. To ask would be to put Fagan in the driver's seat. And he wasn't going to play his little game any longer.

But why, why, *why* did a problem like this have to come at him now? Not that he *ever* wanted to deal with Fagan. But why now, when he was laid up and half blind? He needed to be at the peak of his game to take on Fagan. In fact, he ought to be out there right now investigating Fagan for loan sharking Philip Fairbanks.

He leaned forward, resting his head in the "donut." His son surely deserved to get out of Cook County Jail by now. Perhaps Harry should have reached out to the cops to let them know they weren't dealing with anyone hard-core when it came to Rodney. But then an aggressive prosecutor might have portrayed such contact as witness tampering, even if Harry didn't threaten them like Fagan probably would. Still, at the very least, Harry could've found Rodney a better attorney. The charges should have been dismissed long ago.

So why hadn't he done anything? Was he afraid of losing DaShawn if his father got out of jail? Harry rubbed the tight muscles in the back of his neck. What if Rodney got out and tried to get DaShawn back? Could he convince DCFS? Of course, Rodney would have to show he could provide a stable home for DaShawn. That wouldn't be easy, given his former lifestyle. But didn't Harry want a stable lifestyle for his own son? Harry knew he should want it. In fact, he should be praying for it, praying that Rodney's life would turn around ...

But he hadn't been praying, and now Fagan was forcing his hand.

Chapter 25

THE DAY DRAGGED AND HARRY FELT ANTSY. He wasn't used to sitting around doing nothing. Yeah, he could watch TV with his mirror ... but that got old real fast. And besides, he was too rattled by Fagan's phone call to care about anything daytime television had to offer.

Maybe he'd take a nap ... but as he lay on the bed—face down— his mind drifted to those words he'd heard: *"The nightmare is over."* He was more and more convinced that God had actually spoken to him. After all, his left eye was no longer deteriorating and his right remained stable, but even more than that, those words told him God understood that it had been a real nightmare, which meant He cared and had been with him through it all.

But when he'd asked Estelle if God ever spoke to *her* personally, she'd said, *"All the time ... God's Word is God's word."* Huh, obviously, she was referring to how God spoke to her through the Bible. Well, it was true ... the main lesson God had been trying to teach him was clearly stated in the Bible. *"Surely, I am with you always,"* Jesus had promised.

So what was the difference? Right now, he needed a "word from the Lord" about the mess with Fagan. Could he find it in the Bible?

Rolling off the bed, he walked back to the living room where Estelle had put his Bible on the table. It felt good to walk around a little, even if he had to keep his head down. Maybe when Estelle came back, they should go out for a little walk. Could he do that? He couldn't see why not. "*See*" ... there was that word again. He smiled to himself. Hamlet may have said, "To be or not to be—that is the question." But Harry knew the *real* question was, "To *see* or not to *see!*"

He sank onto the couch, chin tucked to his chest, and opened the Bible. He knew the Book of Proverbs was all about wisdom, how to resolve practical issues. He flipped the pages. Ah-ha, right away in chapter two he saw something that seemed to apply:

Wisdom will save you from the ways of wicked men,
  from men whose words are perverse,
who leave the straight paths to walk in dark ways,
who delight in doing wrong
  and rejoice in the perverseness of evil,
whose paths are crooked
  and who are devious in their ways.

Huh! That certainly described Fagan, but it didn't tell Harry what to do. What was "wisdom" in this situation where his son's imprisonment hung in the balance? Scanning through the verses, another one caught his attention at the end of chapter six:

He will not accept any compensation;
  he will refuse the bribe, however great it is.

There! That was it! It was speaking to him—"*you* should refuse the bribe"—or ... was it meant for him?

When Harry read the verse in context, it referred to how an angry husband could not be bought off by the scheming adulterer who had seduced his wife. Harry was about to turn the page and look for some other nugget of wisdom when he realized that, in reality, Fagan had been raping the neighborhoods by stealing drugs and guns and money from dope dealers for his own profit and then turning those same dealers back out on the streets to continue committing crimes. Now that Fagan had been "caught" and was facing prosecution, he was offering Harry a bribe to subvert justice. And the bribe was great—freedom for Harry's son—but it would be a corrupt compensation.

He sighed with relief. The words did speak wisdom to him. He should not accept Fagan's offer! Embracing that conclusion, Harry felt certain God had again spoken to him, just as clearly as when He'd assured Harry his nightmare was over.

Harry felt giddy with the prospect that God might be as eager to speak to him today as He had to others in ancient times. But Harry realized his challenge was learning how to listen.

ESTELLE CAME BACK THAT AFTERNOON and fixed a dinner of chicken and rice for Harry, then sat down to eat it with him. As they ate, it crossed his mind that he'd managed pretty well while she was gone—got around the house, read, watched TV, listened to music. Was there any real need for her to continue staying over?

Her company! Ahh, yes, that was a good reason! He loved being around her. And though, since the bandages had come off, he was no longer feeling trapped in what he'd felt was his "room with the closing door," Estelle still reached out and touched his arm or shoulder whenever she passed. Once, noticing him rubbing the back of his neck where the muscles were cramping from keeping his head bowed, she said, "Here, let me do that," and gave him the most relaxing, sensuous shoulder and neck massage he'd ever received. And when they sat close enough—like now, at the table—she often took his hand. If he had to give up all that, he might be tempted to put those bandages back on his eyes.

But reveling in her closeness was dangerous. The more time they spent together, the deeper their souls entwined. He loved it … but was it right? Was he tying her down to an invalid?

With his head bowed, he grimaced as though he had just taken bitter medicine. "Uh … Estelle, when we're done eating tonight, maybe you should switch with DaShawn. You understand me? Let him come back home to his own room. He's probably feeling like an orphan by now, don'cha think?"

She let go of his hand. "I hear your words, Harry Bentley, but I'm not sure I know what you really mean." She got up and began to clear the table. "But if that's what you want, I'll be gettin' on up outta here …"

"Estelle, I didn't mean it that way. It wasn't for me—"

"Well then, how *did* you mean it?"

"I love havin' you around. You know that. It's just that …"

"It's just that you're not about to let this relationship go anywhere, are you? But I told you from the very beginning, Harry Bentley, that I wasn't up for you playin' with my heart. If you got commitment issues, deal with them on your own time. I'm too old for that stuff."

"Oh, come on, Estelle. That ain't what I meant. It's just that …" How should he say it?

"It's just that you can't even finish your sentence, Harry. Get real!"

She bussed the dishes from the table, and he could hear her filling the dishwasher … none too gently. Pretty soon she was back slinging a washcloth across the table. She tossed it toward the kitchen sink and stomped into DaShawn's bedroom where Harry knew she was picking up her stuff and grabbing her big ole purse. Before he knew it, she'd be gone. He had to say something!

"Estelle, would you come in here and sit down for a minute? Please don't go off in a huff."

"It ain't me that's goin' off in a huff." She marched into the dining room and slammed his keys down on the table. "Here! Don't worry 'bout me. I'm quite capable of getting a taxi for myself. I'll tell Denny Baxter to bring DaShawn back over here soon as he can … tonight."

In a moment she slammed the door, and Harry heard her stomp down the stairs.

His head sank down into his hands. "O God, what have I done?"

It was nearly eight o'clock when Denny brought DaShawn home.

"Grandpa, you got the bandages off! Can you see now?" DaShawn dropped to the floor to look up at him."

"'Course I can, leastwise with my good eye. Get on up here now and give me a hug. They been treatin' you right over there at the Baxters?"

"Yes, sir. Mr. Denny brought me home."

"That's good, that's good. Thanks, Denny."

"No problem. Glad to do it."

"And you, young man, I'm so happy you're home. But you're gonna have to be my helper now, you know, 'cause I'm supposed to keep my head down like this for two whole weeks."

"Two weeks?"

"Yeah, and that means I can't look up to see what's on shelves or even look you in the eye … except, here … check this out!" Harry picked up his double mirror and turned it toward DaShawn. "There ya go! Gotcha right in my sights, so don't try and get away with nothin'."

They laughed.

"Hey, Denny, I really appreciate you guys keepin' him for a few days, especially on such short notice. You're the best."

"Was nothin'. He was easy to have around. But, hey. I've got an idea. What if the guys all come over here to your place tomorrow night for the Bible study? Would that be good?"

"Over here? Uh ... sure, that'd be great. Hadn't even thought about it. Guess DaShawn could go over to his great-grandma's or read in his room or—"

"Why can't I come?"

Harry chuckled. "'Cause it's just for us men, and you ain't old enough."

"Aw, Grandpa. Just once?"

"I think it'd be okay, Harry. Can't imagine any of the brothers minding. Besides, isn't that the best way to bring up a kid? Let 'em observe a few men's events, you know."

"You mean of the *decent* kind, like eavesdropping on a council of elders or something?"

"*Elders*? Hey, you're the one with no hair left on your head."

"Yeah, but even with this mirror I can see that those streaks of gray have been growin' on you lately."

They both laughed.

"All right, DaShawn. We'll give it a try tomorrow night ... but just this once, okay?"

That evening after DaShawn was in bed, Harry had second thoughts about having his grandson come to the men's Bible study. In the back of his mind, he'd wanted to test with the brothers his conclusions about Fagan and talk about the direction he believed

God had given him from the Bible. Does God really speak that way? He was a new believer, still learning about faith, and these guys had been some of his best teachers along the journey. But he couldn't very well talk about Rodney with DaShawn sitting right there, hearing everything he might say about his dad.

Harry knew life with his mother, Donita, had been a living hell for DaShawn, and the boy was glad to get away from all her drugs, prostitution, and violence, and especially her pimp, Hector. But how had it been before, when Rodney was in the picture? The few times DaShawn had mentioned him, the boy had called him his "old man," but that didn't prove anything. Frankly, Harry didn't know what kind of a father Rodney had been. He'd been out of touch with Rodney for nearly ten years, clear up until Leslie Stuart, the social worker from DCFS, had called on him to take in a little boy named DaShawn, the grandson he never knew he had.

Ten years, and Harry hadn't even seen his son, didn't know he had a grandson. It twisted his heart into a knot. Now … now he had a chance to do things differently with DaShawn. But that still didn't answer whether Rodney had been a good father or not. But there was one person who might know.

Harry picked up his cell phone and saw that the time said eight-forty—probably not too late. He punched in the number.

"Hello," came the thin, wavering voice on the other end.

"Hey, Mama. It's me, Harry."

"Oh, Harry, will you be home from work pretty soon? I need you to take the trash out. You forgot to do it this morning. And I've told you—"

"Mama, Mama. This is Harry. I don't live with you anymore. Remember? I'm sorry I haven't been able to come over recently, but I've had some medical problems with my eyes." He still thought of the problem as having threatened both of his eyes.

"Oh, yes. Estelle told me all about that. She takes such good care of me. She's over here two or three times a week. She says you pay for that. Is that right, Harry?"

"Well … yeah. It's part of her work. She does it as a business, Mama."

"Oh, still, I hate askin' her to take out my trash. That's something a man should do."

"I know, Mama, but I can't do it right now. Maybe I'll have DaShawn come over tomorrow and help you out a little."

"Okay. He's a good boy, but he wears his pants too low."

"I'll speak to him, Mama. It's just a fad, but I don't like it either."

"Well, you do that, but remember he's a good boy."

Yes, thought Harry, *and how did he get to be that good boy?* "I need to ask you somethin' about him, Mama. Did you know DaShawn before he came to live with me? Did Rodney ever bring him to see you?"

"Well, we used to have Christmas together every year. But you didn't come. Why didn't you come?"

Harry sighed deeply. How far the ripples of his behavior had extended. "I shoulda been there, Mama. It was wrong of me."

"Well, Rodney's wife never came to Christmas, either, and I always wondered why. Somethin' wasn't right, if you ask me."

"Hmm. You were probably right. But Rodney … did he and DaShawn get along okay? I mean, did he seem like a good dad?"

"Well, I think so. I mean, he made that boy mind, that's for sure … but he wasn't mean to that baby. Cute as a button, the boy was. Does he still have all that hair? Used to look like the halo of an angel, but … I can't remember it except when he was little."

"No, Mama. He got it cut. You've seen him lots without it. But you're sayin' you think Rodney was a pretty good dad?"

"Well, he was there, wasn't he? And they loved each other. What else can I say?"

"Not much, Mama. That about sums it up, I guess. Now you get a good sleep. I'll send DaShawn over tomorrow. Goodnight."

Harry closed the phone slowly. Yeah, *Rodney was there, and they loved each other*. Of course, his mother's senile summary didn't represent an in-depth case study, but it suggested better parenting than Harry had provided for his own son. And DaShawn certainly hadn't picked up his good attitude and manners from the streets. A caring parent had to have given the boy some input into his life … and he was sure that hadn't been Donita.

A new appreciation for Rodney grew in Harry, but at the same time it gave his heart another twist for missing out on so much. It also complicated what he should do now. If Rodney was a decent person—a decent father—and he got out of jail, Harry couldn't very well object to him taking DaShawn if he wanted him.

So should he help? And how?

Chapter 26

WHEN DASHAWN GOT HOME FROM SCHOOL the next afternoon, Harry sent him over to his mother's as promised to help with the chores, but he was glad when the boy came bouncing back into the apartment again. DaShawn seemed happy to be home ... and Harry realized anew how much he enjoyed having the boy around. Made it hard to think about the possibility of Rodney getting custody if he got out of jail. Well, that was down the road. He didn't have to think about it today. The guys were coming over tonight for Bible study and they had to get ready.

At least they still had Estelle's leftovers for supper, and DaShawn didn't even have to be told to do the dishes. Everything was still generally in good order from Estelle's careful housekeeping, but Harry smiled as he watched his grandson bustle around the kitchen, putting things away and cleaning off the counter.

"How many chairs you want me to put out, Grandpa?"

Harry scanned the living/dining room, using his mirrors like an inverted periscope. "Let's see. The couch can take three, my recliner makes four. I'll stay on this thing." He slapped the legs of his massage chair. "Why don't you bring three of the dining room chairs over and arrange them so we can sit in a circle?"

DaShawn hopped right to it. Obviously, tonight was a big deal.

"I've also got some wooden TV trays in the hall closet. Could you get one and set it up in front of me? I'll use it like a desk to hold my Bible. I can probably write on it, too."

He was thinking he needed to write Rodney. Sending him a letter might be the only way to communicate right now. Rodney could probably phone back—if he had phone privileges—but there wasn't much chance of calling in and reaching him. Harry knew it had been too long since they'd talked. What would he say to his son, anyway?

"Here, Grandpa. Is this what you want?"

"That's it, but it's kind of dusty, isn't it? There's a rag and some furniture spray under the kitchen sink. Could you wipe it off for me?" He watched DaShawn with his mirror. "No, the other cabinet. Yeah, there ya go."

Harry wanted to talk with the brothers about how someone could know he was hearing God's voice and not just his own wishful thoughts. But with DaShawn at tonight's meeting, how could he approach that question? The best example was what he thought God was telling him in the Book of Proverbs about whether to accept Fagan's offer of help to get Rodney out of jail. But he didn't want to talk about that—especially his own ambivalent feelings—with DaShawn right there listening. He gritted his teeth. If only he hadn't teed off Estelle last night, DaShawn would still be over at the Baxters, and he could discuss the subject freely.

But DaShawn was enjoying every minute of it. The door buzzer sounded a few minutes before seven, and DaShawn ran to answer it. "Who's there?"

"It's Ben."

Harry waved the go-ahead, and in a few minutes, DaShawn opened the door to a huffing and puffing Ben Garfield. In his mirrors, Harry caught a glimpse of Ben's bulbous nose and white pompadour hair.

"So this is your home sweet home, *nu*? No, no, don't get up, Harry. Why do ya think I climbed all those stairs? Keep your head down, they're tellin' ya. Ha, ha! Just like the army, huh? *Keep your head and your butt down when you do the low crawl!*" Ben sounded like a drill sergeant. "Here, DaShawn, take these *rugelach* into the kitchen and find a plate for 'em. The boys'll love 'em."

"What's that you brought? Never heard of it before."

"Pastries, Jewish pastries. You never heard of *rugelach*? Ruth sent 'em over. Cut back, she says to me, you need to lose a few. Then she feeds me like this! *Nosh* on these, they're good. Some apricot, some walnut and raisin."

The buzzer sounded again, and Harry heard the rest of the guys coming up the stairs ... yes, all four of them—Denny, Josh, Peter, and Carl—Harry recognized each voice. They were talking loud and sounded like a herd of elephants. He hoped the neighbors were out.

"Come in, come on in here. Door's open."

Harry used his double mirror to view each guy and wave a greeting as they came in.

"Hey, DaShawn," Josh said as he bumped fists with the boy, "you gonna join us tonight?"

"Grandpa said I could."

"Glad to hear it. Us young guys gotta stick together. Right?"

"Ha," said Denny. "I told Harry he oughta let his grandson sit in on a few men's events once in a while. The wisdom of the ages might do him some good."

"Hey, don't you mean the wisdom of the *aged*?"

Everyone laughed as Denny shook DaShawn's hand and greeted Harry.

"Hey, bro," said Carl Hickman as he grabbed Harry's shoulder, "whaddaya puttin' your face in that thing for. It's supposed to go around your neck."

"What are you talkin' about?" said Denny. "He's doin' it right. I helped him set it up the other night."

"Nah, nah. I seen pictures of those things before. They go around your neck. That's what they used to take slaves out of Africa with, a big long 'Y' stick, tied around each guy's neck, from one to the next. As a matter of fact, I think I still got some scars from one right here. Ha, ha!" He slapped Harry on the back. "Hey, how's that eye doin'?"

"Okay, I guess. Help yourselves to some of those … uh, those whatchamacallits—"

"*Rugelach*. I told you that already."

"Yeah, the pastries over there on the table. Ruth sent 'em."

"And they're good, too," added DaShawn through a mouthful.

The *rugelach* disappeared as fast as snowflakes in August. And after a few more minutes of joshing and joking, followed by an opening prayer, Peter Douglass said, "Seriously, Harry, how you doin'?"

Harry hesitated. He still felt awkward about blurting it all out. But they asked.

"Well, doc says things are going pretty good—no infection, no bleeding. 'Course, in my case, good's relative. You understand?" When no one responded, Harry continued. "Four times a day I gotta take this patch off and put drops in my eye. And I ain't kiddin' you when I say my eye looks like a meatball sittin' there in my face. Just like a hunk of hamburger. You wouldn't want to see it."

Everyone remained silent, and Harry regretted being so graphic. The guys obviously didn't know what to say, and he hadn't meant to ask for sympathy. He was just tellin' it like it was. "But you know what ..." He had to get out of this awkward moment. "... it's all good. You follow me?"

There were sighs and several guys moved again in their chairs.

"Well, I don't," rumbled Ben. "Your eye, you say it's like hamburger, but you call it all good? What's with that?"

"I think what he's sayin'," offered Denny, "is that good things can come out of bad situations sometimes. Isn't that right, Harry? Like Joseph in the Bible. His brothers sold him into slavery. He spent all those years falsely accused and in prison. But then God used him to save a lot of people, including his brothers. And he ended up telling them, 'You meant it for evil, but God meant it for good.'"

"Sure, sure, after he was a prince, second most powerful man in Egypt. But *oy veh*! Look at Harry here. He's sittin' there with a hamburger eyeball. Good, smood! That's *mishegoss*."

"Look. I'm sorry I used the word 'hamburger,' and maybe I shouldn't have called it all good. Who knows? But there's actually something I'm strugglin' with that I was hopin' you guys could help me out with tonight. So I don't want to get us off on the hamburger too much. It was just a ... ya know, a figure of speech. Uh... by the way, Ben, you eat hamburger?"

Everyone roared with laughter.

"Yeah, yeah, sure. But it's gotta be kosher."

More laughter.

Ben looked offended. "You laugh. Kosher we don't keep with most things, but kosher beef doesn't carry Mad Cow disease. So there! Might be a clue to what's wrong with you *goyim*. Too much junk hamburger from who knows where!"

"All right, all right, everybody." With a grin on his face, Peter held up his hands. "Let's get back to Harry. Harry, this is your night. We came over here to support you, and that's what we're here to do. How can we help?"

"Well, it's a faith thing or … or a Bible thing." Harry caught a glimpse of DaShawn in his mirror. Maybe he should start back a ways. "I haven't shared this with you guys, but I just about lost my faith over this eye thing. I kept praying for God to reach out and heal me, and I know you guys were prayin', too. But it seemed like every time I turned around, every time I went to the doctor, things were getting' worse. I started wondering if God was there at all. Whether He even existed."

"That's a bad place," said Carl. "I been there before."

"Yeah, you know it's bad. Pretty soon nothin' has any meaning." Harry swallowed the lump that had caught in his throat. "Anyway, when I realized it was more important to me to know that God was with me than if I regained my eyesight, I knew He'd taught me something. And if He'd taught me, then He was there!"

"Hallelujah! Hallelujah!"

"That's right. You got that."

"Anyway, that was my important lesson for the year … maybe for my life. But it wasn't much later that something else happened. I heard God tell me, 'The nightmare is over!' He actually spoke to me."

"Like an audible voice?" said Josh.

"Oh, I heard it, clear as day. I'm not sayin' *you* would have heard it if you'd been sittin' right beside me. Truth be told, I think God spoke it right inside my head. But it was clear, as clear as any of you guys talkin' tonight. No one can make me doubt what I heard. Since then, nothing's gotten worse—in spite of my hamburger eyeball, Ben." He adjusted his mirror to grin at his friend. "But that's not my question. What I'm wondering is, how can we know when God has spoken to us, like from the Bible? Estelle says God speaks to her all the time from the Bible."

"Ah, that's a good one," said Carl. "That's a good one. I want to hear what some of you Bible scholars have to say about that.

Like I heard this old story about a guy who thought he could use the Bible like an Ouija Board."

"Ha!" said Josh. "How'd he do that?"

"Well, he'd close his eyes, flip open the Bible, and put his finger down on the page. And whatever phrase his finger landed on, he believed that was God talkin' to him."

"So what happened?"

"Well, he was wanting to know what to do with his life, so he did his Ouija Board thing, and his finger landed on the verse that said, 'Judas went out and hanged himself.' But the guy didn't think that gave him much direction, so he tried again, and this time his finger landed on, 'Go thou and do likewise.'"

Everyone laughed, DaShawn the loudest.

"There we go. At least my man, DaShawn, here appreciates my comedic career. Give me five, bro."

Harry heard their hands slap, and then Peter Douglass said, "That's actually a good example of taking Scripture out of context."

"So how do we avoid such foolishness?" Josh asked.

"You gotta follow some guidelines," Peter said. "First of all, we need to make sure we're not taking something out of context. Second, we need to ask whether it was said exclusively to one individual, or whether it was God's instruction or promise to everyone."

Harry started to raise his head from the donut. "Whadda you mean?" He put his head back down, but this was getting to his question.

"Well, just because God told Noah to build an ark, that doesn't necessarily mean we should all build arks. Right?"

"Guess not. But what about something like where God said, 'I'll never leave you nor forsake you'?"

"That's a good one, Harry, because God said it to Joshua, so can we apply it to ourselves?"

Josh spoke up. "Didn't Jesus say almost the same thing at the end of his ministry? Something like, 'I'll be with you always'?"

"That's right, and even the words to Joshua are repeated in the New Testament. Someone turn to Hebrews 13 and 5, and read the last part of the verse."

Boy, Peter Douglass sure knew his Bible. Harry flipped his pages. "Here it is. 'Never will I leave you; never will I forsake you."

"Okay," said Peter. "That is quoted from the Old Testament. But in context, it is given as a promise to all believers, just like Jesus' words at the end of Matthew."

This was beginning to make sense. But Harry still had a question.

"What about something more personal?" Harry was thinking about the verses in Proverbs and how they might apply to Fagan.

"Don't get me wrong. I do believe God speaks personally and privately to His children today just as He did in the past. Those words, *the nightmare is over*, could very well have been the voice of God speaking directly to you. Another way God speaks in that personal way is to 'quicken' a Bible verse to us, so we have a deep sense from the Holy Spirit that those words were meant for us."

Ben jumped in. "Wait a minute. You mentioned Noah earlier. Are you saying God could tell someone to build an ark just by them reading what He said to Noah in the Bible?"

"Hmmm, not in that case. God told Noah to build an ark because He was going to destroy the world with a flood. But after the flood, remember the rainbow? It represented God's promise that He would never again destroy the earth by water. So anyone claiming that message, would not be getting it from God. See what I'm sayin'?"

Peter stopped and rubbed his chin thoughtfully. "You see, anytime we think a 'personal word from the Lord' is telling us to *do* something or something specific is going to happen, we need to make sure it's genuinely consistent with the rest of the Bible, because God never contradicts Himself. That's why we need to know His Word. It's the primary test."

Everyone was quiet for a few moments, and Harry scanned the room with his mirrors. "DaShawn! What you doin'? You textin' someone?"

"Yes sir. Just askin' Robbie what he's doing tomorrow."

"Look, if you don't want to be in here, that's okay." *Better than okay!* thought Harry. "You're free to go to your room. No problem. But if you're gonna be in here, you need to be part of what's goin' on, and we're having a conversation that you asked to take part in."

"But I didn't have anything to say."

"That's okay. You can still listen respectfully."

"Yes, Grandpa." The boy closed his cell phone and put it in his pocket.

Peter Douglass was smiling warmly when Harry looked back at him.

"You know we're glad you're with us tonight, young man."

DaShawn nodded.

"So, where was I? Oh yeah, there's a couple of other things I want to mention. One way to test any prophecy that predicts the future—and that's what we're talking about here—is whether it comes true. Hold on a minute. I gotta find something." He turned the pages in his Bible. "Here we are, Deuteronomy 18 and 21...

You may say to yourselves, "How can we know when a message has not been spoken by the Lord?" If what a prophet proclaims in the name of the Lord does not take place or come true, that

240

is a message the Lord has not spoken. That prophet has spoken presumptuously. Do not be afraid of him.

"So in your case, Harry, part of whether it was the Lord you heard or just your own wishful thinking will be whether those words prove true. Hear what I'm sayin'?"

"Yeah. Well, so far things have turned around."

"That's good, but Paul tells us in 1 Thessalonians 5 to test prophecy. This presumes it can be for real, but it also acknowledges that we could be mistaken. Another way to test prophecy is to submit it to other wise believers who are grounded in the Word. If God speaks to their hearts to confirm its validity, that adds more weight. Personally, I sense the Holy Spirit confirming the truth of the word Harry heard, and I pray it's true."

While Peter had been talking, Harry had been ticking off in his mind the ways the other "words from the Lord" might be true, the ones from Proverbs he'd applied to Fagan. They seemed to pass most of Peter's five or six principles, but the idea of testing them with other mature believers seemed all the more important. But how could he do that without putting the whole thing out in front of DaShawn?

Once the brothers had left, clapping him on the back and shaking hands with DaShawn, Harry called his grandson over to him. "I know that was some pretty deep stuff. You glad you came?"

"Yeah. Those pastries were good."

Harry gave him a squeeze. "How many did you have?"

"I dunno."

"That's okay. You head on to bed now. School tomorrow."

"Yeah. Good night, Grandpa."

"I love you, son."

And DaShawn was like a son to him, such a joyful experience. Harry got up and moved to the couch. He had to change positions sometimes. Then he remembered that he was going to write Rodney. He needed to trust God with the outcome. And the more he thought about it, writing Rodney and offering to try and find him a better lawyer didn't involve any moral issues. He didn't even need the words from Proverbs to go forward with that.

He got back up, found a tablet and pen in his desk, and took them to his massage chair with the TV tray writing table situated in front and began to write.

"Dear Rodney, I want to ask your forgiveness for not doing more to get you out of jail. If you agree, there's a lawyer I know who might help ..."

Chapter 27

WEDNESDAY WAS A TEACHER INSTITUTE DAY. Why they needed one when school had been in session only a week, Harry had no idea, but he was glad to have DaShawn around. "Face down" was getting old. Harry felt like he was confined in a straight jacket. What was supposed to be a relaxing massage chair twisted him like the rack. By mid-morning, the daytime TV was as entertaining as a toothache.

"Isn't there anything better on that tube?"

DaShawn handed Harry the controller. "Here, Grandpa, you try. Can I go over to Robbie's?"

"It's raining out, isn't it?"

"No, it stopped."

"Well, is his mom home?"

"I dunno. I'll see."

But before he opened his cell phone, it rang in his hands. "Yeah?"

"You should answer with hello." Harry whispered loudly.

DaShawn got up and headed down the hall, away from Harry's interruptions. "Yes, Miss Estelle, we're doing okay."

Estelle? Harry frowned. What could she want with DaShawn? Why didn't she call him on his phone?

In a moment, DaShawn came bouncing back into the living room. "Miss Estelle needs help cooking lunch for the shelter. Can I go down there?"

"Now?"

"Yeah. She wants me to help her."

What was going on? There were lots of women at that shelter who Estelle could recruit if she needed help. She usually had one or two scheduled for each day. So what's with that?

"How would you get down there?"

"She said Josh Baxter's comin' down right now to work on something at Miss Gabby's six-flat, and he could give me a ride if I'm downstairs waitin' when he comes by. But he's in a hurry."

"Well, that gets you there. But how will you get home?"

He spoke into the phone again, then glanced up. "She says she'll make sure someone gives me a ride. Maybe Josh when he comes back up this way."

"Okay. Good enough for me. You do what she tells you, now."

DaShawn was out the door and down the stairs like a bird from a cage.

Harry got up and watched his feet take him to the bathroom, then wandered around the apartment wishing he could have gone with his grandson. Maybe he should've. Maybe he could use his mirror to see the stoplights and check the traffic. Maybe ... Oh, that was crazy.

He wandered into DaShawn's room. The boy hadn't made his bed. Should've had him do that first. It was no good turning into a couple of bachelors. They needed to maintain some order. Mess can depress!

Still keeping his head down, he started to leave the room when he noticed a thick book on the shelf by the door. He picked it up ... Estelle's Bible. What was it doing here? Surely she'd need it.

He should've sent it with DaShawn. Estelle's name was inscribed in the front on the top of the title page along with her old South-side address. He flipped through it … boy, she had a lot of verses marked with a yellow highlighter. He ought to read his Bible more.

Harry shuffled back toward the living room, turning the worn, dog-eared pages between which were sandwiched little memen-tos—a pressed purple and yellow pansy, a faded picture of an elderly couple with definite family resemblances. He studied it closely. Is that what Estelle might look like when she got old? Not bad … kind eyes, gentle smile, content. Like mother, like daughter. Estelle would be someone to grow old with, wouldn't she?

He sat down on the couch, still turning the pages, feeling a little guilty for snooping. Ah … a yellowed newspaper clipping with a picture of a smiling basketball player, ball tucked under his long arm: "Michael Williams, 1993 MVP, Wendell Phillips High School." So Leroy—or Michael, as he was called until recently—was a hoopster. Would he ever recover from his burns—and his troubled mind—sufficiently to play again? Harry shrugged. At least he could take him to some games when this eye stuff was over. Leroy might like that.

Harry was setting the Bible aside when he noticed one more item tucked inside the back cover. He pulled out a napkin from Riva's Restaurant on Chicago's Navy Pier, the place he'd taken Es-telle the night he'd planned to propose to her. He turned it over and saw she'd been doodling, perhaps when he'd left her to go to the bathroom. But it wasn't the swirls and curlicues around the edge that caught his attention. It was the words in her flowing script: "Estelle Williams, Estelle & Harry, Harry & Estelle, Estelle & Harry Bentley, Estelle Bentley."

Breathe, Harry! Breathe! In spite of what's written on that napkin, you still gotta breathe. Ahhh! What had she been writing that for?

Like a schoolgirl with a silly crush, she'd been playing with their names ... and ... and imagining they were married.

That had been before she'd known about his eye, before he'd decided he couldn't burden her with his problem, especially if it showed up in his right eye, too. But ... had she really loved him that much? Would she have said yes that night?

O Lord, the things that might have been! The older I get, the more paths not taken I can look back and see. Tears were spilling out of his good eye and perhaps his bad one, too. He missed her. He missed her bustling around the house. He missed her touch on his shoulder. He even missed her fussin' at him. Maybe he'd been too hasty getting her to switch with DaShawn. She'd probably still be here if he hadn't suggested ... actually, if he hadn't *sent* her away.

There was no getting around it: He'd been the one who sent her away!

But would she really have said yes to his marriage proposal? He again studied the napkin where she'd tried out the sound of his last name. At least she wasn't one of those women who scorned taking the name of their husbands. She was his kind of partner. They could've made a great team together.

He put the napkin back in the Bible and placed it on the arm of the couch. She would need her Bible, and he ought to figure out some way to send it to her. On the other hand, if he did nothing, she'd have to come by and get it herself. Then he could see her again. But what would he say? Especially now that he'd seen that napkin. But that was silly, putting more meaning in a doodle than the paper was worth.

And yet, was there a way to reclaim the path he'd not taken? Was there still a chance for him and Estelle?

DASHAWN CAME IN AT ABOUT TWO-THIRTY carrying a plastic Jewel shopping bag filled with food Estelle had sent home with him … "because they're leftovers I need to clean out of the refrigerator," she'd told him.

But DaShawn said he'd helped peel the potatoes for the tub of potato salad and the green beans and the chicken were still warm. "That's what we had for lunch today, Grandpa."

"And how about this chocolate cake?"

"I dunno. She just put it in."

Yeah, thought Harry, *she had to get rid of it. No, she's still looking out for us.* "Why don't you put it in the refrigerator. We can have it for supper."

Harry heard the refrigerator close.

"Hey, Grandpa, can I go over to Robbie's now?"

"Check with his mom." Harry was bored, but it wasn't fair to keep DaShawn around just to entertain him.

DaShawn ran off to his room and came skipping back a moment later. "She wants to know if I can stay for dinner. She said she'll bring me home afterwards. Can I?"

Harry tried not to show his disappointment. "I guess, but I want you home by eight. You've got school tomorrow."

THE NEXT DAY WAS JUST AS TEDIOUS until Harry's door buzzer sounded in the early afternoon. He clicked off the TV and buzzed his guest in without checking who it was with the intercom. Certainly it was Estelle, coming for her Bible.

But the slow tread on the stairs wasn't hers. It paused for a minute or so on each landing of the three flights.

Curious, Harry took his mirror but was startled to see who his visitor was when he opened the door.

"Pastor Clark! Good to see you."

There he stood, thin and a little haggard in his cardigan sweater, gray slacks and loafers, looking like the old Mr. Rogers. Harry swung the door wider. "You didn't need to climb all the way up here. But come on in."

"Well, I wanted to check on you personally, and ..." He had to stop and catch his breath. "... and since they tell me you have to keep your head bowed, I thought I'd better ... whew ... I thought I'd better drop by and cash in on all this praying you're sending up."

"Ha, ha. Can't claim to be using much of my time praying, head bowed or not, but I'm glad you dropped by. Here, you better have a seat over there on the couch. Can I get you some coffee or water, soda, something else?" He hoped SouledOut's co-pastor was okay. His white skin seemed paler than usual.

"Water would be fine. I've pretty much cut out the caffeine. But you don't have to go to any trouble."

"It's no trouble." Harry moved into the kitchen and started filling a couple of glasses. "You want a straw? I gotta use one 'cause I can't tip my head up. But I've learned to get around pretty good with these mirrors. Hope you don't mind lookin' at the top of my head, though."

"Well, it's a little bright and shiny, have to say that."

"See, now there you go. I was even able to shave this morning. How 'bout that? Only one little nick in the back."

The pastor took the glass of water Harry handed him and took a sip. "Ah, that's good."

Harry turned his massage chair around so it was facing the couch instead of the TV and set himself up with his mirror. "Just pretend we're talkin' by Skype."

"Oh, yeah, that's that computer video thing. You got it?"

"No, but I heard it's pretty cool." Harry shrugged. "Don't know who I'd call, though."

"I know who I'd call, a pastor friend of mine in Malawi ... if he could get a good connection. We sometimes email." He waved his hand as though he were dismissing the subject and took another sip of his water. "So, tell me about your eyes. I've heard snatches, but tell me the whole story."

Harry told him, right from the beginning.

When he was done, the pastor just sat there nodding for a few minutes. "I can imagine that must've been pretty scary."

Lots of people had expressed genuine concern for Harry, and he appreciated it, from every person. He knew they cared. But he remembered the tears that had trickled down Pastor Clark's face when he'd returned to church after his heart attack, and he knew the man had "been there." He'd understand what Harry'd been through. He was going to ask him about it, when the pastor said, "So, how's this affecting you and Estelle?"

Whoo, was this guy psychic or something? No, unless it was just a coincidence, it had to be the Holy Spirit.

"Uh ... Estelle? Yeah, well, I don't know." Harry swallowed and was glad his head was down so the mirror wouldn't reveal the liquid pooling in his eyes. "I guess the thing is, I don't want to tie her down to me and my problems. It's the least I can do."

"You mean your eye problems?"

"Yeah. You know, she's got enough on her plate with her son and all. You know 'bout him gettin' burned, don't you?"

Pastor Clark nodded. "That was terrible. But are you saying you don't think you can't be any support to her on that?"

"Well ..." Harry hadn't thought of it that way before. He blew out a long breath. "Actually, my involvement may have been the cause of the incident. I mean, it looks like one of my old enemies from my days on the force tried to retaliate and get to me through Estelle. Her son just got caught in the middle. But … that's another story."

Pastor Clark was quiet for a moment. "Sorry to hear that. But what makes you think Estelle doesn't need your support now?"

"Huh. Can't be much support to her like this, can I?"

"Is that what she'd say?"

"Probably not."

"But you don't want what you're going through to be a burden on her. Is that it?"

"Yeah, pretty much."

"How'd you make it this far?"

"Well, I … actually, I had to learn that God's been with me through it all."

"Oh yeah? You sure about that? I mean, are you sure He's been with you?"

What was going on? Harry hadn't expected the *pastor* to challenge him on this. But he wasn't going to let those questions throw him.

"Yeah, I'm sure. In fact, God spoke directly to me and told me that *the nightmare is over*. Those were the exact words. I tell you, Pastor, it was amazing! Nothing like that's ever happened to me before."

Pastor Clark chuckled. "Oh, I believe you. Been there myself. But tell me, was this the worst thing you've ever been through?"

Harry considered. "Well … Yeah. I think so."

"And you're sure God's been with you through it all?"

"Uh … now I am, but not for a while there. Kept sayin', 'I believe, but help my unbelief.' "

"Done that, too." In his mirror, Harry saw the pastor's soft smile broaden. "Just one question: If you're sure God's been with

you through your worst time—even spoke to you in the middle of
it—wouldn't that be a pretty safe space to invite Estelle into?"

Harry squirmed. He didn't know what to say.

"Don't answer now. Just think about it. Okay?"

Chapter 28

Pastor Clark stood up, indicating his intention to leave. "Please understand," he said, holding out his hand, "I'm not trying to play matchmaker between you and Estelle. There's a lot to consider as to whether God's calling the two of you together in marriage. But I was just speaking about what sounded like fear over a battle that's already been won. Does that make sense?"

Harry got off his chair, fumbling to aim his mirror in the right direction as he shook the pastor's hand. "I hear you. It's been helpful. Maybe we could talk some more later."

"I'd like that." The pastor took a step toward the door and then turned back. "By the way, are you interested in becoming a member at SouledOut? We're having a membership service for a friend of yours, Gabriella Fairbanks, Sunday after next. We'd be glad to receive you the same day if you want."

"With the Firecracker, huh?" Harry thought for a moment. "I guess I'd be done with this face-down thing by then, but ..." What about Estelle? What if he did break things off with her? Wouldn't that be a little awkward being in the same church? After all, he was only at SouledOut because of her. That he'd found God again was good, but maybe he ought to go to another church. "Could I have a little time to think about it?"

"Sure. You busy a week from today?"

"No busier than you see me right now."

"Why don't I drop by next Thursday? We can talk about it then."

When Pastor Clark was gone, Harry went into the kitchen, popped a can of Pepsi, and put a straw into it. He sucked a few swallows as he paced up and down the hall—head down—telling himself he needed a little exercise. But what Pastor Clark had said about Estelle was the real source of his agitation. What did he mean about *"a battle that's already been won"*?

Harry didn't feel like he'd won anything. But what was it the pastor said? Think about whether inviting Estelle into his space was safe. Huh! He'd thought he was protecting her from "his space," from himself and his circumstances. But ... maybe not. Pastor Clark might be right. The worst of what he'd been through had been transformed when he realized God was right there in the middle of it and even had a purpose for it.

Perhaps being in God's presence and purpose was not something he needed to protect Estelle from. Anywhere with God was a good place for both of them. From a distant memory of attending church with his mother, Harry remembered a line from an old gospel song: *"Anywhere with Jesus I can safely go ..."* The tune was just a bouncy little ditty. But the words were deep.

And they were true! So what had he been doing?

A hot wave swirled through his head causing him to almost lose his balance. He put his hand out to steady himself against the wall.

He'd taken the wrong path. He'd been trying to "protect" Estelle from something he didn't need to fear. Was it too late? Was there any way back? At the very least, he needed to apologize, confess that even though he hadn't meant to, he'd messed things up big time.

Would she forgive him?

Estelle was a gracious woman, but she'd warned him more than once not to mess with her heart. It was a big deal, perhaps too big for her to give him another chance ... unless, unless he proposed to her on the spot. That way she'd know he was serious.

Yeah, she'd know he was serious, but she'd probably say no, thinking he was out of his mind, too many pain pills or something. No, he had to do it right, one step at a time. He had to apologize, and then if she forgave him, he'd have to come up with a really unique time and place to propose to her. But he was gonna do it!

He made his way back into the living room and spotted Estelle's Bible on the end of the couch ... perfect! He sat down to phone her, but first he opened the Bible again and took out the napkin. The ink from Estelle's pen had soaked into the absorbent paper, giving their names a fuzzy look. But there was no question. She was trying out the idea of taking his last name. Maybe it could still happen.

He put the napkin back and dialed her number. It rang and rang and then went to voice mail. "Uh ... Estelle, this is Harry. I was callin' to let you know that you left your Bible over here, and I thought you might be lookin' for it. Also ... also, there's something I need to talk—"

Beep!

What was with the phone companies these days? They didn't even give you enough time to finish your message. With such high prices, couldn't they afford another megabyte or two of memory so a guy could finish what he had to say?

He stared down at his phone. Should he call back and leave the last half of his message, let her know he had something important to say? No. She'd get back to him about the Bible, and he could tell her then.

He closed the phone and tossed it onto the table, then turned his massage chair around to watch TV, but it was all trash. Within minutes he was up again, pacing down the hall, back to the kitchen ... and not keeping his head down very well either. On his second trip, he stopped in the bathroom.

When he came out and returned to the dining room, he noticed the red light flashing on his phone announcing voice mail. How could that be? He hadn't heard it ring. Maybe it was a message from earlier in the day. He picked it up and played it back.

"Hi. Got your message and know you need a ride to the doctor's tomorrow. I'll stop by about 8:30. DaShawn should be off to school by then. Okay? I can get my Bible then. Don't call me. I'm busy the rest of the day."

"*Busy the rest of the day*"? His heart sank. Sounded like she was willing to help him out, give him a ride to the doctor or send food home with DaShawn, but she didn't want to deal with him in any other way.

Leave it alone, Harry. Give her some space.

He knew that's what he should do, but oh, it was so hard. He'd have to wait until tomorrow.

THE BUZZER SOUNDED THE NEXT MORNING before DaShawn left for school, and feeling certain it was Estelle, Harry buzzed her in. But a few moments later, when he didn't hear her climbing the stairs, he thought he hadn't held the buzzer down long enough. He pushed the button again. Then he pushed Talk ... "Estelle, you there?"

"Yeah, I'm here."

"You comin' up?"

"Why? You not ready?"

"No, I'm ready."

"Then bring my Bible down."

Oh, boy, she was still in a snit.

He called to his grandson. "You ready for school? Let's go." It would be good to have him along when he went down to break the ice. Maybe they should even drive him to school. It was only a few blocks out of the way.

But even that didn't help. DaShawn sat in the back, and after they said hello to each other, neither said a thing during the five-minute ride to Bethune Elementary.

After they dropped DaShawn off, Harry kept his head humbly bowed but felt he had to say something. "I put your Bible in the back seat."

"Thanks."

Okay, if at first you don't succeed, try again. "My eye is looking a little better, not so much like hamburger."

"Good."

"Yeah. I noticed when I was putting the drops in this morning."

Harry used his mirror to steal a peak at Estelle. Her jaw was set, and she was busy driving. Too busy, he thought.

"And guess what? ... I could see the bubble, like a pool of quicksilver resting in the bottom half of my eye. And I could see over the top of it, too."

"Hmmm."

Harry waited for a moment. "Strange. I couldn't figure out why the bubble was on the bottom. It was supposed to float to the top, so why was it sitting at the bottom?"

"Guess you'll have to ask the doctor."

"Yeah, I guess." This wasn't getting anywhere. She wasn't about to warm up. He wished she would. It would make it easier to apologize.

They rode in silence for a couple of more blocks, then Harry cleared his throat. "Uh … Estelle, there's something I gotta tell you." He paused.

"Last time you said that, you'd spent the afternoon in a bar—"

"No, no it's not that. It's about my eye. Well, not exactly my eye, but my fear—my fear that it was unfair to burden you with my problems, especially with all you're going through with Leroy."

He checked Estelle again with his mirror and thought the set of her jaw had relaxed a little. "I was afraid, Estelle."

"I know you were, Harry." Her voice had softened. "I know."

"And if this problem had spread to both eyes and I would have ended up blind, I couldn't bear to burden you with that … at least, I didn't think I could because I didn't believe I could live with it myself. But then …"

"Yeah …"

"Then God let me know He was right there with me. He'd been with me the whole time, and I realized His presence was far more important than my physical sight. It was like … like I got a second sight into what mattered most."

They were driving through a rough section of the city, the near Eastside, and Estelle clicked the locks on the doors.

"Everything okay?" he asked.

"Yeah, I just … you know, precaution."

"Sure." He thought for a minute. "Precaution … I guess I was being too cautious about you. Please don't take this wrong, but while I was learning to trust that God was with me, I wasn't trustin' Him for you. I was afraid if things got worse, how would you cope? It'd be too much for you. You follow me?"

"Uh … kinda, but could you break it down a little more?"

His hopes rose. She wanted to know. "Well, yesterday I was talking to Pastor Clark, and he asked me a question I couldn't answer. Basically, he was askin' if God's presence was enough for me, why didn't I think it was enough for you?"

"What? Why didn't you think it was sufficient for me?"

"That's where I was wrong, Estelle. That's what I'm tryin' to tell you. I was pushing you away from me because I wasn't trusting God to do for you the very thing He was trying to teach me."

"So, you're sayin' you didn't think I could handle your eye problem. Well, let me tell you, Harry Bentley, I've faced harder—"

"Hang on, Estelle. It wasn't about you. It was about God—or rather my lack of faith that He would be with you whatever happened to me. Just like He's been with me. I was tryin' to protect you from something that was not a danger. Don't you see?"

She was quiet for a moment, and then she said, "That's what you were thinking, Harry?"

"Yeah, but I was wrong. Can you forgive me?"

She reached over and touched his arm. "Yes. Of course, Harry. I do forgive you. It means a lot that you were trying to protect me, but you're right. The Lord's presence is my best protection. And that's a given."

Her touch nearly made him cry. Swallowing the lump in his throat, he said, "Yesterday I was thinking about this old song: 'Anywhere with Jesus I can safely go.' You know that one?"

"Oh, you mean …" And she started singing a soulful rendition unlike anything Harry'd ever heard. With a laugh, he joined in as the words flooded back.

Anywhere with Jesus I can safely go,
Anywhere He leads me in this world below;

Anywhere without Him, dearest joys would fade;
Anywhere with Jesus I am not afraid.

Anywhere! Anywhere!
Fear I cannot know;
Anywhere with Jesus
I can safely go.

Dr. Racine was pleased with Harry's progress. "Here," he said, swinging a large instrument around for Harry to lean into. It resembled a pair of flat binoculars with large adjustable lenses. "I'll set your left one to duplicate your missing lens. Tell me what you can read from that chart on the wall."

Harry stared. Everything was a little foggy, but he was seeing again with his left eye. He read several lines until the letters were too blurry. The doctor had him do the same thing with the pin-hole shield.

"That's about 20/50, pretty good at this point."

Harry was ecstatic. "And does everything else look good?"

"Looks good to me. And the bubble has subsided enough that I think we could do the laser work today, if that's okay with you."

Ooo, laser. Harry was not at all eager for that. The laser treatment was the one thing that had really been painful in this whole ordeal.

Perhaps the doctor saw the expression on his face, because he quickly said, "I won't do too many. I just want to pin down that area where the detachment was. You don't want that to start again."

"Well, okay … let's go ahead. But speaking of the bubble, I could see it this morning when I put the drops in, but it looked like it was lying in the bottom of my eye."

"Oh, yeah. It might look that way, but it's not. When light comes into your eye and forms an image on the back on your retina, it's upside down, like with a pinhole camera, if you remember. But the brain is a marvelous thing, it turns it right-side-up. However, what you are seeing *inside* your eye—the bubble—is not a projected image. It's actually there. But your brain still flips it—upside down, in this case. When you're sitting like you are now, without being face down, the bubble floats to the top of your eyeball. When you look out, you're seeing the image that comes in under the bubble. Again, your brain flips it and tells you you're looking over the top of the bubble."

Harry played with these mechanics in his mind as a way to distract himself while the doctor began to shoot him with laser. One ... two ... three ...

"There." Dr. Racine finally moved the apparatus away from Harry's face and turned on the room lights. "Twenty-four more shots for a total of eighty-nine. I think that ought to hold you. You okay?"

Harry stood up slowly. "I think so." But he was sure glad Estelle was there to take him home.

Half an hour later, as they drove north through the afternoon traffic, Harry sat up a little straighter, the pain nearly gone. "And one more thing, Estelle ..."

"Yeah. What's that?"

"I'm gonna become a member at SouledOut."

"You what? Get outta here!"

"Yeah. I've decided. Pastor Clark asked me about it yesterday. I'll be joinin' the church Sunday after next."

"Hmm. Harry Bentley, you're a surprise a minute."

Chapter 29

SATURDAY AFTERNOON THE *LAW AND ORDER* RINGTONE on Harry's phone played four times, and he was afraid it would go to voicemail before he found it. "Yeah. Harry here."

"Got your letter."

"Rodney? That you?"

"Yeah. So, who's this lawyer you know?"

The kid sure cut to the chase. Not, "How you doin', Dad? Good to hear from you. Of course, I forgive you." Just, "*So, who's this lawyer you know?*" Guess that's how he'd raised him ... or *didn't* raise him.

"Thanks for callin', Rodney. I didn't know how to get in touch with you any other way since I can't leave the house—"

"What? You gotta be kiddin'!" His laugh was sardonic. "You can't leave the house? What's the matter, you on house arrest or somethin'?"

"Huh. You might call it that. I had some operations on my eye, and it's the doctor that makes me stay in. Plus, I gotta keep my head down the whole time."

Rodney's laugh had a bitter edge to it, and he switched right back to his own agenda. "So, what about a lawyer?"

Harry took a deep breath. "He's someone I met on the job. One of the best defense attorneys in the city. And if what you told me is true, he oughta—"

"It was the truth! What, you think I made all that up? I'm tellin' ya, they—"

"Rodney, Rodney, I wasn't doubting you. It was just a figure of speech. All right? Let me start over. From what you told me, this guy might be able to help. His name is Alan Sondano, a big Swede with yellow hair, but he knows his way around the Cook County court system. He oughta at least be able to get you bail."

There was silence on the other end of the line.

"You still there?"

"Yeah." Rodney's tone had softened. "I was just thinkin' … why you tellin' me this now?"

"That's what I was tryin' to say in my letter. I shoulda stepped up earlier. Shoulda done what I could to get you outta there, but I didn't. So I'm askin' for your forgiveness. That's all."

"Ha! I been here so long, this place's startin' to feel like home. Know what I'm sayin'?" The attitude was back.

"My bad. Seriously, Rodney, I'm tryin' to tell you I'm sorry."

"I know."

Harry waited for a moment. Maybe he needed to say it all over again, straight up. "So, can you please forgive me, son?"

"Yeah. Yeah, I forgive ya."

Harry sighed. It could be read as a brush-off, but Harry took what he could get and felt like an I-beam had been lifted from his shoulders. He drew a couple of deep breaths.

"So, what's this about your eye?" Rodney asked. "What's goin' on?"

Harry tried to explain, and Rodney seemed genuinely concerned. Then Harry asked what was happening on Rodney's deck in Division 9 of the jail. So far he'd been able to avoid most of the violence without hooking up with one of the gangs. "But it's not easy, you know."

O God! And to think I've let my son just sit there.

Harry cleared his throat. "So, what do you want me to do about the lawyer?"

"Anything to help would be good. My case is kinda stuck, if you know what I mean."

"I know. All right, then. I'll call him. He'll know how to get back to you and replace your PD if you want him to. Okay?"

"Yeah. Thanks, Dad."

"And thank you for callin' me back. It's good to hear your voice. Let me know what happens."

IT TOOK UNTIL MONDAY MORNING BEFORE HARRY was able to get through to Alan Sondano. The attorney remembered him, but not so fondly as Harry had hoped. Harry, after all, had usually testified for the prosecution on the cases Sondano defended. But Harry had been a stand-up cop whose collars were legitimate, even if Sondano was often able to get his clients off.

Finally, the lawyer agreed to look into Rodney's case on the basis of a retainer Harry put on his credit card, nearly maxing it out. He'd have to transfer some funds from his retirement account. Boy, he was going through money a lot faster these days than when he was still working as a doorman at Richmond Towers ... and before DaShawn came to live with him. Maybe he'd have to find a part-time job.

Nevertheless, Rodney's forgiveness and engaging Sondano raised his spirits. And the fact that things were again good between him and Estelle made remaining face down almost bearable during his second week—except for the day Estelle came over to cook and found Harry sitting on the couch, watching TV without his mirror.

"What are you doin'?" She sounded as frantic as if he'd dumped a cup of salt into her peach cobbler.

"What? ... What you yellin' 'bout?"

"You! You're not face down! You want to go through this all over again?"

He tucked his chin to his chest. "It was only for a couple minutes. I just sat down here. I didn't even realize ..."

"That's the problem! If you're not aware, you might be messin' up all day long without realizing it. Ahh! You're like a little kid, gotta be watched and checked up on the whole day long. Now get over there in your chair while I fix some dinner."

Harry complied while Estelle dropped her purse on the table and began banging pots and pans around in the kitchen. Her tirade was almost funny, but it bothered Harry. Something wasn't right about this picture.

"So, where's DaShawn?" she carried on. "He should be here watchin' you by now."

"I called him after school and asked him to go by Mom's to help her with the chores. He should be along pretty soon."

"I should hope so. Between you and Leroy, I feel like I gotta be the big mama of the whole world."

There ... that's what was wrong with the picture. "Estelle." Harry made his voice as even and calm as possible. "You're not ... my mama. You were right to correct me for not havin' my head down. That was my mistake, and I welcome your help. But I'm the head of this house, so you need to show me a little respect up in here. You understand me?"

There was silence from the kitchen except for water filling a pan. In a moment, it stopped, and Harry heard the pan get placed on the stove and the *tick-tick-tick* as the igniter lighted the gas burner.

"Estelle, you hear me?"

"I heard ya, but ..."

When she didn't continue after a moment, Harry turned his mirror so he could see her in the kitchen. Between repeated attempts to open a box of pasta, she wiped her eyes with the back of her hand. What was that about? Did she have such a hard time taking a little correction? They needed to work this out. They both needed to be able to correct one another if they were going to be a team, a partnership.

"But what, Estelle?"

"I know I was outta line, but it's just that I worry so much about you."

The pained grimace on her face brought Harry up off his chair, and he approached her, still using his mirror.

"I don't want you to have any more trouble with that eye, Harry. Really I don't. But I'm sorry." She broke into sobs, something Harry never imagined could come from such a strong, self-assured woman as Estelle Williams.

He set his mirror on the counter and put his arms around her, tentatively at first, then pulling her close. "Hey, hey. It's okay. I know you were thinkin' of me, so I'm not mad at you. We just gotta learn how to work stuff out, don'cha know?" He wanted to add, "if we're gonna get married," but instead he gently lifted her chin with the tip of his finger.

"Harry ... Harry." Her voice was a whisper, her eyes wide as they stared into his. "Your head's not all the way down again."

He grinned. "I know, but this'll only take a minute, and it's gonna be worth every second." He planted a long warm kiss on her lips, an "Estellar" kiss, as Harry thought of it, one she'd never forget.

AS SOON AS PASTOR CLARK ARRIVED Thursday afternoon, Harry told him he was ready to go ahead with the membership. "I listened to what you said about me and Estelle, and I think things are back on track. So the membership thing seems okay."

Pastor Clark seemed pleased. He reviewed the membership questions with Harry, asking about his salvation and commitment to Jesus, and then they talked through the details of the ceremony. "Is there a special song you'd like us to sing?"

"Oh, I don't know." Harry thought for a moment. "There is one, one that kinda brought me through the darkest moment with my eye. It's that song, 'Pass Me Not O Gentle Savior.' You know that one? It's on a CD by Fernando Ortega."

"Yes, yes. I think we could do that one." The pastor made a note on a slip of paper in his Bible.

"But be sure the praise team does it slow and soulful, not bouncy like a ditty for Sesame Street. I'm just sayin'"

"Yeah. I think I got you. But why don't you tell me about your 'darkest moment,' as you called it?"

Harry explained how he, at first, decided his sight meant more to him than life itself. But then in his greatest despair, when everything seemed to be going wrong, he'd heard this song saying Jesus means *"More than life to me,"* and he'd realized that was true for him, too. "Of course, I want to see again! But ... it became more important to know God is here with me. And I found myself singing along, *'Savior, Savior ... Do not pass me by.'* And I meant it, a real cry from my heart."

"Hmm." Pastor Clark sat in silence for a moment. "That's deep, Harry."

"Yeah. But the best part was discovering that truth gave me a glimpse into the meaning of my ordeal. Before then, it all seemed so meaningless—so meaningless I began to doubt God's very existence. But when I saw He'd been tryin' to teach me something, it … well, it's hard to explain. But it helped me *know* God's real and proved to me that He'd been with me all along."

"I think I know what you mean." The pastor nodded. "You know about my recent heart attack, don't you?"

"Yeah, some." Harry laughed nervously. "Enough that I worry about you climbing these stairs to see me."

"Don't worry about that. I need to build up my strength. But I had some of the same thoughts you had when I was going through it with my heart. And I was praying for healing, just like you—"

"Yeah, the whole church was prayin' for you."

"I know. But in spite of all that prayer, it didn't happen that way, at least not instantly. In fact, my healing only came by means of the surgery and now my continuing rehab."

Harry wanted to tell him about God's promise that his *"nightmare is over,"* but Pastor Clark continued on.

"I could've died, so I've been studying about all this, and the first thing that struck me was that none of the physical healings Jesus performed when He was on this earth were permanent."

Harry raised his head in shock. "I don't get it. What're you sayin'?"

"Well, think about it. Everyone Jesus healed has since died, right? In fact, the Bible says we're all destined to die—'It's appointed unto man once to die.' So, unless Jesus returns first, we're all going to die, and for the vast majority of us it will be painful, if not physically, then emotionally for the family and friends left behind. Even when Jesus prayed to not go through death on the cross, God said there were higher, eternal priorities that required it. And I think for us, too, sometimes there are higher priorities than getting healed immediately. You know, miracles that will survive for eternity."

Harry frowned. "So what are you sayin' these higher priorities are?"

"You got a big dose of one when God confirmed He was with you. That's His first priority, by the way, growing our relationship with Him so at rock bottom we *know* God exists and is with us, not just in our head, but experientially. That's why Jesus said the greatest commandment is, 'Love the Lord your God with all your heart.' It's all about intimacy with God as a person with whom we have a growing relationship. It's ongoing, and it will last for eternity."

Harry tucked his chin and adjusted his mirror. "Well, I've believed in Jesus for some time, but …"

"I don't doubt your salvation. And for many of us, 'getting saved' was more of a transaction, you know, like the verse, 'Believe on the Lord Jesus Christ and thou shall be saved.' But developing an intimate, communicating relationship with Him is more of a process, and I believe it's God's top priority for each of us."

"Hmm … And number two?"

"The second commandment, of course. 'Love your neighbor as yourself.' That's about healing our relationships with other people. That, too, is eternal."

Harry nodded thoughtfully. Like getting it right with Rodney. "You discover any more 'higher priorities' while God had you down for the count with that heart attack?"

Pastor Clark laughed. "Yeah, I think there'r at least a couple more. Not so sure about their order, but one is about discipleship, what the Bible calls 'being conformed to the image of God's Son,' as Romans 8:29 says. Or 'being transformed by the renewing of our minds,' like it says in Romans 12:2. This is character development: becoming like Christ in our attitudes, responses, openness, and lifestyles. You follow me?"

"Yeah, I think so."

"And the other one is about spreading God's Kingdom—you know, preaching the Gospel, ministering to the poor, the sick, those in prison. Working for justice and peace. All those things are eternal. In fact, Jesus said that on judgment day, God would say, 'Depart from me, I never knew you,' to those who failed to do the work of the Kingdom. It's that important."

Pastor Clark leaned back in his chair and turned both palms up. "Of course, some people start at different places. Some are all into doing good works. Others focus on trying to be righteous—the Christian character piece—but ultimately all those efforts come to nothing without a personal relationship with God and reconciled relationships with other people, particularly those closest, like family. I've seen people burn out on the mission field while destroying their family, and I don't think that's a godly priority."

Harry felt as if his mind was being stretched to the bursting point.

"Are you saying that next time I feel like I need a miracle, God may not answer me the way I want because He's more concerned about these priorities?"

"More than that, I'm saying if He doesn't answer as we expect, perhaps we should change our prayers and ask Him to transform our circumstances into a real miracle in one of *these* areas."

Harry blew out a deep breath. "Well, guess I'd have to say I got my miracle, then."

"From what you told me, I think you did. But it's okay to keep on praying for your sight to be restored. Jesus taught us in the Lord's Prayer to pray that we will not be led into the time of trial and to be delivered from the evil one. And the Apostle Paul said, 'With thanksgiving, present your requests to God'—"

"Ah, yes, the thanksgiving piece. We talked about that in men's Bible study recently."

"Very important. So we can ask. In fact, God wants us to ask. He isn't interested in seeing us suffer, but sometimes there are more eternal issues at stake."

Pastor Clark checked his watch. "Oops. Gotta get out of here. I have a meeting with Pastor Cobbs in fifteen minutes. You good for Sunday?"

"Far as I know." Harry got up and walked the pastor to the door. "Thanks for comin' by. This has been good, real good."

"Will you be able to lift your head by Sunday? Not that you have to."

Harry laughed. "If I haven't forgotten how. I'm supposed to be 'freed' tomorrow."

Freed tomorrow. The words seemed to hang in the air after the door closed. If what the pastor had said about higher priorities was true, maybe he was already free.

Harry went into the bathroom to put drops in his eye. He was getting pretty good at it by now. He removed his patch and stared at himself in the mirror. The hamburger effect—even most of the redness—was gone from his left eye. When he closed his right eye, forcing himself to look through his damaged one, he could see the remains of the bubble, lying like a shiny puddle in the "bottom" of his eye. Harry made a fist and peeked through it as though it were a small telescope. By opening it just enough to admit a pinhole of light, he was able to see. He peered around the bathroom, reading the labels on the toothpaste tube and the shampoo bottle.

He could see ... and with only a slight distortion in the center. He took a deep breath. Even if his vision got no better, that would be okay ... kind of a reminder of what God had brought him through.

Chapter 30

HARRY SAT IN THE PASSENGER SEAT OF HIS RAV4 as Estelle drove him to the eye clinic Friday morning.

"You sound like a hive of honeybees," Estelle said. "What's that you're humming?"

"Who, me? Oh, sorry. Just an old Bob Dylan tune, you know: 'Any day now, any day now, I shall be released.'"

They both laughed.

"But you'll notice I'm keepin' my head down until my prison door has been officially opened by Dr. Racine."

Two hours later, after some extensive testing, Dr. Racine did open that door. "Everything looks like your macula has flattened out nicely, and there's no evidence of further tearing or detachment to the retina. Your other eye looks fine, too. You even scored about 20/40 on the vision test for your bad eye, once we substituted the right lens. So, are you ready to come up for air?"

Harry glanced at Estelle who was sitting in an extra chair pretending to read a magazine. "You mean I don't have to be face down any longer?"

"Not for any reason I can see."

Estelle grinned and shook both fists in front of her as she heard the news.

"I do want you to be careful, though," said the doctor. "No heavy lifting for a couple more weeks, and no airplane travel during that time. You still have some of that bubble in there, and at higher altitudes where the air pressure is less, it would expand, possibly damaging your eye. But don't worry ... it'll be fully absorbed in a few more days."

"Sounds good. Uh ... just one thing. When I was doing that vision test, there was still a little distortion and fuzziness right in the center of my vision. In fact, the only way I could read some of the smaller letters was to focus above or to the side of each one, like I was playin' dodge ball with the letters."

"Hmm." Dr. Racine nodded soberly. "That's not uncommon. The macular hole probably destroyed some of those central cells, and they don't regenerate. However, over time, some of the surrounding cells may migrate in to cover that area some. Still, that's a pretty good score for someone who's had as much trauma in their eye as you've suffered."

True. When he was looking through the big lenses, he'd been able to see fairly well. Maybe God was going to leave him a little reminder of what they'd gone through together, like Jacob in the Bible, who had to live with a limp after wrestling with God all night. But that wouldn't be so bad. It was an experience worth remembering.

But Harry still had a question. "Without that big contraption, I still can't see a thing. When can I get a lens put in?"

"Why don't you come back next Wednesday, and we'll measure you for one. The girl out front can set you up with an appointment. It'll take about five or six days to get the lens back, and then we can insert it. Does that sound okay?"

272

Harry's shoulders sagged. He wanted this thing over. But he shrugged. "And in the meantime I can, what? Punch pinholes in my credit card?"

Dr. Racine laughed. "Yeah, either that or you can walk around holding a big magnifying glass in front of your eye. You might be able to focus with that."

"I don't think so. How about the patch?"

"You don't have to wear that thing if you don't want to. It was only necessary at the beginning when your eye had to be protected."

Huh. But what good was his eye until he got that lens put in? He might as well wear the patch, cut down on the blurriness.

Harry had fleetingly imagined he might be able to drive home with the black patch over his left eye, but he hadn't anticipated that the doctor would again dilate *both* eyes. The moment he stepped outside into the daylight, he squinted and tucked his head.

"Harry, he said you don't need to be face down anymore. You can look around."

"Not without some shades."

He found a pair in the glove compartment of his car, but they weren't dark enough to keep him from squinting, and he still found himself riding most of the way home with his head down.

Harry let Estelle take the car over to her place when she dropped him off at his apartment, thinking he could get it back Saturday. He climbed the dim stairwell alone, enjoying for the first time the cheap decorator prints the management had hung on each landing. By the time DaShawn burst in from school, his eyes were recovering from their dilation and they decided to go out for dinner, just the two of them. They could walk.

Being free was a thing to celebrate.

BUT THE NEXT MORNING WHEN HARRY CALLED about getting his car back, Estelle said, "Unless you especially want it in your parking lot, it's okay over here on the street."

"But I've got a lot of errands today. Don't forget I've been out of commission for two weeks. There's shoppin', and I've got to take that massage chair back, and—"

"Harry, I don't have time to run you all over the place. I've been out of commission, too, you know, takin' care of you."

Harry pulled the phone away from his ear and stared at it a moment as though that might give him a clue as to what Estelle was talking about. "Estelle, I'm not expecting you to drive me around anymore. I'm free, remember?"

"But you can't drive. You've only got one eye."

"No, I've got two eyes. Remember what you said about not speakin' death? I've got two eyes. Just because I'm wearing a patch over one ... oh, forget it. Listen, lots of people drive with only one eye. You can even get a license with only one good eye."

"Yeah, but ... You can?"

"Yes. You can. I told you that before."

"Oh, yeah. But is it wise, Harry? And as far as that chair goes, you're not supposed to be lifting anything over twenty-five pounds for a while. And I know it's heavier than that."

Harry sighed. "All right, Estelle. There's plenty I need to do around here. But what about Sunday? I'm supposed to become a member at church this Sunday."

"I know. I'll pick you up. You and DaShawn be ready."

HARRY AND DASHAWN WERE READY when Estelle arrived Sunday morning, but Harry decided not to get into the issue about him driving. He didn't need another "moment of intense fellowship" with Estelle before his membership ceremony that morning. Apparently, she wasn't up for it either, because when they got to church, she drifted away to greet some Manna House residents who had come.

Harry spotted Gabby Fairbanks and headed for her. He frowned as he got close and saw a bright red scratch going down her face. "So what does the other guy look like, Firecracker?"

"Ha! It was just Jodie's cat goin' after one of my curls." She dismissed it with a wave, then pointed to his patch. "You should talk, Mr. B. Where'd you get the pirate outfit? It's not even Halloween yet."

He had tried leaving it off earlier that morning before leaving the house, but the seriously out-of-focus images in his lens-less left eye were so distracting that it seemed more comfortable to wear the patch.

Gabby studied him through squinted eyes. "Are you okay?"

"Oh, yeah, yeah, I'm fine. If Estelle would just give me back my car keys. That woman! Thinks I can't drive with one eye."

They both laughed, and Harry moved off to find a seat.

Before the service actually started, Estelle came and took the seat beside him. That was good, because for the moment they didn't need to talk.

Before Harry realized it, the initial worship time was over and Pastor Cobbs, the short, sturdy African American pastor, announced they were going to receive new members into Souled-Out's fellowship that morning, and would Gabrielle Fairbanks and Harry Bentley please come forward?

Harry stood and grinned across the room at the Firecracker as she stood up, gaping at him in surprise. As they met at the front, she murmured, "You didn't tell me!"

He grinned broadly at her. "You didn't ask." Apparently, the pastors hadn't told her either.

Jodi and Denny Baxter came up to stand with them. Pastor Clark gave a little talk about the meaning of church membership, reminding the church that this brother and sister were each going to take their place as essential members in the Body of Christ. Then he prayed and asked the membership questions, to which both Harry and Gabby answered in the affirmative.

Harry was a little taken aback when everyone stood, clapping and cheering.

When the applause died down, Harry thought they were done, but Pastor Clark spoke again. "As most of you know, this brother has gone through quite an ordeal with his eye lately." He pointed at Harry. "This morning he's still wearing a patch on his eye, but he's out and about. That's a big improvement over the last two weeks when he had to remain face down twenty-four/seven to allow his eye to heal after several operations. And for a time, he wasn't sure whether he'd ever see out of that eye or not. And—am I right, Harry?—there was some concern that the problem might develop in the other eye, too, leaving you totally blind."

Harry nodded and stared at his shoes.

"Well, while he was goin' through it, the Lord spoke to him powerfully and assured Harry that He was right there with him and was caring for him. Harry's asked if we could sing a song that ministered powerfully to him during that ordeal. 'Pass me not, O gentle Savior, Hear my humble cry; While on others Thou art calling, Do not pass me by.'" The praise team struck a cord, but Pastor Clark held up his hand to signal for them to wait another moment. "Do you mind, Harry, if I take a minute to say something about the origin of this song?"

Harry shrugged and smiled. He was eager to hear about it himself.

"This song was written by Fanny Crosby back in 1868. And the thing about Fanny Crosby is, she was *born blind*. And if you'll listen to the words, it's about Bartimaeus, a blind beggar who cried out to Jesus for mercy. He didn't just say, 'Hey, Jesus, if You've got a minute.' No, the Scriptures say he shouted and yelled, 'Jesus! Son of David! Have mercy on me!' He caused such a big disturbance the disciples were going to shut him up until Jesus called him over and healed him, restoring his sight."

Pastor Clark turned to Harry. "I don't know if you knew the background of this song, Harry."

Harry shook his head. It was all new to him.

The pastor looked back at the congregation. "As you sing today, think about the words. Fanny Crosby never received her physical sight, but she got a deeper insight, a greater miracle, actually. As the last verse says, she came to realize there was something more important than physical sight. The Savior did not pass her by, and His presence meant more than life itself."

Harry was so blown away by this story he could hardly sing as the music group gently carried the song ...

> *Pass me not, O gentle Savior,*
> *Hear my humble cry;*
> *While on others Thou art calling,*
> *Do not pass me by.*
>
> *Let me at a throne of mercy*
> *Find a sweet relief;*
> *Kneeling there in deep contrition*
> *Help my unbelief.*

Harry gulped. The woman who wrote these words was blind! And she had cried, *"Help my unbelief,"* just like he had. She knew what it was like. She really knew! The lump in Harry's throat was so big, he couldn't sing anymore, and the tears swirled in his good eye, spilling down his cheek and leaking out from under his patch during the last verse and refrain. Seeing how it had moved him, Denny Baxter gave Harry a hand stepping down off the platform as they headed toward their seats.

Once he sat down, Estelle reached out and gripped his hand, but Harry barely noticed. All he could think about was that the Savior had not passed him by either. Jesus had come to him and had given him that greater miracle … His very presence.

The last verse still echoed in his head …

> *Thou the spring of all my comfort,*
> *More than life to me,*
> *Whom have I on earth beside Thee,*
> *Whom in Heav'n but Thee.*

Chapter 31

B Y TUESDAY, HARRY HAD TALKED ESTELLE INTO giving back his keys, and he'd caught up on most of his errands, including taking the massage chair back to the rental place. Why pay $35 a day for something he no longer needed? As it turned out, it was easy to disassemble the chair into three pieces that weren't too heavy for him to carry down to his car.

And as much as he'd appreciated the brothers coming to his apartment for Bible study when he had to be face down, it felt like a luxury to go over to Peter Douglass's place that evening. In recent weeks, they'd sometimes detoured from their regular chapter-by-chapter progress through the New Testament—some detours had been on Harry's behalf—but they were finally at Second Peter, chapter three. As they got into it, Harry realized it was all about the return of Jesus, "looking forward to a new heaven and a new earth," and how we should live in light of eternity.

Harry wanted to jump in and tell the brothers what Pastor Clark had said about God's priorities for eternity. He was ticking them off in his mind to be sure he remembered them—intimacy with God, reconciled relationships, conforming to the character of Jesus, and working for the Kingdom—when he realized the Bible study time had ended, and they were taking prayer requests. Josh prayed for the next weekend as some of the shelter residents and children moved into their own apartments in the building Gabby Fairbanks called "The House of Hope."

Some of the guys hadn't heard the whole story, but even Harry appreciated Josh's review of what had happened since God gave Gabby the vision of using the inheritance money from her mother's estate to buy a six-flat apartment building. She and her boys already lived in one apartment, and Josh and Edesa Baxter were going to move into another unit so he could function as the property manager. The other four apartments were to be used for homeless women with children who had come through the Manna House shelter, gotten themselves stabilized, and were ready to live in a place of their own. The City of Chicago had even approved the House of Hope as part of their Supportive Housing Program, with the HUD Trust Fund subsidizing rent monies and Manna House providing the needed social services.

Denny jumped in. "And I've got that little shop in my basement—and a nice router—so Josh and I are building a large wooden sign to fit into the stone arch above the doorway with the words, 'House of Hope,' carved into it."

"All right! That'll be great," said Carl.

As Harry listened, he felt amazed and proud of the Firecracker. She was a real mover and shaker! And, as far as Harry could tell, what she was doing was genuine Kingdom work. Maybe that was why God had allowed all the trauma in her life—including ending up in the shelter herself for a time—and then performed all the miracles it had taken to launch the House of Hope.

Hmm ... miracles for God's priorities. There was something to that.

ESTELLE INSISTED ON COMING WITH HARRY the next day when he went for the tests necessary to order his new implantable lens, but she didn't object to him driving, though Harry sensed she was a little nervous. Twice she put her hands out and said, "Watch—" before realizing Harry had already seen the traffic situation they were approaching.

When the exam was over—this time without dilating Harry's eyes—they returned to the car and Harry said, "You wanna go see Leroy while we're down this way? You've been paying so much attention to me, he probably needs a visit."

She turned to him with a surprised look on her face. "You sure you're up for that?"

"Of course. Why not?"

"I don't know. I guess today just seemed like such a big thing."

Harry shrugged. Getting "fitted" for a lens implant *was* a huge milestone in his recovery, but ... "The tests were nothin', really. Seems like the best way to celebrate is to get back to normal life. So let's go."

Estelle grinned. "You're on."

When they got to the burn unit at the county hospital, Leroy was away from his bed. A nurse told them he was having a therapy session in the whirlpool. "He's the star of rehab, these days. Should be back in twenty minutes or so."

Harry looked at Estelle. "You want to wait?"

She checked her watch and grimaced. "I canceled my knitting class this morning, but I thought I'd be back from your eye clinic in time to fix lunch."

"Why don't you call the Firecracker and see if she can get Precious to sub for you on lunch?"

"She's 'Miss Fairbanks,' Harry."

"What? You call her Gabby."

"That's different."

"Ah, she don't mind. I always call her the Firecracker, and she calls me Mr. B. We're good friends."

Estelle wagged her head. "Whatever. I'll call and see what I can work out."

Harry sat in a chair by Leroy's bed while Estelle went out into the hall to make the call. The heat and humidity in the burn unit was almost unbearable, and the smell of death—at least of dying flesh—turned Harry's stomach. Why put up with it when Leroy wasn't even there to talk to? He got up and followed Estelle into the hall. When she'd worked out a plan for lunch, he motioned to her to follow him to an air-conditioned waiting room. "The nurse said she'd call us when Leroy gets back."

Harry picked up a tattered, outdated magazine and flipped through it, then tossed it aside. "You know, Estelle, we need to talk about what's gonna happen when Leroy is discharged."

She heaved a sigh, a far-off look in her eyes. "I know I do, Harry. He's always on my mind."

"I said 'we,' Estelle. We're both in this, just like you hung in there with me while I was goin' through it. Together, we can work it out together."

She nodded, and Harry saw a glisten in her eyes.

The door opened, and the nurse motioned to them.

SINCE HARRY WAS RESTRICTED from doing any heavy lifting, he was off the hook for the moves going on over at the House of Hope that weekend. But Saturday afternoon was going to be a chorefest anyway. At least, that's what Harry planned. He and DaShawn would sleep in late in the morning, then he'd let DaShawn watch TV or whatever. But after lunch they'd go over to Mother Bentley's, vacuum the old lady's floor, carry out the trash, help her pay her bills, and clean out the refrigerator. Having been freed from his face-down confinement, Harry was still running on buzz.

DaShawn had not been so enthusiastic. "Do we have to, Grandpa? I was just over there the other day helpin' her."

"I know, and your great-grandma appreciated it, too. But this time we'll go together and get a lot done in no time at all. When we're finished, we'll come back and do our place. Then ..." He needed an incentive. "Then we'll go out for pizza and take in a movie. I saw the preview for 'Happy Feet.' Oughta be fun."

"Aww, Grandpa. I was gonna play with Robbie tomorrow."

"Well, you still can. We'll just do the chores in the morning." So much for sleeping in.

The boy pulled a pout. "I don't know why I have to work on Saturday anyway. Seems like school's my work. And I gotta do it every day, all week."

Harry shrugged. "Too bad, buddy. One way or the other, the chores gotta get done, so you choose."

DaShawn didn't choose, so Harry let Saturday morning take its leisurely course, planning to do the chores in the afternoon. But the phone call he got while he was cleaning up after lunch changed his ambitious plans.

"Mr. B, sorry to bother you, but Philip was mugged this morning, and ... and the cops are back here askin' a lot of questions, and I don't know how to answer them, and I just wish someone who knew—"

"Wait a minute. That you, Firecracker? You're sayin' Philip got mugged?" He sank into a chair at the table.

"Yeah. They've been checking him out in the ER for the last few hours. Some thugs worked him over pretty bad, but the doctors say he's gonna be okay. They're tryin' to find a room for him right now, and—"

"Where are you? What hospital?"

"Weiss Memorial. That's where they brought him in the am-bulance. Lucy found him in the pedestrian underpass—you know, the one in the park by Richmond Towers. Denny and Jodi were here earlier, but they had to go help move people into the House of Hope, but I was hoping you—"

"Gabby, Gabby. Calm down, Firecracker. I'll be there soon as I can. Okay?"

"Yeah. Thanks, Mr. B. Oh … any chance you could bring Es-telle, too? I'd just, well …"

"I'll give her a call and see if she can come. You just take it easy, now. Everything's gonna be all right." Harry hesitated a moment before hanging up. "You know the Lord's in control. He's there with you … and I'm prayin'."

"I know, Harry. Thanks."

Harry closed his phone and was halfway out of the chair when the last thing he'd said to Gabby echoed in his mind. He sat back down and prayed, not only for the Firecracker, but also for her no-good husband, Philip.

When he was done, he called, "DaShawn!" His grandson had disappeared into his room as soon as they'd eaten, probably hop-ing Harry would forget about the afternoon of chores. "Guess what, DaShawn? I think you got your wish. Give Robbie a call, and if it's okay with his mom, you can go over there for a while. I gotta go help Miss Gabby. But we're still gonna do those chores sooner or later. So don't be whinin' when the time comes."

DaShawn bounced out of his room as fresh and chipper as the "Happy Feet" penguin.

Harry hadn't expected it to take so long to get to the hospital, but by the time he dropped off DaShawn and got to Estelle's, she was busy doing something and couldn't come out for a few minutes. He sat in his RAV4, drumming his fingers on the steering wheel. Something stunk about the mugging. He opened his phone and dialed his old police partner.

"Cindy, Harry here."

"Hey, Harry. No more favors." She laughed.

"Oh, you sound just like one of Santa's elves."

"But I ain't, so what's up?"

"Look, I think Fagan's still out terrorizing the civilians. You follow me?"

"You mean he's showin' his ugly face in public again?"

"Yeah, well, this may be worse than that. Now he may be rearranging other people's faces." He told Cindy what he knew about the possibility of Philip getting a loan from Fagan, that it was pretty obvious he hadn't been able to pay it back, and Philip had just turned up in the hospital after a pretty cold beating.

"I doubt Fagan would've done that himself," Cindy said. "But Andrew Mercer and Tyrone Taylor—both Fagan boys—were late reporting for duty this morning. And Andrew had a very puffy, red eye that's gonna turn into a shiner as dark as that patch I saw you wearing. Did your mark say whether he tagged his attackers or not?"

"Don't know. I haven't seen him myself, yet. But I'll ask."

"Okay. I'll let you know if I hear anything else here on the 'home front.'"

"Thanks, Cindy. Oops. Here comes Estelle. Gotta go."

But by the time they drove down to Weiss Memorial Hospital and found Philip's room, it was three in the afternoon.

The police had gone, and Philip Fairbanks looked a mess—bandages around his ribs, his right arm in a cast and supported out from his body with an awkward-looking brace. His head had been shaved and wrapped in bandages except for his face, which was a mess—swollen nose and eye, scrapes and cuts. He appeared to be asleep.

"Sorry it took so long," Harry whispered to Gabby. "The cops finally lay off?"

"Yeah, they left a while ago. Guess I managed." The Firecracker stared wearily at the man in the bed. "He's so pumped full of painkillers, you can't wake him."

Estelle approached the bed and put a hand on Philip's shoulder for a moment. Then she turned back to Gabby. "We're not stayin', honey." She opened her arms to wrap Gabby in a hug. "Just wanted to let you know there are a whole lot of people prayin' for Philip right now. And if you need anything—*anything*—you let us know, you hear?"

The Firecracker sniffed a nod, then lowered her head onto Estelle's shoulder and sobbed. Harry stood back, feeling awkward watching such a vulnerable moment. When Gabby finally recovered and wiped her eyes, Harry motioned her to follow him out into the hall.

"You know who did this, don't you?"

She shrugged. "I told the police it seemed like a random mugging to me. But they said nothing had been taken from his wallet." As she caught his drift, she slowly nodded her head. "But if you're right about Matty Fagan …"

Harry tipped his head to the side and squinted with his good eye. "I know I'm right. What's it been … four weeks since Philip met with Fagan? Fagan never gives anybody that long to pay back what he loaned 'em. I've got my ex-partner on the case, seeing what she can find out." Harry shook his head. "The sooner Internal Affairs gets that rogue off the streets, the better for everybody."

Chapter 32

MONDAY. HARRY FROWNED AT THE STACK OF BILLS he'd just opened. A couple were overdue because he'd been "out of commission." It stung his pride to be late ... and to have to pay the fees. But he might as well get it over with.

Halfway through writing the checks, the door buzzer made him jump. Distracted, he buzzed open the vestibule door and went back to the bills. Probably DaShawn coming home from school. Why the boy hadn't used his key didn't even cross Harry's mind.

But the footsteps coming up the stairs clearly weren't DaShawn's. Harry frowned, went to the door, and pulled it open.

"Rodney?"

"Hey."

"What ... how'd you get out so soon?" Harry opened his arms ... a little, wanting to give his son a hug, but not wanting to force it.

Ignoring Harry's move completely, Rodney stopped in the doorway and gave the interior of the apartment a once-over.

"Guess it looks a little different from where you been crashin', don't it? Hey, you want a Pepsi? I could make some fresh coffee. Come on in here and have a seat. Let me just get those newspapers off the couch."

Rodney finally took a couple of long strides across the room and sat down on the edge of the couch without leaning back. His expression was blank as he again looked around and then focused on Harry. "Your eye still botherin' you?"

"Nah, it's better. I just wear this patch 'cause I lost my lens in that eye so everything's a huge blur. But tomorrow I'm supposed to get a new lens put in, you know, like they do for old people who have cataracts. Should be able to see again after that." He stood in the middle of the room, then shrugged. "So, you want something to drink?"

"Water'd be good."

From the kitchen, Harry spoke over his shoulder. "How'd you get out so soon?" It suddenly occurred to him that Rodney might be here to take DaShawn.

"That lawyer you found, guess he didn't have no trouble gettin' the charges dropped."

"Dropped? You mean you're not out on bail? Don't have to go back to court?"

"No, nothin'."

"That's great." But Harry wasn't so sure. If Rodney had been completely cleared of all charges, it would be a lot easier for him to gain custody of DaShawn. Wouldn't have to prove he was a fit parent or anything. Beads of sweat tingled on his scalp as he brought the glass of water in to Rodney. "You're not on probation? Don't have to check in with a PO or anything?"

Rodney made a sideways grin, shrugged, and shook his head. He took a long drink. "Ah. Even the water's better on the outside. I think they put stuff in the water at the county."

"Whaddaya mean? What kind of stuff?"

"Oh, you know, saltpetre to keep the sex down, and who knows what else to drug us up."

Harry waved his hand dismissively. "Saltpetre's an urban legend. It don't do nothing to ya."

"I don't know. There's some strange stuff goin' on up in there."

Harry sat down in his recliner. "Well, I'm glad you're out. So what's next?" He dreaded Rodney's response.

"I dunno." Rodney hung his head. "But … I wanted to thank you for gettin' me out. And I thought I'd drop by and see DaShawn." He surveyed the room again as though he might have missed him. "He in school?"

Harry checked the clock. "Yeah, but he should be home in the next twenty minutes or so." Man, there it was: DaShawn. What was Rodney gonna do? "I'm sure he'll be glad to see you … and find out what you got planned."

Rodney nodded, letting his gaze return to the floor. "Don't really have anything planned yet. This was kind of a surprise. Know what I'm sayin'?" He glanced up at Harry again. "A good surprise, though." A faint smile drifted across his face, the first one Harry had seen.

"So, you gonna look for a job, or what?"

Rodney shook his head. "From what I hear, everything's pretty tight around Chicago right now. Thought I might head on down to Atlanta and see a couple brothers I used to know when they lived up here. Get my feet back on the ground, you know, and go from there."

"They sound like the same guys who made you late for your court case and got you picked up."

"No, Dad. It was the weather, not them. They're stand-up dudes. They're workin'. One's married and got a kid, even."

Harry took a deep breath and plunged in. "What's this mean for DaShawn?"

"Well, I don't mean to be leavin' you holdin' the bag and all, but I gotta get my head together, settle down, find a good job.

Know what I'm sayin'? Maybe I'll come back up this way, and he can see me as often as he wants. I dunno. You up for keepin' him a while longer?"

"Oh, I'm good with that. He's into school and church. We got a good church. And you know, your grandma's here. He goes over there and sees her a lot."

"Hmm. How is Grandma? S'pose I oughta go see her, too. She still live in the same place?"

"No. She moved down this way." The DaShawn question seemed to have passed for the moment, much to Harry's relief. "So how'd you know where to find me?"

"Ha!" Rodney smiled again. "Remember that hundred bucks you sent me? The paper sayin' it had been credited to my commissary account had your name and address on it."

"And you saved that?"

"No. I just remembered it."

"Remembered it?"

"Yeah. I was trying to imagine where you lived. And I knew it was somewhere around here."

Harry shook his head and studied his feet. What did that say about himself, that his own son had to *imagine* where he lived? The fact that Rodney had any interest at all in imagining where he lived put him to shame for his neglectful parenting.

A thunder of footsteps rose up the stairwell.

"Hey, that'd be DaShawn, now."

Rodney stood up. "How you know?"

"Ha, ha. When you can't see with your eyes for a while, you learn how to see with your ears, notice things you've never heard before."

A CELEBRATION SEEMED IN ORDER. DaShawn and Rodney both voted for pizza.

"Got just the place. Don't think either of you've been there," Harry said as he drove them to Gulliver's on Howard Street for Chicago's famous pan pizza.

Surrounded by a museum of antique light fixtures and marble busts, Harry watched DaShawn's eyes follow his father's every move. Obviously the kid idolized him and hungered for his attention. But why? His dad had been in jail, hadn't been able to take care of him, hadn't even written to him. Harry had been the one to step in and provide stability and love. Sure, he was glad Rodney was out and hoped the best for him, but … why was DaShawn looking to his father instead of to him? He felt as jealous as a thirteen-year-old who couldn't attract the attentions of the girl who had eyes only for the school "bad boy."

But that's foolishness, he told himself. Rodney would soon be gone, and DaShawn would remain with him. They did have a good relationship—grandson and second-chance "dad." He should be thankful for what God had given. That's right … he needed to remember to always give thanks. Hadn't he learned that was the way to build his faith and trust God for His continued blessing?

Rodney slept on the couch that night, and the next morning Harry made coffee. He couldn't eat or drink anything because of the lens implant procedure scheduled for later that morning, and coffee was all Rodney wanted. But Harry sat at the table with him while he sipped his cup of joe.

"So, how you gettin' to Atlanta?"

Rodney blew into his cup. "Bus, I guess."

"I'm going down that way to my eye doctor. You want me to drop you off at the station?"

"Nah. I'm good. I'll take the El to the Loop."

"Got enough money?"

Rodney nodded. "At least they didn't keep the cash I had on me when they picked me up. Sometimes it just disappears, you know, even if it's on the inventory."

Harry checked DaShawn who sat at the other end of the table shoveling Cheerios into his mouth as if he were the only person in the room.

Frown lines deepened in Harry's forehead as he turned back to study his son's face. "I'm gonna be praying for you, Rodney. That's the least I can do at this point. In fact, if you want, I'd like to begin by prayin' for you right now. You cool with that?"

Rodney shrugged a shoulder.

Harry didn't quite know what that meant, but Rodney hadn't said no, so he reached out and put his hand on his son's arm.

"Dear God, You been mighty good to me, far better than I've deserved. You brought my grandson to me and gave me the sight to see my son one more time. I wanna thank You. And I want to ask your forgiveness for not being the father I should've been, but now my son's a man and a dad himself, so I want to ask You to bless him. Bless him with your presence that means more than life itself, more than sight or anything else. Help him come to know your love and to receive Jesus into his life. Save him, Lord, and keep him safe on the streets. Help him find a good job, and at the right time, bring him back to us to find all to be well with his own son. Amen."

When Harry looked up, there was a hint of tears in Rodney's eyes, and he was nodding his head. "Thanks ... Dad."

ESTELLE SEEMED TO UNDERSTAND why Harry couldn't talk about his time with Rodney as they drove to the eye clinic one more time. In fact, they didn't talk about anything until the *Law and Order* ring of Harry's cell phone sounded.

"You want me to get that?"

"Yeah, would ya?"

She listened for a moment. "No, this is Estelle. He's driving right now. Want me to put you on speaker?" She listened a little longer without turning on the speaker. "Okay, I'll tell him. Thanks." She closed the phone and turned to Harry. "That was your old police partner. Cindy, she said. She wanted you to know she hasn't found out anything more about that incident last Saturday, but she thinks you're right. She'll get back to you if she comes up with anything more."

Harry drove on, nodding.

"So was that about the attack on Philip Fairbanks?"

"Yeah. I asked her to check out a few things about Fagan's possible involvement."

"You still think he was behind it?"

"Can't prove it, but yeah."

When they got to the eye clinic, the check-in, signing of release forms, and pre-op took over an hour, but the surgery itself lasted fewer than fifteen minutes. Harry was surprised when the surgeon said, "I think that will do it, Mr. Bentley. Everything looks fine. Dr. Racine probably went over the post-op details with you, but let me review. Your vision may be blurry for a few days, but it should clear up. Here are some drops you'll need to put in your eye for the next six weeks. No heavy lifting. Keep any water out of your eye when showering for a couple of weeks, and wear this protective bandage at night. And of course, since there's a slight increased risk of retinal tears or detachment following lens implant, I know Dr. Racine's going to want to see you … Let's see, when did he schedule you …?"

Harry's stomach knotted. He didn't remember anything about an "increased risk" of the hell he'd just come through.

"Oh, here it is. You're supposed to see him on Thursday. But I don't think there'll be any problems. Everything went smoothly."

Harry reached up and felt the thick bandage that had been taped over his eye. "You think my black eye patch would give me enough protection?" He pulled it from his shirt pocket.

"I suppose that's sufficient. We just don't want you to accidentally bump it when you're asleep."

The doctor removed the bandage and helped Harry position his patch. Harry stood up, not sure whether he felt a little woozy or what.

"You okay? You think you can walk on your own? I could get a chair for you."

"No, I'm good." No way was he going to be rolled out in a wheelchair. He took a few tentative steps and became more sure of himself. Outside in the waiting room, he found Estelle. "Let's go home. But you gotta drive."

"You done already?"

He didn't answer but headed for the door. When they got in the car, he turned to Estelle. "Before you start the engine, I need you to pray for me."

"O Lord Jesus!" Estelle clapped her hand over her mouth, then spoke through her fingers. "What happened? Didn't it work?"

"He thinks everything's fine, but … I got a little shaky when he told me the surgery increased the risk of more retinal problems. Somehow, I never heard about that. I was so eager to get my vision back. But like you say, I want to speak life, not death. I want my faith to grow, so we need to pray."

"Yes! Yes!" She turned and put both hands on Harry's head. "In the name of Jesus, we rebuke you, Satan, and the doubt and fear you would plant within us. And we rely on You, Lord, to complete the good work You have begun. And for that, we need a miracle, Lord. So in your mercy please deliver us from the Evil One. In the precious name of Jesus, amen."

Harry blew out a long breath. "Thank you, Estelle." He leaned his head back on the headrest and closed his eyes. "We can go now."

As Estelle headed the car back up Western Avenue, Harry thought about the miracle Estelle had prayed for. For some reason he felt a deep peace that God had already granted her request … no matter how it worked out.

Chapter 33

Harry stared into the bathroom mirror. His gray, horseshoe beard could use a trim, and he needed to shave his head again … otherwise he appeared rather rakish with that black patch over his left eye. *Huh.* He'd save it for Halloween and dress up as a pirate. But right now, he was going to have a look at his eye.

He took off the patch.

"Ahh, not too bad. Just a little bloodshot." He leaned closer and thought he could see the place on the side where the doctor had inserted his new lens the day before. Amazing! The brightness of the bathroom light still drove him to squint that sensitive eye, but could he see out of it?

He closed his good eye, and gazed around. He *could* see! A little foggy, as though the room had filled with steam from a too-hot shower, but he could see! He could actually see! From the little stand by the toilet, he picked up an old copy of *Reader's Digest* and realized he could read the article titles on the cover. There was a slight warp and blur to the letters at the very center of his focus, and inside he really couldn't make out the regular text, but … he could see.

"Thank You, Jesus. Thank You! Thank You! Thank You!" The words came tumbling out again and again. He couldn't stop.

Harry checked his right eye. No distortion there, no blind spots anywhere. His problem had not spread.

Without replacing the patch, he walked into the living room. Though it seemed out of character—or maybe he was changing— he felt so overwhelmed with gratefulness that he knelt on the rug and stretched himself out flat on his stomach, hands extended before him and began to blubber, "Thank You, Thank You, Thank You, Jesus," tears flowing freely.

How long he remained prostrate on the floor before his gratitude had all spilled out, he had no idea. But when he stood up, he felt purged of the nightmare with all its horrors, and he wanted to get on with life. God was so good! Before this, he'd never really known how good God was. But it was worth knowing, and not just "knowing," like a fact to be stored in his memory, but as an experience to be cherished forever.

The hint of a question flitted through his mind: Would he have chosen to go through what he'd gone through if—given who he was—that was the only way for him to experience such intimacy with God? Would he have pushed the "go" button if he'd had the choice before it all started?

"Yes ... yes, I think I would." And his "goin' through" wasn't like a trip from which one comes home with nothing but snapshots and memories. It was an intimacy that had been established, existed still, and could continue into the future.

Harry had no illusions he'd "arrived" at some spiritual plateau where he'd never again cry out, "I believe, but help my unbelief!" or struggle with heart-stopping doubt. He knew from Bible stories there'd be days when it seemed as if God was silent and distant. He didn't know what to say about that. And he didn't pretend to be able to explain why seemingly innocent people—especially children—suffered personally or from great natural disasters.

Some mysteries were beyond his explanations, perhaps incomprehensible by any human until God revealed the answers in heaven. But ... he wasn't going to let his limitations cancel the truth of what he'd discovered—that God was with him and loved him even when all seemed lost.

He felt like celebrating! He wanted to get on with life ... he was ready for it. And it needed to begin with Estelle. She had stuck with him, prayed for him, and nursed him through the whole thing, all while he struggled with fear and ambivalence about their relationship. That had to end. He was ready to tie the knot. But first he had to ask her!

He got up from the floor and went to his bedroom dresser. Where was the ring he'd planned to give her? Ah. There it was. Opening the box, light flashed from the diamond. He grinned ... he had to do this right. But where? And how? He wanted to take her completely by surprise. He'd blown proposing to her at a fancy restaurant or on a cruise boat while fireworks arched over the harbor. So what was left? It needed to be someplace beautiful and unusual—and at a time when Estelle least expected it.

"O Lord," Harry said out loud, "this is how I'm going to celebrate your gift to me, by taking a step of faith into my future."

But where, where, where? *Hmm.* A while back, he'd picked up a brochure from a rack advertising all kinds of stuff to do in the Windy City. Where had he put the thing?

He spent an hour looking for it without any success before DaShawn came home from school needing help with his math homework.

He was still helping him when his phone rang.

The Called ID said Estelle. "So what time do you have to go in tomorrow, Harry?"

"Uh, let's see. Oh yeah, my appointment's at 11:10."

"Mmm. Wish I'd have known earlier so I could get someone to be on lunch for me. I've called on Precious so many times lately, I'm afraid I'm using up all her good will."

"That's okay, Estelle. You don't need to come with me tomorrow."

"But what if you can't drive home again?"

"I don't think that'll happen. I'm actually seeing pretty well, and my eye's feeling pretty good."

"Yeah, but—"

"Now, we're not goin' there, Estelle. Faith, remember? I'm believin' everything's gonna be good."

She was silent for several seconds, then he heard her sigh. "You're probably right, Harry. That's good. There's a time when the Holy Spirit nudges us to exercise faith. But just call me, okay?"

"You got it, Babe. By the way, I love you."

"Harry!"

"What? You got your speakerphone on or something?"

"No, but—"

"Then, I love you … even if the speaker's on. I still love you!"

He closed his phone and chuckled to himself. It was good to finally have the brakes off. He made a wry face at DaShawn. "Who you lookin' at, boy?"

"You gonna marry her, Grandpa?"

"You just finish your math. I gotta go cook dinner."

He made a stew he thought would even impress Estelle if he served it to her. But instead, he and DaShawn took it over to Mother Bentley's to share a meal with her and watch a couple of her TV shows.

It wasn't until the next day, when he got back from the eye doctor with a positive report, that Harry found the brochure in the back of his sock drawer. He had no idea why he'd put it there along with old birthday cards, souvenirs, and all his pin-on numbers from the Ricky Byrdsong 5K "Race Against Hate" that he ran every year. But there it was. He took it into the living room and read through the details. He started to chuckle. Yes! This was it! If Estelle didn't totally freak out, she'd be so flabbergasted she'd never guess that he was about to pop the big question.

He called the number on the brochure and made reservations for the following Sunday evening at 6 pm. Then he phoned Robbie's mom to see if DaShawn could have a sleepover with Robbie starting after church on Sunday. She said it'd be fine, and she'd be sure the boys didn't stay up too late so they'd be good for school the next morning.

His third call was to Estelle, but apparently she was busy because it went to voice mail.

"Estelle, this is Harry, reportin' in like you asked. The doctor says my eye's progressing even better than expected, and I scored a 20/40 on the vision test with my new lens. That's pretty good. He thinks it'll get even better with time. So we can thank God. In fact, we need to do a little holy celebrating, have some fun, don'cha know? So let's go somewhere Sunday afternoon. Be ready at five o'clock. Okay? And—this is important—wear gym shoes and some capris or pants that aren't too fancy. Maybe bring a light jacket if the day's cool. Let's see, guess we're supposed to show up for that Manna House mural dedication or whatever on Saturday, so I'll see you there if you've got any questions. Okay? 'Bye now." He flipped the phone shut.

Harry's grin was so wide it made his face ache. Everything was falling into place.

HARRY AND DASHAWN SLIPPED into the back of the multipurpose room at the Manna House Woman's Shelter. Guests, board members, and supporters had already gathered at the tables drinking coffee or red punch and talking quietly. Harry grinned to himself as he started to make his way slowly through the crowd toward Pastor Clark and Carl Hickman standing in mirrored poses as they examined the mural that covered one whole wall. Both men had a hand on one hip while their other hand supported their chin, head slightly cocked to the side.

From what Harry could see, the mural definitely could stand up to their review. It pictured Jesus as the Good Shepherd, but unlike the usual Sunday school pictures, the sheep were of all different shades of white, black, brown, and tan, some with scraggly, dirty wool, some scrawny and hungry looking, others with bloody or bandaged wounds. With a kindly face, the Shepherd was coaxing them into a pen where they would be safe and warm.

"The guests named this room 'The Shepherd's Fold' after my mom, Martha Shepherd." Gabby Fairbanks stood at Harry's right elbow holding a pitcher of punch to fill people's cups. "The mural fits, don'cha think?"

"Sure does," he said, turning toward her. "And she'd like it, too. How ya doin'?"

"Hey!" Joyous surprise lit up her face, framed by all those wild curls, as she shot him a grin. "You're not wearin' your patch. That's great. Can you see?"

"Better and better each day, thank God."

"I'm so glad, Mr. B! And glad you came today, but … you haven't seen Lucy around, have you? I can't believe she's not here. This whole dedication thing was her idea, and my mom was her best friend."

"No. In fact, I haven't seen her since the picnic." Which didn't surprise Harry. The old bag lady came and went like Chicago's weather.

"You know who painted the mural, don't you?"

Harry shook his head.

The Firecracker nodded toward the two men discussing the painting. "It was Carl Hickman's son, Chris."

"Get out! Didn't Carl tell me his boy used to get in trouble for tagging buildings with graffiti?"

Gabby shrugged. "I wouldn't know. But he's an art student at Columbia College now." She lifted the pitcher. "Guess I better finish my rounds with this."

The Firecracker moved off, but she wasn't the only one to notice Harry wasn't wearing his eye patch. He never did feel very comfortable schmoozing in crowds, and Estelle was busy keeping the snack table stocked with fresh veggies and hot wings. But at least his improving vision was something to talk about, though he wished it wasn't "about him."

He was glad when Mabel Turner called everyone together for a short dedication program for the mural, which included some speeches of appreciation to Chris Hickman for painting it. The event ended with prayer, and people began to slip away.

Harry was finally able to corner Estelle in the kitchen. "So, did you get my voicemail about Sunday?"

"Mm-hm, I got it. Pick up a towel and help me dry these pitchers, will you? You and DaShawn want some of this leftover punch? How about those hot wings?"

"No, thank you, to both offers. I had enough wings already." He grabbed a towel and set to work. "So, is Sunday good with you?"

"Sure, Harry. But where we goin'?"

"Ah ... you'll see. Just wear what I told you."

"I don't know. You—"

She was cut off by a yellow dog, bounding into the kitchen, wiggling its butt and wagging its tail, panting with its mouth a-grin as though the hot wings on the counter had been saved just for him.

"Dandy, get outta here!" Estelle yelled. "Who let him in here, anyway?"

Harry shooed the dog out of the kitchen. "That's Lucy's dog, isn't it?"

"Yep, used to belong to Gramma Shep. But keep him outta my kitchen!"

"Oh, don't go getting' your panties in a knot, Estelle." A gravelly voice followed the dog into the kitchen. "Got any food left?"

"Lucy!" Harry said. "Where you been? Gabby was expecting you at the dedication. She was lookin' for you."

"Yeah, well, I been lookin' for her, too. Where she at?" Lucy pulled off her purple crocheted hat and scratched her head before jamming it back down to her ears.

Estelle grabbed a rag and started wiping the counter, almost finished with the cleanup. "Gabby told me she had to leave early to go down and visit her husband at Weiss Memorial Hospital."

"Well, he ain't there, but I got some intel on him that you"— she stabbed her finger at Harry—"Mr. Former Police Officer, need to know. Hey, Estelle, that coffee still hot?"

A few minutes later, Harry sat across a table from Lucy, who was making short order of a plate of food Estelle had fixed, while Dandy wandered over to the back door of the shelter trying to nose the lid off a garbage can containing enough chicken bones to choke a hog.

"So, what's up, Lucy?"

"You know those two guys that beat up the Fuzz Top's husband?"

"Uh ... didn't know anyone was able to make a positive ID."

"Well, that's who I think did it. Anyway, they was hangin' around Richmond Towers before the attack, and they're back there again today ... just a'fore the lights went on up there in Miss Gabby's old apartment. So I think her man's home from the hospital, and those scumbags are fixin' to mug him again the moment he steps outta the building. So there, Mr. Cop. That's what I seen."

Chapter 34

THE SERVICE AT SOULEDOUT THE NEXT MORNING was "smokin'," as the kids would say. The teens had had a Lock-In the night before and were geeked to share a Christian stomp and rap they had written. The whole congregation clapped and cheered as the "Steppers" performed, but Harry couldn't keep his mind on anything but his plans for Estelle that evening. This was going to be the night. He was going to knock that woman's socks off. There'd be no way she could say no.

But after the service, Denny Baxter cornered him to talk about Philip Fairbanks.

"Okay, this is how I see it," said Denny, ticking off points on his fingers. "If Philip's gambling debts have piled up like Gabby says, and he's deep in debt to this loan shark, and if Fagan's the guy responsible for beating him up last week, and if Lucy is right that some thugs are watching his apartment building, then ..." Denny hacked at the palm of one hand with the edge of the other, as though it were a knife, "then he's gotta get out of that penthouse, don'cha think?"

Harry nodded and pulled at his beard. "But where's he gonna go that they wouldn't find him?"

"What if we could put him in a safe house until he got this worked out?"

"Denny, get real. You have any idea what it takes to set up a safe house and conceal a person's identity?"

"That's just the thing!" Denny was getting animated. "We wouldn't be trying to conceal him, just keep him in an environment where other people are around all the time so nothing would happen to him."

"You can't put the Secret Service on him to guard him day and night! And no man wants a bunch of babysitters taggin' after him."

"Yeah but, what if we invited Philip to stay with us for a few days? We've got the space, and after I mentioned it to Gabby last night, Jodi and I talked. We'd be up for it … for a while, at least."

"Denny, don't you know your own neighbors? Don't you realize who lives just across the alley and one door down from you? That's where Matty Fagan lives."

"Oh, right. I forgot." Denny's brow crinkled in puzzlement. "But don't they say, the best place to hide something is right in plain sight? I mean—"

"Look, it's just a bad idea, Denny. Don't waste anymore time on it."

"Yeah, yeah, see what you mean." Denny shook his head. "I just think we … oh, hey, Gabby."

The Firecracker joined them. "Hi, guys. Sorry to interrupt, but … can I talk to you for a minute, Denny? I'm going to go see Philip this afternoon, and last night you said—" She stopped and looked back and forth between the two men as Harry rolled his eyes. "What?"

"That's just what we were talking about," Denny said. "Harry, here, reminded me that Matty Fagan—the rogue cop we all presume is behind this attack on your husband—lives here in Rogers

Park. In fact, just one street over from our house. He's just across the alley and one house down."

"Fagan lives near *you*?" Gabby frowned. "How do you know?"

"Look, I worked with him on the force. I've been at his house before." Harry sighed. "It's a long story. Tell you another time. But the fact is, Denny's bright idea to get Philip away from those thugs staked out at Richmond Towers would put him in Fagan's backyard. Literally."

"Oh." She nodded her head slowly. "Guess that puts the kibosh on … oh, sorry. That's my cell." She dug in her purse and checked the caller ID. "It's Philip. Excuse me a minute." She turned away and flipped the phone open. "Hello? … Hello?"

A moment later she turned back to Harry, a look of bewilderment on her face. *"Fagan!"* she mouthed, pointing frantically at the phone. Her bewilderment morphed into horror as she listened. She pushed the Mute button and hissed at Harry, "He's got a gun!"

"Who—Fagan?"

She nodded.

Harry grabbed her phone, put it to his ear, and heard a panicked Philip Fairbanks. "Look … Fagan. I already told you. You'll get your money, just put that gun away." With all the noise from the SouledOut people talking around him, Harry couldn't make out the next words from another voice in the background. But then Philip spoke again. "I can't if you shoot me. Please …"

"What's happening?" Gabby mouthed frantically.

Harry held up his hand and quickly headed out of the church to the quieter sidewalk along its front and began pacing back and forth. He put a finger in his other ear and heard through the Firecracker's phone, "You're just an architect or whatever, Fairbanks, you don't need your knees. But I do need my money, and I need it paid on time." Definitely Matty Fagan's voice.

"Just a few more days, Fagan. Please!"

Harry heard a whoosh, and then Fagan said, "Now don't try anything stupid just because we got a rolling audience. They'll soon be gone."

A different voice, more distant, announced, "Route 147, Outer Drive Express to Howard and the Red Line." Harry stopped in his tracks. That was a CTA bus with its speaker announcing to the visually impaired which bus they were about to board.

Harry could hardly believe it. He knew where that was. The 147 bus came off the Outer Drive at Foster and turned north on Sheridan. Its first stop would be just past the Dominick's food store, less than two blocks from Philip Fairbanks' luxury highrise. He'd probably just gone out to the store for something. But having worked as the doorman in Philip's building, Harry knew every square foot of that neighborhood.

He opened his own phone and dialed 9-1-1. As soon as the dispatcher answered, Harry said, "We have a 245 in progress on Sheridan Road, just north of Foster. That's a 245, an assault with a deadly weapon. Patch me through to the responding officers so I can direct them to exactly where it's happening."

"I'm sorry, sir. That won't be possible. Please stay on the line and give me all the information.'

"Ma'am, it *is* possible, now patch me through, immediately, before someone gets shot!"

"But I—"

"Do it now, lady, if you want to keep your job and avoid a personal lawsuit." Harry knew the latter wasn't likely, but why not light a fire under the woman?

A moment later, Harry heard the static-filled transmission from officers en route. He briefly told them he was a retired Chicago police officer who'd worked a couple of blocks from where the incident was happening. "There's a Dominicks on the northeast corner of Sheridan and Foster. On the north side of the store is an access alley going around behind the store. The assault's going down *now*, right at the mouth of that alley. It's gotta be within a few yards of the bus stop there on Sheridan. There's a fence and a telephone pole and a big transformer box. He's probably using those things as cover. But he's right there! And it's a Code 2—urgent without lights or siren."

Through his phone, Harry heard the big engine in the police car jump to a higher RPM as the tires squealed around a corner.

"How do you know all this?" came the distant voice of the officer. "You in an apartment across the street where you can see it or something?"

"More like, 'or something.' No, I'm not watchin' from across the street. You might say I'm usin' my 'second sight.'"

In the background, Harry heard the driver say, "Oh, no. If you've got some wacko psychic on there, you better warn him that if this is a false report, he's going to jail."

"I heard that," yelled Harry, "and this is for real! In fact, I hope you've got some backup, because this guy's armed and dangerous."

The Firecracker arrived at Harry's side just then. "Harry, what—?!"

Harry waved her off and turned his back as he heard the police car skid to a stop—through both phones—and knew the cops had arrived at the right location. "That's it! You're there. It's the alley!" he said into his phone. "North of the store ..."

"Who's the assailant here?"

"The guy with the gun, knucklehead. His name is Matty Fagan, and he's gonna tell you he's on the job and give you a cock-and-bull story about the other guy. But just arrest him!"

"You mean he's a cop?"

"Yeah, he *is* a cop, but he's on suspension. He won't have a badge. But check his ankle. He might have a throwaway."

Yelling and confusion came through Gabby's phone, but Harry could tell that the police had assessed the situation enough to believe his report and were in the process of arresting Fagan.

He closed the phone with a huge sigh and wiped his brow. He felt drained. The Firecracker had gone back inside the church, and he followed her, handed back her phone and sank into a chair. The Baxters and Estelle gathered around him, all talking at once, asking what happened.

Harry frowned, giving a quick rundown of what he'd heard. "Does Philip have you on speed dial, Gabby?"

"I ... I don't know anymore. He used to ... I suppose he still does, but ..." She shrugged.

"Hmm. Don't know whether Philip had the phone in his jacket pocket and Fagan punched him in the chest or what, but somehow the call came through. When I realized what was happening, I tried to figure out where Philip could be." He turned to Gabby. "You said he just got out of the hospital, so it wasn't very likely he'd be too far from home. And I could hear street traffic, so I didn't think he was in the park. But it was the bus that told me the location. They use those speakers to announce what bus it is every time the bus stops. It's for people who can't see, like ... like I was."

Denny frowned and cocked his head back. "How could you hear something so subtle as that over the phone?"

Harry smiled. "Good question. But like I said to my son, Rodney, the other day, when you can't see with your eyes, you pay more attention and begin to learn how to 'see' with your ears."

"Okay. But ... how did you know where the bus was along its route? I mean, it could've been anywhere."

"Not this one. It was the 147 Outer Drive Express. That bus comes all the way from downtown along the Outer Drive without stopping until it exits at Foster and turns north on Sheridan. The first stop on Sheridan is by the back of Dominick's. And that's the only place near Richmond Towers where Fagan could've had enough cover to confront Philip."

Denny shook his head. "Amazing."

Everyone murmured agreement while Harry wiped his sweaty head with his handkerchief. Estelle sighed. "Well, thank the Lord. He must have a plan for your scoundrel of a husband, Gabby, or that guy wouldn't still be in the land of the living."

"But what about Philip?" Gabby asked anxiously. "Is he all right? Did they hurt him?"

"I think he's all right," Harry said. "At least I heard him tell the officer he didn't need to call an ambulance. But they're probably taking him down to the station to make a statement, and then they'll drive him home. Which reminds me ..." Harry stood up. "I need to go down to the station to make sure the arrest sticks."

"And I've got to get the boys home, get them something to eat, and then I need to go see Philip as soon as he's done at the station." Gabby started toward the door, then turned back and gave Harry a hug. "Thanks, Mr. B," she whispered in his ear. "Don't know what magic you worked with those two cell phones, but ... thank you. You probably saved Philip's life. He owes you big time."

She'd no sooner left when Estelle said, "I'm going with you to the station, Harry."

"No, no, better if I go alone."

"Did you hear me, Harry Bentley? I'm going with you."

"And I said you're not. Now listen to me, Estelle Williams, you go home and get ready for tonight. We still got a date, remember?"

Chapter 35

HARRY GAVE A LOW WHISTLE WHEN ESTELLE opened the door for him shortly before five. Instead of one of her usual flowing caftans, she'd followed Harry's requests and dressed in a pair of pale tight-fitting yellow capris with a loose lime-green and black printed top. Her hair was done up in a knot on the top of her head while gold earrings with little red jewels that matched her lipstick dangled from her ears ... all accenting her beautiful, creamy brown skin.

Mm-mm, she was fine!

She even had on gym shoes like he'd asked and was carrying a white denim jacket over her arm. Perfect!

"You're lookin' gorgeous, Babe."

She rolled her eyes at him as they walked toward his car.

As he opened the door, he said, "I was afraid I might be late. It takes so long to book a perp these days. I can't believe it. And Fagan had a second guy with him. Must've kept his mouth shut 'cause I didn't have a clue about him. As it was, the sergeant couldn't believe I heard all that stuff through the phone, anyway." He closed the door as Estelle reached for her seatbelt and went around to the driver's side and got in, picking right up where he'd left off. "But I told him, 'You don't need to believe me. Just take the

312

word of the arresting officers and what they found when they got to the scene.' It all squared with what I told 'em. Then—can you believe it?—that sergeant started speculatin' that I might be in on the whole thing in some kind of a conspiracy."

"Conspiracy? Conspiracy to do what?"

"That's what I said." Harry pulled away from the curb and headed south toward the Outer Drive that would take them down to the Loop. "I just told the sergeant to check the records, and they'd see Matty Fagan was quite capable of committing the whole shakedown by himself."

"Well, at least they didn't lock you up today." Estelle laughed.

"Oh, you know I'd've busted out for this!" He shot her a warm grin.

"Then you better come clean now, Harry Bentley, and tell me where we're goin'."

"Ah, you'll see, you'll see. Uh ..." He pointed over his shoulder with his thumb. "There's a bag of chilled apples on the backseat. Would you get me one? And since it's gonna be much later before we eat, you might want one, too." It was part of Harry's plan, and he was glad when Estelle bit into a crunchy Braeburn.

He exited the Drive at Randolph and found parking in one of the lots underneath Millennium Park. As they climbed the stairs into the late-afternoon daylight, Estelle said, "So, let me guess. Are we going to a concert in the park?"

"You'll see. Just be patient ... and hold on for the ride of your life."

"A ride? I knew it!" She clapped her hands in glee. "We're going on one of those horse-drawn carriage rides all over the city. I've always wanted to do that. Oh, Harry!" She threw her arms around him for a quick hug.

"Hmm ..." Harry's heart skipped a beat. Maybe that would've been a better idea, especially if that was something she'd dreamed of doing. Was it too late to switch? Yeah, definitely too late. He'd stick with his plan.

The huge office building they walked up to gave no hint from a distance what was housed in the ground-level storefront. Harry swung open the door with the sign announcing: "City Segway Tours."

"Here we are!" he said.

"What? What's this? What ...?"

"A Segway tour! We're gonna ride Segways up and down the lakefront and through the parks. Not quite a horse-drawn carriage, but a lot more fun. Don'cha think?"

She surveyed the room filled with rows of the two-wheeled personal scooters, and her mouth dropped open. "Harry ..." Her eyes got bigger as she noticed the video going on the wall showing someone riding one of the electric "transporters," zipping down a path like a magic top balanced on two side-by-side wheels. "I don't know how to ride one of these things!"

"Neither do I, but they promise to teach us. It's supposed to be easy."

"But ... it's been years since I've even been on a bicycle. I'll fall flat on my face. Look!" She pointed to the video screen. "It would take a trained acrobat to keep that thing from falling over."

"No, no ..." Harry was beginning to worry. "It's got gyro-scopes and computers and stuff inside to keep it balanced for you. You don't have to—"

"Good evening, folks." A young man came up to them. "My name's Travis. I'm one of the guides here. Will you be joining us for our six o'clock tour this evening?"

"Yes—"

"No way! I'm not getting on one of those chariots even if you paid me in diamonds."

Harry couldn't help himself from snorting and covering his mouth with his hand. "Uh … yes. I have reservations for two. Harry Bentley." He checked to be sure the little square box was still in his pants' pocket.

Travis consulted his clipboard. "Ah, yes. Here you are … and I see," he wiggled his eyebrows up and down at Harry, "the little note by your name. We'll be sure to take care of everything, Mr. Bentley."

He turned to Estelle. "And you are …?"

"*Not* Mrs. Bentley! I'm Estelle Williams, and I'm definitely not with him!" She pointed at Harry with a determined look on her face. "Not if he's getting on one of those things."

Travis laughed good-naturedly. "Don't you worry about it, ma'am. There's nothin' to it. Anyone can ride one of these. I guarantee you'll do just fine. But for now, let me just tell you about it and demonstrate how it works. Then, if you still don't want to do it, fine. Okay?"

Somehow, the guide's breezy confidence calmed Estelle enough that she didn't walk out the door. But Harry still worried that this time he might have gone too far.

They milled around with the other tourists—both younger and older than themselves—as they all found helmets that fit and signed release forms. "See, see!" Estelle punched her finger on the paper. "Why do we have to sign a release form if these things are so safe? Why do we have to wear a helmet if there's no danger of knockin' our brains out?"

"Why do you put on a seatbelt when you get in a car?"

"Humph! I'm thinkin' you must've already taken a ride on one of these *without* a helmet, Harry Bentley. Did it hurt?"

Harry laughed quietly to himself. Her recovery of her sense of humor eased his tension some. She might have enough spunk after all … he hoped!

Travis guided them outside to an extra-wide open area of sidewalk adjoining the park. Each rider pushed a Segway in front of themselves with its power turned off as though it were a two-wheeled wheelbarrow. Then the guide had everyone introduce themselves by first names. "We wanna get to know one another as a team. And you'll have the time of your lives. I guarantee it." He seemed to say that a lot.

"If it's not the end of my life," Estelle muttered.

Travis demonstrated how to get on a Segway, how it maintained balance for the rider without having to do anything. He even stood still without holding onto the handlebars to show that it remained completely stable.

"But when you want to go forward," he said, "all you have to do is rock forward slightly on your toes. When you want to stop, relax. If you want to go backwards, rock back a little on your heels. To turn right, lean with the handlebars to the right. Left, lean left. It's as simple as that." He then proceeded to do figure-eights. Stopping, starting, and going backwards. "Nothin' to it. It's nowhere near as challenging as learning to ride a bike, or to skate or ski, or anything like that. It's totally intuitive. It was designed for *your* body. I guarantee that within five minutes, every one of you will have mastered these basics and can do what I'm doing right now." He zipped around in circles some more.

Then the guide went from person to person, giving each one individual instruction and helping them up onto their machine.

Harry watched … *and* he watched Estelle watching. As others quickly got the hang of riding their magic platforms, apprehension drained from her face and a glint of determination grew in her eyes.

But when Travis came to her, she said, "No, no. You do him first. If he doesn't crash straight off, I'll give it a try. But I don't want to be the first to go down."

"Ah, you won't, Estelle. It is 'Estelle,' right? Okay, we'll let Harry try first. But I can guarantee you, this is gonna be your day, Estelle. I can feel it comin'."

You better believe it, thought Harry, and he stepped onto the Segway, finding it just as easy to control as Travis had promised. After a minute or two, he buzzed up the sidewalk fifty feet or so and milled around with the other riders, practicing maneuvers. It would be best if he let Travis do the teaching without him looking on too closely.

Before he knew it, though, Estelle scooted up beside him with a big grin on her face. "These are the *bomb*. Where'd you ever hear about this, Harry?"

"Uh, I dunno." They were driving circles around each other and weaving in and out of the other riders. "I've seen 'em down here along the lakefront lots of times. In fact, last spring the Chicago PD bought a bunch of 'em. And I was thinkin', when this thing with Fagan's all over, I might join the force again if I could ride one of these. But I suppose I'd have to be a beat cop again to do it. Don't know about that ... oh. I think we're ready to go."

Since everyone seemed comfortable controlling their Segways, Travis led them south through the park to Buckingham Fountain—still firing its beautiful water cannons 150 feet into the air. They circled a few times and then continued on through Grant Park and under the Outer Drive to the Museum Campus. All along the way, Travis provided a running commentary about Chicago architecture, history, and trivia—mostly for the out-of-towners who were on the tour. Harry and Estelle often hung back or went ahead, making their own conversation.

After that they went up onto the outside deck of Soldier Field—home of the Bears—and rode around it before coming down and going out toward the lakefront. They headed south on the peninsula that used to be a small commuter airport.

Travis herded the group together as they rode and said, "A few years ago, Mayor Daley got tired of fighting the court battles required to close the airport and convert it into additional lakefront park area he thought the city needed. So in the middle of the night, he ordered crews to destroy the runway surface by bulldozing large X-shaped gouges into it. How 'bout them apples?"

Everybody laughed. But Harry pulled up beside Estelle. "You know, I have to admit that it's becoming a beautiful prairie now, but I can't help wondering whether public behavior like that encourages people like Fagan to think they can get away with whatever they want to do."

The sun had set by the time they came around the lake side of the Adler Planetarium at the north end of the peninsula, where they were met by the magnificent skyline of the city as seen across the harbor. Lights in all the buildings sparkled with a rainbow of colors.

Harry grinned. This was exactly what he'd hoped for, the city backed up by a golden horizon rising to a cobalt sky punctuated by the evening's first stars.

"Okay everybody. We're gonna take a break here for a while. So park your Segways over here against the rack and stretch your legs. I'll blow this whistle ..." Travis gave a sample toot. "... when it's time to remount." He nodded knowingly to Harry.

"That was so cool!" Estelle leaned her Segway against another one and stepped back, wobbling a little as she regained her "shore" legs. She undid the jacket she'd tied around her waist and slipped it on against the cool breeze blowing off the lake. "I never imagined it could be so easy to ride one of those things. Guess I owe you an apology, Mr. Bentley." She grabbed his arm and pulled him close to her as they crossed the path and walked down the grass toward the water. "Oh, look at the lighted windows in that building … They spell, 'Go Cubs! Sox!' "

"Yeah. They do that every year." He blinked each eye at the reassuring sight. *Thank You.*

"Here, Estelle. Let's sit here. We can lean up against this tree."

"Oh, Harry, I'm liable to get grass stains on my pants."

"I got just the thing." He pulled out his large handkerchief and unfolded it for her, laying it on the ground with a flourish. "Madame."

She giggled and took his hand as he helped lower her to the grass. Harry glanced back toward the planetarium as he sat down. Travis and the rest of the "team" were nowhere in sight. He'd probably guided them around to the other side of the planetarium with some remote trivia about the stars in the east. Harry knew the whistle wouldn't blow until he and Estelle returned.

She leaned her head against his shoulder. "This is the most fun I've had in a long time, Harry."

"Better than a horse-drawn carriage?" He slipped his arm around her and pulled her tighter.

She nodded. "Lots better. Makes me feel young again."

"So … how many diamonds do I have to pay you for riding that Segway?"

"Whaddaya mean?"

"Well, you know, you said you wouldn't get on one of those things even if I paid you in diamonds."

She laughed like a schoolgirl.

Harry pulled the box out of his pocket and flipped it open with one hand down by his side where she couldn't see. Then he moved it over in front of her until the lights of the city flickered off the radiant setting.

"Would one do?"

After a long silence during which Harry did not breathe, she reached out and took the box. "One is more than sufficient." Her voice was a mere whisper.

"Does that mean you'll marry me, Estelle?"

"If you're askin', the answer's yes."

He lifted the ring out of the box, and slid it onto her finger. Then he pulled her close and kissed her gently on the lips … and she kissed him back.

He couldn't help it. Gratitude bubbled up within him. They'd come so far, he and Estelle … and he and God, for that matter. And this was only the beginning.

"Thank You, Jesus," he whispered. "Thank You."

Acknowledgments

My sincere thanks goes to …

My wife, **Neta Jackson,** for "loaning" me Harry Bentley yet one more time and for the "moments of intense fellowship" we enjoyed as we wrestled with whether Harry would really say this or Estelle would respond like that … or even why Harry wore his eye patch so long. She wrote *Who Do I Lean On?* before I wrote *Harry Bentley's Second Sight,* so my facts had to correspond to hers.

Allen Arnold, Senior VP and Publisher of fiction at Thomas Nelson Publishers, for continuing to support our experiment with "parallel novels" by printing an excerpt from this Harry Bentley novel in the back of *Who Do I Lean On?* Neta's third House of Hope novel.

Carl Fowler, Cheryl Hipp, Neta Jackson, Sue Mitrovitch, Julia Pferdehirt, Larry Waites—readers and editors who improved the story and helped me avoid many blunders.

Dr. Norm Blair, friend and the retinal ophthalmologist God used to restore most of the vision in my left eye after I experienced problems similar to Harry's. Go to www.daveneta.com and click on "I Was Blind, but Now I See … Reflections on Losing My Sight" for a fuller report.